The jewel in the crown

the jewel in the crown

FRANK SIMON

BARBOUR
PUBLISHING

Published by Barbour Publishing, Inc., P.O. Box 719, Uhrichsville, OH 44683, www.barbourbooks.com

Our mission is to publish and distribute inspirational products offering exceptional value and biblical encouragement to the masses.

Printed in the United States of America.
5 4 3 2 1

For Carl Hammert

acknowledgments

I want to thank the people who helped make this book possible:

My wife, LaVerne, first editor and my sweet helpmeet,
Paul Meehan for his expert advice on security systems,
Shannon Hill for her guidance and suggestions,
Alton Gansky for his efforts in the editing process,
My friend and agent, Les Stobbe.

chapter 1

The deserted office was close and oppressive. Gary Nesbitt straightened and pushed the notebook computer back a few inches. He smoothed his sandy blond hair and eyed the screen's cryptic columns of numbers, brilliant white against a black background.

"Did you get in?" John Mason asked, his black face so serious it looked painful. John's heavy, athletic frame towered like an avenging angel.

Gary felt his jaw muscles tense. "No, but we're not going to let that stop us."

"I just saw the display go wild," John said, pointing to the computer.

Gary's blue eyes flicked over the screen. "Those were data packets transmitted by the security system. The system has holes, all right, but I haven't been able to hack into the control program. I can access it, but I haven't found a valid ID and password."

"Did you get anything?"

"Quite a bit, actually. I have the security configuration, but we could have guessed that: electronic locks on the vault and front door, microwave motion detector, infrared motion detector grid, and a surveillance camera. Looks like a job for Sherlock."

John's brown eyes grew very wide. "You mean we gotta go in through the window?"

Gary almost smiled. "Don't see any way around it. I could defeat the front door's alarm, but then we'd trip the infrared grid and probably the motion detector as well."

John nodded. "Okay, okay. Just a thought."

Gary rose and stretched his wiry body. "Grab your gear. Time for some mountain climbing."

John nodded but was obviously not pleased with the prospect. He hefted his backpack and began attaching it to his climbing harness.

Gary snapped his own backpack onto his climbing harness and looked around the room. Then he flipped off the light, stepped to the window, and looked out. Darkness flooded in like a black tide. The cool night breeze, mild for the second week in April, caressed his face. The window glass, removed by John earlier, sat on the floor to one side. Gary looked out at Manhattan's galaxy of lights, then down at the late-night traffic on Fifth Avenue, seventy-six floors below. He felt a momentary twinge of fear as he watched the distant red and white lights of the cars and trucks. He punched a button on his watch. It was almost midnight.

John ran a hand through his close-cropped black hair. "You *sure* you want to do this?" he asked.

Gary nodded. "Absolutely. Come on, we can do it."

"Okay."

John placed the hook of his miniature motorized winch over the windowsill, turned, and climbed cautiously over the edge until he was hanging by his fingers and the slim steel cable that was his only lifeline. "See you."

The electric motor whined, and Gary watched as John bumped his way down the side of the Empire State Building on his three-story trip. After almost a minute, John stopped. Gary rigged his winch and started down. Halfway there, he heard a barely audible *whump*. He stopped beside John and peered in through the large, neat hole cut through the window by the shaped explosive.

Nice work, Gary thought to himself. The lighting inside the office, while dim, was adequate. His eyes made a quick survey of their target. He spotted the motion detector and surveillance camera immediately, both aimed at the tall vault door. However, the camera's fixed field of view did not include the window. Gary couldn't see the infrared motion detector grid, but he knew where the invisible beams would be. He smiled at the popular misconception of ruby-red bars forming an impenetrable electronic fence. *I wish I could see them,* he thought. John nudged him and pointed toward their goal.

Gary reached into his backpack and extracted Sherlock. The miniature wheeled robot was about the size of a DVD player and could be fitted with caterpillar tracks if necessary. Its upper deck, also detachable, was tailored to the mission. Although Sherlock was John's invention, Gary had spent more time practicing with its remote control. Gary lowered the machine through the window and pulled out the controller. In moments Sherlock was scooting silently along the walls underneath the infrared grid, until it was directly under the surveillance camera. A tiny hatch popped open, and a compacted mast extended until the short cylindrical object in its manipulator hung in front of the camera. Gary tapped the joystick, and the cylinder slipped over the lens. A green light on the device winked on, indicating that the blackout iris was closing. The security monitor, wherever it was, would now be dark. Hopefully, the guards would assume it was only a camera failure. There were no alarms—for the moment.

Gary thumbed a switch. The cylinder shifted when the padded gripper released but did not fall. *One down, two to go,*

Gary thought. He retracted the mast, repositioned Sherlock, and swiveled the gripper to pick up a gray box on Sherlock's deck. The pincers closed, and the mast hoisted the device up beside the motion detector and stuck it to the wall with a strip of exposed tape. Two wires hung down, each tipped with a tiny alligator clip. Down came the mast again, and this time Gary picked up a multi-tool unit topped by a microcam. He moved it up beside the motion detector, rotated the drill into place, and cut two holes near the detector's circuit board. Then he extended a pair of miniature forceps, gripped one of the alligator clips, and guided it through a hole and onto an exposed wire. Then came the second wire, and a green LED reported the detector bypassed. *Now for the vault.*

Gary retracted the multi-tool and guided the robot over to the massive steel door, tweaking the joystick until Sherlock was in position. He picked up four wire jumpers and raised the mast beside the lock's control panel. He examined it with the microcam and sighed in relief as he recognized the manufacturer's name emblazoned on the faceplate. He extended the power driver and removed the plate. One by one, he attached three of the jumpers using the forceps, rotated the cutter into place, and clipped two wires. Gary examined the readout on the controller's LCD screen, then keyed in two commands in quick succession. The first inserted a date/time packet into the security system network, resetting the time to 9:00 A.M., defeating the time lock. The second began retracting the locking bars. A muted whining sound drifted out through the window, and moments later the vault door swung open a fraction of an inch.

"Show time," Gary whispered. "Don't take all night."

John grinned, his white teeth glinting in the dark. "Don't get in my way." He detached the descent cable's drum from his winch and carefully let it go. It swept through the window and swung back and forth like a pendulum. He pulled a telescoping pole out of his backpack and attached a compact drill with a circle cutter in its chuck. John eyed the sprinkler heads and extended the pole until the blade was lined up with the water pipe hidden above the acoustic tile. He pressed a button and raised the drill. The blade cut through the light fiberglass easily. John exhaled and retracted the pole. He removed the fiberglass disc and repeated the operation three more times. He exchanged the drill for a pair of pliers and placed a hook with attached wire through the nearest hole and over the sprinkler pipe. The hook settled into place with a faint click. John stowed the pole in his backpack and snapped an empty drum onto his winch. He attached the wire to it and took up the slack until his toes barely touched the sill. Then he pushed off, pulling his legs in at the same time. He swung like a pendulum above the infrared grid.

John placed three more wires and shifted to each one in turn until he was hanging beside the vault. He pulled the massive door open a few inches, then played his flashlight's beam about the vault's interior. Holding the miniature light in his teeth, he reached in with the pole and snagged something. Out came a cloth bag dangling from the pliers. John slipped it inside his backpack. He collapsed the pole and then started coming out, transferring his weight from one wire to the next until he was ready to lower himself back onto the windowsill.

Gary held onto the window frame with his left hand while he reached for John's boots with his right. He missed on the first try and slipped. He pivoted out of control and hit the inside wall, his boots slipping to the edge of the sill. Gary looked down. Sweat beaded on his forehead despite the cool evening. A fraction of an inch of hard rubber was all that prevented him from tumbling into the room and setting off the infrared motion detector alarm. Carefully he pulled himself back and inched his boots to safety. He looked up at John, who hung from the ceiling, his eyes bulging in surprise.

Gary reached in again, grabbed at John's boots, missed, tried once more, snagged one, and pulled it toward the window. In moments John was standing on the sill once more. A car horn drifted up from the street below, sounding thin and far away. John's descent cable and drum slapped against the building's limestone exterior. He swapped winch drums. Then he and Gary started back up together.

"Not a bad night's work," Gary whispered, as if someone might hear them three-quarters of the way up the skyscraper.

"Yeah, but I sure am glad we're done."

The security guard searched for the right key among the myriad circling the ring hooked to his belt as he stood outside the offices of Sheldon Silverman and Company, one of several diamond wholesalers in the Empire State Building. The guard had argued against making a trip up to the seventy-third floor, but his supervisor had insisted. But it *had* to be a faulty TV camera; what else could it be? Why not wait until morning and let the day crew handle it?

The man found the right key, inserted it, and only then remembered. He reached up and punched in the security code on the keypad. He got it wrong the first time, but the green light blinked on with his next try. The guard unlocked the door and pushed it open. His angry scowl faded into disbelief, then fear as he saw the open vault and the gaping hole in the window.

"What the. . . ?" he began, before trailing off into a series of feeble curses. Then he grabbed for his radio.

John knew he should be sleeping since he and Gary had to be up early the next morning. But he hadn't unwound yet, and sleep would be impossible until he did. He thumbed the TV on with the remote and started surfing the cable channels, thinking he might find a movie, what Gary would call "bubble gum for the eyes."

The unmistakable image of a news desk flashed on the screen, and it was not until three or four channels later that something about the image forced John to go back. Behind the female news anchor was a picture of the Empire State Building.

". . .apparently lowered themselves down the side of the Empire State Building, blew out a window, then somehow opened the vault belonging to Sheldon Silverman and Company, diamond merchants located on the seventy-third floor. How much the thieves took is not known at this hour; however, the police investigation is continuing.

"We take you live to. . ."

John jumped up, raced across the room, and banged on the adjoining room's door. "Hey, Gary, get up! We've got a problem."

Gary yawned as he and John got off the elevator on the seventy-third floor. Down the hall a reporter and cameraman waited.

"That's great," Gary grumbled. "Just what we need."

"The vultures have landed," John whispered back.

The male reporter seemed to come to life when it became obvious the visitors were headed for the target office.

"Rolling," the cameraman said.

"Excuse me, are you involved in the diamond heist hoax?" the reporter asked, shoving a microphone in John's face.

"No comment."

The mike shifted to Gary.

Gary felt an urge to evade but knew that wouldn't be right. There wasn't anything wrong with a simple "no comment," but he decided the question deserved an answer.

"I'm not aware of any hoax, but we did conduct a security system test last night at the request of our client."

"And that would be Sheldon Silverman and Company," the reporter prompted.

"Yes. And building security *also* had notice of what we were doing, so there is no hoax."

"Then why did they report the break-in to the police?"

"You'll have to ask them that. Now, if you'll excuse us, we have an appointment with Mr. Silverman."

"One more question. Who are you? Who do you work for?"

Gary considered refusing but decided it really didn't matter. In fact, it was probably free publicity. "SecurityCheck, Incorporated, Northridge, California."

"Has your company ever had a failure like this before?"

"Excuse me," Gary said. He opened the door, waited until John went through, then closed it, blocking out the glaring light and the inquisitive reporter.

The receptionist stared at them. "May I help you?" she asked.

"We're here to see. . . ," Gary began.

"In here, gentlemen," a deep, cultured voice said.

Gary turned to see Sheldon Silverman looking at them through tinted designer glasses. He was not smiling, but then Gary couldn't remember a time when he had. But what the man lacked in humor, he made up in elegance. Gary couldn't guess what the man's suit, shirt, tie, and shoes cost, but he knew they hadn't come from a discount store. Not a hair was out of place on Sheldon's head. He waved toward his office.

Gary and John marched inside and waited while their host closed the door. Sheldon rounded his massive walnut desk and sat down in his executive swivel chair. "Please sit down," he said in what seemed like an afterthought. The young men did as they were told.

Sheldon glowered at them for a few moments, then said, "I'm a respectable diamond wholesaler, and this publicity isn't doing my business any good."

"I'm sorry, sir," Gary said, "but it wasn't our fault. If the

16

security people had followed your instructions, this wouldn't have happened."

This seemed to deflate Sheldon's anger. "Yes, I suppose you're right. What's done is done."

"How bad is it?"

The fire came back into Sheldon's eyes. "It started out as a break-in, then changed to a diamond heist as soon as they checked out my company. Finally the news clowns escalated it to the largest diamond robbery in New York history."

"They actually said that?"

"I believe the words they used were 'according to reliable sources.' You know the rest."

Gary nodded. "They emphasized certain details to boost their ratings."

"You've got it. The real story broke just in time for the morning shows. Now I'm a laughingstock all across America, probably around the world."

"I'm sorry, but I imagine it will die down before long."

"I hope you're right." Sheldon paused. "Do you have it?"

"Yes, sir." Gary thought that was a silly question since he was holding the bag in plain view.

"May I . . ." It was not a question.

Gary got up, handed him the bag, and sat back down.

"The building people are giving me a hard time about the window."

John cleared his throat. "Sorry about the damage, Mr. Silverman, but we followed the rules. Damage to property consistent with an actual break-in is the responsibility of the client, and so on."

"That is correct." Sheldon looked closely at the bag, hefted it, and dropped it on the desk. "You didn't open it, I see."

"No, sir," Gary said, "but I did spot the fine thread you stitched into the neck so you'd know if we did."

"How very observant." There might have been a hint of a

smile, but it quickly disappeared. "However, a handful of cubic zirconia isn't worth a lot."

"That's not the point. Per your instructions, we penetrated your security system and took what you told us to, as proof of what a real crook could have done, which is a *lot* more than what we actually did."

Sheldon tapped the bag with his silver letter opener. "But everything else was locked up."

"Those dinky drawer locks are nothing compared to evading the alarms and opening the vault. We can demonstrate that as well, if you like."

The client leaned back in his chair. "That won't be necessary. So what do I need to do?"

Gary held up a binder. "It's all in our report." He leaned forward and slid it onto the desk. "But I'll give you the breaking news version."

Sheldon leaned back and folded his hands. "Please do." He listened carefully, making an occasional note with his gold pen, and stood as soon as Gary finished.

Gary and John sprang to their feet.

Sheldon reached into his suit's inner pocket, withdrew a folded piece of paper, and handed it to Gary. "I believe you will find this correct," he said.

Gary glanced briefly at the check and saw it had the right number of zeros. "Yes, sir. Thank you."

Sheldon nodded toward the door. "I have a busy schedule, so I must bid you good day. Have a pleasant trip back to California."

"We'll sure try," Gary answered for them.

In moments they were out in the corridor, walking back to the elevators. Gary smiled, thinking of their return to the Valley. His mind sprang into fast-forward. The Empire State Building heist was history. Next stop: Fort Knox.

chapter 2

It was Monday. Gary Nesbitt smiled as he admired the sign on the door which proclaimed "SecurityCheck, Inc." in flowing, futuristic white letters on a blue background. He and John Mason had worked hard to establish their business. It might be tucked away in the back of a run-down office park on Devonshire now, but he was confident they would require larger and finer quarters soon. At the rate they were growing, they would have to add to their staff as well.

Gary tried the door and found it unlocked, as expected, since he had seen John's gray Camry in the lot. He pushed it open and stepped inside. He ignored the dingy beige walls and the water-stained ceiling tiles. Well-worn carpet that had once been dark blue covered the floors, except for the white vinyl tile in the back workshop.

"Finished with your gadgets yet?" Gary asked.

John poked his head out of the workshop at the end of the hall. "Get off my case, man." His scowl held for only a moment, then broke into a broad grin. "I suppose *you've* finished the operation plan and hired our computer expert."

Gary laughed. "I'm working on the first, and we have to talk about the second."

"Okay. When do you want to do it?"

"How about now?"

"Let me put this down." John waved a metal box, which was trailing an untidy bunch of wires. "Want some coffee?"

"If you're buying."

"Yeah. Right."

Gary entered his office and placed his briefcase on the corner of his desk. He walked to the round conference table and pulled out two chairs. John came in holding brimming mugs and set them down carefully.

"Thanks," Gary said as he sat down.

John took the chair opposite and sipped his coffee.

"I've been interviewing hackers ever since we got back from New York," Gary said.

"Any of 'em look promising?"

Gary shook his head. "Not really. Some are pretty good, but not exactly what we need. You know of anyone qualified?"

John frowned and leaned back in his chair. "Maybe, but we have to talk about it first. Have you met Ann O'Brien? She's been going to our church for about six months."

"No."

"Well, Sara and I introduced ourselves to her on her first visit." John's frown eased into a tense smile. "You know the drill: 'Are you visiting?' 'What do you do?'"

Gary smiled. "Uh-huh. I know."

"Right. So she says she's a computer programmer doing short-term contracts but looking for a full-time job. I tell her I'm into electronic hardware, and we discuss the local job market."

Gary leaned forward a little. "Is she a hacker?"

"Yeah, you could say that." John's frown returned. "But there's a slight problem."

"What's that?"

"Sara and I have talked with Ann quite a bit. You know how my wife is—wants to help everyone she meets. Sara says she sensed something going on with Ann. It took a while, but over the next few Sundays she told us a little about her background." John took a sip of coffee. "She grew up in Redwood City. Her father's a high school teacher. Ann's mom was raised in San Jose; they met in college, married, and settled out here. Although Ann grew up in a Christian home, she rebelled. After high school, Ann went away to college, and when she graduated, she took a job at a bank. And here's where it gets sticky."

"Sticky how?"

"She scammed the bank. Big-time. She was funneling money into a fictitious account, which just happened to be hers, and got away with it for several years, until she was out sick one day and another programmer had to work on one of her systems. It took a while, but they eventually unraveled enough to have her arrested. She ended up in prison at Corona."

"I'm sorry to hear that."

John nodded. "Yeah, it's a sad story. One good thing, though, it gave her a lot of time to think. Her parents visited her frequently, and her mother gave her a Bible. She came to believe not long after."

Then he sighed. "But I think you see my concern. Sara and I care about Ann, and she seems to have turned her life around, but who knows if she's really changed?" He shrugged.

Gary felt a momentary twinge of irritation. "John. *I* was in prison, as you very well know."

John fiddled with his coffee mug. "I know, but I've known you for a long time, and you're completely different now. I was part of that prison ministry and saw the changes occur in your life. Take a step of blind faith with our business? That's harder for me."

Gary leaned back in his chair as he mulled over all that John had said.

"Sounds like she has the talent," Gary said. "And we need a hacker. Anything wrong with interviewing her?"

"No. . .just know that I'm not completely comfortable with it."

"I understand. But will you set it up?"

"Sure. Be glad to."

"Good. Now, how is your gadget factory getting on?"

John laughed. "What do you mean 'gadget'? I'll have you know I handcraft only the finest high-tech equipment. I'm almost done with the Fort Knox gear, but how many powered hang gliders did you want? You said you weren't sure at our last planning session."

"I know. One should be enough, but build another one, just in case."

"You've got it. Anything else we need to discuss?"

"Don't think so. Keep up the good work."

They got up, and John returned to his workshop. Gary sat at his desk, logged onto the network, and began reviewing the operational plan for their next job. A few minutes later he heard the front door open. A tall man of medium build with slicked-down brown hair walked past.

"Dan," Gary called out.

Dan Thompson returned and looked in, his brown eyes framed by his thick glasses. The team's communications expert was a quiet man and a loner. Gary knew little about his family. His mother had died of cancer a few years ago, and his father was a retired Navy chief who had spent the latter part of his career at the Navy Electronics Laboratory Center at Point Loma in San Diego. And Dan was divorced, with no children.

"Pull up a chair," Gary said. "I'm reviewing the plan, and I need an update on our communications gear. Are you ready to roll?"

Dan sat in the side chair Gary indicated. "I think so. John helped me with the specialty gear, and he'll pack all my comm equipment in with his stuff."

"Good. You see any problems tapping into the post's lines?"

Dan pushed his glasses up his nose. "Nothing I can't overcome. We've got maps of most of the lines, and we can sniff out the secret ones when we get there. Of course, the secure circuits will be encrypted."

"Right, but we can do enough damage through the regular lines."

"Don't you know it." Dan put his hands on the armrests and started to get up. "That all you need?"

"Yeah, thanks." Then Gary snapped his fingers, "Oh, wait, there is something else. Is Sully coming in today? I never can keep track of his schedule."

Dan settled back in the chair. "I think so. Want to see where he is?"

"What? You mean right now?"

Dan grinned. "Sure. I've been testing a new type of pager that's got a GPS receiver in it."

He got up and pulled a large pager off his belt. After tapping a series of buttons, he placed the unit on Gary's desk.

"I sent a message to Sully's pager asking for its location," Dan explained. He pressed another button and a crude map of the Los Angeles area appeared on the screen. "There. He's on the Hollywood Freeway almost to the Ventura Freeway. Shouldn't be too long, unless he runs into gridlock."

"Very nice. Think that might come in handy?"

"You mean on our next job? I doubt it." Dan laughed. "But it did tell you where Sully is."

"That it did. Thanks."

Dan picked up his pager and walked out.

Gary turned back to his computer monitor and continued reviewing the operational plan. He had the nagging feeling he was overlooking something, but he felt sure the structured walkthrough scheduled for the end of the week would reveal any flaws. He made a trip to the break room, refilled his coffee mug, then returned to his office.

Two minutes later Gary heard the front door open.

"Hey, Sully," he said. "I need to see you."

Moments later Sean Sullivan appeared at Gary's office door.

"Take a seat," Gary told the young Hispanic man.

Sully crossed the room with the easy stride of a dedicated athlete and sat down. "How'd you know it was me?"

"It's my job to know what's going on."

Sully's eyes flicked over to his pager. He smiled. "With a little help from Dan."

"I cannot tell a lie. That gadget is going to be useful."

"If my pager starts cramping my style, I'll leave it at the office."

"Okay, okay. But what I wanted to see you about is the Fort Knox job. I know you're part-time, but I'd like to have you with us for this one. Last time we talked, you still weren't sure. I need an answer now, guy."

Sully sighed. "Yeah, I know. If you had asked me yesterday, I would have said no. I thought I had this stuntman gig in the bag, but I lost out to this dude who couldn't jump a motorcycle over an anthill."

"What happened?"

"He's a friend of the director." Sully's eyes flashed. "I really wanted on that film, man. It's going to be so cool."

"What's it about?"

Sully jumped up and started pacing. "It's set in San Francisco, and there's this *terrific* motorcycle chase over the hills, jump after jump. And they go down some steps, but the best part comes right at the end when the good guy jumps his cycle over a cable car, and the bad dude plows into it, and there's this big explosion."

Gary struggled not to laugh. "So, it's a film about motorcycle racing."

Sully stopped pacing. "Uh, no. It's sort of a teenage coming-of-age slasher. It would have been a nice credit for me."

"Well, I'm sorry you didn't get it."

"You know what they say; don't give up the day job."

"Sounds like good advice to me. So you're in?"

"Yeah, man." Sully grinned. "You think Kentucky is ready for the Kid?"

"Probably not. But a little West Coast weirdness won't hurt them. Since you're on board now, check in with John and Dan so you can get an idea of what kind of wheels we'll need."

"Okay. You mean in addition to a Porsche Boxster?"

"Get out of here."

Sully grinned. "Sure thing, boss."

Gary spent the rest of the day refining the plan. Around five, John stuck his head in the door.

"Ann will be here at one-thirty tomorrow."

"What? Oh, right, the interview. I'd like you to sit in on it."

"You bet. Good night."

"Night." Gary watched him go, wondering if he had been wise in pursuing an interview with Ann O'Brien. The people who worked for SecurityCheck—John, Dan, and now Sully— they were more than employees; they were a team. The failure of one member would not only defeat the operation; it might get someone killed, since breaching security systems was dangerous in the extreme. And there was something else.

Getting past a client's security usually gave access to valuable assets. What would he and John do if something turned up missing? The fledgling company wouldn't survive the scandal.

Gary shut down his computer and stood up. *No use in borrowing trouble,* he decided.

Ann O'Brien pushed an errant strand of her long brown hair behind an ear and stared at the LCD screen on her laptop. A glance at the clock told her she had less than an hour until her interview, and she still hadn't penetrated the firewall. She absentmindedly picked at a broken nail and looked down at it in disgust. She really tried to keep her nails neat and polished, but it seemed like everything she did chipped or broke them. She focused on the screen again, trying to visualize the hardware and software that were thwarting her hacking attempts so far. On a hunch, she made a quick code change, compiled, and executed the revised program. A black command line window popped up, and a series of lines of white text scrolled down. The blinking white cursor sat beside the default directory path of the Security-Check server.

"Excellent," she said to herself. She was in. "Now for some cybersnooping."

Her nimble fingers flew over the keyboard, and at times she paused to make notes in a text window. As a final step, she downloaded a program to the server and executed it. Then she disconnected and printed the text file. *Now* she was ready for the interview.

Gary jumped when the fifteen-minute warning appeared on his screen. Despite his resolve the previous day, he had not been able to stop worrying about the coming interview. Now he would finally get to meet Ann O'Brien and decide if she was right for the team. He waited until 1:25, then went out to the reception area. At precisely 1:30, the front door opened, and a willowy young woman entered. She removed her sunglasses, revealing her blue eyes. Gary recognized her face instantly.

"You must be Ms. O'Brien," he said. "I've seen you around church. Gary Nesbitt."

"I've seen you, too. Nice to meet you, Mr. Nesbitt." She smiled but it seemed strained.

"Please, call me Gary."

She extended her hand, and Gary shook it.

"It's nice to finally meet you, Ann. John Mason is supposed to join us, but he seems to have forgotten." He called toward the back workshop. "Hey, John."

John stepped into the hall, a puzzled expression on his face. Then he looked at his watch. "Oh, it *is* time, isn't it?"

"If you can tear yourself away from your gadgets," Gary said.

"Be right there."

Gary turned back to Ann. "Shall we go in my office?" He led the way inside and over to the conference table. "Please sit down. Can I get you anything—coffee, or a soft drink?"

"Oh, no. I'm fine." She took the indicated chair and looked toward the hall.

John came in and closed the door. "Ann."

"Good to see you, John."

As soon as John was seated, Ann opened a folder and handed them some papers. "My résumé." She sat back and waited while they read.

Gary scanned the pages quickly. The résumé was well done and said she had the right experience. His eyebrows shot up when he reached the education section.

"Bachelor's degree from Cambridge?"

"That's right. Full academic scholarship."

"Wow. That's impressive."

"Thank you."

"What college?"

"Magdalen."

"Wasn't C. S. Lewis a professor there?"

"Yes. He taught medieval and Renaissance literature there after he left Oxford," she answered.

Gary smiled in appreciation. "He was certainly one of the greats. I enjoy reading his books."

The room grew quiet for a moment. As Gary considered how to broach the subject that they needed to discuss next, Ann looked at him evenly and began to speak.

"You've noticed the gaps in my employment history. I'm guessing John told you I served time," she said.

"John told me a little of your background," Gary said, nodding.

"So you're wondering if you can trust me."

Gary maintained steady eye contact. "Yes, it is a consideration in our line of work."

The light in Ann's eyes flickered.

"I can understand your reluctance to hiring an ex-con. I've had reservations about doing this interview, but John insisted."

"Ann, *I'm* an ex-con."

"What?"

Having started, he decided she deserved more. "I defeated the alarm system at a Beverly Hills mansion and made off with a diamond necklace worth millions, but the fence I sold it to cut a deal with the DA and turned me in."

"I'm sorry."

A wry smile came to Gary's face. "Yeah, I was too, sorry I got caught. But while I was a guest of the state, these prison ministries kept coming through. I ignored them at first, but on one particular visit, this big black dude came over and asked if he could talk to me." Gary's smile brightened. "John looked terrified. I found out later it was his first prison visit."

"Hey, you gave me a hard time, man," John said.

"I know, but I remembered what you told me." Gary shifted his gaze to Ann. "There's more to it, of course, but that incident changed my life. I came out of prison a Christian."

"I see."

Gary sensed that she did understand. "So I know a little of what you're going through. Maybe people ought to be more forgiving, but, hey, it's not a perfect world."

"You can say that again."

"Why don't we explore this further? I guess you know what we do. Did John tell you anything about the job?"

"Just that you were looking for an experienced hacker. No details."

"Typical hardware man," Gary said with a smirk. "Brother John doesn't understand geek-speak."

"Hey," John said with a smile.

"Your objection is noted. I'm currently the resident software dude, but we need someone with better skills. Think you can do the job?"

A smile flitted across Ann's face. "Meaning you can't take a résumé at face value these days, what with achievement-enhanced entries and all that."

"Something like that. It's always wise to check."

"Do you want to do a technical interview?"

"Nothing as boring as that. I've got a security monitor program running on my workstation. Show me how you'd go about breaking into it. If you can actually crack it, so much the better." Gary got up and started toward his desk.

"Okay." Ann grabbed her folder, walked around the desk, turned the swivel chair around to the computer, and sat down. She touched a key and the screen saver password box popped up.

John moved around to where he could see.

"Here, let me key in my password," Gary said.

"No problem." Ann's fingers flew over the keyboard. The screen saver disappeared.

Gary stared at the screen, then slowly turned his eyes to Ann. "You know my password?"

"Obviously." She opened her folder and gave him a sheet of paper. "And here are all the other IDs and passwords in use on your network." She paused. "You guys *are* in the security consulting business, right?"

Gary traded glances with John, whose mouth was open. "I thought we were."

"You've got some holes, but all security systems do, so don't feel too bad. It took me a while to hack my way in."

"Uh, thanks."

Ann opened a command window, keyed what looked like a line of gibberish, and hit Enter. A large window opened, displaying line after line of tabular data. She pointed to a line about a third of the way down the screen. "Is that the security program?"

"Yes. How did you do that?"

"I installed one of my programs when I was checking out your network."

She selected the program, opened another window, and scrolled the display, rapidly at first, then more slowly. She overwrote two characters and hit the Enter key. "Okay, I've bypassed the log-in routine. Would you like to try it, or shall I?"

Gary waved toward the screen. "Be my guest."

Ann switched to the security program and activated it. A user ID and password box popped up. Ann hit the Enter key for both entries, and the program displayed its main menu. She then selected the security circuits and disabled each one.

"The security system is now shut down."

"Very good," Gary said. "As a matter of fact, excellent."

"Thank you."

Gary looked at John. "I think we've found our hacker."

chapter 3

It had been a hard week, spent in preparing for the Fort Knox job. But Friday had finally arrived, and none too soon for Gary. He entered the conference room and began setting up the video projector for his PowerPoint presentation. This was the project phase he liked the least, sorting through and reconciling all the details, and making sure the team members understood their jobs. It was plain hard work, but it had to be done. Only then could they enjoy the adrenaline rush of the actual operation. That this was potentially dangerous made him take extra care in the planning.

John came in carrying a mug of coffee and sat down. "Got your dog and pony show ready?"

"Almost. How's everything in the gadget factory?"

"Couldn't be better. Just finished making some black boxes and a special drill for Ann. I think I'm all caught up."

"Did I hear my name mentioned?" Ann said as she came in.

"I was telling Gary about the drill and the electronic taps I made for you," John said.

"You said they were black boxes," Gary said.

"Didn't want to burden you with the technical stuff."

Dan Thompson and Sean Sullivan walked in together.

"Ann, you've met Dan, and I'd like you to meet Sean 'the Kid' Sullivan," Gary said. "Sully is a part-timer, and he'll be our driver on this operation. This is his day job, since in real life he's a Hollywood stuntman. Sully, this is Ann O'Brien, our computer expert."

"Hacker," Ann said.

Sully sat down, reached across the table, and shook hands. "Pleased to meet you, Ann."

"Likewise, Sully." Ann hesitated a moment, then added, "Uh, are you Irish?"

"Of course, don't I look it?" Sully grinned and ran his hands slowly through his black hair. "My grandfather on my dad's side was Irish, from New York. He moved to San Diego and married a woman from Tijuana. So I'm three-quarters Hispanic but named for my granddad. I take it you're the real deal—Irish, I mean."

"Half. My mother's parents emigrated from Russia and settled in San Jose. My dad is Boston Irish with an accent that's pure emerald. He met my mom at San Francisco State, and they got married after they graduated."

"Cool."

Gary tapped the projector with his laser pointer. "Okay, folks. It's time for some blue smoke and mirrors." He started the presentation with an aerial photograph of a tan square building surrounded by a perimeter fence. Emblazoned across the slide in gold, drop-shadow letters were the words "Operation Go for the Gold."

"This is the U.S. Bullion Depository at Fort Knox," Gary said, "and there hasn't been a successful heist there since *Goldfinger*. Thomas Brooks, our army contact, said he didn't want us to be number two." Polite laughter went around the table. "The U.S. Bullion Depository is run by the U.S. Mint, part of the

Treasury Department. We won't be messing with those bad dudes since we're only interested in the army post. The army runs an armor school along with normal garrison duties, and for the history buffs, the post is the home of the Patton Museum.

"We're going to attempt breaking into the telecomm lines, intranets, and selected facilities. Also, we'll take whatever isn't nailed down, if you catch my drift. In particular, we're going to try and make off with an M1A1 Abrams main battle tank."

"Cool," Sully said. "I always wanted to drive one of those."

"Well, I hope you get the chance, since that's a bonus item. Sure you can handle it?"

Sully looked hurt. "You ask this of the world's greatest stuntman?"

Gary laughed. "Please forgive me, Mr. Sullivan. I forgot who I was talking to. I'll consider it in the bag. 'Go for the Gold' kicks off a week from next Monday. Sully and Dan will fly into Louisville next Wednesday to rent our vehicles and start the initial work of penetrating the telecomm lines. John airfreights the equipment to Sully on Thursday, and the rest of us fly out on Friday."

Gary advanced to a slide showing one of the gates. "Fort Knox is an open post, meaning anyone can drive through the gates. However, there are many secured facilities and training areas throughout the installation, and these *are* guarded. Authorized vehicles have bumper stickers; however, the guards sometimes check military IDs. We'll have our photo printing and ID equipment with us, so that should not be a problem, unless they decide to run our serial numbers through Department of Defense databases.

"Now, I've arranged for our normal collection of costumes and disguises: army and delivery uniforms, beards, makeup, and so on. Anyone needing a disguise better check with me pronto."

"You use disguises?" Ann asked.

"Of course. Deception is our stock in trade."

"You actually *make* the costumes?"

"No. We use a shop in North Hollywood that caters to the studios. Costumes for U can make anything."

Gary advanced to a map of Fort Knox. "Dan will describe his plans for penetrating their telecomm."

Dan took the laser pointer. "Here's what we have so far, based on research here plus a quick trip I made a few weeks ago. This isn't complete, and I'm sure much of it is inaccurate, but that's why I'm going out early with Sully. By the time the rest of you arrive, we'll be ready to start looking for all the cracks and loopholes."

Gary leaned back in his chair and listened carefully as Dan detailed his plan with calm efficiency.

Ann took over when Dan finished. Her presentation showed she had done a lot of research on short notice. Gary listened with great interest, glad he had decided to take a chance on her. That she knew what she was doing he had absolutely no doubt.

John got up and, wielding the laser pointer like a baton, detailed all the equipment he would be providing. John had come by his fascination with gadgets honestly, since his father was a lead technician at the Jet Propulsion Laboratory in Pasadena and had worked on several of the Mars rovers. John's interest in explosives had come by way of necessity and hard research, aided by his skill as an expert machinist.

After John finished, Sully jumped to his feet with his usual enthusiasm and showed them the vehicles they would have and what he could do for them. Gary made a few final notes on his laptop, then stood and took the pointer from Sully.

"Okay," he said. "I think we're close to being ready. Now I want everyone to study the detail plan between now and departure. If you find any errors, let me know immediately. Same with suggestions. We've got a lot riding on this. Any questions?" Only silence greeted him. "Okay, let's get back to work."

They stood and started filing out. When Gary saw John

hanging back, he waited until they were alone.

"Something on your mind?" Gary asked.

"You might say that." John's smile looked strained. "You're right about a lot riding on this job. If it comes off without a hitch, we're set for the foreseeable future. It's a terrific contract."

"Yes, and if something goes wrong, we're bankrupt."

"Right."

"We knew that going in, except we didn't realize the preparation would be so expensive. I guess we should have expected it since this is the biggest job we've ever done." Gary forced a smile. "But cheer up. It's going to come off. We start in a week."

"Yeah, but I'll feel better when we get there."

"And *I'll* feel better when I put the Treasury checks in the bank. Now quit worrying."

"I'll try."

Gary watched John go, then started packing up the projector and laptop computer. After he finished, he stopped by the break room to fill his mug with coffee, then returned to his office. He sat down behind his desk, swiveled his chair around, and checked his E-mail. "Twenty-nine new E-mails." Four were spam, so he deleted those without opening them. Then he started reading. About half of those remaining were informational. He composed quick replies for the others and sent them on their electronic way.

The computer clock said it was a little after eleven-thirty, almost time for lunch. Then, after a few more hours in the office, the weekend would start—their first Saturday off in a long time.

The phone gave an electronic warble. Gary picked up the handset, hoping whoever it was wouldn't be in a talkative mood. "SecurityCheck, Gary Nesbitt speaking. Can I help you?"

"Hi, Gary, Thomas Brooks here."

Gary's attention ratcheted up a few notches. "Good morning, Mr. Brooks." He mentally added three hours to Pacific time. "Or I guess I should say good afternoon. How are things in D.C.?"

There was a long pause. "Not so good, actually. The army has cancelled the Fort Knox security review, so I'm afraid we won't be needing your services."

Gary's initial dismay quickly turned to anger. "We have a *signed* contract!"

"If you'll look on page 55 under the heading 'Termination'—it's near the bottom—you'll see that we can cancel the contract at any time."

"Just a minute." Gary pulled open a drawer and fished out his copy. He flipped to the correct page and ran his finger down the turgid legal-speak. "I see it."

"Now it's not *all* bad since there's a kill fee."

Gary groaned. "How much?"

"Ten thousand."

"This leaves us in a bad way. We've spent a lot of money and time getting ready for this job."

"Oh, the department will also pay for your out-of-pocket expenses and a reasonable charge for labor. Listen, Gary, I had *nothing* to do with this, and I'm really sorry about it."

"What happened? Not that it makes any difference."

"The General Accounting Office is auditing Fort Knox, and they questioned why the army was paying civilians to check military security. They recommended we cancel the contract and let base personnel do the job. It's considered hazardous to one's health to ignore a GAO recommendation."

"So the fox is going to guard the henhouse."

Thomas laughed, but Gary could tell it was strained. "Yeah, I guess so. Listen, Gary, I really am sorry."

"Me too. Our preliminary research shows Fort Knox has some serious security deficiencies. You could really use our services."

"Hey, you don't have to sell me."

"I don't suppose there's any chance of reinstating the contract."

"None, at least not during this fiscal year."

"You'll keep us in mind for future work?"

"I will. Well, good-bye."

"Good-bye."

Gary put down the phone, closed his eyes, and leaned back in his chair. Visions of bankruptcy raced through his mind as he quickly reviewed the ramifications.

"Isn't it early for a siesta?" a voice asked.

Gary popped his eyes open and saw John standing in the doorway with Ann, Dan, and Sully behind him.

"We're going out for pizza," John continued. "Want to come along?"

It took a few seconds for Gary to process what John was saying. "Uh, no." His voice sounded flat.

A puzzled expression came over John's face. "I don't believe what I'm hearing. You're the one that keeps saying pizza is one of the basic food groups. I told the guys we were having pizza 'cause I knew you liked it. Come on, we're celebrating."

Gary looked past John at the others. They looked confused as well.

"Something's come up," he said.

"What?"

Gary stood up. "Come in and close the door." He looked out into the hallway. "You three go on without us. John and I have to talk."

They didn't move, and Gary began to wonder if he was going to have to say it again. Then they started drifting off toward the front door. John closed the door. Without a word, the two men went to the conference table and sat down.

"What's wrong?" John asked, his face full of dread.

Gary laid it out for him in succinct bullet points.

John took a deep breath and let it out slowly. "So where does that leave us?"

"In a *real* bad way. I'll meet with our bookkeeper on Monday and get an exact picture, but unless we get some new business—and I mean *real* soon—we're looking at letting everyone go and calling it quits."

"How long have we got?"

"I'd guess a few weeks, tops."

John pounded the table. "This job was supposed to set us up! We've poured *everything* into this company."

"I know, but that's the way it is." A thought came to Gary's mind. He pushed it away angrily, but it kept coming back. Finally he had to accept it. "Is any of this a surprise to God?"

John looked at him as if he were speaking a foreign language.

"Well, is it?" Gary repeated.

"No, of course not. But what are we going to do? This is a disaster here."

"Prayer comes to mind," Gary said, his voice low.

"You're right." John paused. "What about the others?"

"We'll tell them when they get back from lunch."

chapter 4

Ann sat at her desk and stared at the computer monitor, unable to concentrate on her work, work that was not going to last much longer. It had been a miserable weekend, and Monday had brought no improvement. All she could think about was the abrupt end to the job she so desperately needed. Gary had called her into his office, said they would do everything they could to find new clients, but that it didn't look good.

The phone's strident trill made her jump. She hesitated, then picked up the handset. "SecurityCheck, Ann O'Brien speaking."

"Peter Watkins here," a clipped British accent said. "How are you faring in your new employment, Ann?"

Ann felt an icy chill. In her mind's eye she could see Peter, how he had looked during their undergraduate days at Cambridge. She flushed as unwanted memories flooded in, the things she and Peter had done together, things she had found nothing wrong with back then. She felt her eyes narrow.

"How did you find me?"

"What? Is that any way to treat an old friend?"

"Very well. How are *you* doing, Peter?"

"Couldn't be better. As to how I located you, I called your mum in Redwood City. She was most helpful, dear thing."

"I'll have to talk to her about that. Now, why are you calling?"

"Well, I think about you from time to time, quite a bit, actually. We had some smashing times at Cambridge. Remember?"

Ann closed her eyes, again trying to shut out the memories. "That was years ago."

"Yes, I suppose it was, but I haven't forgotten, indeed I haven't. Have you?"

"No, but I'm ashamed of it now."

"I can't believe I'm hearing this. The Ann I remember. . . wait. You haven't gone and gotten religion now, have you?"

"As a matter of fact, I have."

"Pity, since I wanted to fly you over, a bit of a holiday and all that. I've connections with the British Tourist Authority, so it would be all expenses paid. Late April is a little early for tourists, and things aren't crowded. Sure you won't reconsider? I could show you a marvelous time."

"No, Peter."

"Sorry to hear that. So what are you doing now?"

Ann wasn't sure how to answer. What did it matter since she would shortly be unemployed? "My company performs audits on security systems, including actual penetration if the client wants it."

"Really? How interesting."

"It can be."

"What did you say the name of the company is?"

"SecurityCheck, Incorporated."

"That rings a bell, somehow. Wait. New York—a diamond merchant in the Empire State Building. Was that you?"

"I wasn't with them then, but, yes, SecurityCheck did that job."

"Turned into rather a circus as I recall."

"Yeah, but it wasn't the company's fault. Building security fouled up."

"I suppose so, but it *did* give the media muckrakers something to salivate over. Tell me, is your company looking for new business or are you booked up?"

Ann felt her throat constrict. "Well, I'm not in the management end, but I understand the owners are looking for new clients. I could give you Gary Nesbitt's number."

"Yes, please do. I'm in MI5 Security Service, and there's this project I'm doing for the Tourist Authority. Can't be more specific right now, but I'm looking for a security consulting firm."

Ann gave him the number.

"Right, thanks," he said after a slight pause. "But tell me now. Do they know what they're doing?"

"Yes, they do. It's a small company, but every team member is top-notch."

"Including you."

She laughed. "Especially me."

He chuckled. "That's my Ann, or I guess I should say, you once were. Is Gary in today?"

"Yes. I saw him a little while ago. Would you like me to transfer you to him?"

"Yes, thank you."

"Good-bye, Peter."

Ann pushed the buttons on the phone, releasing the call to Gary's office. She leaned back in her chair, closed her eyes, and wondered what the two men would talk about.

Gary replaced the telephone handset. He took in a deep breath and let it out slowly as he tried to put his talk with Peter Watkins into perspective. He had felt a brief spark of hope when the Englishman had explained a little of what he wanted.

Then reality set in. Gary knew that getting this job was a long shot, and besides, Peter had been very stingy with the details, saying only that it was a substantial project. Obviously Peter would research SecurityCheck carefully. He had asked for references, and Gary felt their prior clients would give favorable reports. Maybe there was a chance.

He called Ann and asked her to come by his office. She appeared at his door and seemed nervous.

"Come in and sit down. I appreciate you referring Mr. Watkins to us."

Ann sat in a chair in front of his desk. "I thought it might be a possible win-win," she said.

"I sure hope so." He paused. "Are you all right?"

She nodded, but her look of concern remained. "Did. . .did you and Peter talk any about—us?"

Gary looked at her in surprise. "He said that you and he knew each other at Cambridge."

Ann's face flushed. "Um, yes. He was studying social and political science, but we were both in the same college. He always said he wanted to go into British civil service and work his way to the top. If ambition will do it, he'll make it."

"He sure sounded confident."

"Oh, he's *very* sure of himself. I ought to know."

Gary saw the stricken look on her face and realized the last comment had slipped out. "I see. Ann, I don't mean to pry, but obviously this is painful, and I'm sorry. Lord knows *I've* got plenty of regrets." He hesitated. "Are you having trouble letting it go?"

"Yes."

"If it's any help, it does get better in time." A wry smile came to his lips. "What I did was at least as bad as scamming a bank. That necklace I stole was worth five million dollars, according to the appraisal filed as evidence against me."

"It's not just the money. I was wild back then. *Really* wild."

"So was I." Gary shrugged. "I didn't grow up in the best of

homes, not that it's any excuse for what I did. My dad was an airline pilot, and unfortunately he wasn't a caring father *or* a faithful husband. He and my mom divorced when I was in college. After I graduated, I decided it was easier to take what I wanted rather than work for it. And that attitude is what landed me in prison. Fortunately, that wasn't the end of the story."

"I can't blame a dysfunctional family," Ann said. "I have loving parents and grew up in a good home. I started rebelling in high school, and it carried over into college. And then I met Peter."

"First thing?"

Ann smiled, but Gary saw pain around the edges. "Yes. It was my first year, and I had just met my tutor. When I returned to the Junior Common Room, I heard this charming British accent coming from around the corner. Then came my surprise at seeing him. Peter's Indian ancestry is quite pronounced: black eyes and hair, dark skin. Quite attractive, I have to admit."

"If we get this job, will it cause you a problem?"

A hard look came to her face. "No."

"Good. Then I need to get John up to speed." He reached for his phone.

Ann started to get up.

"Please stay," Gary said. "We need your input."

After Gary placed the call, he and Ann moved to the conference table.

John hurried in and sat down. "What's up?" he asked.

"Thanks to Ann, we may have a shot at a job in England."

John grinned. "That's great. Who's the client?"

"MI5, Britain's internal security service. I just got off the phone with Peter Watkins. He's one of their agents."

"Maybe we should move Ann to marketing."

"Oh, no," she said. "Hacking's my thing."

"What do you think our chances are?" Gary asked.

Ann looked thoughtful. "It seems a little odd that a British ministry would consider an American company, but Peter almost always gets what he wants. If he decides on SecurityCheck, he'll get it approved."

"Any idea what he's like to work for?"

"He's focused. Intense, actually, and he can be quite demanding."

"That's okay, but is he fair?"

"You mean, is he likely to stab us in the back?"

"Yeah. If we commit to an unreasonable client, we could end up in even worse trouble than we're in now."

"Well, Peter doesn't operate by the same code of ethics as we do, but I don't think he'd give you any trouble."

"Know much about his background?" John asked.

"Not a lot," Ann said. "As students we were pretty much wrapped up in university life. I know his father is English from a prominent Midlands family, and his mother was an immigrant from New Delhi."

"You say 'was.' She's dead?"

"Yes, in childbirth. The father's family was relieved since they were against the match from the beginning. This was very painful for Peter; he only talked about it once, when he was drunk."

"So his father raised him?"

"You've heard the term *benign neglect?*"

"I'm afraid I have."

"First, Peter's father hired a governess. Then, when Peter was old enough, it was a series of boarding schools."

Gary leaned back in his chair. "If we get this, we'll have to hit the ground running. Peter said he'll want the work to commence immediately. That could play havoc with our planning and preparation."

"We'd probably be able to use some of the Fort Knox equipment," John said. "That would cut down the lead time."

"I guess, but what about the preliminary research? I suspect we won't have time for that."

"We could do it as we go."

"We may have no choice. Well, we should know soon."

As Tuesday morning dragged on, Gary began to wonder if he would hear from Peter Watkins. Even though he had tried to concentrate on prospecting for new clients, his thoughts kept drifting back to the mysterious Englishman. But when the clock on his computer reached 10:00 A.M., his hope began to fade, since it was 6:00 P.M. in London. Peter had probably ended his workday by now.

Gary jumped when his phone chirped. He slowly picked up the handset. "SecurityCheck, Gary Nesbitt speaking. Can I help you?"

"Peter Watkins here. I certainly hope so, Gary. Ready to talk business?"

Gary took a deep breath. "Yes, I am. Can you hold on a moment? I want to conference in John and Ann."

"Certainly."

Gary set up the connections, then switched to speakerphone. "Okay, go ahead, Peter."

"Right. I've spent all day vetting you chaps, and I'm pleased to say SecurityCheck passed with flying colors. I'd like to hire you to begin immediately."

Gary grabbed a lined pad. "Then I suggest we talk about what you want us to do, and. . ."

Peter interrupted. "May I make a suggestion?"

"Uh, yes, of course."

"You and Ann really should check your E-mail. The document is encrypted for security purposes, but Ann should have no problem rectifying that for you."

Gary turned around and activated his Outlook window. There at the top of his inbox was an unread E-mail. A few minutes later, Ann laid a single page on his desk, which stated the target and the amount to be paid on completion. Gary wasn't sure which piece of information surprised him more.

"Does that seem agreeable? Time is moving on, you know," Peter said.

Gary cleared his throat. "Normally John and I discuss these things before committing; however, I think I can say this is a go. Right, John?"

"Okay by me."

"Good," Peter said. "I *like* working with decisive people. Now, Gary, how many people will be on your team?"

"Five."

"Fire me off an E-mail with their names. . .use the same encryption, please. . .and I'll have you on tomorrow's 5:40 P.M. British Airways flight to Heathrow."

"Tomorrow. I don't think we can be ready by then."

"Oh, come now. All you have to do is trot down to LAX two hours before flight time and off you go. Couldn't be simpler."

"But we've got a lot of equipment we have to crate up and ship, besides the personal preparation."

"I can't pack your bags for you, but I've already dispatched a British Airways freight truck to your location. Show the men what you want shipped, and they'll take it from there."

"But we've got explosives and all *kinds* of sophisticated electronics."

"Not to worry. I work for MI5, so I know how to handle these things. I'll see that your toys arrive at your hotel. By the by, I'm putting you up at the London Bridge Hotel. Nice digs and convenient to the target."

"Uh, I have a question," John said.

"What's that, John?" Gary asked.

"Would someone tell *me* what the target is?"

"Oh, sorry," Peter said. "It's Waterloo Barracks in the Tower of London."

"Uh, isn't that where the Crown Jewels are kept?"

"Right you are. The British Tourist Authority is quite concerned that the Tower security be absolutely top drawer. What with worldwide terrorism plus the odd ruffian out to pinch what isn't his, there *is* reason to worry, don't you know. We can discuss all the details when you get here. So are we all set now?"

Gary settled back in his chair. "We are now. See you tomorrow."

"Actually, twelve noon day *after* tomorrow, but I understand. Good-bye until then."

"Bye."

The line went dead. Gary replaced his handset and waited. A few seconds later John flew through the door, his eyes wide.

"Can we do this?" John asked as he threw himself into a chair.

Gary smiled. "Peter seems to think we can, and I'm sure of it. But you'd better start rounding up all our gear for the British Airways people."

"*What* gear?"

"All the Fort Knox stuff plus anything else you think we might need, and see if you can get us one of those one-man-band TV cameras that reporters use."

"What do we need that for?"

"High-quality video, plus it might come in handy as a prop. Reporters can go places we common folk can't."

"Right. I'll see if Sully knows of a source. Anything else?"

"Be sure we have plenty of C-4. That's something we won't be able to get in England. And check with Dan and Ann. Oh, and speaking of Sully, have you seen him? I have to know if he can go."

Sully stuck his head in the door. "Someone mention my name?"

"Are you available for a job in London?" Gary asked.

"England?"

"Last time I checked that's where it was."

"Cool. Count me in. When do we leave?"

"Five-forty tomorrow afternoon."

"Man, I'd better get busy. Same vehicle types as for the army job?"

"Yes. Large truck and a car."

"I'll get right on it." He turned to go.

Gary snapped his fingers. "Hold on, I want you to do something else as well."

"What?"

"I need some disguises from Costumes for U." Gary closed his eyes. "Let's see. Get me some uniforms: Beefeater, London bobby, utility workers, deliverymen, FedEx, UPS. Oh, and evening clothes for everyone."

"Evening clothes?" Sully asked, as if Gary had said something in Swedish. "You mean, like tuxedoes?"

"Yes, only I think Ann would appreciate a gown." Gary paused. "You *have* worn a tux before, haven't you?"

"Naw, man. Movie scripts don't say anything about wearing tuxes while wrecking cars."

"Well, it's never too late to try something new. Get all our measurements, and ask Ann what kind of gown she'd like." Gary paused. "On second thought, see if she can go with you. She can check the catalogs for English working clothes, and if you two see anything else we might need, order it. But tell 'em it's a rush job. We *have* to be at LAX by 3:40 tomorrow afternoon."

"Okay, boss. After I arrange for the vehicles I'll head on over there."

"Great."

Sully hurried off.

"John, would you make a run to the bank?"

"Sure. How much cash do you want me to get?"

"Ten thousand. We'll change half of it to pounds in London."

48

"Will do." John's tense expression eased a little. "This couldn't have come along at a better time."

"I agree. I think it's the answer to our prayers." Gary smiled. "God seems to operate on the just-in-time principle, which is sometimes uncomfortable."

John stood up. "You got that right. I'll break the news to Dan and see if I've got his needs covered. Then I'll go to the bank."

"Right. Time's getting short."

chapter 5

Gary stifled a yawn as he led the way into London's Heathrow terminal. The clock said 12:10. A ten-and-a-half-hour flight through eight time zones had taken them past midnight and into Thursday. Although he had managed a few hours of sleep, Gary knew he was suffering from jet lag, and the day was far from over. Passengers bustled about the jammed arrival lounge, moving in every direction.

The walk through the web of passageways seemed endless, but they finally arrived at the immigration hall. Gary groaned when he saw the long lines snaking leisurely toward the bored inspectors.

"Man, I didn't think England could *hold* this many people," Sully said.

The man in front of Gary turned his unsmiling face on Sully, then, unspoken admonition delivered, faced forward again.

"Whoa, *what* a look," Sully said. "That rates at *least* a ten on the death-o-meter."

Gary had a hard time not smiling, even though the numbness from their long trip was still with him. The line inched forward in lethargic ripples. At long last Gary reached his turn before the inspector. He handed the man his passport and landing card.

The man thumped the passport with an ancient stamp and placed the landing card in a tall stack. "Enjoy your stay in the United Kingdom," he said without feeling.

Gary took his passport and stepped to the side. The others went through the same ritual. Dan was the last one through.

"Where to now?" Dan asked.

"Baggage claim," Gary said. He spotted a sign up ahead.

A medium-height man in a conservative suit waved. "Ann, over here." He had black eyes and hair and dusky skin.

"Must be Peter," Gary whispered to John. Gary started maneuvering through the crowd toward their client.

Peter's eyes left Ann and fastened on Gary.

He's very sure of himself, Gary thought.

"Gary Nesbitt, I presume," Peter said. "Peter Watkins, at your service." He flipped open his wallet.

Gary glanced at the MI5 ID. "Pleased to meet you," he said. He shook the man's hand and noted his firm grip.

Gary performed the rest of the introductions. Peter handled each one with reserved grace. His confident smile turned quizzical when he met Sully, but he quickly recovered.

Peter turned to Gary. "Well, then, I trust you are ready to begin. We've got the rest of the day ahead of us."

"That's what we signed on to do," Gary said.

"That's the spirit." Peter started walking toward baggage claim.

"Thank you for flying us over first-class," Gary said.

"Glad to do it. Actually, thanks goes to the British Tourist Authority, since they're funding the security work we're doing. I've been learning a lot about tourism in my work of late. It's quite an industry, important to the economy and all that."

"I imagine so."

Peter glanced over his shoulder. "So, Ann, excited about being back in the UK? Bring back fond memories?"

"I'm looking forward to our job and seeing London again."

"That's all?"

"Yes, that's all."

A few minutes later they arrived at baggage claim. Passengers from all over the world packed themselves around the carousels. The buzz of hundreds of voices provided an uncomfortable background.

A tall man with long blond hair tied in a ponytail approached. He had a diamond stud in one earlobe and a smile on his face that was not echoed in his blue eyes.

"Allow me to introduce my associate, Ian Hayford," Peter said. "He'll be assisting me in the Tower evaluation."

Gary looked the man over as Peter made the introductions. Ian had a heavy build that was in no way flabby, and his eyes seemed cold and hard.

Eventually, the baggage for their flight started tumbling off the conveyor and thumping down onto the moving carousel. The Americans grabbed their luggage and gathered about Peter, who led the way outside to two cars parked in a tow-away zone. The sky was gray, and the humidity made the air seem almost solid. Peter directed the dividing up of personnel. Gary and Ann ended up in his car, while Ian took John, Sully, and Dan.

Ann got in the backseat. Gary slipped in beside Peter and buckled in. Peter pulled out and weaved through the airport traffic with a skill and speed that reminded Gary of Sully, except Sully was better. Several minutes later the powerful car roared up onto the M4 motorway. Peter swerved into the inside lane, cutting off another driver who was also in a hurry. He swept past car after car, and several times had to flash his lights to clear the path ahead. Approaching London, the motorway ended, and Peter slowed a little as they took the A4 through Chiswick, Hammersmith, and Kensington, and finally into Westminster.

Up ahead, Gary could see the Houses of Parliament and Big Ben. Peter made a turn on a street parallel to the Thames and took the ramp down into an underground garage.

"Thames House on Millbank," Peter said as he parked the car, "is the home of MI5. MI6, the James Bond chaps, are across the river near Vauxhall Bridge." He turned around in his seat. "I see Ian made it. Shall we retire to my office?"

Gary got out, stretched his legs, and glanced toward Peter, who was talking to Ian. Gary reached down and placed a tiny transmitter and GPS receiver inside the front fender. Ann stepped out and joined him. John came over with Dan and Sully.

"Right, follow me," Peter said.

He led them to the elevators and up to his office. Ian went for extra chairs. Soon they were all gathered around Peter's desk.

"Would anyone like tea, coffee?" Peter asked.

"Nothing for me," Gary said.

Peter looked around, but no one said anything. He turned back to Gary. "So, are you ready to begin?"

Gary glanced at Ann, who gave him a barely perceptible nod. "Almost," he told Peter. "Your E-mail said you wanted a security audit on the Tower of London, focusing on Waterloo Barracks. We're to attempt taking something from the Barracks. If we succeed we get a bonus, and your security will obviously need improving." He grinned. "And if we fail, you can assume a real burglar wouldn't do any better."

"That's bang on."

"So what do you want us to snatch, or can we choose?"

Peter opened a folder and pulled out a large color photo. "I want you to pinch this." He moved the photo in an arc so all could see it. "This is the Queen Consort's Crown, more commonly called the Queen Mum's Crown, one of the most popular of the Crown Jewels." He pointed to an immense gem. "And *that* is the Koh-I-Noor, the most famous diamond in the world. It weighs 105.6 carats and was presented to Queen Victoria in

1849 when England annexed Punjab." He smiled. "As you might imagine, India would like it back, but that is not likely to happen."

"It's the jewel in the crown," Ann said with a smile.

Peter looked at her in obvious surprise. "Very clever, Ann. An Indian diamond in the Queen Mum's crown, just as India was called the jewel in the crown of the British Empire, back in the days of the Raj." He maintained his gaze for a few seconds, then turned back to Gary.

"More recently," Peter continued, "when the Queen Mum died, her crown accompanied the body to Westminster Abbey, and, of course, out came all the Indian nabobs for a few broadsides at the old Empire. Pure opportunism.

"As you probably know, the British Museum has loads of this and that, which various countries want back—Egypt and Greece come to mind. The government considers it pure cheek, of course. We pinched the stuff fair and square, and occasionally paid for it."

An electronic chirp sounded. Both Peter and Ian checked the phones on their belts, but Peter won. He opened the phone and brought it to his ear.

"Peter Watkins here," he said.

He listened for a few moments then said, "I see. I'm quite busy right now so I'll have to call you back. Bye." He clipped the phone on his belt. "Sorry about that. Now, are we clear on what's to be done?"

"I think so," Gary said, "except for the paperwork."

Peter pushed two pieces of paper across his desk. "Here's the contract, one copy for you and one for us. I've already signed. If you and John would complete it." He also handed Gary a check and a plastic card. "And here is your advance and a government credit card for your expenses." He paused. "Do be careful with that."

"Oh, we will." Gary folded the check and stuck it and the

credit card in his wallet. He and John signed both copies of the contract and gave one back to Peter. "Now, we need a document from MI5 stating *exactly* what we are doing, in detail, and that in performing our work, SecurityCheck is not in violation of any laws."

"I think you will find this meets your needs." Peter pushed another sheet of paper over to Gary.

Gary read it over very carefully, then looked up. "That should do it. We have no desire to visit Scotland Yard while we're here."

"Don't blame you a bit. Now, I must warn you about pinching the crown. I want a realistic test, so the security people at the Tower do *not* know what you are up to, and neither do the police. My department is the only one in MI5 that knows about this operation, since we're in charge of the work for the Tourist Authority. So do be careful, won't you?"

"We always are, but thanks for the warning."

"Good. If you succeed, you *must* bring the crown back to your hotel immediately, so I can call off the dogs, so to speak. All clear?"

"I think so."

Peter leaned back in his chair. "Now that we've got our business sorted out, any tourist plans after you complete the job?"

"We discussed that on the way over," Gary said. "We'd like to see the sights in London, take in a play, perhaps tours of Windsor Castle and Hampton Court. Ann suggested we take a side trip to Scotland, maybe even a trip to the Orkney Islands."

"Sounds like a good plan, but England has island getaways as well. The Isle of Wight and the Isle of Man are quite famous tourist stops. Working with the Tourist Authority has really opened my eyes to what England offers." He stood up. "But I'm keeping you from your work. Ian and I will drive you to your hotel." He handed Gary a card. "Here's where you can reach me. My mobile number is on there as well."

Dan slipped back into Gary's hotel room, where the others were waiting, and removed his earphones. "All the rooms are clear. We aren't being bugged."

"Good, but I want a complete sweep every day to make sure it stays that way," Gary said.

"Will do."

"Okay, everyone, take a seat," Gary continued. "First of all, are we all convinced Peter Watkins works for MI5 and that this job is on the up-and-up?"

"I am," John said. "We already knew that MI5's offices are in Thames House, and Peter's name was painted on his door. It seems reasonable that MI5 would be conducting a security review of the Tower of London, especially with world terrorism on the rise."

"I agree. Ann, what about you?"

"I think he's legit. There were MI5 signs on the walls, and the papers on his desk looked official to me. Plus, this is the type of career he always talked about when we were at Cambridge."

"Dan? Sully?"

"He's the real thing," Dan said.

"Hey," Sully said, "you're asking a Hollywood stuntman for a reality check?"

"Humor me."

"Consider yourself humored. That dude looks like the real thing to me."

"Thank you, Mr. Sullivan." Gary turned to Dan. "Did you get anything in Peter's office?"

"A little. I picked up his mobile phone's ID and signaling protocol, as well as considerable data on the network connections in his office. Standard stuff and not very well protected."

"Ann, how did the microcam test out?"

She smiled as she fingered a gaudy pin clipped to her blouse. "I looked over John's shoulder while he transferred the recording to disk. The image is surprisingly sharp and the sound is so-so; you can make out what's said. I even got a shot of Peter's MI5 ID at the airport. I'm impressed."

Gary laughed. "John's gadgets usually work fairly well."

"Thanks," John said. "And speaking of the same, I have presents for everyone." He opened a small box and pulled out five flesh-colored objects that looked like hearing aids. He gave each member one, then picked up his and held it up. "Earphone radios, made to Dan's specifications. Almost undetectable, and notice: no external mike to worry about." He pointed to a tiny crevice. "The microphone is in this little slot right here, and believe it or not, it works even better than the external jobs.

"Each earphone has its own ID, allowing Dan to shift channels remotely. However, they share the same channel by default so we can talk to each other. And, of course, the transmissions are encrypted."

"What's the range?" Gary asked.

"Five to ten miles at ground level, further higher up."

"Good job."

This seemed to please John. "Thanks."

Gary turned to Dan. "Have you got a clean signal from Peter's car?"

"Couldn't be better."

"Good. Sully, you and Dan go pick up the vehicles. Get two sets of keys so our drivers will have keys for both, and make sure the truck has double rear doors. Bring the truck back to the loading dock, and I'll check with the hotel about our equipment."

"Yes, boss," Sully said.

Gary watched them go. Then he pulled his laptop toward himself, put on an earphone with a boom mike, looked up a number on the Internet, and double-clicked it. The phone rang twice.

"MI5 Security Service, how may I direct your call?"

"Peter Watkins, please," Gary replied.

"One moment, sir."

As soon as Gary heard the first ring, he disconnected. *Yes,* he thought to himself. *Peter Watkins really does work for MI5.*

Rain drummed on the roof of the rental truck as Gary surveyed the result of their labors. It had been a rush job, but they had managed most of the truck's conversion tasks by 5:00 P.M. Outside, high on the right side near the back and hidden inside a rectangular housing, John had installed the telescoping mast for the parabolic antenna and low-light microcam, and all around the roof he had placed concealed video cameras. Inside the cargo box, the auxiliary power unit hummed away in a corner, supplying power for all the electronics. A worktable ran along the front and wrapped around the right side, the last five feet detachable. A row of monitors was mounted above the worktable, providing views of outside and the cab's interior. On the left side, the costume locker occupied the front corner, alongside storage cabinets with shelves above and below. The team had set up most of Dan's communications gear, but many unpacked boxes were stacked randomly on the shelves.

It was time for Gary and John to go. "We'll leave you to it," he said.

Ann turned her head and smiled, obviously looking forward to the team's first op.

Gary walked to the back of the truck's cargo box, opened his umbrella, and opened the rear doors. Wind blew rain inside. John stepped down first. Gary followed and closed the doors.

"You're good to go," Gary said.

"Roger," Dan's voice said in the earphone radio.

The truck pulled away from the curb. Gary and John returned to the hotel.

Gary and John monitored the entire op from Gary's room, listening in on their earphone radios but not participating. They watched the red dot representing Peter's car as it moved along the London map on Gary's laptop, the team's truck's blue dot following. A data link updated the GPS positions in real time.

The red dot traced a path that led from Thames House past Parliament and Trafalgar Square to Regent Street, until it winked out in London's Soho district. The blue dot lingered in the area for several minutes then turned south, crossed London Bridge, and entered the Snowsfields National Car Park on Kipling Street, several blocks from the hotel. Gary shut down his computer when he saw the blue dot wink out. He removed his earphone radio and turned it off. John did the same.

"That was nicely done," Gary said. He knew that much from listening in on the radio circuit. The details would come later.

"Yes, it was," John agreed. "And the radio and GPS links are working great, just like Dan said."

They only had a few minutes to wait. John let the excited team members in.

"Grab chairs, everyone," Gary said as he led the way over to a table. "Let's get this debrief over with." He waited until they were all seated. "Dan, you start."

"He lives on the fifth floor of Regent Place, apartment 503, and thanks to Ann, we got a good position. It's up front, just to the left of the main entrance."

"Peter left his mobile phone on," Ann said. "I ran a program to simulate a cellular tower, and Dan homed in with the parabolic antenna."

"Good work," Gary said. "How did the telescoping mast perform?"

"Like a champ," Dan said. "Up and down at the push of a button, and the parabolic antenna and microcam both did great."

"I like what I'm hearing," Gary said. "We've checked out some of our gear. We've vetted Peter, and now we even know where he lives." He grinned. "I think that's enough fun for one night. Let's pack it in. We start the grunt work tomorrow early."

chapter 6

Gary took a long sip of coffee. He felt much better after eight hours of sleep, but his jet lag wasn't quite ready to pack it in. Still, the caffeine did clear away a few of the cobwebs. He scanned the dining room as he waited for the others to arrive. The white table-cloths, silver, and crystal were quite elegant, but that was to be expected in a four-star hotel. A fresh flower arrangement in a large vase graced a table in the center of the room.

Gary turned at the sound of rapid footsteps behind him. John strode across the room as if he were late for something. If he was tired, his wide grin didn't show it.

John took the chair next to Gary. "Top of the morning to you," he said.

Gary smiled. "Try again. I think that's Irish."

"Whatever. So how are you?"

"Still a little tired but a lot better than yesterday. What about you?"

"I feel great, man. I'm really looking forward to this job."

"Glad to hear it."

John's expression turned serious. "What's your gut feeling?"

"It's going to be harder than anything we've ever done before, but we can do it. *And* collect our final check, *and* the bonus."

"That's what I want to hear."

"Are the others coming?"

"Should be. Sully was stumbling around when I left. I asked him to roust everyone out."

"Good. We've got a lot to do today."

"Don't you know it." John looked around. "Here they come now."

Dan and Ann sat on the other side of the table while Sully took the chair on the other side of Gary. The waiter seemed to materialize out of nowhere. The man poured coffee for the newcomers and refilled Gary's cup. Then he took their orders and disappeared into the kitchen.

"What's on tap for today?" Ann asked.

"Tour the Tower of London," Gary said. "Dan will be monitoring from the truck while the rest of us provide the sensor data. Then we document the security setup and look for weak spots."

"Any idea how we're going to break in?"

"Nope. I thought about asking a Beefeater to go get the crown, but I suspect it won't be that easy."

Ann snickered. "Very funny. Actually, they're called yeomen warders."

"Duly noted," Gary said. "Now, does Ms. O'Brien happen to know a way we can break in?"

"Oh, no, not me. The only thing *I* break into is a program."

The waiter returned bearing a large tray and began serving them. Gary waited until he left before bowing his head and offering up silent thanks for his food. When he looked up he noticed Ann looking at him quizzically; then she closed her eyes and looked down. Sully and Dan were already well into their eggs and breakfast sausages.

While the team didn't exactly wolf down their food, they

didn't dawdle either. Soon the plates were empty. Gary had to admit it was an outstanding breakfast, and the service better than any he could recall. Seeing that everyone was done, Gary got up and started for the exit.

Dan hurried to catch up. "Help me with the hotel cameras?"

"Sure," Gary said. "You going to monitor the placement from the truck?"

Dan shook his head. "No, that would take too long. I'll use the laptop up in my room." He held up a paper bag. "Here."

Gary looked inside. "One of 'em looks like a wax apple."

"It is, except it has a camera and mike inside instead of a worm. There's a basket of wax fruit in the lobby." Dan pointed to the next object. "That gray slab is for the outside. It's a pretty good match for the first-floor limestone. And the last one is a fake electrical outlet for the corridor outside our rooms. The apple is easy. Set it on top, and I'll guide you in positioning it. But be careful of the other two. Once you pull the tape off, the adhesive will latch onto the first thing it touches, so make sure the camera is positioned before you stick it on."

"I understand."

"Let's do the lobby first. I'll call you from upstairs."

"Okay."

Gary waited until the others were out of sight, then strolled into the lobby. The manager was standing behind his desk. He looked up as Gary walked past.

"Good morning, sir. May I be of assistance?"

Gary smiled. "Good morning. No, just going to sit for a spell."

"Very good, sir." The man dropped his head and continued his work.

Gary spotted the basket of wax fruit and sat down on a couch across from it. He reached into his shirt pocket and pulled out his earphone radio, placed it in his right ear, and turned it on. A few moments later he heard Dan's voice.

"Gary, are you in place?"

Gary glanced toward the manager.

"Yes," he whispered.

He reached into the sack, pulled out the wax apple, and walked to the fireplace. He examined the painting over the mantle, then went over to the basket. A quick peek assured him the manager wasn't looking. Gary quickly placed the apple on top of the other artificial fruit.

"How's that?" he whispered.

"Great view of the ceiling," Dan said. "Down 80 degrees, clockwise 10."

Gary repositioned it.

"That's got it. Now take a turn outside."

"Roger that."

Gary picked up the bag and walked through the lobby. He pushed through the front door, stopped on the sidewalk, and looked both ways. It was pleasantly cool, and blue skies had replaced last evening's rain.

"Where do you want it?" he asked.

"Either side will do nicely. Go down about twenty-five feet and let's take a look."

Gary turned left and estimated twenty-five feet. He pulled out what looked like a thin slab of stone and saw the barely visible lens recessed into the surface. Leaving the tape in place, he positioned the slab against the building, noting that it blended in quite well.

"That's perfect, right there," Dan said.

"Okay. I'll stick it on." He removed the tape and pressed the slab into place. The camera was almost impossible to see.

Gary went inside and hurried through the lobby. The manager looked up, smiled, and returned to his business. Gary took the elevator up to their floor and stepped into the corridor.

"I'm in the hall," he said.

"Go to the end and point it back toward the elevator."

Gary got in position and removed what looked like an electrical outlet plate. He knelt down and placed the camouflaged camera against the wall.

"It's upside down," Dan said.

"Sorry." Gary turned it around.

"Perfect," Dan said. "Stick it on."

Gary removed the tape and set the plate in place.

"Is John in there with you?" he asked.

"Yeah, we're all in here."

"Okay, let me in."

A door opened down the corridor, and Dan peered out. Gary hurried inside and closed the door.

"What now?" John asked.

"Get on with the tour," Gary said. He turned to Ann. "Have you had time to set up your hacker gear?"

"Checked out and ready to go," she said.

"Good. Dan, how about your surveillance equipment?"

Dan pointed to his table. "Right there: two TV cameras and wideband receivers for everyone. Whatever electromagnetic signals are flying around in there, we'll get on disk."

"Good. Is the truck's command center set up?"

"I have to check out the receivers, but I can do that on the way over there."

Gary turned to Sully. "Mr. Sullivan, think you can drive us to the Tower of London without getting lost?"

"No problem, boss."

Gary stood by the truck's open back doors, his hand on a handhold. He looked all around. Large, fluffy white clouds sailed serenely across the deep blue sky. Sully was up in the driver's seat while the other team members waited inside the command center.

Gary pulled himself up into the back of the truck and closed the doors. The fluorescent lights provided subdued but adequate lighting. A long row of monitors above the worktable presented blank screens. A jumble of stacked boxes sat on the shelves on the left, above and below the cabinets. The auxiliary power unit's turbine hummed away, providing energy for all of the equipment. Dan emptied a nylon bag on the worktable and started sorting out the surveillance equipment. Ann sat to Dan's left, dividing her attention between two laptop computers. John stood well forward, examining the gauges on the auxiliary power unit.

Gary opened a cabinet, pulled out a map, and took it over to the worktable. He smoothed it out and located London Bridge; then he traced the path to the Tower of London. He turned to Ann. "What's the parking situation at the Tower?" he asked.

"Nearly impossible, if you mean right next to it," she said. "We'll have to use a car park."

"There's one on this side of the Thames near the Tower Bridge, and another one across the street from the Royal Mint Coin Museum."

Dan shook his head. "Neither one's close enough. All that stonework, iron, and security gear will limit the transmission range, and I'll lose you completely once you enter the Jewel Room's vault. But I want clean signals up until then."

"We'll be recording our signals, right?" John asked.

"Correct," Dan said, "but I still have to monitor things with my Star Wars gear." He swept a hand about his electronic trove.

"So where do you want the truck?" Gary asked.

Dan pointed to the northwest corner of the Tower complex. "That's the Waterloo Barracks, right?"

"Yes," Gary replied.

"Then I want to be right there." He pointed to the street adjacent to the Flint Tower.

"The police won't allow it," Ann said.

"What about something like a telephone truck?" Gary asked.

"Maybe. But the police are still likely to question us, and I don't think American accents are going to be very convincing."

"You went to school here. Can you fake a British accent?"

Ann paused. "I could probably get away with it, but I think some kind of media truck would work better, say, the BBC."

"Okay, let's do it," Gary said. "Can you and John take care of the signage?"

Ann turned to Dan. "Are we connected to the Internet?"

A smug smile came to Dan's face. "Surely you jest."

"Consider it done," Ann said to Gary. She sat down at one of her computers and clicked the Internet Explorer icon. Her personal home page of customized links flashed on the screen, and a few moments later she was looking at the BBC's home page. After a few more clicks she had located a picture of a camera van. "There we are." She printed the page, then saved the graphic file and opened it with a photo-editing program. A few minutes later she had the BBC signage elements retouched and ready to print.

"John, would you load up the film printer?" Ann asked.

John retrieved a roll of thin plastic film and slipped the end into the continuous-feed laser printer. "Ready."

John collected and trimmed the signs as they came out of the printer.

A speaker mounted to the wall crackled. "Hey, we're doing this sometime today, right?" Sully asked.

Gary grabbed the mike. "Soon. Come back here. We need your artistic advice."

Gary took the printouts from John and went outside with Ann. With Sully's guidance, Gary and Ann peeled the backing off the BBC signs and applied them to both sides of the truck.

"That look official?" Gary asked when they were done.

"Don't know about the Brits, but it would fool me," Sully said.

"Just as long as the bobbies buy it," Gary said. Then another thought came to his mind. "You know how to operate a video camera, don't you?"

"Sure," Sully said.

"Good. When we get to London Tower you'll be Ann's cameraman."

"What?"

"I'll explain when we get there. Get on up front."

"Okay." He returned to the cab.

Ann and Gary climbed into the back and shut the doors.

"We're ready," Gary said. He turned to Ann. "When we get there, it will be up to you two to keep the cops off Dan."

"What if a bobby comes after me?" Ann asked.

"Make like an obnoxious TV reporter until he gives up."

A wry smile came to her face. "Thanks."

Gary grinned. "You're welcome." He grabbed the mike. "Sully?"

"Right here, boss."

"Move out. Is the GPS working on the London map?"

"Looks great."

"Okay, take us over the Tower Bridge and turn left at the Tower's corner."

"Roger. Stand by for takeoff."

Despite what Sully said, the trip across the Thames to the north side of the Tower of London was smooth and sedate. Gary alternated watching his own GPS computer map and the truck's external cameras. "This is it," Gary said.

The truck slowed to a stop with a squeal of brakes.

Gary grabbed the one-man-band TV camera and turned to Ann. "Are you ready?"

"I guess so."

Gary led the way outside and around to the front of the truck. Traffic was getting by this unexpected obstacle, but it was obvious from the honks and waves that the drivers were not happy.

Gary turned toward the Tower's crenellated northern walls.

The stonework was of varying shades of light gray and tan, giving the impression of what the Tower had always been: a fortress. Gary scanned the long wall, spotting the prominent northern towers: Martin, Brick, Bowyer, Flint, and Devereux. And brooding over it all stood the massive White Tower with four domes over its corner towers.

Gary helped Sully with the camera, then handed Ann a mike. Only then did he see what was coming up behind her. He lowered his voice and whispered. "You've got a customer. It's a bobby, and he's not smiling. I'm going back inside."

She glanced over her shoulder. "But. . ."

"You can handle it."

Gary entered the truck and closed the doors. "Patch in the sound from outside," he said.

"Sure thing." Dan flipped a switch and adjusted one of the exterior cameras so they could see Ann, Sully, and the approaching policeman. The man was very tall and looked menacing in his stark black uniform and distinctive conical hat.

"What do I do?" Sully whispered, his voice muffled by the breeze.

Gary picked up the mike. "Act naturally."

"Thanks a lot."

"If he searches the truck, we're dead meat," John said.

"They can handle it," Gary said.

The bobby stopped several paces from Ann. "Here, now," he said, his voice clearly audible through Ann's mike. "What's the meaning of this? You can't impede traffic like this. Move along now."

"But we're with the BBC, doing a documentary on the Tower of London for the British Tourist Authority. It's quite important, and I *must* have these shots. Do say we can stay."

Gary nodded in approval. Her accent sounded good to him, but he realized he probably wasn't a good judge of what Brits sounded like.

The bobby took his time answering, clearly thinking it over. "Well, I don't know. How long will it take?"

"A half hour, perhaps an hour."

The bobby shook his head sadly. "I'm very sorry, miss, but I really can't allow it. You see how you've thrown a spanner into the works, don't you?"

"Oh, come on now," Sully blurted out. "What's it gonna hurt?"

John groaned but said nothing.

Sully clamped his mouth shut, obviously realizing his mistake.

"What's going on here?" the bobby demanded as he started around Ann. "And where are you from, lad?"

Gary picked up the mike. "Head him off, Ann."

Ann scooted into the policeman's path as effectively as an offensive lineman. "Oh, that's easy enough," she said in a hurry.

The bobby stopped with obvious reluctance. "Are you speaking for him?"

"Um, yes. Yes, I am—speaking for him—and the BBC."

"I'm waiting."

Ann smiled at him sweetly and glanced toward the truck. "So am I."

"What?"

"You were wondering about my cameraman?"

"Yes, miss, I was."

"Perfectly understandable; I don't blame you at all."

"Sully's an exchange cameraman from the PBS station in Los Angeles," Gary said into the mike.

Ann gave a barely perceptible nod. "You see, Sully—I mean, Mr. Sullivan—is an American. The BBC has an exchange program with a television station in Los Angeles. We sent one of our cameramen over there, and we got Mr. Sullivan in return."

"Did you now?"

"That's right."

The policeman looked at Sully. "Your name is Sullivan, is it? And are you Irish, then?"

"My grandfather on my father's side was, so I'm one-quarter Irish. The other three-quarters is Hispanic."

"You don't say."

"Actually, I believe I did."

"I'll be taking no cheek off you."

Ann again blocked the bobby's way. "I'm sure he didn't mean anything."

"But. . ."

"And did I mention this program is one of the PM's pet projects?"

The man frowned. "The PM, you say."

"Quite. Anglo-American cooperation and all that, so the BBC brass are most interested that everything go smoothly, not to mention 10 Downing Street."

"Well, now, that puts a different light on things, doesn't it?" He turned around and looked toward the Tower's west side. "Tell you what, see that side street up ahead?"

"Yes."

"Where's your driver?"

Sully cleared his throat. "That's me."

"I thought you were the cameraman."

"Well, ah, I'm the driver also."

"Hmm, jack-of-all-trades, are you?"

"You might say that."

"Well, follow me. There's a taxi queue round the corner, and I'll put you in there."

He spun on his heel and began a quick march.

"Ann," Sully said as he took down the camera rig, "can you hold this?"

"Sure."

Gary watched Ann take the camera and hurry around to the

passenger side. Sully bounded up to the cab, threw open the door, and jumped inside.

Dan picked up the mike. "Sully, we have to stay close to Waterloo Barracks."

"Hey, man. I gotta do what the cop says."

Gary leaned over and pressed the mike button. "Move out, Sully. If we end up too far away, we'll scrub and try something else."

He panned one of the external cameras and watched the wall as the truck followed along after the plodding bobby. The man turned the corner and walked to the head of a long line of taxis where he ordered two of them to move off. Sully guided the truck into the vacated space. Gary turned the camera toward the Tower's northwest corner.

"What do you think?" he asked Dan.

Dan zoomed the camera in. Ancient stonework filled the monitor's screen. "I'm not sure. We're a little farther away but probably close enough."

"Then let's do it," Gary said. "Is our police friend still out there?"

Dan zoomed out and tilted the camera down. "Yes, there he is. Looks like he doesn't want to miss anything."

Gary pressed the mike button. "Ann, Sully, your audience is waiting."

"Got it," Sully replied.

Sully opened the door, got out, and joined Ann, who was standing on the wide green lawn in front of the west wall.

Gary turned to John. "Ready to play tourist?"

"Lead on," John said.

"Where's the cop?" Gary asked.

"He's engrossed in what Ann and Sully are doing," Dan replied. "You're clear."

Gary opened the back doors, stepped down, and ducked behind the truck to stay out of sight. A muted *thump* told him that John had closed the doors. Gary stopped when he got to the front of the truck. Down close to the river he saw a row of shops selling souvenirs and the line to buy tickets. He started walking down the street.

"We going to take the Beefeater tour?" John asked after he caught up.

"Yes. Who knows? We might pick up something useful. Besides, we'll be accompanied in the Jewel House no matter what we do."

"Right."

Gary bought the tickets, and they walked past the wide grassy strip where the moat had once been and through the Middle Tower. Gary looked to the right. The square stone towers of the Tower Bridge rose above the Tower's outer wall. Gary and John strolled through the Byward Towers, where they had a good view of the walls and towers that protected the Inner Ward. There they joined a tour group led by a Beefeater dressed in a dark blue uniform with scarlet piping and wearing a large round hat. He had intense blue eyes and sported a neatly trimmed beard.

"Good morning, ladies and gentlemen, and welcome to the Tower of London," the man said in a booming voice. "We will begin our tour with a brief orientation. The wall behind me guards the Inner Ward, which consists of the White Tower, the Queen's House, the Gaoler's House, the Chapel of Saint Peter ad Vincula, the Waterloo Block, which contains the Jewel House, the Oriental Gallery, the Regimental Museum of the Royal Fusiliers, the Hospital Block, and the Workshop. This wall was built by Henry the Third, and it has thirteen towers. The one you are standing under is the Bell Tower, and up ahead is the Wakefield Tower."

He turned and started walking. "If you will follow me, our first stop will be Traitors Gate, where in ancient times, enemies of the Crown were brought into the Tower."

Gary looked through the gap in the wall at the stone wharf and beyond to the murky waters of the Thames.

The yeoman warder escorted them through a tunnel beneath the Bloody Tower, where the grounds opened up into a roughly square expanse, the center dominated by the commanding bulk of the White Tower with its four tall spires. A large green lawn ran from the inner wall to the tower and down both sides. To the left was the Tower Green in front of the Queen's House and the Gaoler's House. In between ran a walkway and two sets of stone steps leading up to the grass square where the scaffold and chopping block had once been.

The warder led his group past the history-encrusted buildings. Gary found it fascinating, and their Beefeater guide certainly was knowledgeable, as he described those who had been executed or imprisoned in the Tower, people such as Anne Boleyn and, in more recent times, Rudolf Hess. The antiquity of the place intrigued Gary; William the Conqueror had built the White Tower in 1078, long before the Old World realized there was a New.

Finally, the guide stopped before the entrance to the Jewel House. "Gather round, please," he said. "In a few moments, we will enter the Jewel House, which is located on the first floor of the Waterloo Barracks. Once inside the vault, you'll see the Crown Jewels. Please note that photography is strictly prohibited, and loitering is not allowed. Now please follow me."

Gary checked the pen, which held a miniature TV camera, to make sure the lens was not obstructed. He and John drifted to the back of the tour group. After a short wait they walked past a single guard and through the entrance.

"I'm picking up signals," came Dan's voice in Gary's ear. "Video looks good too. We'll see how long it lasts."

Gary and John moved through a serpentine maze that reminded Gary of an airline ticket counter, only this had a lot more class. Tasteful display cases dotted the lobby, and a large-screen

TV projected Queen Elizabeth's coronation.

Finally they arrived at the heavy vault doors. Once inside, Gary spotted a long line of cases. Two moving sidewalks carried the visitors past the crowns and other regalia. Without a word, Gary took one conveyor while John rode the other.

The walls and ceilings were cloaked in gloom, but brilliant beams immersed the regalia in a sea of light. Gary's eyes glazed over as he scanned the crowns, orbs, swords, and lesser but still spectacular objects. The first case contained Saint Edward's crown. Then crown followed orb followed crown followed sword.

At last they reached the fourth case, and there, on the highest shelf, sat the object of their quest: the Queen Consort's Crown, also called the Queen Mother's Crown. It was red with a circlet of white ermine about the base, but these rich details were mere setting. An orb surmounted the crown's arches, and at the top reigned the fabled Koh-I-Noor. Gary's eyes tracked the crown as the moving sidewalk carried him past.

The last case featured the Imperial State Crown, similar in construction to the Queen Consort's, but set with three thousand diamonds. The 317-carat Cullinan II blazed away atop the crown, larger and more brilliant than the Koh-I-Noor but with a less intriguing history. Gary had never seen that many gems on a single object.

Gary stepped off the sidewalk and turned to the guard nearest him. "May I go around again?" he asked.

The guard nodded. "Crowd's light today, so go right ahead."

Gary and John swapped sides and walked back to the start of the conveyors. Gary confirmed what he had suspected on his first trip: All the crowns faced one way. Now he saw what their backs looked like, maybe a little less spectacular, but not much. All in all, the displays were extremely well done. Then he remembered the armored vault doors. *And extremely well protected.* He knew the side walls *had* to be steel and concrete.

After the second viewing Gary and John rejoined the tour

group and followed the yeoman warder out of the vault. The guide's words became a disjointed buzz as Gary's mind rehashed all he had seen, trying to come up with a way to defeat the Jewel House security. It seemed hopeless. Finally, their guide led them back outside.

John sidled up. "That's it," he whispered. "How about cutting out?"

Gary shook his head. "No. I don't want to arouse any suspicion."

At the end of the tour, the yeoman warder bid his charges farewell. Gary and John rushed out the Middle Tower and were once again outside. Gary spotted Sully and Ann up by Legge's Mount, the fortified northwest corner of the outer wall. The bobby was observing their every move.

"Come on," Gary said. "Let's get inside while he's looking the other way."

They reached the truck undetected, climbed inside, and closed the doors.

Dan turned. "Welcome back." He held out his hand. "If you'll let me have those, I'll start downloading."

Gary retrieved his recorder. Dan plugged it into a Universal Serial Bus cable and with a few keystrokes started transferring the data. He took John's recorder and plugged it into another line.

"Great work, guys," Dan said. "The video feed I picked up was excellent until you entered the Jewel House vault. I was even getting signals from some of their security systems, enough to give us a start. But what I'm *really* interested in is what's inside those." He pointed to the downloading recorders. "Oh, and I found something interesting."

"What's that?" Gary asked.

"I think it's a maintenance port on the central office switch the Tower uses."

"Telecom isn't in my skill set. What's a maintenance port?"

"It's used to control the switch, set operating parameters,

check alarm messages, stuff like that. You can even collect call records through it."

"That could come in handy."

"Could save us a lot of time. This one has a dedicated telephone line. Apparently the switch technicians do their maintenance remotely."

"Terrific. I'll add that to Ann's to-do list." Gary took out his earphone radio and turned it off. "Call Sully and Ann so we can get out of here."

A few minutes later Ann entered, lugging the camera, and pulled the doors shut. Gary scanned the TV monitors. Sully ambled past and climbed up into the truck's cab.

A speaker clicked. "Back to the car park?" Sully asked.

Gary took the mike. "Go."

The engine rumbled to life. Sully pulled out of the taxi queue and turned around. The return trip was short. Sully turned into the car park and pulled in beside their car. He ran back and climbed up into the truck.

"Did I miss anything?" he asked.

"Nope, we waited for you," Gary said. "I want everyone up to speed as we go."

Sully rubbed his hands together. "Cool. So what does it look like?"

Gary turned to Ann. "We'll get to that, but first, Dan's found a little something for our hacker."

"Telephone switch maintenance port," Dan said.

Ann's eyes grew wide. "You mean the switch the Tower of London uses?"

"The very one," Gary said.

"Let me see."

Dan pointed to the PC to his left. "I found it using your 'dialing for dodos' program."

"What's that?" Sully asked.

"It dials through the lines assigned to a switch, looking for modems," Ann said. She sat down and typed in a few cryptic commands. Lines of white text scrolled down the text box interface. Several minutes later she turned and looked at Gary. "Didn't you want to tap into the Tower's phone lines?"

Gary nodded. "It's on the task list, providing Dan can find the service panel."

"It's under the street we were on," Dan said. "Probably in a maintenance tunnel."

Ann waved at the PC's screen. "Forget that. I can load a program into the switch to record the phone calls."

"Great. How long will it take?"

"An hour, maybe less. I have all the building blocks I need. All I have to do is add a few lines of code and assemble the pieces."

Gary thought for a moment. "Could you also disable the switch?" He saw she understood what he meant.

She grinned. "You mean like during a heist?"

He nodded. "Yes, if necessary." He knew there were still many problems to overcome before they got that far, but cutting off the Tower's telephone service might prove crucial.

"Nothing could be easier. I'll install a worm program along with the call recorder. Then, issue a command, and the worm brings down the switch's operating system, which cuts off all phone service."

"Great. Get on it after we debrief."

"Will do."

Gary turned to Dan. "What have you got for us?" he asked.

Dan leaned back in his chair. "To start with, they've got closed-circuit digital color cameras all *over* the place. Inside the Jewel House vault, there's a combination passive infrared/ microwave intrusion detector, a heat sensor, plus multiple sound detectors. I don't know how many. I wasn't getting any signals from the cases, but I expect they have motion detectors inside."

"They do," Gary said. "I saw one."

"Okay. First the good news. I think it's likely we can defeat the TV cameras, providing we can tap into their video cables. Chances are good we can also bypass the passive infrared/microwave detectors and maybe the heat, noise, and motion devices. Depends on whether we can locate the data lines."

"What if they're wireless?"

Dan shook his head. "Very unlikely. The vault would cut off the signals." He frowned. "Now the bad news: I don't see any way we can break into that vault. If we could hack the combination and defeat the time lock, maybe, but does anyone really think we can do that?"

Gary looked around. "John? Ann?"

"Not my thing," John said.

"Same here," Ann said. "The vault door is mechanical, not electronic. I might take a shot at the time lock, but that won't do us any good without the combination."

Gary turned to Dan. "What about the TV cables? Won't they be hard to find?"

"No," Dan said. "The location of video wiring is pretty predictable; plus, that stuff is bulky."

"Anything else?" Gary asked.

"That's all so far."

"So what do you think?" John asked Gary.

"The Jewel House is going to be a tough nut to crack," Gary said. "But we knew that when we signed on. All security systems have loopholes, and it's up to us to find and exploit them." He looked at each face in turn. "In my opinion, we're the best security experts, bar none, so it's only a matter of time until we find a way in.

"Now, we're going to take this one step at a time. First, we need a plan to tap the Tower video cables. Dan, I want their communications network unraveled and every weakness identified. Anybody got anything else?"

Again Gary looked all around. He saw concern in their eyes,

but he also sensed their determination to keep going. That suited Gary. He wasn't about to give up on that bonus.

"All right, let's get to work."

Ann turned back to her PC and began coding. At least eavesdropping on the Tower personnel was in the bag.

chapter 7

Gary sat by himself in the hotel dining room, sipping his coffee that had recently been refilled by his patient waiter. It was Monday now, and he was ruminating over the events of the past few days. Saturday, Dan had resumed work on his diagrams of the Waterloo Barracks Jewel House and downloaded the recordings from the Tower's telephone switch. Sully and Ann helped him scan them for useful information, but all they heard were routine conversations.

In the evening, Gary had reminded both John and Dan that heisting the Queen Mother's Crown required tapping into the Tower's closed-circuit surveillance cameras, assuming they found a way to get inside the vault. To Gary's mind, that was a *very* big "if," but it *was* the next logical step.

Then they'd had their first disagreement. Dan suggested continuing their work on Sunday to catch up on their research. Gary told Dan, without fuss or rancor, that SecurityCheck would be standing down on Sunday, and they would pick things up on Monday. Dan had not been pleased, and Sully impossible to read.

He took another sip of coffee, and a rueful smile came to his lips. To work or not to work, that was the question. God told the Israelites they were to work for six days and rest on the seventh, with disobedience punishable by death. Today, the civilized world considered the five-day workweek sacrosanct, but without allocating either of the spare days to God. At the opposite extreme were those who worked seven days a week.

"Good morning," a cheerful voice boomed.

Gary snapped out of his reverie, looked up, and was grateful to see John's smiling black face.

"Good morning to you, Brother John," Gary said. "Seen anything of the others?"

"Nope, but I'm sure they'll be along soon. We've got a lot to do, if we hope to get those video taps planted today."

Gary frowned. "Yeah. Dan sure hammered away at that on Saturday. You'd think he would know by now how you and I feel about Sunday."

"You'd think so." John pulled out a chair and sat down. "You know, he could be probing to see what we really believe."

"He wants to know if we're serious?"

"Could be." John's grin returned. "And if he keeps tromping around on the creek bank, he just might fall in."

"I guess we could pray for that."

"Wouldn't hurt."

Gary caught a movement out of the corner of his eye. Dan walked into the dining room wearing an expression that was hard to read. He wasn't smiling, but he wasn't frowning either. He seemed puzzled. He sat down next to John.

"Good morning," Gary said.

"Morning," Dan said without much feeling.

Ann and Sully came in and took places about the table.

The waiter appeared, poured coffee for the newcomers, took their orders, and left.

"Have you thought about my suggestion?" Dan asked, as if

he couldn't put off the question any longer.

"Sending Ann to fix a telephone problem that we cause?" Gary asked.

"Yes. We've got to have a pretext for getting inside the equipment room. We can't exactly sneak past all those guards."

"What if their telephone equipment isn't in the same room as the video cabling?"

Dan sipped his coffee. "They probably share the same room. I mean, it makes sense to."

"If we focus on the video system, we wouldn't have that worry."

"I *know* that, Gary, but there's no way I can fake a video problem right now."

"I like your idea of getting invited inside; sure would make things easier. Maybe we can arrange it; send them a FedEx package, courtesy of MI5."

"You can't be serious."

"Think about it. The Tower people know that MI5 is reviewing their security. I don't think they'd be surprised if MI5 recommended certain upgrades, maybe even provided the equipment?"

"That's ingenious," Ann said.

"Yeah, not bad," John chimed in.

Dan frowned. "Looks like I'm outnumbered."

"Well?" Gary said. "What about it?"

"Could work. So what are we delivering to the unsuspecting limeys?"

"I'm working on it. Some kind of electronic gadget, but whatever it is, the shipping box has to be big enough to hold a man."

"Are you suggesting. . . ?"

"I'm going to be inside it."

"All right, say we do it. Just how do you expect to get away?"

"I'll use a disguise."

"What kind?"

Gary took a sip of coffee. It was cold, but he barely noticed. "I'm working on that too."

The incessant whine of the truck's auxiliary power unit, although faint, made it hard to concentrate. Gary tried to ignore John's anxious stare. It was hard enough coming up with the hypothetical black box without distractions. Dan wasn't staring, but Gary knew he was growing impatient, as shown by his frequent checks on his communications circuits. And to make matters worse, Gary couldn't decide on a disguise. He had considered, and rejected, utility worker, bobby, and FedEx deliveryman.

"It's almost one," Gary said. "We need a plan."

Ann looked over at him. "What about an improved digital recorder? Greater capacity, improved hardware and software, and so on. You know, new, better than ever."

"That's not bad," Gary said. "I bet they'd buy that, but a digital recorder doesn't take up much room."

"Okay," John said, "throw in some replacement cameras, you know, improved low-light jobs."

"That might work," Gary said. "They do have quite a few cameras." He laughed and patted his stomach. "Think that will account for enough volume?" But even as he said it, Gary felt the twinge of an old fear.

John ran his eyes over his friend's wiry frame. "Yeah, for you. But it sure wouldn't hide me."

"Roger that."

John grinned. "I'll overlook that for now." Then his smile faded. "But how do we make sure they'll take the box where we want?"

"I'll write them a letter of instruction," Gary said.

"That just leaves the disguise."

The answer flashed into Gary's mind like a thunderbolt. "Got it. I'll be a Beefeater."

"Hear, hear."

The British accent was so good it made Gary jump. Turning, he saw Ann's impish smile.

"I'm glad our FedEx delivery person likes it."

"Me?"

"You're the only one who speaks the language."

"I don't know if I can handle a box that heavy."

"Sully will provide the muscle." Gary snapped his fingers. "That reminds me. Sully, we need a shipping container pronto. Take the car and get a box large enough to hide me in. Make it one of those heavy-duty cardboard export jobs."

"I'm gone." He dashed out of the truck.

Gary turned to John. "Rig us an explosive squib so we can blow one of the truck tires. We need an excuse for remaining in the loading dock to give Dan and me enough time."

"I'll get right on it."

Gary peered into the magnifying mirror as he pressed the fake mustache into place. It was black, flecked with gray, and matched the trim beard he had already applied. He moved his head around, making sure the black wig covered his blond hair. Satisfied, he put in the brown contact lenses.

Gary stood up. "Crown me," he said with a grin.

John went to the costume locker, retrieved the distinctive round hat, and placed it on his Gary's head.

"That's amazing," Ann said. "Your hair, the beard, the brown eyes—I'd never recognize you. You look *just* like a Beefeater."

"That's the general idea," Gary said.

"But you sure don't sound like one."

"Let's hope I don't have to talk my way out."

Gary checked the sleeves and belt on the yeoman warder uniform. The crimson piping contrasted sharply with the deep blue that looked almost black.

"I think I'm ready," he said.

"Don't forget the pager," Dan said.

"Right, thanks." Gary picked the GPS device up and clipped it to his belt.

"Ready for me to seal the letter?" John asked.

"Let me look it over," Gary said.

John had created the MI5 letterhead from a cleaned-up video frame Ann had captured in Peter's office. It looked quite good, and Gary thought it should fool the Tower personnel. The letter, from a fictitious MI5 officer, stated what the shipment contained and requested it be stored in the Jewel House closed-circuit TV cable room.

"Okay," Gary said.

John took the letter back, slid it into the FedEx envelope, and sealed it.

Gary glanced at his watch and saw it was almost three o'clock. "Let's get a move on."

He grabbed the blue-and-red FedEx decals and handed them to Sully. "You and Ann apply these to the truck while John and Dan pack me into the box."

"Right," Sully said. "Anybody outside, Dan?"

"You're all clear," Dan replied.

Sully and Ann hurried out, and the doors clumped shut.

"Grab those boxes while I take this down," Gary told John.

He detached the last five feet of the wraparound worktable and stowed it forward. Then he and John erected a random wall of boxes, which hid Dan and the team's equipment.

Gary peered into the large box beside him and eyed the folding chair which rested on a plywood base. Mentally he surrendered his freedom as he contemplated his stay inside this cardboard prison. John looked him in the eye.

"Sure you're okay with this?" he asked softly.

Gary had suffered from claustrophobia all his life. Being in tight places, especially dark ones, had always bothered him, almost to the point of panic. Only in recent years had he managed to control it, but he knew it would never go away entirely.

"I'll be okay," he said finally.

John nodded and helped him inside. "Ready for me to close it up?" he asked.

"Do it," Gary replied, forcing a smile. He removed his yeoman warder hat and placed it in his lap.

John closed the box flaps, plunging the interior into utter blackness. A loud ripping noise told Gary he was now being taped in. Gary felt his heart rate increase. By force of will, he mastered the threatening fear.

"Okay in there?" John asked.

"Yeah. What's the in-flight movie?"

"*Birdman of Alcatraz,* but don't expect a meal. We're cutting back on frills."

"Very funny."

As his eyes grew accustomed to the darkness, Gary saw a dim glow coming from the camouflaged vents. At least he wouldn't suffocate. He heard a scuffling noise and knew John had disappeared behind the box wall. Moments later the engine started, and the truck began to move.

"We're here," Gary heard Dan say over his earphone.

"Thanks," Gary replied.

This warning had been quite unnecessary, since he had felt the truck back up and then stop. The sound of crunching footsteps penetrated the cardboard separating Gary from the outside, and with it a murmur that resolved itself into a querulous voice.

". . .most irregular, if you asks me. Don't recall nothin' about any shipment due today. 'Oo's it from?"

"There's a letter goes with it." Ann's voice sounded confident.

A squeaking sound announced the opening of the doors.

"Coo, look at the size of that thing."

"Here's the letter."

Gary heard a tearing sound, then a long silence.

"It's MI5 business, right enough," the man finally said. "An' I don't muck around with them chaps, if you know wot I mean. But I don't fancy 'auling that all over creation neither."

"Not to worry. My mate and I will truck it for you."

"Now that's right decent. Much obliged to you."

"Only too glad. Now if you'll kindly lead the way. . ."

"Right you are. Mind you, it'll be a tight squeeze some places."

"We're used to that."

Gary grinned as he imagined how Sully was taking this generous volunteering of his services. No doubt he would complain about it later.

The box tilted, and at first Gary thought it was going over. Then it rocked back the other way, tottered a little, and the trip to the cable room began. At first the ride was smooth, obviously over a paved surface. Then came a series of jolting bumps, and Gary realized Sully and Ann were pulling the dolly up some steps. Finally the box leveled out and landed on the floor with a muted *thump*. Gary heard beeping sounds followed by a solid click; then the box moved once more. The clear sound of a door closing and a bolt driving home told him he was finally alone and locked in.

"If you would be so kind," he heard Ann say.

Getting the delivery signature, Gary guessed. Then the sound of retreating footsteps.

"Dan, blow the tire squib," Gary whispered.

"Right," came Dan's voice in the earphone. "Oh, my, seems

we've got a flat tire. Wonder how that happened."

"Just make sure Sully takes his time changing it."

"Roger. Good news, the cable room is right where I thought it was. Let me know when you're ready to proceed."

"Okay. First thing is to get out of my prison."

Gary felt around in the dark, grasped a tab, and pulled. The attached cord ripped through the scored cardboard all the way around the top of the box. Gary pushed, and the top sprang open. Myriads of green and red lights stared at him, bright but offering little illumination. Relief washed over him now that his confinement was over. He stood up and stretched his legs. Then he straddled the box and almost fell when it tipped. His left leg hit the floor, and the box scooted out from under him with a *thump* that was surprisingly loud in the confined space. How he had kept from falling he had no idea.

"What happened?" Dan asked.

"Almost messed up my pretty uniform," Gary whispered in irritation.

"What?"

"I had trouble climbing out."

Gary slipped on his night-vision goggles and looked all around. The light from the LEDs, plus what came in under the door, provided ample light for the night-vision device. He set his Beefeater hat by the door and did a quick check for cameras. There were none. He crept to the door, placed an ear against the cool wood, and listened. All he could hear was his own heartbeat. Satisfied he was alone, he flipped on the lights. He took off his goggles and placed them and the pager inside the concealed pocket of his uniform.

Thick bundles of black cables entered the oblong room from all four corners, and one bundle came through the floor. The bundles merged and split, entering and leaving the various routers, recorders, and switch panels placed about the room.

"Are you getting all this?" Gary whispered. A microcam was

hidden on his uniform, inside the red outline of a crown.

"Am I ever. Now, turn around slowly."

Gary did so, noting the orderly array of equipment along all four walls. Many cable rooms looked like Medusa on a bad-snake day, but this one was neat in the extreme.

"They do nice work," Dan said.

"Don't they, though. Where do you want to start?"

"Good question. The door faces east, and that's the direction of the Jewel House, so start probing the cables on that side of the room."

"Right." Gary pulled out a small electronic device and hurried over to the black bundle coming through the east wall. He picked a cable at random and carefully inserted the test probes.

"Hold it there, I'm getting a picture," Dan said.

"What is it?"

"It's an exhibit of armor—one suit is humongous. Wait while I look it up. Here it is. That camera is in the White Tower. The giant-economy-sized tin suit was Henry the Eighth's tournament armor. Guess he thought that anyone seeing that would die of fright."

"Dan, the meter's running."

"Oh, yes. Well, I'd say you're fairly warm. Try again."

Gary pulled the probes and inserted them into another cable.

"Hmm," Dan said. "That looks like a bunch of dummies on horseback. That's the Line of Kings display, also in the White Tower. Keep going, and pick up the pace. Sully's trying to take his time, but he's got a Beefeater breathing down his neck. Don't know how much longer we'll be able to stay here."

"Roger that," Gary said.

Next came the Spanish Armory display, followed by two cameras in the Royal Fusiliers' Museum. By now, Gary had become adept at inserting and pulling the probes. In the interest of time, he began removing the connection after giving Dan about a five-second look.

"Wait," Dan said. "Go back."

Gary reinserted the probes.

"Bingo. That's one of the second-floor cameras in the Waterloo Barracks. Okay, insert the tap and bury the transmitter inside the cable bundle."

Gary pulled out a tap, inserted the wires, and tucked the plastic box deep within the cables. "How's that?"

"Excellent. Now, the adjacent cables are probably the other Barracks cameras."

Within five minutes Gary and Dan had tapped the remaining cameras on the second floor and those inside the Jewel House vault.

"Great work," Dan said, after checking the latest tap. "That's all of them. Now, see those smaller wires on the outside of the video cable bundle?"

"Yes."

"They probably go to the various detectors: motion, heat, sound, and so on. Pull out the data line sniffer, and let's see what we've got."

"Roger."

Gary took the slim device and picked out two thin cables. He inserted the probes while watching the LCD display. The bar readout suddenly pegged. "Okay, what's that?"

"You're hot today," Gary replied. "That's from a passive infrared/microwave motion detector. Insert the bypass and check the other one."

Gary cut the cable and installed a tiny module, which would transmit a normal signal to the monitoring station. He moved to the next cable.

"That's another one," Dan said.

Gary placed that bypass and made sure both devices were hidden inside the video bundle.

"Any other cables like those two?"

"Not that I can see."

"Okay. That's probably it for the passive motion detectors. That's really all they need for the Jewel House vault and the floor above. Move on to the other cables."

"Dan," Ann's voice broke in. "Sully's almost done."

"Gary, be advised that Sully has the spare on," Dan said. "He's stowing the flat as I speak."

"What about the other sensor lines?"

"Don't have time. We'll wait for you at the car park across the street from the Royal Mint Coin Museum."

"Roger that."

"Good luck. Call if you need anything."

"Don't worry, I will."

After Gary reattached the shipping box's top, he listened at the door but couldn't hear a sound. He put on his Beefeater hat, then turned to the door's lock. He had hoped for a simple double cylinder dead bolt, which he was prepared to pick, but found instead a sophisticated electronic unit. Now he would be forced to trust the electronic passkey that John had assured him would work.

Gary knelt and pressed the plastic box against the lock and waited. Numbers whirled on the LCD display faster than he could read them. Then, one by one, an eight-digit code appeared. Thankful for John's expertise, he punched in the code on the lock's keypad, and the bolt retracted with a solid *thump*. He turned off the light and stepped outside. He looked around, closed the door, and pressed the button to relock it.

"I'm outside the room," Gary whispered.

"Roger," Dan replied.

Gary visualized the location Dan had pointed out on his diagram of the Waterloo Barracks. He was on the lower floor of the Jewel House, so all he had to do was make it to the entrance and slip out. Then he would walk past the Tower Green, down the steps beside the White Tower, through the tunnel under the

Bloody Tower, then across Water Lane and through the Byward and Middle Towers, and he would be home free.

Gary reached the Jewel House entrance, which opened onto a narrow path between the Waterloo Barracks and the Chapel of Saint Peter ad Vincula. Right outside stood a single guard. Gary checked his uniform and felt to make sure his beard and mustache were in place. Last he made sure his hat was on straight.

Gary pushed through the door, walked past the guard, and turned left, maintaining a brisk step until he reached the courtyard surrounding the White Tower. He paused and looked all around. Tourists were everywhere, most in groups, but there were also couples and individuals. Gary glanced to the left and spotted a yeoman warder addressing a tour group in front of the Royal Fusiliers' Museum. Fortunately the Beefeater was facing the building.

Gary hurried off toward the steps leading down to the Bloody Tower. Off to his left, near the White Tower, he saw a small group of tourists waving at him. He shook his head. *They think I'm a Beefeater. Guess that's a good sign.* He looked straight ahead, and after passing the site of the Executioner's Block, he saw a round blue hat coming up the stairs. It was another yeoman warder. Gary froze, unable to move, as more and more of the Beefeater came into view. The man was leading another tour group and seemed unaware of the intruder, but Gary knew that would change soon.

"I've got a problem," he whispered, just loud enough for the mike to pick up. "I'm cut off. There's a Beefeater in front of me and one to the side. If they see me, they'll know I'm not one of them."

"Copy that," Gary heard John say. "Hold on, we'll think of something."

"Don't take too long."

●—○—●

John released the button and set the mike down. Nothing could be heard inside the truck except the muted sounds of traffic on Royal Mint Street. "Any ideas?" he asked.

Ann shook her head.

"We need some kind of diversion," Dan said.

"Yeah, but *what?*" John's angry scowl melted into embarrassment. "Sorry."

Dan nodded. "That's okay."

"Hey, I know," Sully said.

John turned to him. "What?"

"Hey, this is Sully the stunt dude." He turned and dashed for the rear doors.

"Wait," John said. "Where are you going?"

"Take too long to explain. Tell Gary help's on the way."

He was through the doors before John could stop him.

chapter 8

Gary looked straight ahead. The Beefeater was still coming, and Gary expected a cry of alarm at any moment. He turned around and started walking toward the Jewel House when he remembered the tourists over by the White Tower. He glanced in their direction, and again they waved. He took a deep breath and headed toward them, hoping they were not British. When he got close, he saw they were Asian—Japanese, he guessed. *This might work,* he thought. *At least it's worth a try.*

"Gary?" John said. "Sully is working on a diversion, but you've got to give him time."

"I'll do the best I can," Gary whispered as he smiled at the tourists.

●——○——●

Sully ran across the car park with only a vague idea of what he wanted, when he slid to stop. A young man in leather pants and jacket had just come in off the street riding exactly what Sully had in mind. The stuntman's eyes roved over the blue Yamaha

YZ450F dirt bike, so clean it looked new. *Well, maybe it is*, Sully thought. The man parked his bike, padlocked it to a pole using a heavy chain, and walked off.

Sully ran to the truck, grabbed the bolt cutters, and hurried back, shielding the tool beside his body. He looked around and, seeing no one close, cut the shackle and removed the chain. After replacing the cutters, Sully returned and hot-wired the ignition. He kicked the starter, and the powerful Yamaha roared to life.

Twisting the throttle, Sully let out the clutch and roared toward the car park exit. He turned west on Royal Mint Street and raced toward the north side of the Tower of London. He heard a wild shout, and out of the corner of his eye saw the bike's owner running toward him, flailing his arms. Sully accelerated and wove in and out of the dense traffic.

Gary smiled as he approached the tourists. They were obviously a family: father, mother, an adolescent boy and girl, and a child barely past the toddler stage, who seemed in utter awe of this tall man in a striking blue-and-red uniform.

The father bowed, followed by his wife and the older children. The baby of the family continued staring, then broke into a grin of pure joy.

Gary smiled and said, "I say, may I be of assistance?"

The man beamed and bowed again.

Ann sounded pained over the earphone. "That accent is horrible. I hope you're not talking to a Brit."

"Please to excuse, but we are desiring of a question, if it is permitted," the man said.

"Never mind," Ann said, obviously amused in spite of the situation.

"But of course. Ask away, chap."

"This construction is most wonderful to observe," the tourist began, pointing toward the White Tower. "If you please, who was built and when was he doing so?"

Gary thought he understood. "Righto. This magnificent building is called the White Tower, and it was originally built by William the Conqueror. And am I correct that you want to know when it was built?"

The man gave a quick, shallow bow. "Thank you very much. Yes, I am desiring to know the timing of construction."

"Ah, yes, my good man, and so am I."

"Please to beg your pardon?"

Gary took a step back, looked up at tower domes above him and whispered, "That's your cue, Ann."

"Oh, sorry, the year was 1078," Ann said.

Gary returned his gaze to the man. "William the Conqueror began building the White Tower in 1078."

"The building is of great age then."

"Indeed it is."

"Why is named 'white,' if you please?"

Gary waited.

"Don't know," Ann said in his ear. "I'll look it up."

Gary didn't have time to wait. His eyes flicked over the tall building. "The White Knight, one of William the Conqueror's most loyal subjects, built the tower, and so it was named for him. Quite simple, really."

"It's built of white Caen stone," Ann said in his ear.

Gary made a show of looking at his watch. "Well, I really must be going."

The man looked distressed. "Oh, please to wait. We are desiring to know where the head-choppings were accomplished."

Gary knew the answer to that question. He looked over his shoulder and, as he expected, the Beefeater he had seen coming up the steps was standing at the site of the Executioner's Block, talking to his group of tourists. Gary turned back. "It's over where that chap is standing. I'm sure he will be glad to answer all your questions."

"Please to accept our thanks," the man said.

"Don't mention it."

Again, the family bowed several times, except the baby, who was still fascinated by Gary. Then the tourists moved off toward the Block's site.

Gary's ears perked up at a shrill noise. The sound of a screaming motorcycle engine seemed out of place amid the ancient walls and buildings. Gary turned back to the Beefeater who had been in front of the Fusiliers' Museum. He had finished his talk and was shepherding his tour group straight toward Gary. Gary could see the man clearly now, and a puzzled expression came to the warder's face.

Gary whirled around and began walking as quickly as he dared toward the entrance to the Jewel House.

"I say there!" came an urgent cry from behind him. "Who are you?"

Gary kept up his pace.

"Halt!"

Sully extended his left leg and made a sliding turn as he approached the Middle Tower entrance. Tourists scattered out of his way like frantic chickens. He leaned forward over the handlebars and twisted the throttle wide open. The dirt bike screamed over the cobblestones, and in seconds he was past the Byward Tower. Up ahead, tourists were coming and going through the Bloody Tower. Again he made a sliding turn, roared under the portcullis and through the tower. He saw the White Tower off to the right and the steps leading up to the Tower Green dead ahead. He knew Gary had to be up there somewhere.

"Outta my way!" Sully shouted, but he knew the screaming

engine was a far better warning.

Sully popped a wheelie as he raced toward the stairs. At the last moment he laid the bike on its side and slid to a stop. He jumped up, then rode up the steps. Glancing all around, he shot past the back of the White Tower. In the blink of an eye he saw three Beefeaters, and he knew one had to be Gary. The man near the Jewel House stood stock-still, staring straight at Sully. The other two yeoman warders abandoned their groups and ran toward Sully.

"Here, you! Halt!" screamed the one on the right.

Sully put a finger to his chest and mouthed: "Me?"

This seemed to infuriate the man, his face now almost as red as the piping on his uniform.

Sully waited two more heartbeats, then twisted the bike's throttle and let out the clutch. He flashed past the nearest Beefeater and came around in a sliding turn, the rear wheel spewing grass and dirt high into the air. He thundered past the Beefeater who was still screaming at him and continued on toward the warder who was running toward him from the site of the Executioner's Block. Sully dodged him, turned and did a figure eight about both men, then came to a sliding stop between them. Both Beefeaters charged.

Sully cut a wide circle around the men, coming around until he was facing the steps leading down to the Bloody Tower. There he stopped. Straight ahead he saw a man in a Beefeater's uniform disappear down the stairs. Sully grinned. The diversion was a success; now for the grand finale.

He watched the charging yeoman warders, waiting, and just before the leading man reached him, Sully popped a wheelie but quickly lowered the front wheel and wound the powerful bike up as tightly as it would go, aiming for the exact center of the stairs that led down. Time seemed almost to stop when the motorcycle soared out into space over the heads of startled tourists. The ground dropped away steadily. Sully's eyes locked onto the touchdown spot near the Bloody Tower. Up ahead he spotted Gary disappearing through the tower's exit.

Sully's sensation of time returned to normal as he executed a near-perfect landing. He roared under the tower, passing Gary, and a split second later laid the bike on its side in a slide which left broad streaks of rubber on the pavement. Then he accelerated out through the two gates.

Not bad, Sully thought to himself. *The Kid still knows his stuff.* He knew Gary would have no trouble getting out after that show.

Gary hurried through the Byward and Middle Towers and past the ticket booth, expecting a cry of alarm at any moment. He walked past the waiting taxis with what seemed like agonizing slowness. Finally he reached the corner and turned right. The car park was only a block away, but it seemed like a mile. Shouts inside the Tower complex drifted over the Tower's high walls, as if a giant hornet's nest had been knocked down. Finally Gary crossed the street and entered the car park. The truck's back doors opened as he walked up, and Sully jumped out, a broad grin on his face.

"Welcome back, boss," Sully said. "How'd you like the show?"

"I think it was risky, but I'm glad it worked." Gary looked through the open doors and saw John's worried expression. "Let's get inside." Gary jumped up into the truck, and Sully climbed in and closed the doors.

"Man, am I glad to see you," John said.

Gary smiled. "And I'm glad I'm here for you to see. I thought you were going to have to bail me out of Scotland Yard." He paused and turned back to Sully. "How in the *world* did you find a motorcycle on such short notice?"

Sully's grin grew wider. "No problem. I borrowed it."

An alarm bell went off in Gary's mind. "What do you mean by 'borrow?' " He thought he knew the answer and was not looking forward to dealing with the situation, but it had to be done.

Sully hesitated. "Uh, I didn't exactly ask the dude."

"Meaning you took it without permission?"

"Uh, yes. But I didn't damage it any, and I returned it."

"That's not the point, Sully. The police would call it stealing."

"Hey, man, I didn't *keep* it," Sully said, almost shouting. "What's the big deal? I got you out of trouble, didn't I?"

"Hold it down," Gary said. "Now listen, I don't want *anyone* taking things without permission."

"If I hadn't borrowed that bike, the cops would have got you for sure. That what you want?"

"If that's the only choice, yes."

Sully's eyes narrowed. "This part of your religion? Don't steal?"

"Yes, it's a commandment from the Bible."

"Well, doesn't it *also* say not to tell lies?"

Gary took a deep breath. He was sorely tempted to tell Sully to do what he was told but decided his question deserved an answer. "Yes, the Bible says that too."

"Okay. Both you guys tell lies."

"You mean what we do to check out a client's security?"

"Yeah. What about that?"

"Lying *is* wrong," Gary said. "But what we're trying to do is to help our clients develop effective security systems. To do this, we have to act like the bad guys, up to a point. That means deceiving the people who try to stop us. Also, our clients allow us to destroy *their* property, and we're even allowed to use devices prohibited to ordinary citizens. But we do not steal or perform other immoral acts, such as intentionally injuring someone. We have to try to work within the law whenever possible. Do you see what I'm getting at?"

"I think so." The way Sully said it told Gary that most of his anger was gone.

Gary grinned. "I appreciate your help, but in the future, please stay within the guidelines."

Sully nodded, a tentative smile coming to his usually cheerful face. "Yes, boss."

"Look, John and I *really* value your contributions to our team. We couldn't do this job without the Kid."

This seemed to embarrass him. "Yeah, well, I like you dudes too. So you ready for me to drive us back to the hotel?"

Gary turned to John. "I'd like to talk to the motorcycle's owner. . .see if we can make things right with him."

"I agree," John said, "but who knows when he'll be back? I don't want to wait around till all hours."

Sully cleared his throat. "Ah, I think we can expect the dude back here pretty quick."

"Why is that?" Gary asked, dreading the answer.

"He saw me take it."

Gary shrugged. "Well, I guess that will help us get it over with."

"Looks like your wish is granted," Dan said. He was looking at one of the monitors.

Gary turned and saw a young man in leathers walking across the street with a bobby in tow.

"John, get some money."

"How much?" John turned and started spinning the combination on the cash box.

"Oh, how about five hundred pounds."

John opened the box, counted out the notes, and gave them to Gary. "Who gets to do this fun little job?" he asked.

Gary looked around. "Ann."

"Me? Why do *I* have to do it?"

"Because you speak the language," Gary said.

"But what do I do?"

"First we wait until the cop leaves."

"Can you pick up what they're saying?" Gary asked.

Dan shook his head and pointed to the speaker. "Nope, I turned the gain up, but they're too far away, and the ambient sounds are too loud. You can catch a word now and then, but that's all."

The team watched the monitor in fascination as the owner pointed to his dirt bike then began waving his arms around. The bobby wrote in a small notebook and occasionally looked up to ask a question, which had the effect of renewing the windmill impersonation. Finally the policeman finished writing, touched the brim of his hat, and walked off in the direction of the Tower of London.

Gary turned to Ann. "Now, go tell him you know who took his bike, and you're sorry it happened. Then ask if he'll take two hundred pounds for his trouble, but head him off if it looks like he wants to take advantage. If Sully says the bike's not hurt, then I know that's the case. You can go up to five hundred if you have to, but. . ."

Ann held up her hand. "I think I understand."

"Good." He touched his hand to the brim of his Beefeater hat. "Carry on."

Ann rolled her eyes at the terrible accent and took the money. She pulled her earphone radio out of her purse and put it in her ear. Then she left the truck.

Gary watched the monitor as he started changing out of his Beefeater uniform. Ann scooted across the car park and began waving. The young man slowed his bike when he saw her.

"Wait a moment. I must have a word with you." Ann's voice came clearly from the speaker.

The man stopped and shut off his engine but remained astraddle the bike. "What about?" he demanded.

"I know who pinched your bike."

"You do? Where is he? I want a word with him."

Ann looked the bike over. "Lovely machine, don't you think?"

"Leave off with the bike. I want the chap what pinched it."

Ann smiled. "I'm *afraid* you are stuck with me." She again examined the motorcycle. "Doesn't *look* damaged."

The man crossed his arms and glared. "Says who? Could be pranged proper for all I know, an' who's going to pay? Tell me that."

"Oh, really?" Ann stretched the last word way out. "I suppose *now* you're going to tell me that a Yamaha YZ450F is as delicate as a pram."

"You know about dirt bikes, do you?"

"I know a rugged machine when I see one. How about we go visit a bike shop and see if your precious has been injured in any way, shall we?"

"Well, I don't know. . . ."

"I really *am* sorry. It was naughty of my friend, I know, but he really is a nice chap at heart. Said you had a really top-flight machine."

"He did?"

"He did. Now, I have a suggestion."

"Oh, and what might that be?"

"Please accept my apology on his behalf, seeing as how there's no harm been done. *Do.*"

The man sat there for a good five seconds, then waved his hand and said, "Oh, all right." Then his eyes narrowed. "But tell him to be keepin' his hands off my bike in the future."

"I will, and thank you."

The man kicked the starter, and the bike's engine roared to life. He tapped the transmission into first gear, let out the clutch, and was gone.

Gary grabbed the mike. "Well done."

Ann turned toward the truck and smiled. Gary hung up the Beefeater uniform and pulled on his slacks and sport shirt. Ann hurried back and entered the truck. She handed Gary the five hundred pounds.

"That was some nice negotiating," Gary said. "Would you like to help us in working out client contracts?"

"I think I'll stick to hacking," Ann said, "and the occasional Brit impersonation."

"Guess that's our loss."

The speaker crackled. "Welcome aboard Sully Air, flight double-oh-seven, nonstop service to London Bridge Hotel. Please sit back and enjoy the flight. Attendants, prepare for immediate departure. Sully Air waits for no one." The truck moved out of the car park at a brisk pace.

Guess he's back to normal, Gary thought.

He sat down in front of his mirror. First he pulled off the black wig, since this was the easiest part of removing his disguise. He set it on its foam form and placed both inside a box. Then came the slow and somewhat painful process of peeling away the beard and mustache. He stowed these as well and began working on the residue adhesive with a cotton swab.

Dan flipped through all the Jewel House cameras. "This is great," he said to Gary. "I think we're ready to plan the heist."

"Good," Gary replied, mopping his face with a towel. "I hope we can figure out a way to do it." He tried to sound optimistic, but he still had no idea how they could pull it off, even with the ability to use and control the Jewel House cameras.

chapter 9

Gary picked up the remote, collapsed into an easy chair, and thumbed on the TV. The hotel set was about average, in that the picture was fair and the colors not too garish, but definitely not high definition. It took Gary only a half dozen or so jabs of his thumb to find a BBC news bulletin.

". . .have no idea of the mystery rider's identity. He entered the Tower of London grounds around three-thirty and made several circuits of the upper Tower Green on his motorcycle before yeomen warders were able to chase him off."

The video cut from the female reporter's talking head to a clip showing a red-faced Beefeater standing at the top of the stairs beside the White Tower, pointing down toward an out-of-focus shot of the Bloody Tower.

"I thought 'e was a cropper for sure, I did. Took off on 'is machine—must have been thirty feet in the air at one point—and landed down there almost to th' Bloody Tower." The man shook his head. "Don't see how he managed to keep from crashin'."

The phone on the table chirped.

Gary pressed the mute button and grabbed the phone. "Hello."

"Gary, this is Dan. We've got a visitor."

Gary's interest level kicked up a notch.

"Ian Hayford," Dan continued. "Picked him up on the outside camera, and he just passed through the lobby. Thought you'd want to know."

"Thanks. Better warn John."

"Will do. Were you expecting him?"

"No, but it's got to have something to do with today's operation."

"Wouldn't be surprised. Recommend you put your hearing aid in."

"I will. Bye."

Gary hung up the phone and looked at the TV. A man was standing in front of a weather map, pointing to various locations in England and Scotland. Animated rain clouds dotted the screen. Gary punched the TV off. He went to his dresser, picked up his earphone radio, inserted it in his right ear, and turned it on. A knock sounded at his door.

"Is that Ian?" Gary whispered.

"No, it's John," Dan said.

Gary hurried over and opened the door.

"Wonder what he wants?" John asked, lowering his voice even though they were alone.

"Got to be something to do with Sully's wild ride."

"Ian just got off the elevator," Dan said. "He's heading for your room, Gary."

"Roger that," Gary whispered.

The sound of three solid raps echoed. Gary resisted the urge to hurry but instead took his time walking to the door. He opened it and tried to look surprised. Ian's ponytail and diamond earring seemed to add to his sinister appearance.

"Ian," Gary said finally, extending his hand, "please come in.

107

What can I do for you?"

Ian's smile did not carry through to his cold, hard eyes, making Gary wonder if the man had any other expression.

"Gary," Ian said. "John."

"Ian," John said. He shook the man's hand.

"Won't you sit down?" Gary asked, pointing to the sofa and easy chairs.

Ian shook his head. "Thanks, I won't be here that long. I'm here for two things, actually. One was to see how things were progressing. The other was. . .how shall I put it? Mild curiosity concerning a rather bizarre happening at the Tower of London. No need for details, but can I assume that you chaps are doing swimmingly, getting your teeth into things, so to speak?"

Gary laughed, trying to sound relaxed. "Please tell Peter things are under control. As to your second question. . ."

"Yes?"

"Whoever caused that ruckus at the Tower seems to know what he's doing, whoever he is."

Ian nodded, and his shark smile widened a little. "I see. Well, I shan't trouble you any further. I'll be telling Peter he's hired the real thing, in my opinion."

"Thanks."

"Not at all. Oh, almost forgot. There *is* just one more thing, a trifle, really."

Despite what he said, Gary was positive Ian was *not* in the habit of forgetting things. A steel-trap mind rested behind those predator's eyes.

"Technicians at the Tower are scheduled to extend the closed-circuit TV system, and this will require a complete re-cabling in the Jewel House. I understand they're quite tidy people; you know, a place for everything, and heaven help you if anything's *out* of place. Tightly wired, I think you Yanks say."

"Interesting, but why tell us?"

"Consider it background."

"Okay. Uh, when will they start?"

For long seconds Ian stared at Gary. Then he said, "Wednesday morning, eight o'clock sharp. Not that it will impact your work, of course."

"Not in the slightest."

"Well, cheerio." Ian turned and let himself out of the hotel room.

"I got it all on disk," Dan said over the radio.

"Good," Gary said. "You *did* sweep the rooms after we got back, didn't you?"

"Of course." Dan sounded hurt. "I know my job, Gary, and there are *no* bugs. I'd stake my life on it."

"Take it easy. I just wanted to be sure."

Gary removed his earphone radio and turned it off.

John did the same. He shook his head, and his face twisted into a strange amalgam of worry and anger. "That tears it. It was bad enough before, but now it's impossible. No way we can heist that crown before Wednesday. So what are we going to do?"

"Hold a powwow, and since Dan heard all that, I imagine Ann and Sully are up to speed by now."

The gentle knock seemed on cue.

In spite of everything, a wry smile came to Gary's face. "Come in," he said.

The door opened and Dan came in, followed by Ann and Sully.

Gary walked toward the table. "Pull up chairs, everyone, we've got work to do." He saw the look of defeat in their eyes and knew he had to do something about it. "Anyone in the dark about what's happened?"

"No," Dan answered for them.

Ann shook her head, and Sully just sat there with an angry scowl on his face.

"Man, this stinks," Sully said.

"Couldn't agree with you more," Gary said. "But we're not

giving up. Now, I want to hear some ideas."

"We've got until sometime Wednesday morning to heist the crown, right?" Ann said.

"Right."

"And we've figured out a way to defeat the closed-circuit TVs and the passive motion detectors."

Gary nodded. "That we have, but we still need a way past the Tower walls and guards, and then there's the vault itself."

Ann smiled. "What are those fan-looking things in the truck?"

Gary cocked an eyebrow at her. "Okay, I'll play your little game. Those are the engines for our hang gliders, as if you didn't know. What did you have in mind?"

"Do you think it might be possible to land on top of the Waterloo Barracks using those contraptions?" Ann asked. Her smile, while not exactly smug, threatened to cross over the line without warning.

Gary examined the problem at warp speed. "Yes," he said. "Now that you mention it, I believe the Barracks is vulnerable to an air assault. I mean, who would even *think* of such a thing?" He turned his eyes on her. "Except you. That is brilliant."

"Thank you."

"What about the sensors we haven't bypassed, and getting into the vault?" John asked.

Ann smiled. "What was it Yogi Berra said: 'It ain't over till it's over'?"

"Okay," Gary said. "We've got the rest of today and until tomorrow night to do this. Now, let's get with it."

It was Sully who finally suggested a way to get inside the vault. "Look at this," he said, holding out a Web page printout. It was a picture showing the ceiling somewhere inside the Waterloo

Barracks. "You think they armored the vault ceiling?"

Gary took the graphic. "Good question," he said. "There's no reason to. The main threat is at ground level. According to the blueprints, the ceiling is stone arches plus the flooring above. That really should be adequate, especially when you add in the TVs and all the other sensors."

"What if the ceiling *is* armored?" John asked.

"Let's be optimistic. So how do we do this?"

John examined the picture. "Most of what we need we have, but not everything. I'll need access to a first-rate machine shop and our client's credit card for supplies."

"No, use cash. I don't want anyone following a paper trail back to us."

Ann looked away from her PC. "I can go rent the shop."

"Thanks," Gary said. "You'll need a disguise. I'll help you with that."

"Okay."

Gary turned back to John. "Now, what about the security devices?"

"Assuming Dan can neutralize the cameras and passive systems, that leaves the active motion detectors, which I'm sure I can bypass."

Gary glanced at his watch and saw it was nearly 11:00 P.M. "Are you sure you can make your new gadgets by tomorrow evening?"

"I think so," John said, "but I'll need you and Sully to help."

"What about the active motion detectors?"

"I suspect there's a beam fence around the second-floor perimeter. The beams are probably microwave, but photoelectric and infrared are possibilities, so I'll allow for all three. Substitute an alternate beam source, and you can break the real one without setting off an alarm."

"Okay, that sounds good. Next step. . . ?"

"That should give us access to the floor above the vault. Cut through the floor and stone vaulting, then use Sherlock to snitch the crown."

"You will, of course, flesh all this out, won't you?"

"Of course. Don't I always?"

Gary looked at the picture of the Barracks ceiling. "Okay, big guy. It's you and me playing Spiderman on top of Waterloo Barracks."

"Beats climbing down the Empire State Building," John said.

"That it does. What are you going to make tomorrow?"

"We already have a super-quiet drill. What we need is a high-tech saw and some spare high-capacity battery packs."

"So, you blow the window, bypass the beam motion detectors, we dig through the floor using the new gadgets, and then it's all up to Sherlock."

"Basically."

"Okay. One more question: How does Sherlock snatch the crown? I mean, since I'll be operating the little guy, I need to know."

"I'll rig a circle cutter and suction cup. Cut the glass, lift it out, and poise the derrick for a little high-stakes fishing. Lift the crown very slowly, and the motion detector won't go off."

"And Sherlock won't set off the heat detector?" Gary said.

"Not if he's at ambient temp when we lower him, and he will be by that time. So now we have the crown, and all we have to do is egress. What could be easier?"

"That's a roger. Let's wrap it up for tonight. Tomorrow we build your gadgets and finish the operational plan, such as it is."

Gary stood, and the others filed out.

Gary stared at the array of John's handiwork, which had taken most of Tuesday to machine and assemble in the machine shop Ann had rented for the week. Sherlock sat in the center of the workbench with a new circle cutter and miniature derrick attachments. Flanking the robot were two high-capacity battery packs and the new saw. John went through one more demonstration of how to assemble the new equipment and the techniques for cutting a hole in the case and removing the crown.

"Very nice," Gary said. "You also attached a vacuum to the drill?"

"Right. We can't let any debris fall into the vault."

"Well done."

"Couldn't have done it without help." John turned to Sully. "Especially our gofer. What was it—four trips out to get everything?"

"Five, but who's counting?" Sully replied. "Hey, on film shoots I spend as much time fetching stuff as I do on stunts. But I tell you what, you do nice work." Sully waved at the arrayed equipment. "If you ever want to break into special effects, let me know. I can hook you up with some FX wizards."

"Think I'll stick to the real side of things," John said, smiling.

Gary glanced at his watch. "We need to scoot. I want to get a walk-through in with the others before dinner."

"Right," John said.

"I'll go get the car," Sully said.

On the trip back to the hotel, Gary watched fluffy white clouds sail serenely across a cobalt blue sky. He had his window down so he could enjoy the cool fresh air. The walk back to the hotel was pleasant.

When they reached their floor, Gary went to his room, changed out of his oil-stained clothes, and called the others in. One by one they entered and took seats around the table.

Gary spread out a map of London, an aerial view of the Tower, and the detailed drawing Dan had spent so many hours on. "Okay, let's see if we can do this without a single bobble. Everybody ready?"

The others nodded, except Sully, who said, "Blast off."

"I'll take that as a yes," Gary said.

The walk-through went smoother than Gary expected. Sully described dropping Gary and John off, then the trip to the car park near the Tower. Gary and John would fly to the Jewel House using the hang gliders. Dan assured them that radio reception would not be a problem at this stage. He recited his role in disabling the passive motion detectors and defeating the surveillance cameras. Ann was available to assist John and Gary if necessary. John recited his tasks without a hitch, and Gary was pleased that he managed his part.

"That was excellent," Gary said when they were done. "Shall we adjourn for dinner?"

There were no dissenting votes.

Gary sat at the table in his room and pored over Dan's detailed drawing of the Jewel House. He glanced at his watch. It was a little after 8:00 P.M. According to plan, they were to leave the hotel in evening clothes at 8:30, to provide cover for their return in the wee hours of the morning. Gary jumped when his phone gave an insistent electronic trill.

"Hello," he said.

"We've got a problem," John said.

"What's wrong?"

"Fog's rolling in. Ann happened to be watching a newscast and caught the report. Should have picked up on it earlier, but we've been so busy. Anyhow, Ann went outside, and she said it's going to be *real* bad."

"I see," Gary said.

"Do we scrub? I mean, we have to, don't we?"

Gary thought that over. Conventional wisdom said they should, since landing hang gliders on top of a building at night was hard enough, even with night-vision goggles. But doing it in fog pushed the odds over the edge—almost. Gary smiled. John had prepared for even this, fitting the gliders with special blind-flying instruments. The question was, were he and John foolhardy enough to go ahead regardless?

chapter 10

Gary held his door open, and Ann, John, Dan, and Sully filed inside. Gary stood before them and saw varying degrees of fear and worry in their faces. But he knew the team's window of opportunity was razor thin. They had to strike now or not at all. What they did was inherently dangerous, but Gary felt confident he and John could have managed the hang gliders in clear weather. But what would the fog do?

"Gary, you can't be serious," Dan said. "There's no *way* you can find the Tower in all this fog, let alone land."

"Now, hold on," Gary said. "Let's take this a step at a time. It won't be as easy, but I can still find the Tower *and* land on the Jewel House roof."

"How?" Dan asked. "Airliners can't fly in weather like this, can they?"

"I know, but flying a hang glider is a tad easier than landing a 747. I'm an instrument-rated private pilot, so I know what I'm talking about."

"Does that enable you to see through fog?"

"Nope, but John equipped the gliders with modified GPS

receivers that are accurate to within fifteen meters or less."

"What about altitude?" Sully asked.

"GPS gives you that too, but John installed radar altimeters, which are much more accurate. And the gliders have the normal flight instruments: turn-and-bank, airspeed, aneroid altimeter, and magnetic compass. Listen. It will be difficult and a little dangerous; I can't deny that, but we can do this."

"What about John?" Ann asked. "Is he as qualified as you are?"

"I've flown hang gliders before," John said. "All I have to do is follow Gary."

"John," Ann said, "you *can't* follow him in this fog."

Gary held up his hand. "Take it easy. I'm aware of the problems, but John and I can work something out." Gary turned to John. "But I need two things: help getting ready, and you have to promise me something."

"Shoot," John said.

Gary smiled in appreciation of his friend's positive tone. "First, the promise. You've got to rely on your instruments. I've warned you about disorientation during instrument flying. Can you trust your instruments rather than what you're feeling?"

"You mean the sensation of turning when you're not?"

"That's *exactly* what I mean. Trust me. Once we're in the soup, you'll *swear* you're in a turn. You have to trust your instruments, or you'll crash. Can you do that?"

John hesitated. "I think so."

Gary shook his head. "No good. Either you trust the gauges, or we scrub."

John's face turned grim. "I can do it."

"Good. Problem two: I have to do the navigating, which means you'll have to follow me in the fog. We need some way for you to know where I am. Any ideas?"

"What about a strobe?" Sully suggested.

"That might work," John said. "But fog diffuses light, making it hard to tell where the source is."

"Okay, could we direct the light through a tube to make a beam?" Gary asked.

"I think so. That won't eliminate the diffusion, but the strobe would definitely be brighter when you're directly in line with it. Then, all I'd have to do is stay within ten feet or so and search for the brightest flashes."

"You guys are really going to do this?" Ann asked.

"Of course," Gary said. "It's just a matter of being prepared. Speaking of that, we need to get cracking." He glanced at his watch and saw it was past eight-thirty. "We're late leaving as it is, so let's move it. Everyone down in the lobby, pronto."

They all ran out.

Gary rushed through dressing. He clipped on his bow tie, secured the cummerbund, and shrugged into his coat. He examined himself in the full-length mirror, then hurried out into the hall. They were all there, even Sully, who seemed quite respectable in a monkey suit. And Ann looked very nice in her aqua gown.

"Okay, people," Gary said. "Let's put on our show for the hotel staff."

Dan bowed stiffly and offered Ann his arm. The team took the elevator down. Gary led the way through the lobby and turned down the night clerk's offer to call for taxis. They paused at the door to don raincoats, then walked out into the fog. They hurried to the car park, changed clothes in the truck, and got to work.

It took John over an hour to modify a strobe, and a quick test proved the theory. In another hour he had the strobe securely mounted on the propeller guard of Gary's hang glider. Gary glanced at his watch. It was almost twelve-thirty, time to head for Hyde Park if they expected to be airborne by one.

"Okay. Ann, you take the car," Gary said. "I want it in the car park across from the coin museum, just in case. After Sully drops John and me off, he'll come back there. If everything goes according to plan, we'll touch down on the Jewel House roof around eight to ten minutes later."

Ann nodded.

"Stay close," Gary said. "Sully will guide you to the car park, then drive us to Hyde Park. Dan, have you got the box for the crown ready?"

"Right here," Dan said, holding up a sturdy aluminum container with a hinged lid and lock.

"Good," Gary said. "All right, team. Let's do it."

Ann and Sully stepped outside. Gary followed Ann on the monitor until she disappeared into the fog less than halfway to the car.

The truck started, and Sully backed out, turned, and drove slowly to the exit. Gary looked over Dan's shoulder. The dot marking the car started moving. Gary could barely make out the car on the monitor. He rubbed his sweaty palms on his dark blue coveralls.

The trip to the car park near the Tower went without a hitch. Ann turned into the entrance while Sully slowed and made a U-turn on the deserted street. Dan hunched over the map display on his PC. The truck's location was marked by a blue dot.

Dan grabbed the mike. "How are you doing, Sully?"

"Can't hardly see anything." Sully's voice sounded tense in the speaker. "I'm following the stripes on the road when I can see them."

"Don't worry, I'll guide you."

"Please do."

"Okay, we're passing the Tower now. Keep going straight. We'll be taking Byward Street to Lower Thames Street."

"Roger."

Lower Thames became Upper Thames Street, then Victoria

119

Embankment. They turned right at Waterloo Bridge, and Sully drove them north past Covent Gardens until they finally reached Oxford Street and turned left.

About a minute later Dan grabbed the mike. "Sully, we just passed Marble Arch. Hyde Park is dead ahead."

"Roger."

Gary glanced at the map. In less than a minute it would be up to him and John. Suddenly a verse from Proverbs popped into his mind: "Pride goes before destruction, and a haughty spirit before a fall." But was he being prideful? he wondered. It was certainly an easy trap to fall into, but on the other hand he was sure he could fly to the Jewel House and land in one piece and enable John to do the same.

"Are you praying, Brother John?" he asked softly.

"Ever since we left the hotel."

"I hear you. I say go. How about you?"

"Go," he replied.

The truck came to a smooth stop.

The speaker crackled to life. "We're here, guys," Sully said. "I'll come back and help with your gear."

"Okay," Gary said.

He inserted his earphone radio and turned it on. John did the same. Sully opened the back doors and looked in.

"We'll take the gliders," Gary said to him. "Can you carry our backpacks?"

"Sure," Sully said.

Gary grabbed the nylon straps that bound the light gray parts of his disassembled hang glider and lifted. Even with John's thorough engineering, it was quite a load. Gary slipped on his night-vision goggles, stepped down from the truck, and led the way out into the park. The clammy mist cut him off from all visual references except what was at his feet. The damp air seemed almost solid.

"Radio check," Gary whispered.

"Read you five-by-five." Dan's voice was clear and strong in the earphone.

"How are we doing?"

"Bear left about five degrees."

"Roger. You copy that, John?"

"Affirmative."

Less than a minute later Dan said, "You're at the takeoff spot."

"Roger," Gary replied. "Thanks."

Gary set his hang glider down, undid the straps, and began assembling the frame. Several minutes later he finished attaching the Dacron wing and checked his work, including the all-important flight instruments.

After John finished his assembly, Gary asked, "You ready?"

"Lead on," John replied.

Gary turned to Sully. "As soon as we're strapped in, hook our backpacks to the ring attached to the engine mounts."

"Got you."

Gary strapped into his harness, slipped under the limp wing, and hooked the harness to the glider's frame. Then he lifted the ungainly aircraft, and Sully attached the backpack.

"You're good to go," Sully said.

Gary waited while Sully assisted John.

"All set," John said.

Gary flipped on the switch, activating the strobe.

"It's working," Sully said.

"Right. Let's get this show on the road."

Gary trundled around underneath the hang glider until the magnetic compass read 160 degrees. He set the choke on the two-cycle engine and pressed the starter button for a few seconds, then let it up. The engine was so quiet it made little more sound than an oscillating fan, which it greatly resembled. He braced his feet against the insistent nudge of the propeller. Gary waited a few seconds, then turned off the choke. The engine purred along beautifully.

"Stand by," Gary said.

"Roger."

"On my mark. One—two—three—go!"

Gary opened the throttle and started his takeoff run. The sodden air blew past his ears, and his boots squished through the wet grass. The hang glider lifted clear of his shoulders. A few more steps and the straps tugged him into the air. Gary's heart was pounding so hard it seemed almost audible.

His eyes zeroed in on the instruments. Good, he was on course, now some twenty feet in the air with an indicated airspeed of thirty knots. The turn-and-bank instrument was reading as it should—the needle was vertical, with the ball centered. But what about John?

"You okay?" Gary asked.

"Yeah, right behind you, man. Don't stop suddenly, you hear?"

Gary laughed, his tension easing a little. "No fear of that." At the moment, he felt okay, more or less.

"You know what birds do on a night like this?" Gary asked.

"No, what?"

"They walk."

"I hear that."

Gary began a gentle turn to the left as he continued his climb-out. He watched the slow turn of the compass wheel and stopped when it read 90 degrees. A glance at the GPS readout confirmed he was exactly on course. They would pass just to the north of Buckingham Palace with St. James Park dead ahead. A few minutes later the GPS display told him they were abreast of the palace. The radar altimeter read five hundred feet above the ground. Gary wiped the accumulated water droplets off his night-vision goggles and peered at his watch. Time to check in with the mother ship.

"Star Chamber, this is Gooney Bird One; how do we look?" Gary had decided on the Gooney Bird call signs because albatross antics reminded him of a hang glider, ungainly on the ground but agile in the air.

"Gooney Bird One, you are on course, on time." Dan's voice sounded far away in Gary's earpiece. "I have you passing Buckingham Palace as we speak."

"Roger. What's your location?"

"Not quite to Marble Arch. We're not exactly buzzing along."

"Hey," Sully interrupted, "I'm doing the best I can."

"At ease, Mr. Sullivan," Gary said. "Star Chamber, keep an eye on us."

"Roger that."

"Gooney Bird One out."

Gary angled a little more to the left as he approached the Thames to make sure they stayed well clear of Big Ben. About a minute later the GPS had them over Whitehall.

"Stand by, John," Gary said. "We're almost to the Thames. Don't forget our course change to the left."

"I'm ready."

"Gooney Bird One, this is Star Chamber," Dan's voice said. "I have you over the Thames near Charing Cross. Please confirm."

"Star Chamber, this is Gooney One. That's a roger. How are you doing?"

"A little better, but it looks like you'll beat us there. We're still on Regent Street, but Sully's driving as fast as he can."

"Hey, give me a break," Sully said. "I left my X-ray eyes at home."

"Take it easy," Gary said. "If you guys pile up we've had it."

"Roger," Dan said.

"Gooney Bird One out."

Gary watched his GPS readout change. The west longitude decreased rapidly as the hang gliders approached not only the Tower of London, but the prime meridian, the longitude that ran through Greenwich Observatory that divided east from west. However, they would not actually reach longitude 0 degrees, zero minutes, and zero seconds. Waterloo Bridge passed unseen beneath the aviators.

"John, stand by for a right turn to 100 degrees."

"Ready."

"On my mark. . .now."

It was the last turn they would make before arriving at their destination. *Then* the fun would begin. Even with GPS, the rooftop landing on the Jewel House would not be easy since the width of the Barracks was barely within the GPS margin of error. And although the roof's slope was gentle, it had all sorts of obstacles. A bad landing could easily result in a broken leg—or worse, if either pilot fell off and tumbled to the ground below.

The GPS longitude continued to wind down while the latitude remained almost constant. They were nearing Blackfriars Bridge. Gary scanned the other instruments. *Looking good,* he thought. His gaze returned to the GPS readout, and his heart froze. The display was blank.

Gary punched the backlight button. Nothing. He disconnected the battery pack, then reseated it firmly. It made no difference. As a last resort he rapped the case, then pounded it. The GPS receiver was dead, and that was that.

"John," Gary said, "we have a problem. My GPS fritzed out."

"Are you sure? Did you check the battery pack?"

"John, I've checked everything. It's dead."

"What are we going to do?"

"Let me think a second." Then he felt an inner prompting. *Lord, help us,* he prayed in response but without hope. Then a strange idea popped up unbidden. They still had a working GPS receiver; it was just on the wrong hang glider.

"John?" Gary said.

"I'm right here, buddy."

"Brother John, you're going to navigate us to the Jewel House."

"What? I can't do that."

"Yes, you can. Keep me updated on our coordinates, and I'll

take it from there." He paused as another thought occurred to him. "Are you still praying?"

"I haven't stopped."

"Good. Keep it up. Okay," he continued, "now tell me when we reach 0 degrees, 4.567 minutes west longitude. That's the meridian the White Tower is on. We're going up that meridian by flying due north. Since there's no wind, your compass should read 6 degrees. Then. . ."

"Wait," John interrupted. "If we're going due north, how come the compass reads 6 degrees?"

"Because the magnetic variation for London is 6 degrees west. When the magnetic compass reads north, true north is 6 degrees to the right."

"So, when the compass reads 6 degrees, then—"

"You've got it. Also, keep an eye on your GPS readout. After we turn, the longitude should read exactly 0 degrees, 4.567 west. If it reads more, we go right, and if it reads less, we go left. One-thousandth of a minute equals about six feet, so be sure the last three digits are 567."

"Got it. I just hope I can do it."

"You can do it. Where are we? Just tell me the longitude."

"Hold on. It reads 5.010 minutes west."

"Okay, that means we've got about a half nautical mile to go. Now, here's what we're going to do. Precision GPS gives our location, plus or minus ten meters or so."

"Ten meters. That's about thirty feet."

"Almost thirty-three, but that's close enough."

"We could miss the Jewel House entirely with that much error."

"That's why we're going to map it."

"With what?"

"My radar altimeter. The walls and buildings will cause the readings to drop suddenly when we fly over. I'll call off each building, and you make a mental note of the GPS readings.

We'll use those to plan our landing approach, adjusting for your distance from me."

"You sure this will work?"

"Trust me."

"Gooney Bird One, this is Star Chamber."

Gary had wondered how long it would take for Dan to check in. "Go ahead, Star Chamber."

"Don't want to bother you guys, but is there anything we can do?"

"Negative," Gary replied.

"Have you considered scrubbing it this evening?"

Gary could see from his watch that they were nearing the turn point. He didn't have time for this. "Considered and re-jected, Star Chamber. Leave this frequency clear until we're down. Gooney Bird One out."

Dan reached up and flipped the switches to cut all transmissions to Gary and John. Now he could only listen.

As he expected, the airwaves weren't silent long. "Dan, can't we do something?" Sully asked.

"You heard the man. The operation is still a go."

"But. . ."

"Just get us to the car park without running into something."

"Dan, this is Ann."

"This is Star Chamber; go ahead Irish One."

"Oh, yeah, I forgot. Where *are* you, Star Chamber? Over."

"Irish One, this is Star Chamber. We're turning into the car park now. Over."

"I see your lights now. Irish One out."

The truck came to a stop. Dan turned to the back and waited. A few moments later, the doors opened and Ann and Sully came in. Sully pulled the doors shut.

"Grab some chairs," Dan said. "Now we wait."

Gary made a slight correction to his heading. "John, watch your readout. When the last three digits read 571, we'll make a gentle left turn until the compass reads 6 degrees. Hopefully that will put us close to 4.567 minutes west."

"Roger that."

"Hang in there."

A few heart-pounding moments later Gary's earphone clicked. "Coming up on 571. . .now."

"Roger. Turning to the left now. Stay with me, bro."

"Got you in sight."

Gary pushed his control bar gently to the right, which lifted the right wing and caused a bank to the left. He watched the magnetic compass begin turning. The numbers decreased with agonizing slowness. Finally Gary rolled out on a heading of 6 degrees.

"How does it look?" he asked.

"Longitude reads 566," John replied.

"We overshot a bit. Keep an eye on your readout while I correct."

Gary turned to 4 degrees and waited.

"There. Exactly 567."

Gary came back to 6 degrees and went over the layout of the Tower grounds in his mind. First came the wharf, then the moat and the outer wall, followed by the inner wall. After that, roughly in the center, came the White Tower, and finally Waterloo Barracks.

Gary had been descending gently since Waterloo Bridge. The radar altimeter read less than four hundred feet now, the vertical distance to the Thames below. Gary leveled out. A few seconds later the radar altimeter reading dropped suddenly.

There's the wharf. The readout dropped again, then went back up, marking a wall. Then it did it again.

"We're past the inner wall," he told John.

The altimeter dropped to three hundred twenty feet. That had to be the White Tower. Then the reading went back up, but not to the previous reading since the ground level was rising.

"John," Gary said. "Note the latitude on my mark." The distance to the ground dropped suddenly. "Mark." He watched for the increase. "Mark. Did you get it?"

"Sure did. The first latitude is 51 degrees, 30.510 minutes north. . ."

"The last three digits will do," Gary interrupted.

"Okay, the second was 518."

"Great," Gary said. "That marks the south and north walls of the Jewel House. How far behind me are you? Measuring from your GPS receiver."

"Uh, about six feet."

Gary estimated it was another six feet to his radar altimeter, so that meant the true latitude readings were short by about two-thousandths of a minute. "Listen, all we have to do is come in with a latitude reading of about 512, and we should be lined up with the center of the Jewel House roof. Piece of cake."

"Whatever you say."

"Okay, here's what we're going to do. You remember what the Waterloo Barracks looks like, right? Oblong towers on each end, a higher center section with two towers to the south, and the north side extends out and up. The north side of the Jewel House roof slopes gently and has several obstacles."

"I've got the picture."

"Good. That's our target. We're going to come in from the west, staying clear of the square tower, and land on the roof. Understand?"

"Roger. Ready when you are."

Gary took a deep breath. He wiped the mist off his goggles

and peered at his instruments. They had to descend to within about ten feet of the highest obstacle on their path, Devereux Tower, then swoop in over Waterloo Barracks and land on the roof without hitting anything or falling off.

Gary listened intently as John read off the GPS coordinates, waiting for just the right moment.

"Okay, stand by for a 180-degree turn to the left," Gary said. "Now."

He began a gentle turn while continuing his descent.

"Gary!" John shouted. "I've lost you. I can't see the strobe."

"Go to full throttle and pull up! There are obstacles all around us."

Gary shoved his throttle forward to its stop.

"What do I do?" John asked, sounding like he was on the verge of panic.

"Listen to me. Keep climbing until your altimeter reads four hundred feet. I want you to fly to the White Tower and orbit until I locate you. And remember your instruments."

"Okay. What then?"

"First things first. Do you remember the coordinates?"

"Yeah, 51 degrees 30.483 minutes north, 0 degrees, 4.567 minutes west."

"Perfect. Now do it. I'll come and find you."

"Right. Okay, I'm climbing now, and the GPS readout is changing in the right direction. What direction should I be going?"

"Somewhere around 120 degrees, but just fly the GPS readout. Make the numbers go in the direction you want. When you get to the Tower, maintain altitude, and do big lazy circles. I'll come to you." But without GPS, he knew this would not be easy.

He climbed to five hundred feet and began crossing the unseen Tower site, mapping it as best as he could using the radar altimeter to identify the walls and buildings. It took several passes for Gary to locate the White Tower with an acceptable degree of certainty. The next step was to find John.

"John, are you over the White Tower?" Gary asked.

"Yes."

"Good. Break out your flashlight, and when I give you the signal, turn it on and point it backwards. Got that?"

"Yeah."

"Okay. Tell me when you're ready."

"I've got it," John said about a minute later. "Now what?"

"Maintain the White Tower's latitude, and fly to 0 degrees, 4.517 west longitude. That will put you about three hundred feet east of the tower. Then do a 180 and fly over the tower with your flashlight on. I'll find you and get out in front. Okay?"

There was a slight pause. "Yeah."

"Start now. Let me know when you reach 517."

"Roger."

Gary felt sweat popping up in his armpits. He began a rapid descent, heading almost due east on a path that would take him close to John, hopefully without a collision.

Less than a minute later, John radioed, "I'm there."

"Okay, make your 180, and turn on your taillight," Gary said.

"Roger that."

Gary reached four hundred feet and leveled out. He hauled his hang glider around in a tight turn and rolled out on a course toward John and the White Tower. He wiped his night-vision goggles and peered into the roiling green mist.

"John. Pull your throttle back to half speed."

"Roger. Got my light on."

Gary left his throttle at full, hoping he would see the glow in time to avoid a midair collision. A few seconds later the green image seemed a little brighter, but he wasn't sure. He slewed the hang glider into gentle turns to either side of his course, then steadied up when the glow seemed brightest.

Gary brought his throttle back a little. Without warning, a circular steel grill materialized out of the mist. It was the protective shield around John's propeller, and he was headed straight for it. Gary instinctively cut the throttle and pulled back hard on the control bar. His hang glider dove underneath the other craft.

"Hey," John said, "was that you?"

"Maintain your course."

"But—"

"Maintain your course, and look for my strobe."

Gary leveled out, shoved the throttle to full power, and pushed the control bar forward to climb. When he reached four hundred feet he leveled out, cutting his throttle and waiting for his airspeed to bleed off.

"I see something!" John shouted.

Gary rammed his throttle forward. "Quick, match speeds before you lose me." After a few moments he pulled his throttle back a little.

"I've got the strobe," John said with obvious relief.

"Okay, now we begin our approach, just like before, except don't get lost this time."

"Don't worry. I'm sticking with you like glue."

"Roger that. Now, give me our coordinates as we descend. Ready?"

"Ready."

"Cut to half throttle."

Again they began their approach to the unseen Jewel House. Gary's mind raced, checking and rechecking every detail as he dictated the altitude and course changes. They dropped ever lower, closer and closer to obstacles that could force them out of the air and hurl them to their deaths. Finally they were within fifty feet of their goal.

"Follow me in," Gary said. "Cut your throttle. Now. Remember the flare procedure."

Gary pulled his throttle back to idle and pushed the control bar forward to slow down. He peered into the mist, looking for the roof. At first, all he saw was endless fog, then a dark shadow appeared off to the right. It was the edge of a roof, and they were low.

"Pull up!" Gary shouted. "Full throttle."

Gary shoved the bar forward and went to maximum power. The hang glider lurched upward, barely clearing the roof's edge.

"Cut power," he said.

Gary started flaring out. He dodged an angular projection. The sloping roof loomed closer. He killed the engine and pushed the control bar all the way forward. The hang glider slowed, then stalled. Gary landed heavily, and his boots went out from under him on the slick roof. He fell hard, and the wing collapsed around him like a shroud. He was down, but in all the noise he had no idea what had happened to John.

"John?" he said quietly.

"I'm here under this bedsheet."

Gary turned off the strobe, unhooked his harness, and crawled out from under the sagging wing. John's glider was several feet away, barely visible. A few moments later John struggled out and stood up.

"Boy, am I glad to be down," he said in a whisper that carried through the air as well as over the radio.

"You and me both."

"Thanks be to God."

"Amen to that."

"Gooney Bird One, this is Star Chamber," Dan said, his voice clear in Gary's earphone. "What is your status?"

Gary smiled and turned in the direction of the car park. "Gooneys One and Two are on the ground and mighty glad of it."

"Us too. You had us worried, guys."

Gary looked at the strange green image of John's face and saw a nod of relief.

"That's a roger on your last," Gary said with feeling.

chapter 11

Gary reached underneath the limp wing and felt for the hook that attached his backpack to the engine mounts. It wasn't easy to find amid the maze of pipes, straps, and tubing, but finally his hand closed around it. He slid the locking tab back and pulled the nylon bag free. He stood up, slipped on a pair of latex gloves, and looked over at John.

"Come on," Gary said.

"Hold on. This hook's tangled up in something."

Gary looked all around and listened. All he could see was a tiny island of roof amid a sea of dripping fog. If the noise of their landing had caused an alarm, it wasn't apparent. The rustling sounds coming from underneath John's hang glider grew steadily louder.

"Hey, hold it down," Gary whispered. "What's wrong?"

Something snapped.

"Hook was tangled up," John said. "But I got it." He dragged the pack out and stood up. He pulled on his gloves.

Gary led the way across the gently sloping roof until the central section of the Barracks emerged from the fog. He pulled a tape measure out of his pack and handed the end to John, who held the tape against the stonework while Gary paced near the roof's edge. He stopped at thirty feet and lowered the tape to the roof.

"I've got it," Gary said.

He reeled in the tape and snapped his backpack onto his harness. John appeared out of the mist with his backpack already on. He pulled out his miniature motorized winch and checked it over.

Gary removed his own winch, attached it to the front of his harness, and crept to the raised stone parapet that marked the sheer drop to the ground. He peered over the edge, but all he could see was a few feet of the wall—the rest was lost in the fog. Gary set his hook, climbed over the edge, and transferred his full weight to the thin cable. He pressed a button and watched the glistening stonework slide past as the motor paid out the wire. When he reached the window, he removed his night-vision goggles and stowed them in his backpack. John dropped into position beside him. Gary scanned the interior, noting the display cases and banners arrayed around the room. The floor directly above their first-floor target was clear.

"Star Chamber, this is Pickpocket One," Gary whispered. "We're on the outside looking in. Do your magic. Over."

"Pickpocket One, this is Star Chamber. Roger your last. Wait one."

Gary tried to ignore the growing discomfort caused by his sodden clothing. The seconds seemed to crawl by.

"Pickpocket One, this is Star Chamber. Sorry for the delay, guys. I had to record enough video from the first- and second-floor cameras to provide loops showing empty rooms. The loops are playing, and I've checked all the cameras. Looks good. I didn't see a thing when I cut them over. Also, I've bypassed the passive motion detectors on both floors. It's all yours, guys."

"Roger, Star Chamber. This is Pickpocket One out."

Gary looked over at John and nodded.

John drilled two holes in the side of the window and bolted metal clips to the stone, then turned back to the window.

"Star Chamber, am I clear to blow the window?" John whispered.

"Affirmative, Pickpocket Two," Dan replied. "But remember guys, the Jewel House has duplex video cabling. If you trip an alarm, the cameras automatically switch over to the alternate cables, and the security honchos will spot you."

"We'll remember," Gary replied. "Pickpocket One out." He turned to John. "You may proceed with your violence and mayhem."

John narrowed his eyes. "Ha. You're just jealous 'cause you can't do the Gandalf stuff."

Gary grinned. "Will you get on with it?"

John reached into his backpack and pulled out a handful of what looked like sticks. After wiping the window, he stuck the first shaped explosive to the window. One by one the remaining charges went up until they formed a rectangle. Then John very carefully inserted detonators and attached the wires to an electronic generator. Finally, he attached two suction cup handles to the glass.

"Ready?" John asked.

Gary grabbed the handle on his side. "Ready."

John cradled the generator in his left hand and grasped the other handle. He jabbed the firing button with his thumb. A barely audible *whump* sounded, and the window section shifted slightly. Gary and John lifted the severed chunk of glass clear. John took both handles, slipped the glass into the metal clips, and then stowed the handles and generator. Gary looked through the hole. From this moment on, they would not say a word until they were outside again.

Gary reached into his backpack and pulled out the microwave detector. Dan had told him the active motion detectors would likely be microwave, so that's what he would try first. Gary pulled out the receiver's antenna and slowly inserted the device into the room. He picked up a signal almost immediately. He moved the antenna around until the signal peaked. The beam was about a foot from the wall, allowing plenty of room for countermeasures. He moved the device up six inches and found the next beam. After locating the beam nearest the center of the hole, Gary marked its position. He looked over at John, who nodded.

Gary stowed the detector and brought out an oblong box. He removed the protective tape strips, reached inside, and pressed the transmitter against the wall. He then flipped a tiny switch and watched. A trapdoor opened, and four jointed arms extended and began searching for the invisible microwave beams. Each arm inched into position independently while the heads sought alignment. One by one four LED indicators lit up. Four of the microwave beams were now bypassed, giving the intruders a thirty-inch gap through the invisible fence.

John drilled two more holes above the window and bolted a sturdy metal bar to the stone, its end extending over the hole. Then he snapped together alloy beam segments and bolted the unit to the bar, forming an upside-down, lopsided T. The beam extended into the room almost six feet. After attaching two diagonal braces, John moved the miniature trolley winch along the track, making sure it rolled smoothly. He turned to Gary and smiled, motioning for him to come closer.

Gary placed his boots on the windowsill and shuffled to the center. He removed his backpack and handed it to John, who hooked it on an eyebolt. Taking a firm grip on the rail, Gary released the descend cable from his winch. John paid out the wire from the trolley's winch and attached it to a ring in Gary's harness.

Gary leaned back as the winch paid out until he was nearly horizontal. He inched his boots sideways until he straddled the hole, then crept upwards. John pressed a button, and the winch began reeling in the wire. Gary flexed his knees until he was doing a horizontal squat. The winch stopped. Gary moved one foot through the hole, extended it, then did the same with the other.

His body swung in small arcs, suspended from the winch, his balance almost perfect. John gave him a push, and the winch's carriage carried him inside between the motion detector's beams. The trolley reached the end and stopped. Gary held onto the beam, drew in his feet, turned sideways and pressed the button to lower himself to the floor. He removed the hook, reeled in the wire, and pushed the winch back outside.

John hooked Gary's backpack to the winch and sent it through. John's pack came next, then John repeated Gary's gymnastics. Gary guided John's legs and helped him to stand up. John grinned and held up a thumb. Gary answered in kind.

They picked up their backpacks and tiptoed to the center of the room. Using a laser range finder, John marked out a two-foot square. The men unloaded their backpacks. Gary set Sherlock and its controller aside while John assembled the saw and attached a vacuum unit to the drill.

John drilled two small holes and bolted the saw's track to the floor. Then he attached the saw, lowered the blade, and engaged the automatic drive. The saw started with almost no sound, and the supersharp blade made hardly a whisper as the carriage glided across the floor. Gary knew this part would take a while, since each pass dropped the blade only a fraction of an inch. John had estimated forty minutes for all four cuts.

After completing two parallel cuts, John drilled a hole and installed a support bar using an expansion bolt. Then came twenty more agonizing minutes for the other two cuts. Finally the saw made one last pass, and the block dropped a fraction of an inch. John removed the saw and set it aside. He took one side of the bar while Gary took the other, and together they lifted the floor section clear.

Gary looked inside and saw the top of the stone arch, part

of the Jewel House ceiling. He eyed the stone-and-mortar struc-ture, glad this was John's responsibility and not his.

John examined the stonework and marked out a roughly two-foot square opening following the mortar joints. Then he drilled a hole partway through the stone nearest the center and inserted an expansion eyebolt. He removed the bar from the floor section and attached it to the eyebolt with a length of steel cable.

John stretched for a few moments, then started converting the drill into what looked like a handheld router. Gary steadied him while he began the tedious task of grinding away the centuries-old mortar. The zigzag cut went deeper and deeper until the cutout section began to move. The cable snapped tight but held. John froze, holding the router perfectly still.

Gary looked at him, wondering what was wrong. John pointed to the stone that formed one corner. Gary looked and saw a hairline crack in the mortar. If they lifted the section out, that stone would drop like a bomb and crash through the display case below.

Gary froze. He knew the slightest movement would dis-lodge the stone, but there was no way he could grasp it. The sec-onds ticked off in agonizing slowness. Finally an idea came to mind. It was risky, but it was their only hope.

Gary looked at John and held up one finger. He pointed to the router and made a slow motion with his hand. Then he held up two fingers. He pointed to the bar that held the stone section and made a quick upward movement. He pointed to the loose stone and made a grabbing motion. John stared at him for long seconds; then he slowly nodded.

John eased the router out of the cut. The loose stone moved a little when the router bit finally came free. Gary exhaled, got down on his hands and knees, and inched forward until he was over the stone. It was now or never. He looked up at John and nodded.

Gary's eyes focused on the stone. He saw John get set out of the corner of his eye, but the sudden heave almost caught Gary by surprise. The arch section shot upwards, and the stone broke free at the same instant. Time seemed to slow to a crawl. Gary saw the stone begin its downward plunge. He threw himself prone, thrust his arms through the hole, and grabbed. His right hand closed around the stone, but he couldn't hold on. He grasped with his left hand, got a grip, but it was too heavy. Just in time he brought his right hand around. He had it—barely.

Two big hands grabbed him under the armpits and pulled. Gary rolled to the side and set the stone down carefully. He looked up at John's round eyes and smiled. John pointed to Sherlock. It was Gary's turn.

"That was close," Ann said.

Dan leaned back and exhaled slowly. "I'll say. But one thing I've learned working with these guys. They're good, very good."

"No argument from me," Sully said.

Dan scanned through the monitors showing the real video feeds from both floors. The color pictures looked great, but that was to be expected from the latest digital low-light cameras. Dan watched Gary hover over Sherlock, preparing the robot for its journey down into the vault.

Gary attached a monofilament line to a ring on the top of Sherlock. The other end led to what looked like a stubby rod and reel mounted on a metal plate. Gary positioned the plate at the hole and secured it with clamps. Then he peered into the armored vault below. The Queen Mother's Crown was almost directly below, and even in the subdued lighting, glimmers of light flashed from the countless facets of thousands of diamonds and from the Koh-I-Noor itself.

Gary lowered Sherlock until it hung suspended from the line. He pressed a thumb switch, starting the robot's leisurely journey down to the glass case. Sherlock spun lazily as the line paid out. Finally Gary retarded the descent, then shut off the motor when the line went slack. Sherlock now rested on its rubber treads.

Gary picked up the remote control and gingerly lined the robot up with the crown, then backed up about a foot. He engaged the miniature derrick, hoisted the cutter assembly off Sherlock's back, and swung it 180 degrees until it was squarely over the crown, then lowered it to the glass. Gary pressed a button and watched a gauge as the attached hose provided vacuum for the suction cup feet.

Satisfied that the unit had a secure grip, Gary deployed the glass cutter attached to the central mast. The combination diamond wheel and ultrasonic head made one silent circuit. Gary saw the derrick dip slightly as it received the extra load of the severed glass. He engaged the drum and lifted the slab clear using the motor's slowest speed. Gary swiveled the derrick, set the glass down, and cut the vacuum to the suction cups.

After returning the cutter assembly to Sherlock's back, Gary brought the derrick back around and lowered the hook into the case with agonizing slowness. Several minutes later it was in place. Gary turned the derrick, moving the hook under the crown's arches. Ever so gently he took up the slack in the line. Then he paused to rub the accumulated sweat from his hands. John's smile seemed a strange combination of encouragement and concern.

Gary pressed a button that engaged the reel at a rate below the motion detector's threshold, according to John's calculations. At first Gary couldn't tell if anything was happening, but then the crown moved slightly. Fully two minutes passed before it lifted clear of the shelf. On the way up, the crown spun lazily one way then the other, its diamonds sending glittering shards of light about the dimly lit room.

After what seemed hours, the derrick motor finally stopped. Gary looked closely, making sure the bottom of the crown was clear of the display case.

Gary placed Sherlock's controller on the floor and punched the thumb switch to begin hoisting the robot. The monofilament line ran smoothly through the rod's eyelets and onto the drum. Gary released the switch when Sherlock reached the top. He exhaled quietly and smiled.

John had the crown's box out with the lid open. Gary lifted Sherlock clear. John removed the crown, placed it in the box, then closed and locked the lid. Gary unhooked Sherlock and released the miniature hoist. These he returned to his backpack. John disassembled the tools and made sure they and the battery packs were securely stowed. Last he slid the crown's box into his pack.

Gary nodded toward the window. They tiptoed over to the monorail with their packs. They would exit the reverse of the way they entered: John first, then the packs, and Gary last. John attached the wire's hook to the ring in his harness. The winch whined and hoisted him up to the trolley. He glided through the hole in the window with surprising ease, and his backpack soon followed.

Gary hooked his pack to the trolley and was about to send it through when he heard a faint whine, and his pack began to bulge. One of Sherlock's actuators was running. He had forgotten to turn off the robot's controller. Fortunately, that was the last thing stowed. He opened the pack and reached for the remote, but it tumbled out, propelled by Sherlock's derrick. Gary made a wild grab but missed. The controller hit the floor with a loud crack and skittered across the floor.

Somewhere an electronic siren began whooping. Gary

looked around the room in horror.

"Come on!" John shouted.

Dan saw Gary suddenly appear in what had been the picture of an empty room. He grabbed the mike. "Hey, Gary, get out of there. The cameras have you." He turned to Ann. "Nuke the switch."

"Already on it," she said. Ann hit the Enter key and waited for the reply. "That switch is history. At least the guards won't be calling out on the landlines."

Dan pulled a laptop over and clicked a button on an application monitoring the mobile phone towers. "Good job. And I'm overriding all the mobile phone services. All they'll be able to get are busy signals."

"What do we do now?" Sully asked.

Dan looked around at him. "Sit tight and hope they make it out." He looked up at a monitor and watched Gary shove Sherlock's controller back in the backpack and send the trolley out the window.

Gary jumped up on the windowsill, and John helped him through.

"What are we going to do?" John asked.

"Keep going," Gary said. "They haven't caught us yet."

Gary snapped on his backpack, and John did the same. Gary hooked up his winch and set it to max speed. He slipped on his night-vision goggles and watched the shiny green stonework slide past.

"You there! Halt!" The urgent command drifted up from below.

Gary looked down and caught a glimpse of an angry face looking up. The fog's clammy curtain cut the man off.

"Come back here," the disembodied voice shouted.

The winch reached the top and shut off. Gary hauled himself over the low stone parapet and stood on the slick roof. John struggled over and joined him.

"Do you need any help?" Gary asked.

"No, I can handle it."

"Hurry. Get ready for takeoff."

"But how are we going to do this?"

"I'll guide you. Now move it."

John lumbered off into the mist.

Gary stripped off his gloves and stuffed them in a pocket. He removed his backpack, then lifted the wing and scurried underneath. He hooked his pack to the ring below the engine, attached his harness, and struggled to his feet. He turned around, and to his horror, he saw John coming toward him lugging his backpack.

"My hang glider's busted," he said, almost in a shout.

Gary felt a fresh jolt of adrenaline. "What's wrong?"

"Gas leak. I must have snagged the fuel line earlier."

chapter 12

G ary knew they had to do something—and quick. They had a short reprieve because it would take a while for the guards to get up on the roof, but he knew they would have company soon enough.

A thought popped into his mind. At first he pushed it aside as a sure invitation to a painful death. But the thought came back, and the more Gary considered it, the more he saw the possibilities. It was dangerous, but then that was their stock in trade.

Somewhere a door slammed open. Gary knew their chance of escaping, however slim, was rapidly slipping away.

"Come here," Gary told John in a harsh whisper. "Hook your backpack beside mine."

"But—"

"Just do it."

John reached under, felt around, and finally secured his backpack to the ring under the engine.

Gary thought he saw a faint glow; then he was sure. "Follow me," he whispered. He led John back toward the center section of the Barracks, away from the disabled hang glider.

"Coo, what's this?" a faint voice said. "Smells to high heavens of petrol, it does."

"Look underneath," another voice said. "Mind your step now."

Gary breathed a tentative sigh of relief and hoped the discovery of the other glider would provide the time they needed. He continued shuffling across the roof until the wall materialized out of the fog, then turned around.

"Hook up your harness beside me," Gary whispered. "We're flying out together."

"What? We'll never make it."

"Yes, we will. Now hook up."

John reached up and fastened his harness. Gary engaged the starter, and the engine sprang to life instantly.

"Now, listen carefully," Gary said. "We're going to take off just like we planned. When we reach the parapet, jump and pull your legs up. Leave everything else to me. Understand?"

"Yeah, I guess so."

"Trust me."

There was a slight pause. "I do."

"That's the spirit. Ready?"

"Yeah."

Gary ran the throttle all the way forward. "Run!" he shouted, not caring who might hear.

It took a few awkward steps, but John finally got in sync with Gary's rapid strides. The wind began to fill the wing, lifting some of the glider's weight off his shoulders. Gary's breath came in ragged gasps as he pumped his legs as hard as he could. The left wing brushed past a dark shadow.

"Halt!" The cry came from somewhere behind them.

Gary caught the pungent odor of gasoline. Then two more shapes emerged out of the fog, the disabled glider and the other guard.

"Now look here!" a startled voice shouted.

The guard ran toward the fugitives. Gary angled more toward the roof's edge, hoping to avoid the man. Then the parapet flashed into view.

"Jump!" Gary shouted.

He did, and he felt John push off a fraction of a second later. Gary pushed forward on the control bar as hard as he could. The hang glider jumped into the air a few feet. Gary's legs hit the charging guard and threw him aside. He pulled the bar back to level the wallowing craft, airborne thanks to ground effect, which provided extra lift close to the ground. He knew they would stall if they flew out of it. The parapet flashed beneath his feet.

Gary pulled the control bar back and shoved it to the left, to dive away from the building. Ever so slowly their airspeed crept up. He leveled the wing, but their descent continued a few more seconds. The ground appeared.

"Lift your legs!" Gary shouted.

Finally the glider started climbing. They were airborne, but he knew they could never clear the unseen wall up ahead. Their only hope was to turn left and fly through the gap between Waterloo Barracks and the wall. But were they past the Barracks? Gary wondered. He thought they were, and every second took them closer to the wall.

Gary began a slow turn to the left, then tightened it and rolled out on a southerly heading. Provided they were in the gap, they now had enough airspace to climb out of the Tower's confines. Gary's thundering pulse eased a little, and he began to hope they might make it. But what then? His GPS was shot. That was a thought he had been pushing aside, but now it came back with a vengeance. Then he remembered how he had mapped the Tower grounds.

"Star Chamber," Gary said, "tell Sully-man to make tracks for Hyde Park, and we'll meet you there. Gooney Bird One and Two out."

Dan reached up and cut off all transmission circuits to Gary and John. He turned to Sully. "You heard the man. Get this heap moving."

"I'm gone." He jumped up and ran to the back.

"What about the car?" Ann asked.

"Leave it," Dan said. "We don't have time."

Sully threw open the doors, jumped out, and slammed them. A few moments later the engine roared to life. "Hold on to your hat," Sully said over the speakers.

Dan scanned the external cameras and saw the fog was as heavy as ever. Sully turned onto the deserted Royal Mint Street, but despite Sully's brash words, their pace was anything but rapid.

When the radar altimeter registered a second sudden drop, Gary knew they were over the Tower of London's outer wall. The reading increased, then increased again. Now they were over the Thames. Gary smiled. He had a plan.

"Brother John," he said.

"Yeah? Hope you've got some good news, 'cause I could sure use some."

"I think I can get us to Hyde Park more or less in one piece."

"That's what I've been praying for."

"Thanks. By all means, keep it up."

"But how can you do it without GPS?"

"It's called dead reckoning. Pilots were using that *way* before GPS and all the other fancy gadgets."

"I'm not sure I like the 'dead' part."

Gary chuckled. "Not to worry. It just means that if you fly

at a known speed in a known direction, you can predict your location even if you can't see it."

"But how precise can that be? I mean, what about the compass and the airspeed indicator? They're not all that accurate."

"Yeah, and a whole lot more besides. But we have an ace in the hole."

"What's that?"

"The radar altimeter. It indicates objects below as dips in the distance to the ground. Like right now, we're over the Thames, heading west. There, we just passed over London Bridge." He chuckled again. "Our hotel's almost close enough to chuck a rock at."

"So we follow the river until we turn off for Hyde Park?"

"That's the general idea," Gary said. "Now let me concentrate on business."

"Right."

"But keep on praying."

"Don't you worry; I will."

The sound of an emergency Klaxon drifted up from somewhere behind them, but the fog made it sound thin and far away. *That didn't take long,* Gary thought. He wondered how far the police would spread their dragnet, and how fast. Being the object of a manhunt wasn't in the contract, and with Gary's image on disk, he was currently tagged "it."

Gary leveled off at exactly five hundred feet, according to the aneroid altimeter. He flew a generally westerly course but angled to ensure he would cross the Thames's south bank. Each time he angled, he returned to the river and repeated the maneuver, so he always knew which side he was on, then counted off each bridge until he crossed Waterloo Bridge. Here the river took a sharp turn to the south. Gary turned to follow, held that course for fifteen seconds, then turned west. Ahead lay Whitehall, assuming his dead reckoning was correct.

The radar altimeter's readings rose and fell as the hang

glider flew over buildings. Then the reading increased and stayed that way.

"We're over St. James Park," Gary said.

"You sure?" John asked.

"Would I kid you?"

"Yeah, lots of times. But this time I believe you."

"Thanks."

Gary turned a little more to the south. There was one more signpost he was hoping for. The seconds dragged on, and the radar altimeter maintained a nearly constant distance to the ground. Then it dipped and stayed that way for a while.

"We're over Buckingham Palace," Gary said.

"Almost there."

"That we are. I better roust out our ground crew. Star Chamber, this is Gooney Bird One. I'm on long final approach, gear down and locked. What is your location? Over."

"Gooney Bird One, we're nearing Oxford Street. Sounds like you'll be down before we can get there. Over."

"No problem, Star Chamber. We'll see you when you arrive. Gooney Bird One out."

The radar altimeter reading shot up. They were past the palace and over the surrounding parkland. Gary pulled the throttle all the way back and pushed the control bar forward. The hang glider slowed, then began a rapid descent, mushing along on the verge of a stall.

"Are we going to crash?" John asked.

"Relax. Everything's under control," Gary replied.

They began giving back the comfortable altitude cushion that had kept them above harm's way. Now the worst that could happen would be to land in a tree or water. The first didn't worry Gary. It might be painful, but they would survive. But a water landing was different, since they might get tangled in the glider and drown. And Hyde Park had two water hazards: Round Pond near Kensington Palace and the aptly named Serpentine, which was longer than Hyde Park was wide.

When the radar altimeter read twenty feet, Gary pulled back on the control bar and went to half throttle. The hang glider leveled out, and the airspeed increased to twenty-five knots.

"Get ready," Gary said. "Remember, you have to run when we land, or we end up eating grass."

"Don't worry."

Gary eased back on the throttle and watched their altitude bleed off. He peered through the fog, alert for anything in their path. His heart began to pound as he sensed the invisible ground approaching.

"Water!" John shouted.

Gary saw it at the same time. He jammed the throttle full forward and pushed on the control bar. "Lift your legs."

Gary hiked his up. The hang glider nearly stalled again. The airspeed indicator jiggled and slowly increased—one knot, then two. Gary nudged the control bar forward and to the left. The hang glider staggered upward a few feet and began a sedate turn to the right. Gary extended his legs and watched the still waters sweep past. Then he saw what he'd been looking for: the shoreline. He chopped the throttle.

"This is it!" Gary shouted.

Gary pushed the control bar forward in one progressive motion. The hang glider slowed rapidly, then stalled. Gary hit the ground and ran until the glider stopped moving. The deadweight now rested on their shoulders.

"Okay, you first," Gary said.

John disconnected his harness from the hang glider and ducked out from under the drooping wing fabric. Gary got loose, unhooked both backpacks, and came out into the open.

"Boy, am I glad *that's* over," John said.

"You and me both. Now all we have to do is wait for our ride."

"I wish they'd hurry." John sounded very tired.

Me too, Gary thought. Then it hit him. They were safe, after enduring an extremely difficult operation, where much had gone wrong. But they had prayed, and they had overcome every danger, *and* they had the crown. He pressed a button on his watch and saw it was 3:41. It had taken a little less than two hours to snatch the crown, but it had seemed much longer.

"We did it," John said with feeling. "We get the bonus *after* all."

"We sure earned it," Gary said.

"You bet we did."

"Hey, you goonies," Dan's voice said, "how about cutting the radio chatter."

"Yes, Mother," Gary replied. "Where are you anyway?"

"Just past Marble Arch. Where are you?"

"I haven't the foggiest, except we almost ditched in the Serpentine. We're somewhere on the northeast side."

"Okay. Keep transmitting, and I'll get a fix on you."

"But you said. . ."

"I changed my mind. Humor me."

Gary shrugged. He had always felt self-conscious doing radio checks. "One. . .two. . .three. . .four. . .five. . ." He waited a second then began again.

Gary heard two-tone Klaxons several times while they were waiting, but none were close. He used the time to disassemble the hang glider and bind the pieces with Velcro straps.

A short time later Dan broke in. "Okay, I've got a pretty good fix on you. Help is on the way."

But it was five long minutes by Gary's watch before a dark green shadow emerged from the fog. He tensed, then relaxed when he saw it was Sully.

"Took you long enough," Gary said, trying for a light tone.

"Hey, Dan's fix on you wasn't all that great," Sully said. "He had you guys a few hundred feet north of here, and close doesn't count in a fog." He patted the pager clipped to his belt. "Fortunately he knew where *I* was."

Gary laughed. "Well, I'm happy to see you too."

Sully was silent for a moment. "Yeah, uh, you guys had me worried. Danger is my business, but you two are *way* over the top. Glad you made it."

"Thanks, Sully," Gary said.

It seemed that all the accumulated tension was now draining away, but the operation was not yet over, and it wouldn't be until they handed the crown to Peter. And to do that, they had to evade the police and get back to the hotel.

"Brother John, if you'll take the backpacks, Sully and I will tote the hang glider," Gary said.

"Okay," John said.

Gary and Sully picked up the awkward bundle of rods, wires, Dacron, and engine.

"Sully," Gary said, "you lead off."

"Will do. Hey, Dan, talk us in."

"Roger. Start walking north."

"Terrific," Sully said. "Which way is north?"

"Just start walking. I'll guide you."

A few minutes later they were all inside the truck's command center.

"Gary, that was a *fantastic* escape," Ann said.

"Thanks, but we still have to get back to the hotel." He turned to Dan. "What's our situation?"

Dan leaned back in his chair. "It was already bad, but now it's worse. I've been monitoring the scanners, and the police have most of central London cordoned off. I'm really surprised they could move that fast. Apparently we've touched the British version of the third rail." He waved at a blank monitor. "I was able to eavesdrop at Waterloo Barracks until they found the taps. Bobbies, guards, yeomen warders, you name it—all *over* the place. It was like a stirred-up beehive."

"Why don't we turn the crown over to the cops?" Ann asked.

"That would forfeit the bonus," Gary said.

"Why? You and John made off with it."

"We have to give the crown to Peter. If we're apprehended, or we give up, it proves their security is adequate, in which case we don't get the bonus. That's the deal." He turned back to Dan. "Do we have a way out?"

"Maybe. We're inside the police dragnet, and they'll start sweeping toward the city center any time now. They've posted guards on most bridges, but I didn't hear any mention of Westminster. If we can get across that, we *might* make it back to the Snowsfields car park. It's the only hope we've got."

"I'll take a slim chance over none. Come on, guys, let's go for it. Sully, get us out of here."

Sully hurried out.

"What about the car?" Ann asked.

"We'll pick it up later."

Gary, John, and Ann took seats around Dan. Gary looked up at the GPS map of London, his eyes tracing the various ways back to the hotel. They would keep going until they could go no farther.

chapter 13

Gary watched the slow movement of the blue dot, which marked their GPS position on the London map overlay. They were nearing the Houses of Parliament and Westminster Bridge.

"I don't like it," he said. "Are you *sure* Westminster Bridge is clear?"

Dan shook his head. "No, but I didn't hear it mentioned."

Gary leaned over the map Dan had marked up. Every bridge in central London had a red X on it *except* the one next to Parliament. "You'd think this would be the first one they'd barricade. It's right in the heart of government."

"You'd think so. Maybe I missed it, or the police could have blocked it on their own. Or maybe they overlooked it. Who knows?"

"We can hope." Gary grabbed the mike. "Sully, keep a sharp lookout. We're nearing the bridge."

"Got my eyes peeled and diced, boss."

Gary glanced up at one of the monitors as they crossed onto the bridge. He split his focus between watching the computer map and the forward camera's view of the never-ending fog. Every moment he expected the dripping curtain to part and reveal waiting police. But the far end was clear as well.

"Where to now?" Sully asked.

Gary wanted to stick to the back roads, but most of the streets led toward bridges and the police. He traced out a route to Union Street for John. "What do you think?"

"I don't see anything better," John said.

Gary keyed the mike. "Sully, keep on Westminster till you get to Blackfriars Road. Then turn left, go to Union, and turn right."

"You're the boss."

Gary's eyes traced the route on the screen, searching for ambush points. Union Street was less than a half-mile from the Thames, so how far from Blackfriars Bridge would the police roadblock extend? He watched the snail-like progress of the truck's blue dot on the GPS map. Finally they reached Union and turned. But despite his worries, they made the turn onto Union without incident. Union Street changed to Newcomen, and they lumbered past Guy's Hospital. Up ahead, the street curved and became Snowsfields. One block beyond was Kipling Street and the entrance to the car park. Their goal was in sight.

Sully followed the curve onto Snowsfields, and since they were close to the Tower Bridge, they had to be near the greatest concentration of police patrols.

Gary grabbed the mike. "Sully, kill your lights."

"Hey, I can barely see the stripes as it is."

"Do it. Use your goggles."

"Okay." He didn't sound happy.

The forward monitor went dark.

"Stay sharp, folks," Gary said. "Keep us posted, Sully."

The truck's pace slowed even more. "I see a crosswalk—must be Kipling Street. Almost there, guys. Whoa!"

"Emergency vehicle," John said.

"Yeah, running without his Klaxon," Gary said.

"All the better to sneak up on us."

"What do I do?" Sully asked.

Gary took the mike. "Sully, any idea where they are?"

"I heard tires sliding, then nothing."

"Sounds like they pulled over," John said.

"Could be a checkpoint," Gary said. "Or they could be waiting for someone to enter the car park."

"I don't like it."

"Me either. Sully, back up a little and shut down."

The truck started moving.

"Think the cops heard us?" John asked.

"Not if they're still inside their car."

The truck came to a stop, and a few moments later Sully climbed inside the command center.

"What we need now," Gary said, "is a diversion to draw the car away." He turned to John. "Did you pack any of your high-intensity strobes?"

"Yeah, two. Focused beams with momentary outputs of two hundred thousand watts, enough to fry your eyeballs if you're looking right at them."

"How far away could you see it in this fog?"

"I don't know, probably in the same league as the spotlights they put on police helicopters." John's eyes narrowed. "What are you thinking?"

"What if we put one on Sherlock and rigged an explosion sound effect?"

"Ah, then when the cops go investigate. . ."

"Exactly," Gary said.

"But Sherlock's not expendable."

"Don't you worry. I'm not *about* to sacrifice your little friend."

"Which way do you want the strobe to face?"

"Backwards." Gary turned. "Dan, can you record us an explosion for Sherlock's audio output unit?"

"Nothing could be simpler."

156

John dug Sherlock and its controller out of Gary's backpack and started to work. In fifteen minutes he had the strobe and its Fresnel lens mounted on the robot's back deck.

Dan handed John a USB cable. "Tell Sherlock to sip slowly," he said. "This sound file packs a wallop."

John grinned. "My buddy can take it." He plugged the USB cable into Sherlock's side and downloaded the file. "See, not even a hiccup."

"I'm impressed."

"Are we ready?" Gary asked.

John stood up and worked the kinks out of his legs. "Guess so."

Gary picked up Sherlock by the recessed handle in the robot's front and cradled the controller in his other arm. "Sully, help me."

Sully picked up Gary's night-vision goggles and got the door. They stepped outside into the clammy darkness. The goggles slipped into place, turning the darkness into a green circle of wet pavement. Sully disappeared inside the truck, leaving Gary all alone with Sherlock and a plan that didn't seem as hopeful as it had a few minutes ago.

Gary walked past the truck, got up on the sidewalk, and crept cautiously toward the corner. When he got there he stopped and listened. All he could hear was the soft dripping of condensation, but he knew the police had to be out there lurking in the mist. He set Sherlock down in the street and checked all systems. The robot seemed no worse for wear after its earlier trials.

Gary engaged the drive and watched as it disappeared into the fog. He looked down at the LCD display transmitted from the robot's miniature camera. At first all he could see was a moving circle of glistening pavement. Then suddenly, a tire loomed large and menacing. Gary maneuvered Sherlock past the back of the car until he saw the curb. The caterpillar treads crawled up the concrete and hoisted the robot onto the sidewalk. Gary guided Sherlock close to the side of the car and kept going until it was well past.

Gary shut the drive down and took a deep breath, then jabbed the auxiliary button. A surprisingly bright flash lit up the fog, accompanied with what sounded like an explosion, complete with subsonic shock waves. An engine roared to life and tires whined on the wet pavement. A blue pulsing light joined a two-tone Klaxon as the car fought for traction.

"Okay, guys," Gary said. "Move it." He heard an engine start somewhere behind him.

Then he remembered Sherlock. He engaged the robot's drive and shoved the throttle all the way forward, his eyes glued to the LCD screen. Cracks in the sidewalk flashed past, and Gary barely avoided a light pole. He saw a dark shape off to the left—a litter can. Gary cut the drive, and Sherlock slid to a stop. He leaned the joystick over to the left, moved the throttle forward, and scooted Sherlock in close beside the container. The robot's rear-facing camera picked up blue flashing lights. The unseen car slid to a stop. Doors opened and closed.

"What was it?" a faint voice asked.

"Could have sworn it was an explosion, but I don't see anything."

Gary could see a flashlight's glow on the LCD display. The man was very near John's pride and joy.

"Keep looking," the first voice said. "I'll take the street. You search the sidewalk."

The flashlight's glow increased on the display, and finally Gary could make out a shadow that gradually resolved itself into a man in a raincoat.

"Hello, what have we here?" came the tinny voice captured by Sherlock's microphone.

Down came a grasping hand. Gary jabbed the auxiliary button. He jumped at the resulting flash and reverberating sound, even though he had expected it.

"Ow! My eyes! My eyes!" The speaker crackled.

Gary engaged reverse, threw the joystick over, and backed Sherlock out in a sharp 90-degree turn. Then he centered the stick and shot the throttle all the way forward, racing past the disabled policeman. Soon all Gary could see in the display was the sidewalk edge and a little of the street below. When Gary estimated Sherlock was near his location, he slowed and started it across the street, stopping when it reached the curb. Gary stepped into Kipling Street and walked along the curb until he spotted the familiar squat object.

He picked up the robot and listened for a few moments. The muffled voices were farther away now, past the still-flashing blue glow coming from the unseen car. Gary hurried through the car park entrance. Though the garage was lighted, the fog still made seeing difficult. Finally he spotted the truck. Sully opened the rear doors and Gary climbed up.

Sully closed the doors, and Dan flipped on the interior lights. Gary was glad to see they were already dressed in their formal clothes. John took Sherlock while Gary went forward and started changing into his tuxedo.

"Is the crown ready?" Gary asked.

"Yes," Dan said. "The box has a built-in transmitter, but I also hid one inside the crown to be on the safe side." He locked the box and gave Gary the key.

"Good." One of Gary's fears was that something would happen before they could hand the crown over to Peter. Now that they had gotten this far, he didn't want to leave anything to chance.

Gary finished dressing and donned his raincoat. He picked up the crown's box and tucked it under his arm. "Everyone ready?" he asked.

"Lead on, gov'nah," Sully said.

"Your accent's worse than Gary's," Ann said.

"Move it, people," Gary said.

Dan turned off the lights and shut down the auxiliary power unit. Gary led them outside and toward the car park's rear exit while Dan locked up. After a brief debate with John, they decided to take the longer route past Guy's Hospital and up Borough High Street rather than risking Weston Street. Only when they reached the hotel did Gary begin to believe they had really made it. They passed into the lobby, exchanged greetings with the night clerk, and went up to their floor. That left one more thing to do—make the all-important call to Peter.

"Everybody in my room," Gary said. "Dan, go get your laptop so we'll know what's going on."

Dan rushed off. Gary opened his door and ushered the others inside. They sat around the table. Gary placed the box in the center and looked at his watch. It was 4:55. In another half hour it would be official sunrise, although the fog would delay the sun's appearance. A few moments later Dan rushed in, the open laptop in his hands.

"We have visitors," he said. "Peter and Ian are through the lobby and on their way up."

"Police must have called him," Gary said. "Better hide your PC. No point in letting any of our secrets out."

Dan nodded but continued to stare at the screen. "They just got off the elevator and are coming this way." He snapped the lid shut, slipped the laptop under Gary's bed, hurried over, and sat down.

Three firm raps sounded at the door.

Gary walked to the door and opened it. Peter looked reasonably fresh, despite the early hour, and his suit was immaculate. Ian stood behind and a little to the side. He held their raincoats.

"Hello, may we come in?" Peter asked.

"Please do," Gary replied. He waved toward the table. "I was about to call you."

160

Peter stepped inside and his eyes went immediately to the box. Ian's eyes did likewise, and a hint of a smile came to his lips but one devoid of warmth.

"I take it, then, that you have the goods," Peter said.

"That we do," Gary said.

"Well done, chaps, extremely well done. May I see the prize?"

Gary laughed. "Of course. You're the one we pinched it for."

Peter eyed him. "Steady, old boy. You're getting the vocab, but the accent is—how shall I say it?—atrocious."

"I keep telling him that," Ann said.

Peter looked at her and smiled. "Doesn't listen very well, does he? Well, no matter. Now, shall we?" He nodded toward the box.

Gary inserted the key, twisted it, and opened the box. He stared at the sparkling facets of thousands of diamonds. Peter carefully lifted the crown. The Koh-I-Noor blazed with light, drawing attention away from all lesser gems.

"Magnificent," Peter said. He gently replaced the crown, closed the lid, and locked it. He removed the key and, after a brief hesitation, pocketed it. "Now, I really must be off so I can put out the fires you chaps have started." He reached for the box.

Gary put his hand on it. "I'd like a receipt, if you don't mind. This *is* part of the Crown Jewels."

Peter laughed. "Rather, old boy. I expected you might."

He snapped his fingers, and Ian gave him a sealed envelope. Peter opened it and pulled out two pieces of paper. He gave one to Gary and unfolded the other.

"I believe you will find the amount correct," he said.

Gary ran his eyes over the check. Yes, this part of the bargain was *definitely* in order. "Thank you, Peter."

"Thank *you*. Your work will enable us to plug some rather nasty holes in our security. We're fortunate it was *you* rather than an actual thief."

He spread out the paper and signed it. Gary took it from

Peter and read it carefully. It was on MI5 letterhead, and it acknowledged the receipt of the Queen Consort's Crown by Peter Watkins. It included a description of the crown plus a complete inventory of all gems, including weight. At the top of the list was the 105.6 carat Koh-I-Noor.

"Is that satisfactory?" Peter asked.

"Quite satisfactory," Gary said. "Thank you."

"Don't mention it. Now, I'm afraid Ian and I really must be going. I assure you: London is in an uproar over this, and as I said, the officials know nothing about the MI5 security audit."

"We understand. You'll have our official report in a day or two. We have all the data we need; it's only a matter of making it pretty."

"Right. No rush. I'll look for it at your convenience." Peter picked up the box. He started to turn, then hesitated. "Oh, don't be alarmed if you should see something about this on the telly. I've got a lot of calls to make, and the media are *not* at the top of my list."

"No problem. We'll lay low until the all clear."

"That's the ticket." Peter smiled. "I'll ring you up when it's safe to come out. Well, cheerio."

Gary went to the door and opened it. Peter hurried out with Ian right behind him. Gary closed the door and turned.

"Well done, everyone," Gary said. "Get some rest, and don't worry about setting an alarm. The cleanup can wait."

After they filed out, Gary undressed down to his boxer shorts and T-shirt. He hung up his tuxedo and shirt, then debated on whether or not to shower. He knew he should, but fatigue won out. He turned off the lights and threw himself into bed.

chapter 14

Gary stared up into the dark shadows and finally decided he couldn't sleep. He turned his head and focused on the alarm clock beside his bed. It was a quarter to six. The sun was up now, but there was no evidence of that fact. The windows seemed as dark as when he had gone to bed.

Gary got up, flipped on the lights, and turned on the TV. The screen flashed and steadied, showing a car commercial featuring people who seemed incapable of sitting still while driving. He jabbed the mute button and began serious surfing. A few clicks later he stopped when a picture of the Tower of London flashed on the screen. He pressed the mute button again.

". . .daring early morning raid, broke into the Jewel House vault and stole the Queen Mother's Crown. Scotland Yard believes at least two people were involved in this unprecedented robbery. Surveillance cameras caught a picture of one of the men as he fled the scene."

Gary felt an increasing sense of dread, despite Peter's earlier warning.

"The police are following up all leads, but the perpetrators have not been apprehended as of this hour. When asked how they got past the Jewel House's elaborate security. . ."

Gary pressed the mute button and tried to reassure himself that Peter probably had not reached the media yet. Maybe notifying the various police agencies was taking longer than expected. Then another thought hit him: What if Peter had been in an accident? The fog certainly made driving dangerous.

Gary remembered Dan's PC was under the bed. He hauled it out, took it over to the table, and sat down. Seeing it was still on, he jogged the mouse to end its sleep mode and started the camera program. The corridor outside was deserted. He switched to the lobby camera and froze. A man in a raincoat was speaking to the night clerk while four uniformed policemen waited behind him. Gary turned up the speaker volume.

". . .I'm concerned about my other guests," the clerk said.

"Not to worry," the plainclothes officer said. "That's why I'm waiting for the Special Branch and MI5 chaps. They know how to handle these things."

A man in work clothes approached the desk holding his hat. "Excuse me, but the police on the dock say I'm not to leave. I've got deliveries to make, mate."

"And you are?" the officer asked.

"Produce delivery," the desk clerk answered for him. "I can vouch for him."

"Sorry, no one goes in or out unless authorized by MI5 or Special Branch. Those are my orders."

The deliveryman nodded and backed away.

Gary flipped to the outside camera. The fog was alive with indistinct blue flashes. They were trapped. Fighting his growing fear, he grabbed the phone and punched in John's number. It rang six times before a groggy voice finally answered.

" 'Lo."

"It's Gary. Get in here, and bring the others."

"What's wrong?"

"The police have the hotel surrounded, and there are cops in the lobby."

"What?"

"Just do it. Now hurry."

Gary slammed down the phone and switched back to the lobby camera. The officer was mumbling something into his radio mike, but Gary couldn't hear what it was. His mind raced ahead. He got his wallet and pulled out Peter's card. He grabbed the phone and punched in the office number. The phone chirped three times before the voice mail picked up.

"Hello, Peter Watkins here. Sorry, but I'm on holiday for a fortnight, beginning the eighth of May. If you need immediate assistance, please call. . ."

Gary hung up, and his mind began connecting the pieces at warp speed. The media might be out of the loop, but the Metropolitan Police should have gotten the message by now. *And now Peter's gone on vacation?*

Gary cycled through the hotel cameras again. The situation in the lobby and outside remained the same. When he flipped to the corridor, he saw Dan and Sully approaching. John stood behind them doing something to Ann's door. Gary jumped up and ran to his door, opening it just as Dan was about to knock.

"Come in," Gary said in a low voice. Dan and Sully hurried past. Gary leaned out into the corridor. "John."

John looked around but shook his head. Something clicked, and he pushed Ann's door open. Gary waited. Soon John emerged, closed the door, and came running.

"Ann's not there. I knocked for several minutes and got worried when she didn't answer," he said, agitated. He came inside and held up an earphone radio. "She left this behind." He stuck it in his pocket.

Gary closed his door. "Come on, sit down." He pointed toward the table where Dan and Sully stood waiting. Gary waited until they were all seated. Then he took his seat in front of the PC.

"What do you mean?" Gary asked.

John's eyes flashed. "I'm not sure what is going on, but Ann's not here. And none of the possibilities are good. Either something bad has happened to her. . .or to us. What if she sold us out? What if she and Peter set us up?"

"Now hold on. We don't. . ."

"*Hold on!* What do you mean, hold on?"

"Calm down. Getting mad won't help. We've got to all stay focused."

John's shoulders slumped. "You got some secret plan?"

"Not yet, but I need to bring you guys up to date. I called Peter's office, and his voice mail message says he's on vacation."

John frowned. "Surprise, surprise."

"One possibility is that Peter scammed and informed on us."

"With Ann's help."

"We don't know that for sure. We need to consider all the options," Gary said, forcing himself to remain calm. The mere idea that Ann might have betrayed them stung. He knew he had to maintain control or they were lost.

"Isn't there *anything* we can do?" John asked.

Gary shook his head. "Not at the moment. The hotel is surrounded. The police are waiting on MI5 and Special Branch to get here."

"MI5, that's a laugh. Suppose Peter will come in off vacation and give them a hand?" John started to say something more, then stopped. "Hey, what about the receipt for the crown?"

"I'm thinking that MI5 will assume it's a forgery. If Peter is involved in this, he'll have covered his tracks. They have my face on video, plus there's all kinds of evidence in the truck. And if they can't locate Peter, they'll say we eliminated a witness."

"Looks like we're boxed in."

Gary looked around. "Any suggestions? Anybody?"

Dan shook his head.

Sully looked at Gary. "You really think Ann is in with Peter?"

"What I am is worried. I don't know what to *think*. We have so little information right now." Much as he hated to admit it, Gary couldn't think of any way around John's arguments. Surely if she went down to the lobby or left the hotel for some reason, she would have seen the police and come back to warn them. He glanced at his watch. It was now five minutes after six. How much longer did they have? he wondered.

"Gary," Dan said.

Gary looked up. "What?"

"Something's activated the radio net." Dan pointed to the flashing icon. "May I?"

Gary shoved the laptop over to him.

"Can anyone hear me?" came Ann's unmistakable voice.

"What?" John exclaimed.

"Hush," Dan said. He inserted his earphone radio and turned it on. He cranked up the volume on the PC.

"This is Dan. Go ahead."

"Ann here. I'm in the truck, almost to the hotel. I know what's happening, and I'm executing a diversion. Do you copy?"

"I copy. But what. . . ?"

"No time; I'm almost there. Get ready to cut out. Got that?"

"Got it."

"Out."

"What's going on?" John asked, his eyes very round.

"I guess we're about to find out," Gary said.

The others gathered around Dan so they could watch the screen.

"I'm across from the entrance," Ann announced over the speakers. "I'm coming inside now."

Dan shifted to the outside camera. The fog was beginning to burn off. A dark shape crossed the street and entered the hotel. Dan punched up the lobby camera. A woman in a raincoat headed straight for the Scotland Yard commander.

"Is that Ann?" John asked.

Gary looked at the image closely. "I guess so, but it sure is a good disguise."

The woman's shiny black hair complemented her light brown skin, and her rapid stride said she was all business. She held up her ID for the policeman.

"Edwina Dunn, MI5. Are you in charge here?"

Gary shook his head. It *was* Ann.

The man seemed to come to attention. "Commander Duncan Akers, Southwark Borough, at your service."

Ann put her hands on her hips. "Well, I *hope* so. What are you doing here? The Special Branch chaps are already searching Waterloo Station."

"Dispatch said the suspects were here." He swept his hand around the lobby as if this explained everything.

"If I might—" the night clerk began.

Ann held up a hand. "Not now. I'll attend to you in turn." She turned back to the commander. "I want your officers over at Waterloo as soon as can be managed."

"But—"

"No buts. Is the chain of command in any way unclear to you? If so, I will gladly take it up with Peter when he comes off holiday."

"Peter Watkins?"

"*Yes.* Peter Watkins. Now *please* unstop your ears. The suspects have gone to ground at Waterloo, and Special Branch is searching the station. I want you to form a perimeter about the station straightaway. If the suspects get away, it will be your neck. Now get a move on."

"Of course. Right away." He fled from the lobby, taking his four officers with him.

Gary watched Ann turn to the night clerk. "Yes?" she asked. Her tone was subdued, but it held a hint of steel.

"Well, I don't wish to interfere in MI5 business, but I saw the bloke you are looking for go upstairs about an hour ago. He—Gary Nesbitt is his name—and four others came in dressed to the nines. Been out on the town, or at least that's what I thought till all this blew up."

"Upstairs, did you say?" Ann said.

"Why, yes."

Ann turned to the deliveryman. "What are *you* doing here?"

The man clenched his hat. "Well, as I was tellin' the police earlier, I was cartin' in produce when—"

"If you were delivering produce, may I presume that the dock doors are open?"

"Why, yes. Can't make deliveries otherwise."

Ann returned her gaze to the clerk. "And the police came before or after you opened the dock?"

"Um, they came in after."

"So the dock was unguarded, at least for a while."

The clerk hesitated for a moment. "Well, yes, I guess it was."

Ann smiled. "Then may I suggest that is why the suspects are down at Waterloo Station rather than up in their rooms."

"But it's not my fault," the clerk stammered.

"Never mind that." Ann looked about the lobby as if mentally photographing it. Then she looked right at the camera and gave an almost imperceptible nod.

She turned back to the clerk. "However, I must report this. Take me back to the dock. I'll need a complete description of everything that happened after you opened the dock doors."

"Will you be needing me?" the deliveryman asked.

"If you please. Now, press on. I haven't got all day."

The clerk led the way out of the camera's view.

Gary jumped to his feet. "Come on."

"What about our stuff?" Sully asked.

"We don't have time," Gary replied.

"But my earphone radio is in my room."

Gary hesitated. "Okay, grab it, but that's all. Meet us at the stairs."

Gary opened the door and ran to the stairs with John. Dan followed, lugging his laptop. Sully came last, working his radio into his ear.

"Keep it quiet," Gary whispered.

Gary led the way down to the first floor, inched the door open, and peered out. He saw no one. He dashed through the corridor and lobby and up to the front door, where he paused and listened. Nothing. He opened the door and stepped outside. Although the fog was lighter now, thick patches still remained. Gary crept along until their truck emerged out of the mist.

"Take the wheel," Gary told Sully. "Everybody else in the back."

Sully jumped into the cab, and the engine rumbled to life. Gary opened the rear doors, waited for the others to climb up, then joined them. He closed the door, and Dan flipped on the lights.

"She even fired up all the systems," Dan said. Views from the hotel cameras occupied three of the monitors.

"Here she comes," Gary said, pointing to the lobby monitor. He went to the back doors and waited.

"I've got her on the outside camera," Dan said. "She's crossing the street."

Gary let her in. "Very well done," he said as he closed the doors. Then, remembering their earlier discussion, he looked at John and saw his stricken expression. He knew they were thinking about the same thing.

"Thank you, Gary," Ann replied.

She hesitated when she said it, making Gary wonder what she was thinking. But more urgent thoughts flooded his mind. He grabbed the mike. "Move out, Sully."

The truck lurched into motion. "Where to?" Sully asked.

"Just drive."

"Okay."

"But stay away from Waterloo Station and the Thames," Gary added.

"I ain't no dummy."

Gary smiled in spite of their situation. He set down the mike. "We need a hiding place."

"Indeed," Ann said.

Gary looked all around. "Any ideas?"

"Say we find a place," Dan said. "What good does that do? As far as we know, Peter's got the crown, and the cops will still find us sooner or later."

Gary turned to Ann. "How long did you rent that machine shop for?"

"A week," she said.

"Do you still have the key?"

She went to her purse, grabbed something, and returned. "Yes." She dropped it into his hand.

"Very good," Gary said. "This will give us some time to regroup."

He took the mike. "Sully. Make for the machine shop."

"Right, boss."

A few minutes later they pulled up outside a dilapidated building off Old Jamaica Road. John got out and unlocked the dingy white garage doors and pushed them open. Sully drove the truck inside. Gary, Ann, and Dan stepped down and joined Sully. John closed the doors. Gary led them to a worktable. It was dank and cool, but it wasn't a jail cell. Gary stood while the others sat around the table on tall lab chairs. He wasn't looking forward to the first thing they had to discuss, and he knew from John's expression that he felt the same way.

Gary scanned each face and finally stopped at Ann. "We're in deep trouble, folks, but we're not giving up. We need to take stock of where we are and start brainstorming. There's *got* to be a way out. But first we have something else to take care of."

Again he saw that strange expression on Ann's face. "Ann, I owe you an apology."

"Gary—" she began.

"No, please let me finish. When we found out you were gone, we considered the idea that you sold us out." He stopped for a moment.

"Hold on," John said quickly. "*I* was the one who accused you. Gary took your side."

"There's more to it than that," Gary continued. "I thought so too. I didn't *want* to, but all the evidence seemed to point that way."

"I understand," Ann said in a low voice, blinking back tears. "I'm hurt, but in all fairness, I'd think the same way if I were you." A weak smile came to her lips. "Leopards usually don't change their spots, right? But 'with God all things are possible.' He changed me." She looked around at all of them; then her gaze came back to Gary. "Am I right?"

Gary thought Dan and Sully looked uncomfortable. He smiled. "Yes. I know that from personal experience."

"Will you forgive me for what I thought?" John asked.

She nodded. "Yes."

"Um, yeah. Me too," Sully said. "That was wrong. Sorry."

"Same here," Dan said. His face was very red.

"Okay, apologies accepted, guys," Ann said. "But we have some pressing business here."

"Thank you," Gary said. "Uh, I suppose it doesn't matter, but how in the *world* did you get past the police?"

Ann took a deep breath. "I'm tempted to say it was luck, but I really think it was providence. After I took a shower, I decided to check the hotel cameras. I fired up my PC, clicked on the outside camera, and saw a flashing blue light stopped beside the front door but no Klaxon. I suspected it was for us, and I panicked.

"I pulled on some coveralls, grabbed a pantsuit and my PC,

and ran down the back stairs. When I got to the loading dock, I saw this guy unloading a truck. I hid until he went inside, and then I snuck past. I saw more emergency lights out on the street, but the fog hid me. I ran all the way to the truck. Fortunately I had my car keys, which also had keys for the truck. I know I should have probably called you guys, but I panicked and went into autopilot."

"Yes, you should have. That was *some* dangerous stuff you pulled off." Gary paused, wondering if the timing was right to discuss her action. He decided to wait. "Any police at the car park?"

"No. Apparently they were sure they had us trapped at the hotel." A scowl came to her face. "We can thank Peter for that, I'm sure. When I got inside the truck, I fired up the auxiliary power unit and all the electronics. Then I called Peter's office and got the vacation message. That's when I *really* knew he did it. But it gave me an idea. I knew the police were Metropolitan Police Service—Scotland Yard—but MI5 and Special Branch had to be in charge. I remembered we had a video of Peter's ID. I had to work fast, but I copied a frame, fixed it up on the photo editor, and printed it. Then it was a matter of my appearance."

Gary looked over her dark skin and black hair. "I wondered about that. Been into my makeup?"

"Yes."

"You did a great job for such quick work. I almost didn't recognize you."

"Yeah, but I was still worried the clerk would."

"You didn't give him a chance."

"That was the idea." Ann stopped and snickered.

"What's funny?" Gary asked.

"Just wondering how that commander is going to explain why all his men are outside Waterloo Station."

Gary laughed. "Just following orders from above."

The smile disappeared from Ann's face. "But what are we going to do now? We're not in jail yet, but we are kinda hot."

"Yeah, and right in the big fat middle of London."

"Don't forget the truck, guys," Sully added. "You can bet they have the description and plates by now."

Gary came around and sat down beside John. "Absolutely. First order of business is to disguise the truck. Mr. Sullivan, do you *happen* to know anything about making movie props?"

Sully grinned and stroked his mustache. "Yeah, man. You want a new truck?"

"That's the basic idea. How hard would it be?"

Sully ran his eyes over the boxy white truck. "Not hard at all, if we can get the right supplies. Hey, props only have to look right; they don't have to work."

"Good. You're in charge of the makeover."

"And after that?" Dan asked.

Gary clenched his teeth. "*Then* we go after Peter."

chapter 15

Gary looked around the metal-topped worktable. "Okay, we need to get rolling. We can't do without this truck if we hope to catch Peter, but we sure can't go out and rent another one with every cop in Britain looking for us. So what kind of truck? We need something the police won't look twice at, so that rules out a James Bond creation."

Sully leaned back in his chair. "Oh, I don't know. If we had a truck like that, the police would never catch us. Cut in the rockets, and away we go."

Gary rapped on the table with a hammer. "Let's get serious now. Give me something that will work."

"It's easier to say what *won't* work," John said. "Delivery trucks are out; same for heating and air-conditioning and so on. They look too much like what we've got."

"What about a tank truck of some kind?" Ann asked. "You know, like heating oil or compressed oxygen or nitrogen."

"That's not bad," Gary said. "We could look on the Web for ideas."

"Yeah," Sully said, drawing the word out. "You *did* say you want something the cops won't mess with, right?"

Gary eyed him suspiciously. "Basically. Why?"

"What about a sewage pumping truck? I bet the cops wouldn't mess with *that* bad boy. Probably help us out in traffic too. 'Outta my way, dudes, I'm full of—' "

"I get the picture," Gary said.

"I like it," John said.

Gary couldn't help smiling as he turned to Ann. "What do you think of Sully's modification?"

"Should work," she said. "It's gross, but it will do what we want."

"What supplies will you need?" Gary asked Sully.

Sully turned and looked the truck over. "Lotta sheet aluminum, paint, and pookie and a bunch of other stuff. I'll make a list."

"Okay. What about the plates?" Gary asked.

"That'll be easy," Ann said. "I'll scan our current one in for a template, then search the Internet for an actual number used by a London area sewage pumping service."

"Good idea, and let's use the company's name as well."

"Right. I'll also get the VIN number."

"Yeah, that too." Gary paused. "Okay, I think that's got most of the tasks, but there's something else I want to do—check out Peter's apartment."

"You think he's there?" Dan asked.

Gary frowned. "Only if he's an idiot. No, you can bet he's long gone, but maybe he left a clue where he went."

"You mean now?" John asked.

"The longer we wait, the colder his trail gets."

"So who gets *this* choice assignment?"

Gary looked over at Ann. "Ann and me. I want everyone else working on our honey truck."

"Need some burglar gear?" John asked.

"That, and a lot of luck and prayer."

Gary looked all around Oxford Circus, checking for danger as he waited for his eyes to adjust from the dimly lit underground. Brilliant white clouds sailed across a deep blue sky. *Good,* Gary thought. *No police in sight.* He examined his dark hands against the sleeves of his white dress shirt and decided he would pass for a New Delhi transplant. Ann's makeup had required only a slight touch-up to match. Gary's conservative gray suit and her light blue pantsuit seemed a reasonable adaptation of current London styles, at least for the business set. He shifted the briefcase containing Ann's computer to his right hand.

"That way?" Gary whispered. He might look like a resident of India, but he certainly didn't sound like one.

"Yes," Ann replied. "A couple of blocks, I think."

Their trip to the edge of Soho, at Ann's suggestion, had been by foot and tube.

"Any idea how we're going to get in?" Ann asked.

"Not until we get there," Gary said.

They crossed with the light and continued up Regent Street. Gary eyed the entrance to the apartment building as they walked past. They stopped at the next corner.

"That's what I suspected," Gary said. "Electric door lock."

"Can we get past it?"

"I think so. We'll stand next to the speaker like we're buzzing a resident; then I'll try this." He pulled a black plastic box out of his pocket. It had a single red button on it.

"One of John's gadgets?"

Gary smiled. "Yep. He guaranteed it would work or my money back."

"I guess we'll see."

Gary turned and led the way back to Regent House. Seeing no one near, he hurried up the front steps and stopped inches from the door. He eyed the lock's striker plate and placed the box next to it. He jabbed the button and heard the catch release.

"All right," he whispered. He pulled the door open and held it while Ann ducked inside. They rode the elevator up to the fifth floor. The corridor was deserted. Remembering Dan's detective work, Gary hurried to the front of the building, and there on the right was apartment 503. They paused and slipped on surgical gloves.

Gary examined the door lock. He reached into his coat pocket and pulled out a thin zippered case filled with lock-picking tools.

"What, no high-tech?" Ann whispered.

"Mechanical dead-bolts don't speak high-tech," Gary answered.

In less than a minute the bolt slid back with a solid *thump*, and Gary slowly opened the door. Looking inside, he saw an entryway, a combination dining area and kitchen, and either a laid-back living room or a formal den. But there was no sign of life, nothing on the dining room table or the kitchen counter. Gary tiptoed inside, waited for Ann to slip past, then closed the door.

Gary motioned for Ann to wait. She nodded. He crept down the narrow hallway to the back, wincing each time the wooden floor creaked. There were two doors at the end. He pushed open the one on the right and saw the bathroom. It was clean and orderly. Gary knew that the other door had to lead to the bedroom. He crept up, listened, then threw the door open. The room was as neat as the rest of the apartment. Even the bed was made.

"He hasn't changed any," Ann said.

Gary jumped and turned around. "I'd appreciate a little warning."

"Sorry."

Gary spotted a tower computer sitting on a large desk.

"He certainly believes in computing horsepower," Gary said. He mentally cataloged the various drives: DVD, CD-ROM, zip, and the ubiquitous but largely useless three-and-a-half-inch floppy.

"Yeah, can't get a laptop with all those devices," Ann said. "Okay if I go to work?"

"Have at it." He handed her the briefcase. "I'll check out the apartment."

Ann removed her laptop from the briefcase and placed it on the desk close to Peter's computer. She attached a network cable between the two machines and began booting them. The various drives began whining.

Gary checked Peter's bedroom closet but saw nothing besides an orderly array of suits, shirts, and slacks. He then searched the desk drawers. Ann scooted back so he could look inside the center drawer.

"This guy has a thing about neatness," Gary said.

"He always did. Psychologists have a word for it, but I don't want to go there."

"Right." Gary pawed around inside the drawer. An orderly stack of bills rested in one corner, behind a sheet of postal stamps and a fountain pen. In the other corner was a single three-by-five card. "What's this?" He pulled it out and held it up to the light. "It's a series of numbers, and all but the last one is crossed out."

"May I see that?" Ann took the card. "Interesting. Starts with '21' and the last one is '32.' Wonder what that means?"

"If you don't know, I sure don't."

Peter's monitor flashed. "Here's the Windows log-in screen. What do you know, Peter logs on as the administrator. Figures. He's always been a control freak. Let's see if he uses a password." She clicked the OK button. "Yes, he does. Probably changes it weekly too."

"That mean you can't log on?"

She turned in the chair. "Do you remember my interview?"

Gary smiled. "Uh, yes, I do. Carry on."

Ann keyed a series of commands on her computer, and the hard drive on Peter's computer chattered a bit. Ann tabbed to the password field, pressed three keys in sequence, then clicked OK. The computer began loading the administrator's settings.

"Cool," Gary said.

Remembering his own work, he checked the bedside table, then made a tour of the front of the apartment, finishing up at the bathroom. When he entered the hall, Ann was perched on the edge of her chair, keying entries into Peter's computer faster than Gary could follow.

"I thought I was fast with a keyboard," Gary said.

Ann glanced around and grinned. "Hey, I believe in working computers as hard as they'll go, but the keyboard's *still* the slowest input device."

"Found anything?"

"Not sure." She pointed to her laptop. The disk drive light was flashing furiously. "I'm copying all his files over to my machine, including the deleted ones. A lot of the files are encrypted, but not all."

"Okay."

"I also found some CDs. Probably useless, but I stuck them in the briefcase just in case. Right now I'm checking out his temporary Internet files and cookies."

"Was he a big Internet surfer?"

"Does Microsoft sell software? Peter has *always* insisted on being on the cutting edge." She pointed to the modem sitting beside the computer. "Broadband ADSL."

"Nice. Still active?"

"Yep, although I haven't used it yet. Windows and the Internet service provider are carrying on their usual digital chitchats." She paused. "Are you done?"

"Yeah. Didn't find a thing. This place is so neat I'd almost expect him home later, except I know better."

Ann glanced at a progress bar on her computer. "The download is gonna take about a half hour more. He has a *lot* of data on his hard drive."

"That's okay. Take your time."

She glanced at the front door. "You don't think Peter would send the police by his apartment, do you?"

Gary shook his head. "I doubt it. Focusing too much attention on us might blow back on him. He fingered us at the hotel, but I don't think he'll do more than that unless we get hot on his trail, which seems unlikely."

Gary brought over a chair and set it close to the desk, where he could keep an eye on the front door. He began pondering what they would do if they couldn't track Peter down. That was not a pleasant prospect, since Peter's disappearance would surely reinforce the case against the Americans. Gary's video image was all the proof the police needed, even if Peter never turned up.

"Gary," Ann said.

He reined in his imagination and looked around. "Yes?"

"Look at this deleted cookie. It has Peter's name and address, E-mail address, phone number, and several dates. One says 'shipping date,' and it's tomorrow."

"Oh? Does it identify the Internet site?"

"No, but it lists a company: CryoSystems, LTD."

"What is that?"

"I don't know. Shall we find out?"

"Be Peter's guest," Gary said with a smile.

Ann fired up Internet Explorer and selected a search engine from Peter's home page. CryoSystems Limited was the engine's first hit. Ann clicked on the link.

"Hmm, looks like they manufacture refrigeration equipment, but they specialize in cold rooms, blast freezers, and chillers."

"Why would Peter be interested in that stuff?" Gary asked.

Ann scooted her chair back a little. "Good question. Doesn't seem related to MI5 or security." She pointed. "There's a place to log on. Suppose Peter's one of their customers?"

Gary shrugged. "Give it a shot."

"Okay." She leaned forward and keyed in "Peter Watkins," and a single *x* for the password, and clicked the log-in button. A message box popped up saying "Incorrect Password."

"Well, at least we know the name he used." Ann pointed. "And there's where we can get the password." She clicked on a link that said: "Click here if you've forgotten your password." An Outlook message popped up with the "To" box filled in with a CryoSystems E-mail address and a subject line that said: "NEED PASSWORD." She clicked the Send button, and the E-mail disappeared from the outbox. Every few seconds Ann pressed the F5 key to refresh. Several minutes later an E-mail popped up in the inbox.

Ann double-clicked on it. "Well, well, well. The password is 'kohinoor.' She logged onto the CryoSystems site and found a link marked "Orders." She clicked on that.

"Hmm," Ann said. "Looks like Peter Watkins of Mountain Light Exporters Limited has purchased a prefabricated cold room, but the shipper isn't specified. The order is to be picked up at the dock tomorrow at 8:00 A.M."

"The cookie you found is for the shipper, not CryoSystems."

"Right, and the shipper's name isn't in the cookie."

"Wonder how many shipping companies are in the London area?"

"We probably don't want to know. Maybe there's another way to find out."

"How?" Gary saw her expression change. "Oh, never mind. Do your thing."

Ann transferred a file over to Peter's machine and installed a program. She double-clicked on the resulting shortcut, and a rather bland window opened, devoid of all buttons except the standard Minimize, Restore, and Close. A few moments later a file structure appeared. She expanded the folder named "Deleted Messages" and arranged the messages in date order, most recent first.

"Why not use Outlook to view the deleted items?" Gary asked.

"These are the permanently deleted items."

"Oh, yes, of course. Silly me." He scanned the list. "He sure sends a lot of E-mails."

Ann opened the top one. It was a message to a colleague at MI5 requesting the inclusion of a digital camera in next year's budget. The next item was equally mundane. She kept hitting the down arrow key, displaying progressively older E-mails.

"Hey, here's something," she said. "Sent on Monday at 7:54 P.M. to someone at martinshipping.co.uk."

Gary leaned closer to the screen. "That was after Ian dropped by to warn us about the recabling in Waterloo Barracks."

"Right. Peter's instructing them to pick up the shipment at CryoSystems on Thursday—tomorrow—at 8:00 A.M."

"That's all it says?"

"Yes. Apparently he arranged for the shipping earlier but left the date open. So let's see what we can find over at Martin Shipping's site."

She entered the company's URL and hit enter. "Suppose he used the same name and password?" she asked.

"Give it a shot."

Ann keyed Peter's name and "kohinoor" for the password. The site displayed the summary of a shipment to be picked up at CryoSystems. She clicked on the "Details" link.

"And there we are at last," she said. "One prefab cold room, model such and such, consisting of three export crates, blah, blah, blah, to be shipped by truck to Le Havre via the Chunnel. Pretty clever."

"Right. Peter knows he can't get out by plane or boat. At

least, it would be very dangerous. But the police can't check everything." Gary pointed to the screen. "There's no way they can inspect all the freight that England exports."

"Wonder what the final destination is?"

"I don't think we care. We'd better catch Peter before he gets to France, or we never will."

"Yeah."

"Look at the dimensions on those boxes. There's plenty of room for Peter to hide inside, with some kind of air supply, plus food and water."

"Why not ship the crown by itself? Why does he have to go along?"

Gary shrugged. "My guess is he's not going to let that diamond out of his sight until—" He turned to Ann— "Say, what *does* he want it for?"

Ann leaned back. "That's a good question. The obvious reason is money, either ransom or a collector willing to pay big bucks for it. But Peter's ego is wrapped up in this. Somehow this is supposed to increase his power and prestige—maybe tied into returning India's pride. You can bet on it."

"Got it. And what *we* want is the crown back and Peter behind bars."

"So what's next?"

"Talk it over with the others. How much longer before you have everything?"

Ann glanced at the download progress bar. "Doing pretty good. I'd say ten or fifteen minutes."

Gary rapped on the garage doors. Ann shifted her PC to her other arm. An eye appeared in a weather-beaten peephole and turned from side to side. Something on the other side rattled and clicked. The right-hand door opened on squeaking hinges, revealing Sully and, behind him, a bizarre-looking vehicle. Gary and Ann stepped inside.

"What do you think?" Sully asked as he closed the door and fastened the padlock.

John finished a cut with a saber saw and removed a long section of aluminum skin. The truck's cargo bay looked like it had tangled with a metal shredder. Bare ribs formed an oval skeleton where the original box structure had been, and all sharp corners were gone. A few strips of sheet aluminum hinted at the shape to come.

"Sully's been a real help," John said. "It's amazing how fast you can change a truck's appearance. When we're done, I bet not even the factory would recognize it." He pointed to something that looked like a small wardrobe. "He even installed us a chemical toilet up front."

Gary walked past John until he could see the entire interior. Yes, it was coming along nicely, and he was glad to see that most of the original cargo space had been preserved.

"You guys have made a lot of progress," he said.

John looked past Gary to Ann. "So, find anything at the apartment?"

"Yes," Ann said. "It looks like Peter's going to stow away in a freight shipment to Le Havre, leaving 8:00 A.M. tomorrow."

"So we need this by morning," Gary said. "Think we can do it?"

"Don't see why not," John said.

Gary became aware of something nudging him. He snuggled deeper into the toasty sleeping bag and drifted back to sleep. The nudge came again, harder this time. Then he heard John's voice.

"Get up."

Gary's grogginess vanished in an instant.

"What's wrong?" he asked as he unzipped the bag and wriggled out.

"More bad news. Dan's recording a BBC broadcast as we speak."

Gary struggled to his feet and wiped the sleep out of his eyes. He looked at his watch and saw it was a little after 7:00 P.M. A glance at the truck showed it nearly complete. He looked in through the camouflaged opening in the back. Then his nose wrinkled.

"What is that *smell?*"

"I'll explain later," John replied. "Go on in."

Gary ducked and climbed inside through the rear hatch. Dan saw him coming and motioned to the chair next to him.

"Have a seat," he said, "and get a load of this." He turned up the sound from the broadcast.

Gary sat down. John stood behind him. The picture on the monitor flashed and jiggled for a moment, then steadied. The female anchor looked at the camera while clips of the Jewel House ran in the background.

"Earlier today, MI5 officials, working with the United States FBI, released the names of five of the suspects in the Tower robbery. All are employees of Los Angeles-based Security-Check, a security consulting company owned by Gary Nesbitt, a convicted thief, and John Mason. Nesbitt and Mason entered the UK last week along with three SecurityCheck employees: Ann O'Brien, also an ex-convict, Dan Thompson, and Sean Sullivan.

"Officials refused to say how the robbers got past the Tower's elaborate security systems but vowed that the perpetrators would be apprehended.

"Peter Watkins, MI5 agent in charge of Tower security, was called off holiday in Brighton to head up the investigation. He had this to say."

The video cut to a close-up of Peter with the White Tower as background.

"Well, well, the elusive Mr. Watkins makes his appearance," Gary grumbled.

Peter's dark eyes looked right into the camera lens. "MI5 was aware of security shortcomings at the Tower of London, but we are completely taken aback by the audacity of this assault on the history and veneration of the Crown Jewels. We have, indeed, suffered a bitter blow for now, but mark my words—MI5 and Special Branch will not rest until the perpetrators are brought to justice." Here he paused. "Hear what I say: The Queen Consort's Crown will *not* leave England."

The reporter's talking head returned. "In other news. . ."

Dan clicked the stop button.

"Old Pete's really twisting the knife," John said. "We snatch the crown for him, he tips the police, and now he's going to personally track us down."

"But there's all that stuff Ann got off his computer."

Gary turned to him. "What do you want to bet he's swapped his computer out for a clean one? As for the files we copied, we made it up. He's got us cold, and he knows it."

"So where does that leave us?" John asked.

"Same place as before, except we're in deeper. Listen, Peter still has to get away with the crown, and right now, the only leads we've got are CryoSystems and Martin Shipping."

"Yeah, I guess that's right."

"So did you and Sully finish the truck while I was sleeping?"

John grinned. "Sully is an absolute whiz. Come and see."

Gary followed him outside and stepped back until he could see the whole thing. Gone were the boxy cargo body and conservative white paint. In their place were authentic-looking dials, hoses, and valves. "Farringdon Sewage Services, Ltd." was emblazoned on the "tank" in black letters. It certainly *looked* like a pumper. The dirty yellow paint job, complete with what looked like caked-on grime, gave the truck a well-used appearance. Again he caught a whiff of something unpleasant.

"That's amazing," Gary said. "The smell?"

John laughed. "Sully's in charge of that department."

Gary turned to their driver.

"Hey, it's gotta look *and* smell like the real thing," Sully said. "We don't want cops looking at it up close and personal, right?"

"Yeah, but where. . .what—?"

"I suggest you let it be," John said. "It's sanitary and not so bad once you get used to it."

"How much is left to do?" Gary asked.

"Just the plates and the VIN. Ann's already done them, so all I have to do is put them on."

"Okay." Gary looked all around.

Ann sat at one of the tables, hunched over her PC. Dan took a box from Sully and disappeared inside the faux tank.

"Listen up," Gary said. "I know everyone's tired, but we've got to have a council of war." Ann came over. Gary waited for Dan and Sully to stow the box inside the truck.

"It's been a long day, so I'll make this short," Gary continued when they emerged. "As you know, we're in deep trouble unless we can catch Peter with the crown. Well, it seems our good friend is back off holiday, vowing to nail us if it's the last thing he does.

"Now, the only lead we have is the possibility he's going out inside a CryoSystems freight shipment at 8:00 A.M. tomorrow. Our only hope is to stop the truck and call the police."

"What if the police open up the crates and nothing's there?" Dan asked.

"I'm not sure. What do you suggest?"

"If we get close enough, I should be able to pick up the crown's transmitter."

"That would help." He looked at Ann. "Have you looked up CryoSystems?"

"Yes," she said. "They're in Gravesend, southeast of here. I printed a map, and there's a place we can park within sight of the dock."

"Excellent. Now, we'll play this strictly by ear since we don't have the time or resources to do anything else. Any comments, suggestions?"

"One comment," Ann said. "It probably won't help, but I think I know why Peter scammed us. Remember that card we found with the crossed-out numbers?"

"Yes."

"Turns out the number 32 is part of Peter's password on the MI5 network. Since we've got secure connections into the phone network, I decided to see if I could hack into his work account. I guessed his ID would be 'pwatkins.' That's a common convention. I tried 'kohinoor32' as the password, and it worked.

"I found several deleted E-mails addressed to a member of the Bangalore Cobras. That's a dissident-slash-terrorist group that wants political power in India. Among other things, they want the Koh-I-Noor back, and their comments about the former Raj are not at *all* polite."

"Well, I guess that explains Peter's motive," Gary said. "And we know what we have to do tomorrow." He looked at Dan. "What time should we get up?"

"Gravesend is roughly ten miles from here," Dan said. "I'd say 6:00 A.M. should give us plenty of time."

"John, how are our finances?"

"No problem at the moment. We have almost all our cash—dollars and pounds."

"Good. We have to assume our credit cards, even personal ones, are hot, so watch those expenditures. That's all I have. See you guys in the morning."

John remained with Gary while the others drifted off.

Gary lowered his voice. "What do you think our chances are?"

John leaned close. "Not so hot."

Gary turned his head and looked at what their truck had become and then turned back to John. "Hang in there. We're *not* done with Peter Watkins."

chapter 16

Gary stifled a yawn with some difficulty, but he did feel better after almost eight hours of sleep. They had driven out of London into a blazing red-and-orange sunrise that stained a vast flotilla of clouds scarlet along the horizon. The warm red tones dissolved into deep blue overhead before fading to a somber gray in the west. And while Gary saw the glory, his mind was on other things.

The command center looked much as it had before the truck's drastic remodeling, but the ceiling and floor angled in now to accommodate the tank shape. Fortunately, the aromatic enhancement had been confined to outside. Gary looked up at the forward monitor as Sully slowed down entering Gravesend on A226.

"How far to the turnoff?" Gary asked.

"Couple of miles," Dan said. He pulled his computer closer and pointed to two superimposed red dots on the screen. "Well, what do you know. I'm picking up the crown *and* the box. We've got him."

Gary nodded. But much as he wanted to agree, somehow he

couldn't shake his feeling of apprehension. He tried to convince himself it was simply a reaction to all they had been through, but then he looked at Ann. She seemed on edge as well. Gary chided himself. It *had* to be nerves.

Sully turned off the highway. The roads grew progressively narrower and ill-maintained as they made their way through the stark and run-down manufacturing district.

"We're getting close," Sully said.

Gary consulted the map overlay on Dan's PC, then looked up at the forward monitor. Yes, CryoSystems was just beyond the building on their left. The chain-link fence up ahead enclosed the property.

Gary grabbed the mike. "Stop here."

The brakes squealed as the truck came to a sudden halt.

"What's wrong?" Sully asked.

"I don't want to be seen. Back up and find something for the pumper to do."

"Gotcha, boss."

The truck starting backing. Gary looked at the rear monitor. "There's a manhole cover in the alley behind us and to your left. See it?"

"Just a minute. Yeah, I'm on it."

The truck continued a few more feet. A door opened, then slammed shut, and Gary followed Sully on the monitors. Sully grabbed a large hose and tugged it toward the manhole. He looked up at the hidden camera and grinned. "Sully the sewer man, at your service," he said.

He grabbed a pry bar off the truck, levered up the manhole cover, and shoved it to the side. He slipped the hose down the shaft. He turned toward the truck and held his nose, then loped off and deployed a series of orange cones.

"That look okay?" he asked.

"Fine," Gary replied. "Now act like you're doing something."

"Man, you're hard to please." He sauntered over to the right side of the truck and began playing with the valves and levers.

"A little less *Keystone Cops*, please."

Sully adopted a more professional demeanor.

Gary turned to the others. Both John and Ann seemed tense. Dan was checking the transmissions from the crown, but Gary could tell he was listening.

"This doesn't feel right," John said.

"I agree," Gary said. "Ann? What about you?"

"I don't like it. We're picking up signals from the crown, but maybe Peter found the transmitters and planted them." She paused. "Also, he could have left those deleted files on purpose. He knows what I can do."

"Well, if it *is* a trap, he obviously set it up before the heist. Why?"

"Extra insurance, in case we got away from the police."

"Or it could be exactly what it seems: a way for him to get out of England with the crown. If he *is* inside that shipment, I'd say his chances are excellent."

"Not if we tip the police," Ann said. Then she smiled. "Of course, if he's *not* on board, *we* could get caught, and we still wouldn't know where he is."

"Are you saying we should scrub?" Gary asked.

"I don't think we can take the chance."

Gary looked at John.

"I agree," John said. "I say follow and watch out for a trap."

"Said the mouse as he sniffed the cheese," Gary said. "Okay, we play it for real. So what's next?"

"We could use Sherlock to reconnoiter. I can attach one of our color cams to his telescoping mast."

Gary glanced at his watch. It was 6:30. "Okay, but get a move on. The truck will be here soon." He turned to Ann. "And I want you to drive rather than Sully. If we have to talk our way out of trouble, Sully wouldn't stand a chance."

"Okay," she said. "I'd better change."

John removed Sherlock from its storage box, grabbed a video camera, and began working.

It was now almost seven. Gary guided Sherlock alongside the battered curb, thankful for the light traffic. A passing truck had forced him to tuck the robot underneath a parked van, but that had been the only delay. Gary divided his attention between the grainy image from Sherlock's microcams and the monitor displaying the color picture from the mast camera.

"I think that's close enough," John said.

Gary shoved the joystick over. Sherlock turned obediently and climbed through a jagged gap in the curb. The robot trundled through the high weeds until it was hidden from the road. Gary elevated the mast, and the chain-link fence around Cryo-Systems came into view. He zoomed in on the loading dock. A few minutes later a semi drove in through the gate.

"Martin Shipping," Gary announced. "Right on time too."

The truck made a wide turn and backed up slowly to the dock. The driver jumped down, climbed the steps to the dock, and opened the trailer's doors. Over the next twenty minutes a forklift hauled assorted crates into the trailer. Last aboard was a huge container that required two forklifts, one at each end.

"That one has the crown," Dan said.

"Or at least the crown's transmitters," Gary said.

"Whatever."

"Get Sherlock back here," John said.

"Right." Gary lowered the camera, spun the robot about on its treads, and shoved the throttle forward. Sherlock lurched and bucked as it shot through the weeds and bushes. Gary slowed the robot for the curb, then cranked the speed when it reached the street. John checked the monitors for traffic, then ducked out through the camouflaged door.

"Tell Sully about our change of plans," Gary told Ann.

"Okay."

Ann looked like a sanitation worker, complete with stained coveralls and the fragrance to match. She let herself out and hurried over to Sully.

"Gary wants me to drive," Ann's voice announced through the overhead speaker.

"Why?" Sully asked.

"In case we get stopped. You know, I speak the language."

Sully looked up at the camera and waved. "You got a point, boss."

He stowed the hose, and he and John replaced the manhole cover. John scooped up Sherlock while Sully gathered the traffic cones. They came inside, and Sully secured the door.

Dan pointed to the PC's map. "He's moving out."

"No rush," Gary said. "He won't be burning up the highway."

"What route do you think he'll take?"

"There are several possibilities, but he has to end up on M20 because that's what goes to the Chunnel freight yard at Folkestone. Most likely he'll take A227 to A2 and M2, then drop down to M20 on A229." Gary pointed to the red dots on the screen, which had just turned south. "Okay, the truck's far enough ahead." He took the mike. "Ann, you can pull out now. Looks like he's heading for A227."

"I see it on my display."

Ann pulled into an alley, turned around, and drove out of the industrial zone. Gary watched the truck's blue dot creep down the map display parallel to the red dots of the shipment. A few minutes later their target merged with A227.

"You can cut over to the highway now, but stay back," Gary said into the mike.

Ann turned onto the next major street, drove less than a mile, and entered the southbound traffic on A227. The distance to the red dots gradually increased.

"He's turning onto A2," Gary said.

"Looks like he's headed for Folkestone," Ann said. "How far back do you want to be?"

"Make it about two miles. No need to close the gap until he gets near the freight terminal."

"Roger."

A short time later Gary watched the red dots turn onto A229, then several miles later merge with M20. All the external cameras showed heavy traffic in both directions, much of it trailer trucks. The broad four-lane motorway cut through the London suburbs, which soon gave way to the green countryside interspersed with peaceful farms and small towns. Gary focused on the forward screen, his eyes drawn to the white stripes flashing past. Ann had them tucked in between two large trucks, and everything looked normal. If everything went according to plan, in less than fifty miles they would have Peter.

The miles to Folkestone ticked off, each one bringing them closer to an irreversible decision. Finally they were less than ten miles from the exit to the Chunnel freight terminal. *So far, so good,* Gary thought, wiping his sweaty hands on his trousers. So why did he feel so nervous?

Dan turned to him. "How long are we going to wait?"

Gary fixed his eyes on John.

"You decide, man," John said. "Looks to me like Peter's making his move, but if you're worried, I'm worried."

Gary spoke into the mike. "Ann, what do you think? Is that Peter up there, and does he have the crown with him?"

She hesitated then said, "I don't like it. Somehow this doesn't seem like Peter. But if it *is* him, and he gets across the channel, he's gone."

"Yeah, right."

Gary turned back to John. His friend had his eyes closed, and Gary knew without asking what he was doing. Gary closed his eyes and sent up an arrow prayer for guidance. Then he opened his eyes and took the mike. "Okay, Ann, start closing. I want that truck in sight ASAP."

"Roger," Ann replied.

The engine noise increased, and the rumble from the tires picked up. "Patch me into police emergency," Gary said to Dan.

"Let me locate a tower I can spoof." Dan pulled his PC over and began switching frequencies and checking signal strengths. "I think I can use this one." He flipped a switch, and a reassuring dial tone came from the speaker. "Hey, they think we're for real." He handed Gary an earphone and boom mike attached to the PC.

Gary slipped on the headset and positioned the mike. He glanced at the rearview monitor, and something caught his eye. The dial tone disappeared as Dan punched in the 999 emergency number. Gary looked more closely at the monitor.

"Kill the call!" he shouted. The phone went dead, cutting off a woman's voice.

"What's wrong?" John asked.

Gary reached forward and zoomed the rear-facing camera. Several miles back and approaching rapidly, a helicopter flew low over the motorway. An ominous thumping sound rose above the noise of the traffic. It increased in volume, rapidly accompanied by an insistent whine, which caused loose objects to vibrate.

Gary grabbed the mike. "Take the next exit! It's a trap." He turned to the forward monitor. The Martin Shipping truck was in plain view, plodding along as if nothing was wrong. Gary could see flashing blue lights in the distance.

"I'm picking up encrypted transmissions," Dan said. "Can't tell what they're saying, but it's got to be the police."

"Yeah, and we know who they're after."

"Gary," Ann said, "there's a roadblock at the next exit. What do I do?"

Gary scanned the monitors. Emergency lights formed a solid line up ahead, complementing those coming up from behind.

"Take the exit. Bluff your way through."

"I'll do my best."

The traffic on the motorway slowed to a crawl. Gary trained the forward camera to the left and zoomed in. A long column of traffic inched its way onto the exit ramp. Two police cars blocked all but a narrow lane, with others positioned farther down. Finally Ann had to stop. They were sandwiched between a delivery truck and a car. Gary watched the checkpoint. It took the police several minutes to clear each vehicle.

"Not good," Dan said. "Sure hope our getup works."

"Have faith," Sully said. "This pumper looks *and* smells like the real thing."

"What about the plates?" Dan asked.

"They'll check out," Gary said. "Farringdon Sewage Services is a real company, and Ann looked up the registration on one of their trucks. Her operator's license should pass muster too."

"I sure hope so."

The traffic column inched forward. Gary watched in fascination as the officers questioned the driver of the delivery truck. The minutes oozed past and nothing seemed to happen. Then one of the policemen waved to the driver and pointed to the side. The truck pulled over clear of the exit. The driver climbed down, walked around, and opened the back of his truck.

"Ah," Gary said. "That truck's the same model and year as ours. I sure hope our camouflage works."

"It will," Sully said.

At the policeman's order, Ann pulled forward and stopped. Dan turned up the volume on the speaker.

"Step down, please," the man said.

Ann opened the door and got out.

"May I see your license, miss?" the man said.

"Right, officer. Anything wrong?"

"Can't rightly say."

Gary stared at the monitor. The policeman seemed only

inches away. In the nearest police car, Gary could see an officer holding a mike. The man got out, took a careful look at the side of the truck, and walked up to his partner.

"It checks out, mate," he said. "Farringdon Sewage Services of London owns this lorry."

"Right," the other policeman said. He was still holding Ann's driver's license as if unsure whether to return it or not. "One thing puzzles me. What are you doing on the motorway to Folkestone?"

"We've had it now," Dan whispered.

"No, we haven't," Sully said. He reached up and twisted a chrome handle. There was a faint gurgling sound.

Gary turned from Sully and looked at the monitor. Both officers looked shocked, then disgusted. One covered his nose with a hand.

"Oh, that's horrid," he said.

"Sorry, mate," Ann said quickly, "but I *am* a bit full right now, don't you know. Built up some gas, I suppose. Happens every now and again. Can't be helped."

"Never mind," the officer holding his nose said. "Get moving."

"Yes. Yes, of course. May I?" Ann held out her hand. The officer returned her license.

"Hurry it up, will you?"

"Be gone in a jiff."

She bounded up into the cab and drove slowly away. The officers' eyes remained glued to the truck until it was well clear.

Gary took the mike. "Ann, that was marvelous."

"Thank you, but without Sully's ploy, we could have been in trouble. Where to now?"

Gary looked at John, who shrugged.

"Back to the machine shop. Then we'll decide. And take the back routes."

Gary turned back to the bank of monitors. Then his gaze drifted over to something he had seen earlier—the chrome lever that had hurried them through the roadblock. He looked around at Sully. "That's a toilet flush handle."

Sully grinned. "I had to use something. I thought that was appropriate."

"Hmm, I guess so. But where did. . . ?"

Sully held up a hand. "You don't want to know."

Gary shook his head. "No, I guess not. I can't smell anything in here, but apparently there's quite a whiff outside."

"That's putting it mildly. Don't worry. I'll take care of everything back at the machine shop."

"Good. Please do."

chapter 17

Sully locked the machine shop's garage doors and walked back to the worktable. Gary stood there and looked at each team member in turn. They seemed worried but expectant, as if Gary knew what to do next. He didn't, and he had every reason to be afraid, but somehow he wasn't. In the quietness of the trip back, he had prayed—mostly because he had run out of ideas, and prayer always gave him peace—but so far, nothing more.

Sully sat in the vacant lab chair, completely subdued for the first time in Gary's memory.

"What now?" John asked.

Gary had been expecting that question. "The plan is still the same. We *have* to catch Peter or spend the best years of our lives rotting in a British prison."

"And exactly *how* are we going to do that?" Dan asked sarcastically. "We don't have a thing to go on."

"That's not exactly true," Gary said. "Peter's having a hard time getting out of England; otherwise, he'd already be gone. The Chunnel ploy was good, and he stood a fair chance of getting out that way. But being supercautious narrows down his options. Now we have to figure out his real escape route."

"You got any suggestions?" John asked.

"How does anyone get off an island?" Gary asked. "Assuming they can't fly."

"But can we assume that? I mean, what about a private plane?"

"Private aviation has security too. Peter would be taking a big chance if he tried that. But the obvious way to get off an island is by boat."

"Well, duh," Sully said, a tentative smile on his lips.

Gary smiled in spite of his inner tension. "Glad you could join us, Mr. Sullivan. As you so eloquently point out, boats are kinda handy. If Peter's going out that way, we can rule out passenger ships and ferries, for obvious reasons. So that leaves boats or ships like tankers and freighters. A roll-on-roll-off container ship would be a good choice."

"A boat might work," Ann said. "There are thousands of fishing villages all around England and Scotland."

"Yes, but that limits you to destinations like Ireland—not likely—and France. France is a possibility, although I'm sure the French are cooperating with Britain on this."

"So you're suggesting a freighter or tanker?" John asked.

"Yes, but not in a major port like Southampton or Liverpool." Gary looked at Ann. "I recommend we start researching shipping and harbormaster sites for arrivals, say, within the next seven days. One thing we can be sure of: Peter isn't going to stick around any longer than he has to."

"You've got that right," Ann said.

"And we have to abandon the machine shop," Gary said. "Peter doesn't know about it, but he probably suspects we're in the area. Plus, it makes me nervous being in London."

"When do you want to leave?" John asked.

"Let's aim for sundown. Things are harder to see then, and

there should be enough traffic to hide us."

"What about the truck's appearance?"

"Let's change it, just in case." Gary glanced at Sully. "I don't think our disguise has been compromised, but why chance it?"

"Okay," Sully said. "What do you want?"

"I don't know. Just pick something that won't take too much time."

"What about a lubrication truck?" John asked.

Sully snapped his fingers. "Yeah, that would work. Replace the big hose with some small ones, some reels and a few pipes, new signs, and a paint job—"

"I'll leave that to the experts," Gary interrupted. "And would you do something about the aroma?"

"Sure, no problem."

Sully walked over to the truck and began examining the rear superstructure in great detail.

"I'll start on the research," Ann said.

"Wait, there's something else I want you to do first."

"What?"

"We might have to do some swimming, and we're not equipped for that. We need dry suits, fins, masks, and snorkels."

"For you and John, I presume."

"Right. I'll write down our sizes. And you'll need help. That stuff is heavy and bulky." Gary turned to their driver. "Sully."

He turned. "Yes, boss."

Ann tried to convince herself that she and Sully were inconspicuous. She wore a plain dress and a blond wig, with enough makeup to change her appearance without attracting attention, she hoped. Sully certainly looked different with a wig and full beard that covered his thin mustache. Gary had tried to get him to shave it off, but Sully had absolutely refused. Though his casual clothes were a little rumpled, he fit in well with many of the other passengers on the tube.

"Our stop's coming up," Ann whispered in his ear.

He nodded, obviously remembering Gary's warning about not speaking.

At first, Ann had been surprised by Gary's decision to get diving gear, but now she understood the reason. If Peter planned on escaping by sea, Gary and John might have to swim. She shuddered at the thought and hoped it wouldn't come to that. But if it did, London was the safest place to buy the equipment.

Ann stood up. The train rumbled into the station with brakes screeching and came to a stop. Ann stepped out and walked toward the escalators with Sully close by her side. When they reached the street, Ann saw that the sky still had a few blue patches, but heavy clouds were rolling in. Fortunately, they didn't have far to go. Ann hurried through the heavy pedestrian traffic toward the shop she'd located on the Web, Davis Diving Equipment. She pushed open the weathered door, and a tiny bell tinkled.

A young man with stringy blond hair looked at Ann without much interest. "Help you with something?" he asked.

"I hope so," Ann said. She took out a piece of paper and placed it on the counter.

The man peered at the list a few moments, then looked up. "This for you and the gentleman?"

Ann almost laughed. "Obviously not. Look at the sizes."

"Right. Half a sec."

He disappeared into the back and was gone so long Ann began to worry. But the periodic thumps and bangs reassured her that he was trying to fill their order rather than calling to report suspicious characters. Finally he returned with a large stack of boxes and dropped them on the counter. Ann opened each one, checking to make sure she had everything. She examined the dry suits carefully, making sure they were the right size and undamaged.

"Is everything in order?" the clerk asked with a hint of irritation.

"Quite. I shall require these tied into two bundles, if you please."

He frowned and went into the back again. Ann pulled out the stack of pound notes John had given her. The clerk returned with twine and tied up the bundles. He wrote up the bill, took Ann's money, and returned her change. His work done, he said, "Come again."

Ann nodded as she lifted one bundle. Sully grabbed the other bundle and followed her out of the store. Ann began to retrace her steps to the tube station when something caught her eye.

"Wait here," she said. "I see something else we need."

She headed for an appliance store.

Gary finished looking over the diving equipment and looked up at Ann. "Excellent." His eyes went to the shopping bag. "What's that?"

Ann pulled out a cardboard box containing a coffeemaker and several bags of Kona coffee. "Thought this might come in handy."

Gary smiled. "I'm sure it will. Thanks."

She nodded. "Made any progress?"

He shook his head. "Not a thing. Come on into the spook shack."

Sully stepped down from the truck dressed for work and minus the beard. He joined John in working on the parts required to convert the truck's appearance. Gary and Ann stepped around the work in progress and entered the back of the truck.

Dan looked around.

"Think you can keep us out of trouble while we do some supersurfing?" Gary asked.

"Sure," Dan said.

His answer landed inside Gary's head like a brick. Gary wanted more than anything to be sure, but he was anything but. Peter's options might be limited, but how could five foreigners hope to elude the full force of British authority? Then another thought hit him. Peter, and presumably Ian, undoubtedly had weapons. Ann pulled up a chair and started working on her laptop.

Gary sat down beside Ann. At first he had trouble concentrating with all the construction going on outside, but soon the noise faded into the background. The sheer flood of data pouring out of his screen dulled his senses. Minutes dragged by, then hours. Gary stared at the computer screen with bleary eyes, his brain suffering from overload. Even after eliminating major ports, that still left Peter a lot of options. And what if Gary's assumptions were wrong? Picking a port like Southampton offered certain advantages. Although police presence would be higher, there were also more hiding places.

"Man, the Web is crawling with weirdness," Dan said. "I'm getting probes from all *over* the place."

"Is our server compromised?" Gary asked.

"Not a chance. We were secure before, but *especially* after Ann's modifications."

"Any indication we're the target?"

"I'd say no, but it's impossible to be sure. It's hackers—a whole *bunch* of hackers—with nothing better to do. Hot news brings out the sharks, I guess. Did you know the media's named our caper the 'Crown Jewels Heist'?"

"No."

"Yeah. I've been following it on the BBC and in newsgroups. We're hot-hot-hot."

"How nice."

"Well, you've been wanting name recognition. Now you've got it."

Gary started to reply but stopped when he saw something familiar. "What's that?"

Ann looked over as Dan cut in the audio for the BBC newscast.

". . .bullet-riddled car was found just before noon near the gas works in Nine Elms. Bloodstains matching Agent Watkins's type were found on the front seat. MI5 officials have been trying to reach Watkins since late yesterday, without success. His partner, Ian Hayford, has also gone missing. Scotland Yard suspects Gary Nesbitt and his accomplices are behind the disappearances."

A handheld shot panned past the fender's bullet holes, around the door, and finally zeroed in on the rusty brown splotches on the driver's seat.

"Scotland Yard remains confident that the Crown Jewels Heist suspects will be apprehended and brought to justice. Meanwhile, in other news. . ."

Dan cut the audio off. "What do you suppose *that* means?"

"It's Peter's way of turning up the heat while he escapes, he hopes." Gary turned to Ann. "Where is Nine Elms?"

"South and west of here," she said, "near Battersea Park. Peter probably figures we're holed up near there."

"He's not far off." Gary glanced at her screen. "Any luck yet?"

"Maybe. Remember Peter's connection to the Bangalore Cobras?"

"Yes. How deep do you suppose that goes? I mean, is it only a business deal, or is he politically involved?"

"I've been wondering the same thing. Could be he thinks the political grass is greener in India because he's disillusioned with the British civil service."

Gary's expression dissolved into a wry smile. "Maybe he thought he'd be director of MI5 by now."

"You think you're joking, but that's the way he is."

"I believe it." He nodded toward Ann's PC. "What have you got?"

Ann glanced at the screen. "On a hunch, I did a search on all ships outbound from India with ports of call in England. There are a dozen or so over the next few weeks, but one in particular caught my eye."

Ann turned the PC. Gary saw that it was a harbormaster report for Chennai, India.

"Where is Chennai?" he asked.

"Used to be called Madras. It's on the east coast of India at about the latitude of Bangalore. The tramp freighter *Bhima* left there several weeks ago, transited the Suez Canal, and made stops at Tripoli and Casablanca. Guess where its next port of call is?"

"I bet it's not New York."

"Not even close. Motor vessel *Bhima* is due into Plymouth at 1:00 P.M. tomorrow, docking at Trinity Pier to off-load a mixed cargo: mostly rice, but also cloth, shirts, pants, and so on."

She brought up an aerial picture of the ship. Gary examined the ship's stark lines, the red waterline and gray sides that were more rust than paint. An untidy array of booms and cables adorned the main deck like metal weeds. A dirty black smudge trailed away behind the single stack.

"And when will the good ship *Bhima* be departing?"

"At 10:00 P.M."

"Are they taking on cargo?"

"None from Plymouth. They took on citrus at Tripoli and Casablanca."

"I see." Gary considered all the hiding places aboard a ship, and the many ways to board without being seen. "So you think this is Peter's way out?"

Ann hesitated. "I think it's possible. In a way, Plymouth would be ideal since it's so near international waters. A few miles steaming, and the ship's in the open Atlantic and free from British authority."

"Peter's fooled us before. He planted the Chunnel scheme on us; what if the Bangalore Cobras is more of the same?"

"That occurred to me, but I don't believe this is a plant."

"What about that card with '32' on it? That's not a plant?"

Ann smiled. "Lots of computer users have a favorite password, which is why network administrators make you change them. Some users bend the rules by simply adding a number. Since it's only the number, Peter probably thinks his password is safe."

"Okay, I guess that's reasonable."

Gary leaned back in his chair. The pieces *did* seem to fit. His earlier uncertainty flowed into hope, then made the leap to conviction—but conviction tinged with caution.

He stood up. "Let's run this by the others."

Gary stopped at the closed hatch and knocked. He had no desire to be spray-painted since Sully and John were still working on the truck's exterior.

The handle twisted, and the hatch opened. Sully stood there with a spray gun in one hand. He pulled the respirator down around his neck. "Come take a look," he said. "We're almost done."

Gary and Ann stepped out. Dan made one last check of the monitors before joining them.

The tank was now a grimy red. Rows of hoses lined the side with signs identifying each one. Above the hoses, large black letters proclaimed: "Beaufort and Company Lubricants."

"Are you done?" Gary asked.

"Almost. Been waiting on John, or we would have finished an hour ago."

"Hey," John said with a wide grin, "some of us take pride in our work."

"Whatever," Sully said.

"What about the license plates?" Gary asked.

"Done," John replied. "Same drill as before. Beaufort is a real company, and we used the same tag number as one of their trucks."

"Good. You guys at a stopping place?"

"Yeah."

"Okay. Ann may have a lead on where Peter's going."

John looked at her. "Wonderful. We sure need a break."

Gary led them to the worktable and waited while they settled.

"Go ahead," he told Ann.

Ann presented her findings and conclusions in easy-to-follow logic. Gary watched the others closely. John was in agreement, he could tell, as was Sully. Dan was a little harder to read, but at least he wasn't kicking up a fuss.

Ann finished and turned to Gary.

"That's a nice piece of research," Gary said. He turned to the others. "Anyone got anything else—comments, criticisms, other possibilities?"

"What's the plan?" John asked.

Gary began filling out a mental to-do list. "First, we're not coming back here, so when John and Sully finish, stow *everything* inside the truck. Second, Ann drives us down to Plymouth. Sully, you can be her assistant after we get clear of London, but keep your mouth shut if we get stopped."

"My lips are sealed," Sully said.

"Good, keep them that way. When we get to Plymouth, we'll check out the waterfront, visually and electronically. Then, it's fly-by-the-seat-of-your-pants time."

Gary snapped his fingers and turned to John. "That reminds me. Did you fix the GPS on my hang glider?"

"Nope. Been too busy with other things. I'll take care of it once we're under way."

"Good. That's all I've got."

John and Sully hurried off to finish the paint job and other trim details. Dan ducked through the fake tank's hatch and sat down before his array of monitors.

Gary lowered his voice. "Still think Peter's in Plymouth?" he asked Ann.

"Yes. I'm more convinced than ever."

Gary nodded. "Good. So am I."

chapter 18

Rain thundered against the machine shop's flat roof, proving the forecasters accurate for a change. The clouds had begun to roll in by midafternoon, and they unleashed a driving rain shortly thereafter. Gary zipped his raincoat up as high as he could, then unlocked the garage doors and pushed them open. A wind gust threw a chill spray into his face, and icy rivulets ran down his neck, chest, and back. Gary looked toward the west, but dark, dreary clouds had swallowed the sunset whole. Somber gray faded into ebony, shrouding all but the immediate vicinity. The truck's engine rumbled to life.

Gary hunched his shoulders as if this would stem the raindrops sneaking past his raincoat collar. It did no such thing. Ann backed the truck out. Gary watched impatiently as the dull red hulk slid past. Finally the truck was clear, and Gary closed the doors and, almost as an afterthought, locked them.

He ran to the back and rapped on the hatch. It opened, revealing John and Sully. Dan glanced his way, then returned to his monitors. Gary ducked and jumped inside, almost falling when his shoes slipped. John grabbed his arm and handed him a towel. Sully slammed the hatch.

"Man, what a night," John said. "I feel sorry for Ann."

"Can't be helped."

Ann's voice came through the overhead speaker. "Are we ready to go?"

Dan turned to Gary. "You need to see this."

"In a minute. Tell Ann we're ready."

Dan took the mike. "Roger. Move out."

Gary removed his raincoat and dried as best he could with the towel. He walked over behind Dan and scanned the monitors. They had decided on a back-roads route running roughly southwest then west until they reached the M3 motorway.

"How's it look?" Gary asked.

"Quiet until a few minutes ago," Dan replied. "But now I'm picking up encrypted radio transmissions."

"Oh? Anything on the emergency scanners?"

"Routine stuff. A few car wrecks, and there's a fire near Kennington Park."

"That's near our route. We'd better tell Ann."

"I already did." Dan traced a route on the PC screen. "We're detouring to the east about a half-mile."

"I have a bad feeling about this," Gary said.

"You think it's a police dragnet?" John asked.

"More likely MI5 and Special Branch, but yes. It's possible they suspect we're holed up near where they found Peter's car." Gary turned to Dan. "Did you do any radio direction finding?"

"Line of bearing only, so I don't know exactly where they are. But the bearings and signal strength suggest somewhere around the Nine Elms district."

Gary felt the first touches of fear. "Sounds like a dragnet to me."

"Probably, with a perimeter of about two or three miles."

"Yeah. A semicircle around the south bank of the Thames, plus checkpoints on all the bridges."

"Hey, guys," Ann said. "The road's barricaded three or four blocks up ahead. There's a police car, and they're detouring all traffic to the left."

Gary looked up at the forward monitor and saw the flashing light. He keyed the mike. "Ann, turn left at the next street and slow down."

"Okay."

Gary turned to John. "They're funneling traffic to the major streets where the checkpoints are."

"Should we go back to the machine shop and wait it out?" John asked.

Gary shook his head. "No, we don't have time." He bent over and examined the map overlay on Dan's PC. "I figure the perimeter is set up along A202."

"So, how do we get past?"

"Find a hole, which isn't likely, or create a diversion." He turned back to John. "Can you rig me a flash and explosion effect?"

"You mean like I did for Sherlock?"

"Yeah, only with more sound if you can manage it."

"Leave it to me—and Dan."

"Coming right up," Dan said.

Gary took the mike. "Ann, take us past Benhill Road."

"Roger."

Gary, Dan, and Sully watched the south-facing monitor while John gathered parts out of the cabinets. The truck trundled past Benhill.

"Just as I thought," Gary said. "Checkpoint."

Less than a minute later they crossed St. Giles Road. Two blocks down, barricades and police cars blocked the road.

"They're diverting traffic back to Benhill," Gary said.

"This street ends in one block," Ann said.

"Turn right, go one block, and right again. Stop just short of St. Giles."

"Roger."

Dan turned and handed John a USB cable. "Here's your sound file."

"Thanks," John said. He took the cable and plugged it into the sound amplifier. "Downloading now. Going, going, gone." He unplugged the cable and looked at Gary. "It's all yours."

Gary toggled the mike switch so Ann could hear. "Listen up, this is what we're going to do."

Gary ignored the cold, damp shirt under his raincoat as he walked down the cross street. He crept up to the corner and took a quick peek. A long line of traffic inched along toward the waiting police. Red taillights and flashing blue emergency lights reflected off the shiny black pavement. Gary turned the corner and hugged the shadows as he hurried toward the barricades. He stopped beside a parked car and squatted down, which screened him from the idling traffic to his right. But only the shadows hid him from the police less than fifty feet away.

He brought up John's contraptions, a modified bullhorn with a large strobe mounted on top and a Fresnel lens covering the light to focus the beam. Gary squinted and peered through the spotting scope. The crosshairs danced around the four officers standing on either side of the gap in the barricades. Up ahead, almost to the checkpoint, was a truck much like theirs before Sully's modifications.

"I'm in place," Gary whispered.

"Roger. We're standing by." Dan's voice came clearly through the earphone radio.

"Remember, after I fire this thing, ease up to the corner. When the police take off, hightail it. I'll meet you on the other side."

"Roger," Dan said.

"On my mark." Gary lined the crosshairs up on the nearside officers. "Three. . .two. . .one. . .mark."

He shut his eyes and mashed the switch. A blood-red image raced along his optic nerve accompanied by a reverberating crash only slightly diminished by the earphone radio and earplug.

"Go," Gary heard himself say, but the word sounded odd and hollow in his ringing ears.

He lingered a moment. The police were running toward the truck Gary had noted earlier. He turned around and ran through the rain back the way he had come, sticking to the shadows.

"It worked," Dan said. "The police are running toward Benhill. We're moving out."

"Don't stop," Gary said, his words coming between ragged breaths.

He rounded the corner and slowed down. The light dropped off rapidly, now that the traffic was behind him. Up ahead, one feeble streetlight illuminated the falling rain and the nearby buildings and cars, leaving all else in inky blackness. Gary paused and slipped on his night-vision goggles. The shadows flashed into surreal shades of glowing green. He continued at a fast walk as he caught his breath. The sound of approaching Klaxons seemed oddly remote because of his ear protection.

Gary looked back and saw a green shape race around the corner. Suddenly the image exploded in green. He raised his goggles a little and squinted into the flashlight's glare.

"Halt!" a voice shouted.

Gary could barely hear the officer over the background Klaxons. He removed his earplug, and in his haste dropped it. Ignoring his burning lungs, he started running through the frigid rain, searching the street ahead. Although the block was short, he had no illusions about outrunning the man behind him, not while carrying the heavy strobe. Then he saw a narrow alley about midblock. On he ran. Now he could hear his pursuer's footsteps. He glanced down and saw the strobe was recharged.

Gary dashed into the alley, caromed off a wall, and whirled around. He walked backward while watching the narrow pathway. The man raced into view, and his flashlight blinded Gary's goggles. Gary transferred the strobe to his right hand, covered his left ear, and jabbed the button. The flash found its way in around the edges of the goggles while the sound crashed and reverberated in the narrow brick canyon.

The flashlight beam bobbed around frantically as the man stumbled and finally fell. The flashlight clattered across the pavement and slammed up against the curb, its beam pointed down the alley toward Gary like an accusing finger. Two more shapes rounded the corner, each carrying a flashlight. The sound of running footsteps echoed down the alley. Adrenaline raced through Gary's veins. He whirled around and ran all-out. Far up ahead he saw a brick wall.

"Stop there!" a voice ordered.

Gary ignored the command and kept running. The wall seemed so far away, impossible to reach in time. Each ragged breath caused hot jabs in his side. He splashed through a deep puddle, slipped, and almost fell. He reached up with his free hand and wiped the rain from his goggles. Finally, he reached the wall and looked back. In the light-sensitive goggles, the three flashlights looked like green floodlights. The officers were close now, not more than fifty feet away.

Gary faced the wall, balanced the strobe on top, and threw his legs upward. He clung to the top, put a leg over, and straddled the wall. He looked back. The leading officer crashed against the brick and grabbed Gary's boot. Gary tugged and twisted, and his foot slipped free, causing him to lose his balance. He snatched the strobe and tumbled down on the opposite side, landing on his right shoulder. A sharp pain lanced deep into his brain.

Gary rolled over and staggered to his feet. He looked back and saw fingers gripping the top of the wall. Then a head appeared. Turning, Gary ran toward the street. Up ahead, heavy traffic flowed in both directions. His lungs burned, and the sharp jabs in his side dimmed the pain in his shoulder. He heard pounding footsteps behind. He saw two policemen, quite close now.

Gary drove himself harder. The street loomed like a barrier, the heavy traffic blocking his escape. A bus pulled up on the far side and started unloading passengers. Gary reached the street, ripped off his goggles, and jammed them into a raincoat pocket. He picked a narrow gap between cars and held up his free hand as he dashed into the street in front of a car. It slid to a stop, horn blaring. Gary continued across and ducked behind the bus. Its doors thumped shut, and the bus began to pull away. With the last of his energy, he raced to the front and pounded on its side. The bus stopped, brakes squealing. The doors opened and the driver looked down in irritation.

"So what's the hurry, mate?"

Gary ran up the steps. "Had to catch this bus," he gasped, in time with his rasping breaths.

The driver closed the door and merged with the traffic. "Well, can't say as I blame you. Ain't a fit night out, you ask me."

Gary took a deep breath, wincing at the pain. "No argument from me on that." Gary looked through the rear windows. Two dark shapes were standing on the sidewalk, waving frantically.

"What brings you to these parts, Yank?" the driver asked.

Gary tried to smile. "Sight-seeing."

The driver shook his head. "Takes all kinds, I suppose." He nodded toward the fare box. "The fare."

Gary looked at the box, then realized he didn't have any

money. "Ah, I don't have my wallet with me."

The driver glared at him. "Well, you can't ride without payin', now, can you?"

"Sorry. If you'll stop, I'll get off."

"That I will." The bus squalled to a halt and the doors opened. "Off with you, now."

Gary dashed down the steps, through a deep puddle, and onto the sidewalk. The bus roared away in a cloud of damp diesel smoke. Gary looked around quickly. A few blocks away he saw flashing emergency lights. He hurried to the corner and turned south on a side street.

"I'm clear now," he said softly.

"Glad to hear it," Dan said. "You had us worried."

"*You* were worried. I thought they had me for sure. Where are you?"

"To the south. Keep walking, and we'll come get you."

"Right."

After a few more radio checks to give Dan bearings, Gary spotted the truck coming through an intersection. It turned left at the next street and disappeared.

"I see you," Gary said. "I'm a block north."

"We're waiting," Dan said.

Gary checked traffic, then crossed the street and ran to the next block. There sat the truck, hiding in deep shadows. He hurried to the back and rapped on the hatch. Sully opened it and looked out, beaming.

"Hey, dude," he said, "way to go."

Gary stepped through, and Sully closed the hatch. John took the strobe.

"You didn't hurt it, did you?" John asked, a twinkle in his eye.

Gary couldn't help smiling, as relief flooded over him. "*No, I didn't hurt it.*"

Then John's grin turned somber. "Glad you're back."

"You and me both."

"Can we leave?" Ann said over the speaker.

Gary turned off his earphone radio, and Dan handed him the mike.

"Roger that," Gary said. "But stay well south until we're clear. Then pick up M3 at Kempton Park Race Course south of Heathrow."

"Roger."

chapter 19

Gary woke with a violent start, and it took him several moments to realize where he was. Then he recognized the smiling black face looking down at him. The high rumbling whine of the tires brought everything rushing back like a flood.

"Come on now, I'm not that frightening, am I?" John asked.

Gary managed a grin. "Compared to what?"

"Very funny."

Gary started unzipping his sleeping bag. "Ah." He grabbed his tender shoulder. "Man, that's sore."

"I'm not surprised." John handed him a bottle of aspirin and a mug of water. "Here."

Gary took two pills and washed them down. "Thanks."

"Don't mention it."

Gary crawled out and stood up. He stretched carefully and rubbed the sleep out of his eyes. "Where are we?"

"About forty miles from Exeter."

Gary looked at his watch and saw it was almost 11:30 P.M. "How's Ann holding up?"

John chuckled. "Fine, if you don't count being talked to

death. Sully took what you said seriously about helping her stay alert."

Gary remembered the conversation when they had stopped outside London to send Sully up front. "Any friction?"

"Not that I can tell. They've been talking movie stuff mostly. Ann seems to be enjoying it."

"Good." Gary scanned the monitors. The low-light cameras provided a decent view of the truck's traveling oasis of light, especially with aid of a nearly full moon. An oncoming car blossomed into color, then faded out to red taillights as it swept past. The stars twinkling against the jet-black sky were a comforting sight.

"Not much traffic," Gary said.

"Yeah, well, it is nearly midnight, plus we're not on a main motorway."

"When did it stop raining?"

"Around Basingstoke. Forecast for Plymouth is clear for the next day or so."

"Well, that's a blessing, I guess."

"I'd say so. You ready to spell Dan and me?"

"Sure, but you're not going to get much sleep. You should have gotten me up earlier."

"You needed it more."

Gary snapped his fingers. "Did you fix the GPS on my hang glider?"

John attempted a hurt look. "Didn't I *say* I would fix your GPS?"

"I believe you did."

"Then it's fixed. Your kite is ready to roll."

"Fly."

"Whatever. Now take over for Dan before he zones out on us."

John pulled out his sleeping bag and started unrolling it. Gary walked over behind Dan.

"Anything I need to watch out for?" Gary asked.

"Nope. Been real calm." He waved a hand toward the array of meters and LCD readouts. "Emergency channels are quiet, and nothing encrypted since we left London. Mobile phone coverage is spotty."

"I'll take your word for it. Go get some shut-eye."

Dan stood up. "Will do. I've set alarms for suspicious radio signals. If any go off, get me up."

"I will."

Gary sat down.

It took only a few minutes for him to relax, and then the tendrils of weariness began to creep back. He yawned and looked around. It was a little warm, even though the air-conditioning system was working properly. The low murmur from the air ducts together with the auxiliary power unit's hum only lulled him further. He got up and filled his mug from the coffeemaker. He sipped cautiously and found it hot and strong—too strong. He debated whether to make a new pot but decided it wasn't worth the trouble. He sat back down and panned the cab camera around. Sully was waving his arms around in rhythm with his moving lips. Ann seemed attentive, to the extent her driving would allow. Gary looked up and saw that Dan had cut off the speaker. Rather than disturb the others, he inserted his earphone radio and turned it on.

". . .that's not all," Sully said. "I *tried* to tell the director he had the camera dolly too close to the impact point, but would he listen? Noo."

"Wait a minute," Ann interrupted. "This alien invasion throws the world back into the Dark Ages, and their headquarters is Los Angeles?"

"Yeah, and the Bugs have built this humongous wall all the way around L.A."

"Made out of old cars?"

"Uh-huh, mainly SUVs plus some semis and buses."

"Okay, and the good guys are attacking from a rebel base in Las Vegas."

"You've got it. Anyhow, since the Bugs have knocked out everything electrical, that means the rebels have to use medieval weapons. They build this trebuchet, sort of a catapult thing, and they use it to fire their guys over the car wall."

"Sounds like that would hurt."

"Naw, see, they're on bicycles with wings. Once they're over the wall, they pedal like mad, driving a propeller, and glide down behind the enemy lines. Then they fry the Bugs with flame-throwers, credits roll, and Hollywood saves the world again. Special effects to the rescue."

"You actually *flew* on that bicycle contraption?"

"Yeah, that part was real. The director considered using a span wire but decided that wasn't realistic enough. I went to a hang gliding club near Carmel, took a few lessons. Then we modified one of those fixed-wing gliders by attaching a bicycle to it."

"And that really worked?"

"Hey, no problema. Our FX guys did a great job on it. They pulled me up in the air with a winch; then I cast off and glided down right past the camera. They got a *great* tracking shot of me landing. You can even tell it's me if you look close."

"Cool."

"Way cool."

"Mr. Sullivan," Gary interrupted, keeping his voice low. "Might I have a word with our driver?"

"Hey, dude, didn't know you were with us," Sully said. "Dan leave you in charge of the spook shop?"

"Yeah. He and John are sleeping. You done with your story?"

"Fade to black."

"Thank you." Gary paused, but a thought nibbled at the back of his mind. "But. . ."

"But what?" Sully asked.

"You said something about the camera dolly being too close to the impact point. What was that all about?"

"Oh. The script called for one of the flying bikes to crash. Really messy scene—hair, teeth, and eyes. We had a real trebuchet, so the director had them load it with a junk glider plus a dummy and a couple of gallons of Technicolor blood. He wanted the camera near the impact point so he could get a tight close-up."

"What? That's crazy."

"Tell me something I don't already know. He has our FX wizard fire a test shot, and they mark where it lands. Then they move the dolly over about ten feet. The director figures the real shot will hit the same place, since nothing's changed."

"I could comment on that, but I won't."

"Good. You couldn't have talked him out of it either. Anyhow, the FX guys fire the trebuchet, and the shot goes way up, then starts back down. The cameraman tilts the camera up to follow the glider, but the camera doesn't move as it comes down."

"The glider's coming down on top of him."

"You got it. Just in time he jumps off the dolly, plows into the director, and they both sack the gaffer for a twenty-yard loss on the play. Cut. Crew takes a break while the director and screenwriter do a quick rewrite."

Ann giggled.

"What's so funny?" Sully asked.

"Did that really happen?" she asked.

"Yeah, basically. Hey, it's a weird business."

"What happened to the camera?" Gary asked.

"Wiped out the magazine, but the camera body was okay. All they had to do was put on a new magazine and continue the shoot. I do my big scene; then the star fries all the Bugs with his flamethrower, and the rebels tear down the car wall. Then our hero rides into L.A. on his steam-powered motorcycle and does a victory lap around the coliseum."

"Wait a minute. Steam-powered motorcycle?"

"Remember, the Bugs knocked out everything that uses electricity."

"Sorry. I forgot. This saw wide release, I take it."

"Naw, art houses mainly."

"I'll bet. Now, if I could have a word with our driver."

"Yes, Gary?" Ann said.

"How are you holding up?"

"I'm doing fine."

"Good. I want you driving when we enter Plymouth, but Sully could spell you for a while."

"I'm all right. We're only about seventy miles out."

"So, we'll be there around 12:45?"

"I think so. We hit the M5 this side of Exeter, and it's major motorways the rest of the way."

"That'll help."

"Too bad it isn't daylight. Devon and Cornwall are really beautiful, quite different from the rest of England. Rolling green hills and tiny fishing villages with streets so narrow you can't drive on them. Cornwall was a refuge for the Celts, same as Wales, when the Saxons invaded."

"Been here before?" he asked.

"Several times when I was in school. Cornwall and Wales are my favorites. And we're not far from Land's End, the western-most part of England, not counting the Isles of Scilly."

"Where are they?"

"About twenty-six miles west of Land's End. Never been there, but I'd like to someday. The Isle of Wight and the Isle of Man are more popular, but I'll take small and quaint over gaudy. Climate's better too. They grow lots of flowers there."

"Sounds nice," Gary said.

He settled back in his chair. Changing his mind about making coffee, he got up, dumped his mug, and went through the ritual of operating the coffeemaker. He watched the dark brew start streaming into the pot and savored the welcome aroma. He waited impatiently. Finally the stream slowed to a drip, and he refilled his mug. He sipped and decided it was definitely worth the trouble.

Traffic picked up a little after Ann merged with M5 outside Exeter, but it was still light. They crossed the river Exe, and a few miles later took M38, their motorway into Plymouth, approximately thirty miles away. Gradually the countryside gave way to housing and business. Ann slowed down. Soon they were inside the city. The truck's blue dot crept along the GPS generated overlay map, following M38. Up ahead, an arrow pointed to the off-ramp to A386. Moments later Ann took the turn.

"Where to now?" she asked.

"Take us down to the port of Plymouth," Gary said. "Drive past the entrance road."

"Roger."

Gary turned off his earphone radio. He walked over to John, knelt, and shook him gently.

His friend's soft snore stopped abruptly, and his eyes popped open. He yawned. "Where are we?"

"Entering Plymouth."

John struggled out of his sleeping bag and stood up. It took several shakes before Gary got a mumbled response out of Dan. The truck leaned going through a gentle turn.

"We're almost there, guys," Ann said.

Dan stood up and stretched. He sat down, scanned the monitors, then looked down at the map overlay. He took the mike. "Stop somewhere past the port entrance."

"Roger."

A few moments later the truck stopped. Dan pressed a switch, and the mast supporting the parabolic antenna and camera shot up into the early morning sky. The wide-angle view revealed the port offices, the passenger and freight buildings, and the piers. The moon painted the scene in shades of milky white in sharp contrast with the inky shadows.

"Not much going on," Dan said.

"At one o'clock on a Friday morning, I'm not surprised," Gary said. He picked up Ann's port manager report. "Let's see." He looked up at the monitor. "The *Bhima* will dock at Trinity Pier; that's the one on the left."

"The one even with the back of that ship on the right?" John asked.

"Yeah. Guess that's a roll-on-roll-off at berth number one. The empty slot next to the west wharf is berth number two for roll-on-roll-off and cruise ships. How about a close-up on Trinity Pier."

The image bounced a little as the camera zoomed in.

"Okay, there's the transit shed for Trinity Pier," Gary said. "That would be a great place to hide, but it's a little obvious."

"I doubt Peter is expecting us," John said. "Ann said he probably doesn't know she broke into his MI5 account."

"Maybe, but there's more than one way to pick Plymouth as a likely way out. We've underestimated Peter twice already, and I'm not going to do it again."

"You're both assuming he's here," Dan said. "Who says that Indian ship has anything to do with Peter?"

Gary looked at him. "You're right, it is an assumption. But it's the only possibility we've got right now. So, if you've got a better idea. . ."

Dan shook his head. "Not me. But, for that matter, Peter may have already escaped."

A wry smile came to Gary's lips. "You're full of good cheer, aren't you?"

"Just trying to be realistic."

"Okay, then how about getting on with your electronic snooping?"

"To hear is to obey," Dan intoned. He reached up and positioned the mast antenna.

"I guess there's a first time for everything," Gary said.

Dan gave no indication he had heard, and Gary knew from past experience that he may not have; such was his level of concentration. Static came from the speaker.

". . .transit shed secure, returning to base."

"Base, aye."

"They've got at least a two-man security team using unsecure radios," Dan said. He pointed to the monitor. "Look, there he goes. Must have been checking that building on Trinity Pier."

Gary watched as the guard left the pier and started walking past an open storage area. He had about a thousand feet to go before reaching the port office buildings.

"Zoom in on that car," Gary said.

"The one on the pier?"

"Yes."

The extreme magnification caused the car's image to shake. "Looks like a Buick, and the sticker identifies it as a rental."

"Backed into the parking slot."

"Quick getaway, maybe."

"Maybe," Gary agreed. "Picking anything up from the shed?"

"Just a minute." Dan tweaked the antenna and began trying different frequencies. "Aha. There's a mobile phone in line with the center of the shed."

"You sure it's inside?"

"Probably, unless it's coming from out in the harbor."

"Is it Peter's?"

"It's not the one he had in London, but he could have gotten another one."

"Yeah, or maybe it's Ian's."

"You think he's with Peter?" John asked.

Gary nodded. "You bet I do."

"Okay, so what's next?"

"Look inside that shed." Gary turned to Dan. "Tell Ann to find us a place to hide."

Dan pressed a switch. "As soon as I lower the mast."

chapter 20

Gary replayed the video recording again with Dan's electronic filter applied. "I see it," he said, pointing. "The shed has an air vent up high just under the roof. But assuming Peter and Ian are inside, won't they see something when you remove the grill?"

"No," John said. "That end of the shed is in deep shadow."

"What about the noise?"

"That metal roof is going to be making all kinds of noise in this wind. They won't hear a thing unless you fall out of the rafters."

"I believe I can avoid that."

John smiled. "I certainly hope so."

"What if they've got a light?"

"Unlikely. My guess is they have night-vision goggles, but even if there is a light, they shouldn't be able to see us. It's a large building, and Dan says they're near the center. And since our goggles have infrared illuminators, you won't have any trouble spotting them even if it's pitch-black in there."

Gary wished he felt as sure as John sounded. "I guess we'll see. What next?"

"Sherlock will do the scouting. Lower him down, and I'll go find the bad guys."

"Sure you can handle Sherlock?"

"I *made* Sherlock."

"Yeah, but I've got a better touch."

"Look, I can take care of my buddy."

It was Gary's turn to smile. "Me or Sherlock?"

"Both of you. Now quit worrying."

"Okay, so Sherlock finds them, you guide me in, and I zap 'em with the pepper-spray-tear-gas combo. Then Dan calls the cops."

"Right, and hope Peter has the crown with him."

Gary paused. "Yeah, that part worries me. If he doesn't, I don't want him talking his way out of this, like saying we kidnapped him and Ian, and he got cut when we grabbed him."

"Kinda hard to make it stick with that rental car outside."

"Bet the car's clean. Peter could claim *we* rented it."

"Hey, if you're going to be that gloomy, what difference does having the crown make? He could *still* say we kidnapped him to ensure our getaway."

"Yeah. Well, it's the best we can do." Gary turned to Dan. "What do you think?"

"I don't see anything better, but remember, we don't know how fast the cops will respond," Dan said.

"I'll hit 'em with the spray again, if necessary," Gary said.

"What if they're armed?"

Gary took a deep breath and let it out slowly. "Pray I get 'em first."

"I'll leave that to you and John." He paused. "But be careful, both of you."

"Thanks, we will."

"So is it a go?" John asked.

Gary pushed his remaining doubts aside. "Yes."

"Who drives?"

"Sully."

At 2:05 A.M., Sully eased the truck up on the sidewalk, as close to the fence as he could. They were on the east side of the port next to an open storage area about three hundred feet from the transit shed on Trinity Pier. To the west, low buildings sprawled across the point of land that separated the port from the Hoe, a sweeping park adjoining the Royal Citadel. The lone port guard had finished his rounds five minutes ago, and everything seemed peaceful.

Gary scanned the monitors one last time and patted his coverall pockets to make sure he had the pepper spray. "Are we clear?"

Dan checked all his readouts. "You're good to go."

"Thanks." Gary inserted his radio earphone and turned it on. Then he grabbed his night-vision goggles and hurried to the back. He opened the hatch and stepped out into the cool night air. When John joined him, they unclamped the ladder and used it to climb to the top of the truck. Under the bright moonlight, the port's buildings and piers stood out in sharp relief against the shadows.

"I need help," John whispered.

"Oh, yeah."

Together they lifted the ladder, swung it up, and lowered it over the fence, resting the top against the truck. Gary stepped onto the ladder and backed down cautiously. John followed with a grace that surprised Gary. He pulled the ladder clear, and Sully drove off.

Gary scanned what he could see of the port complex then whispered, "All clear."

John nodded and picked up his end of the ladder. They hurried over open ground and along the back of the transit shed, which was about the length of a football field. Gary was breathing hard by the time they reached the far end. John took the ladder and placed it against the wall. He stepped up the rungs with hardly a sound and started working on the vent. After almost ten minutes, the last screw came free. John lifted the vent clear and lowered it. Gary set it aside, well clear of the ladder. John came down, removed Sherlock from his backpack, and handed it to Gary.

Gary took his time climbing the ladder. He reached the top, slipped on his night-vision goggles, and looked in through the vent opening. The nearby metal joists and rafters stood out in bright green while those farther back faded into shadow. The central load-bearing girder provided a narrow pathway and ran the entire length of the building. Orderly piles of boxes and crates jammed the floor below with aisles in between for fork-lifts. Most of the interior was open storage, interspersed with tall steel shelving units. As expected, there were no lights. The building's frame squeaked and groaned in the gusts.

Gary crawled along the girder, pushing Sherlock along in front. Upon reaching the first supporting post, he held Sherlock out to the side and pressed a button. Soundlessly, the robot lowered itself by unreeling a thin nylon cord. After it reached the floor, Gary threw the cord down to be retrieved automatically. Sherlock was John's problem now.

Gary looked around and spotted a tall shelving unit within reach of the nearest roof joist. He edged out on it and reached down with one foot, then the other, and finally transferred his whole weight. Gary winced as the top emitted a muted creak. He listened a few moments but heard nothing except the wind and the roof's restless groaning.

"Sherlock is halfway there," John's voice whispered in Gary's earphone. "Nothing so far."

Gary turned around and started climbing down the shelves. Upon reaching the bottom, he paused, then crept toward the next aisle over, parallel to the one Sherlock had gone down. He cautiously peeked around the corner. It was clear all the way to the far wall, three hundred feet away. But according to Dan, there was a mobile phone at the one-hundred-fifty-foot mark.

Gary stepped into the aisle and began tiptoeing, listening and looking for any sign of life. He approached the midpoint with agonizing slowness but dared not move any faster. He scanned the orderly stacks of freight, most of it higher than his head, and paused at each cross aisle, making sure each was clear before proceeding. Finally, only ten feet remained. Gary stopped.

"Sherlock's in position," John whispered. "Waiting for your mark."

Gary reached up to his radio and flicked the microphone with a fingernail, transmitting a *click* to John.

"Roger that. Easing Sherlock forward. Now I'm seeing something. Yes, two figures, one facing away, one looking in my direction. Don't think he's seen me. Can't tell who they are, but it has to be Peter and Ian. Wait! The one facing Sherlock is moving. He's armed."

Gary glanced all around, looking for the nearest cover. There was much to choose from, but no quick way out if he got trapped.

"Now the other guy is turning," John said. "They're wearing night-vision goggles. I'm pulling Sherlock back."

Gary heard the familiar whine of the robot's drive motors going all-out and started backing up. Rapid footsteps sounded off to his right. He turned around and started running. The sounds from the robot cut off abruptly. Gary kept going.

"I see 'em. They're still coming my way," John said in a whisper. "Get out of there."

I would if I could, Gary thought. *Lord, help me.*

Both men were well past him now, racing down the next aisle over. Their echoing footsteps slowed and finally stopped. Gary slid to a stop. The element of surprise was gone now, and that made it unlikely Gary could hit both Peter *and* Ian with the pepper spray—either one, for that matter.

"I'm calling the police," Dan announced over the radio.

Gary wondered what the response time would be, but he wasn't optimistic. A lot could happen in fifteen or twenty minutes, most likely his death. He looked toward the vent—over a hundred feet away, but it seemed more like a mile. A long thin shadow extended past a crate, enlarging rapidly into a sinister shape.

Gary saw the gun arm coming up; he whirled around and ran. Up ahead he saw a cross aisle. The soft pop of a silenced gun sounded behind him. The bullet buzzed past his left ear and smacked into a crate. Gary dived for the opening, hit the floor hard, and rolled. Two more shots chipped the concrete behind him. Ignoring the pain in his shoulder, he scrambled to his feet.

"I'm coming in," John said over the radio.

"Stay put," Gary said, making no effort to keep his voice down.

"But. . ."

"That's an order."

Gary heard running feet and looked around frantically. The nearest shelving unit had an empty shelf about ten feet up. He started climbing. The sounds of pursuit were closer now, and a shadowy figure skidded around the corner. Gary hurtled upward and onto the shelf, hauled his legs in, and rolled to the side. The shelf heaved upward with two metallic shrieks. He looked down and saw jagged holes where he had been only a moment before.

Gary scrabbled farther into the shelf. Someone was climbing up behind him. Up ahead boxes blocked the way, but to the side a narrow opening appeared between crates. He turned and wriggled through. The next shot hit a box behind him. The opening ahead led to the main aisle Sherlock had come down. Gary reached the edge and peered down. The other man was waiting for him. Gary jerked back. Three bullets ricocheted off the shelf above. He grabbed a box and shoved it over the shelf's edge. Gary heard the expected *thump*, the cry of the man below, and the sound of metal skittering across concrete.

Frantic scrabbling told him the man behind him was getting close. Gary grabbed the edge of the shelf, pulled himself out, and glanced down. The man on the ground was searching frantically for his pistol. Gary clawed his way upward on the remaining shelves and slid onto the top with an all-out leap, landing with a loud sheet-metal clatter.

Gary jumped up and looked toward the vent, still almost one hundred fifty feet away. The shelving unit continued on for another twenty feet, and beyond that lay a vast section of open storage with tall stacks of palletized cargo. The building's central girder ran along a foot above his head. In the far distance, he saw John walking along the beam.

"Go back," Gary said. "You can't help me."

"I'm coming anyway," John answered.

Gary heard a sound, looked back, and saw a hand gripping the top. He leaped for the girder, grabbed, and swung his legs around it. He pulled himself around on top and stood. Looking down, he almost lost his balance. The four-inch-wide girder seemed impossibly narrow, and a fall, he knew, would be fatal. It was ten long feet to the next roof joist, and beyond that the shelving unit ended. A clatter behind and below announced his pursuer.

Gary slid his feet over the girder like a tightrope walker, reached the joist, and swung around the metal post that ran up to the roof. A bullet ricocheted off something up ahead. Without looking back, Gary continued out over the jumble of boxes and crates below. Another bullet buzzed past his ear.

A sudden movement on the floor caught his attention. The other man was tracking him, obviously waiting for a good shot. Unless he did something quick, Gary knew he was a dead man. He looked all around and spotted a tall pallet of boxes, a little to the left and some six feet below. He steeled himself for what he had to do. He could hear the man behind him clearly now. It was time to go.

Gary leaned to the left, pushed off, and spread his arms and legs. He landed hard, and the lightweight boxes gave a little, the stack rocking alarmingly. For a moment he thought it would fall, but it teetered in a precarious equilibrium. Somewhere below boxes gave way, and the tilt increased.

He glanced back. The man on the girder was at the roof joist and about to come around. Gary looked down, and the boxes leaned even more. The man on the ground was aiming his weapon. Gary lunged, toppling the stack. The man saw it coming, and his shot went wide. Gary sprang for a lower stack, hit, and tried to hold on, but it fell as well.

The concrete floor rushed upward, and Gary braced for impact. The man below disappeared under the avalanche of boxes. Gary flattened the box he clung to and rolled off onto the concrete, ending up on his side. With a furious flailing, a head appeared, and for the first time Gary got a good look. It was Peter, recognizable despite the night-vision goggles and the mask of hate he wore. Peter brought his pistol to bear, obviously relishing the moment.

Gary thrust a hand inside his pocket, drew out the pepper spray, and pressed the valve without taking aim. A fog shot out a little off target. He turned the can, but Peter saw it coming and tried to twist out of the way. He cried out when the spray struck the side of his head. He staggered to his feet, turned, and ran.

"Ian!" Peter shouted as Gary raced toward the exit. "Help me."

Gary looked up. Ian leaned against the roof support, again taking careful aim. Gary rolled to the side and caught a glimpse of the muzzle flash. Concrete chips stung his face. He slammed up against a pallet and looked all around, but there was no place to hide. He could see that Ian's gun was pointed right at him, and he knew the next shot would not miss.

Something struck Ian in the chest, bounced off, and clattered to the floor. The pistol's muzzle flashed twice, but both shots went wide. Gary looked around and saw John walking along the girder about twenty feet from Ian.

"Look out!" Gary shouted.

Ian brought his gun up, and John swung around the roof support. Ian fired twice more. Gary jumped to his feet and looked around for something to throw until he realized he was still holding the pepper spray. He threw the can as hard as he could. It arced up and struck Ian on the side of the head.

"Ian!" Peter shouted. "Come here. Now!"

Ian hesitated; then he turned and ran back across the girder. Upon reaching the shelving unit, he jumped down and fell hard. He sprang up and scrambled to the edge, then climbed down and ran out of the building. Moments later an engine roared to life and rubber squealed. The sounds quickly diminished.

"Are you okay?" John asked.

"A little sore," Gary said. "How about you?"

"Not a scratch."

"Not that I'm hurrying you, but the police will be here soon."

"Yeah, after Peter's disappeared again."

"Later."

"Yeah. How about fetching my flashlight?" John asked.

"So, *that's* what you hit him with."

"Yeah, wish it had knocked him off."

"Me too." Gary searched around amid the tumbled boxes and finally spotted it. He jammed the flashlight into a pocket and scooped up his pepper spray.

"Don't forget Sherlock," John said.

"Where is it?"

"Just a minute." John brought out the remote control and backed the robot into the aisle.

"I see it." Gary worked his way around the debris and picked up the robot.

"Need any help?" John asked.

"No, I can make it."

Gary jogged back to the shelving unit he had climbed down earlier, getting there before John. He climbed up to the top and waited.

"Here," Gary said.

He handed the robot up. John took it and continued on to the vent. Gary pulled himself up on the joist, eased over to the girder, and joined John. Gary looked out at the moonlit port, then down the ladder to the pier below.

"Dan, come and get us," Gary said.

Angry, frustrated thoughts whirled about in Gary's mind, until a still, quiet impulse overrode them. Then he realized he and John were alive, when they could have easily been killed. He thought over what had happened and knew he could not account for their survival except by God's providence.

chapter 21

Sully parked the truck on a narrow country road north of Plymouth and came around to the back. Gary let him in.

"Glad you guys made it out," Sully said.

Gary closed the hatch. "By all rights we shouldn't have," he said.

He walked over to the coffeemaker where Ann was filling her mug. He waited until she finished, then poured himself some and took a sip. Now that the present danger was past, a solid weariness settled over him like a suffocating blanket. He looked at his watch and saw it was a little after 3:00 A.M., and he marveled that he and John had been gone for less than an hour. Even now, he couldn't explain how they had escaped death. Then something seized his jumbled thoughts and directed them elsewhere. *No,* he admitted to himself, *I don't know how, but I do know who. It's by God's grace that John and I are here. But what now?*

"Are you all right?" John asked.

Gary looked at him in confusion. "What? Oh, yeah. Sorry." He took a long sip from his mug and sat wearily in the only remaining chair.

"I'll keep this short," he began. "Dan and Sully know most of what happened." He paused and his gaze flicked over Ann. "Ann's research was dead-on. Peter and Ian *are* planning on escaping aboard the *Bhima*." He quickly reviewed the encounter inside the transit shed.

"What do we do now?" Dan asked when Gary was done.

"That, indeed, *is* the question," Gary said. "First, though: Is Peter still planning on using the *Bhima,* or does he have another way out?"

"He *can't* go out on the boat, can he?" Sully asked.

"I guess that depends on what the police come up with," Gary said.

"Is there anything to implicate us?" Dan asked.

"No," Gary said, grateful for some good news. "We got out with all our gear."

"Maybe Peter or Ian left something behind."

"Nothing but a few spent shell casings, and that won't tell the police anything."

"Peter will stick to his original plan," Ann said. "Escaping like this is just his style."

"I agree," Gary said, "and there are lots of ways he could do it. The crew could smuggle him aboard or they could pick him up elsewhere."

"You mean at sea?" John asked.

"That's the most obvious way," Gary said. "Or they could fake engine trouble and pull in at another port." He saw John's look of concern. "I know the possibilities are expanding, but it's a whole lot better than Peter disappearing completely."

"Can't argue with that," John said.

"So, we need to get busy."

"Obviously we have to keep the freighter under surveillance," Dan said.

"Right," Gary said. "There's a tall building on the west side, across from Trinity Pier. What if we stick one of your microcams up high on the wall?"

"That'll do for starters, but we'll also need a transmitter on the ship *and* a microcam if you can manage it."

"How do we get aboard?" John asked.

"We've done harder things," Gary said.

"Yeah, but not with every cop in Britain hot on our trail."

"First we do the building, then worry about the freighter. But right now, we all need to grab some z's. Let's set a watch and rotate every two hours. I'll take the first one."

"Let me," Ann said. "I'm more rested."

Gary decided not to argue. "Okay. The *Bhima* is due in at 1:00 P.M., so I want everyone up by nine. That should give us plenty of time to place the camera."

He watched as the others, except Ann, pulled out their sleeping bags. Only after he dragged his out did he realize how exhausted he was.

Gary opened his eyes with a start. He rubbed his eyes and looked at his watch. It was almost 9:00 A.M. He came out of his sleeping bag and stood up. Then he noticed the distinctive smells of eggs, sausage, and fresh coffee. His stomach emitted a loud rumble.

"Whoa," Sully said, stepping back. "Who let the tiger out?"

"What's that I smell?" Gary asked.

"Breakfast from the Golden Arches," John said. "Ann made a food run."

"Thanks."

"I also picked up some work clothes for you and John," Ann said.

"What kind?"

"Cornish fisherman."

Gary nodded. He poured himself a mug of coffee, took a

long sip, and set the mug down. His mouth watered as he hurriedly unwrapped a sausage-and-egg muffin. He took a large bite and munched away. "Oh, that tastes good." Gary wolfed down the rest of the muffin and grabbed another one. "What's been happening?" he asked.

"The Crown Jewels Heist is still hot," Dan replied. "Nothing new, so they keep running the same old clips over and over. Your mug comes up a lot."

"Thanks."

"Don't mention it. Besides you, they typically show a guard outside the Jewel House, the Queen Consort's Crown, Peter's car with the bloody seat, and various MI5 guys looking very serious and saying they'll bring us all in if it's the last thing they do."

"Any *real* news about us?"

Dan scooted back in his chair a little. "Indirectly. The port manager said that persons unknown broke into one of the transit sheds and damaged some cargo. All the police found was a few spent shells. The investigation is ongoing, and so on."

"Do you get the impression the police are linking this to the heist?"

"I don't think so."

"They're treating it like a bungled burglary," John said. "Ann did some serious searching, various media, newsgroups. Nothing."

"Plus my scanners are relatively quiet, and I'm picking up almost no encrypted radio signals," Dan added.

"Good," Gary said. "So, next task is planting the spy cam."

Gary sat down beside Dan and looked up at the monitors. Ann had just completed the second leisurely drive past the port of Plymouth on Millbay Road, and there had been no indication of police activity. Low warehouses surrounded the port, giving way to taller buildings near the city center. Multiple grids of narrow streets collided with one another at every conceivable angle, adding a sense of quaint disorder to Plymouth's historic waterfront.

"Still nothing?" Gary asked.

"Quiet as a graveyard," Dan replied.

"I'd prefer a different idiom."

"Fresh out. Seriously, I haven't heard a thing for some time now, other than routine status checks."

"I guess that's good." He reached over and keyed the mike. "Ann, Sully, how do things look?"

"All clear," Ann said over the speaker.

"Okay," Gary said. "We're going in. Keep a sharp lookout."

"Roger," Ann said.

Ann circled the block, came back heading east, and turned right at the port entrance. Gary scanned the monitors anxiously as Ann followed the perimeter road past the inner basin and the car marshalling yard, which was jammed with tiny cars awaiting transportation. The road curved around to the south past the passenger terminal. Gary looked up at the forward monitor. Ahead were berths one and two. The roll-on-roll-off ship was still tied up but riding high in the water. Ann slowed as she drove out onto the wharf. Ahead towered a tall building parallel to the wharf.

Gary took the mike. "Stop here a moment."

"Roger." The truck came to a smooth stop.

Gary's eyes swept the monitors. Across the outer basin was Trinity Pier and south of that the Military Pier and marina.

"Where do you want to put the camera?" Gary asked.

Dan tilted the forward camera and zoomed in. "Up high on the corner of that building."

Gary turned to John. "Ready to do your thing?"

John smiled and flexed his fingers. "Anytime."

Gary keyed the mike. "Proceed. John will guide you in."

"Roger," Ann said.

She brought the truck around in a wide, right-hand circle and edged in beside the north end of the building. The truck slowed to a crawl.

John's eyes alternated between two monitors, one showing the diminishing gap to the building and the other aimed up high where the camera would go. "Can you move in a tad closer?" he asked Ann.

The gap narrowed to almost nothing. The truck inched into position and finally stopped.

John reached over and pressed the switch to deploy the surveillance mast. The microcam's view opened up to a wide panorama. John stopped the mast at forty feet, then turned the camera and focused on the side of the building. The image in the monitor swayed and jittered.

"That wind going to bother you?" Gary asked.

"Hope not," John said. "Once the tape hits the wall, that camera's there forever." He turned back to the close-up of the building, grabbed a small remote control, and pressed a button. A square plate with attached camera entered the monitor's field of view. John stopped the plate less than an inch from the wall. It swayed and bobbed and almost touched the building.

"Whoa," John said. He backed the camera away and wiped his hands on his jeans. "More wind than I expected. Last thing we need is to attach it cockeyed."

He waited. Several minutes later the wind died and the oscillations of the mast slowed and almost stopped. John pressed the button. The plate came into view and kept on going. Still the lull held. The plate hit the building and stuck. John released the robot's grip, then pressed the button to lower the mast.

"Let's check it out," Dan said. He flipped a switch. A bird's-eye view of Trinity Pier flashed onto the monitor above his head. "Very nice." He tilted the view up and down, then panned around to the left. "Man, we can see nearly the entire port."

John performed a tiny bow. "Thank you, thank you."

Gary took the mike. "Ann, get us out of here."

"Roger," she replied.

The truck began inching backward.

A rust-streaked gray ship danced in the extreme telephoto view, two tugs maintaining station off either bow. The monitor's inset clock said 12:26:41.

"They're on schedule," Gary whispered to Dan.

"Yeah."

The compact convoy passed Drake's Island to port, then lined up on Plymouth Port's channel. The *Bhima* slowed even more, its bow wave diminishing to a narrow white line that soon disappeared in the light chop. A few minutes later the freighter crept past Military Pier, and by the time it reached Trinity Pier it was almost dead in the water. The port-side tug dropped back and began pushing the ship's stern to starboard.

"Are they going to back in?" Dan asked.

"Have to, if they're going to tie up on the port side."

"Oh. Nautical things aren't my bag."

Roiling white water spread outward from the *Bhima's* stern, and it began backing into the berth with both tugs pushing from the starboard side. Sailors on deck threw lines to workers on the pier, who pulled them in. Next came the attached hawsers. The ship inched into the berth. Finally the dockworkers made it fast.

"One-oh-five," Dan said. "Not bad."

"Yeah. Now we wait."

Gary and John hovered over Dan's shoulders as they watched yet another replay of the edited footage from the surveillance camera.

"Here they start the unloading," Dan said. "From about

one-forty-five until just after six, they unload the holds, and the forklifts cart everything into the transit shed." The time code on the monitor jumped a half hour. "Now, here a ship's derrick hoists mystery container number one aboard, despite the fact the port manager's report says they aren't taking on freight."

"Could be supplies," Gary said. "Provisions for the crew, spare parts."

Dan clicked the Pause button with his mouse and looked around at him. "Maybe, but what if our good friend Pete's in that box?"

"Yeah, I know. Keep going."

Dan clicked the Play button. "And here's box number two. It took four crewmen to haul this one aboard. Looks kinda heavy from the way they're struggling." The monitor's picture jumped again. "And here's the last one, loaded by derrick. Again, a crate large enough to hold a man and whatever else he wishes to smuggle on board."

"That's all of them?"

"That's a roger. Crewmen have brought assorted boxes and bags aboard, but none large enough to hold a man."

"What about a crown?"

"Oh, that's different. Most packages were large enough for that, and, of course, Peter could be coming aboard later, closer to sailing time."

"I don't like it," John said.

"Me either," Gary said. "Peter knows we're after him, so this could be a trap. On the other hand, this may be his only way out. He certainly went to a lot of trouble setting it up."

"What if we tip the police?" Ann asked.

"Do that, and the police will likely catch *us*. And even if Peter *is* aboard, there's a good chance the police wouldn't be able to find him. There are just too many places to hide. The Brits can't very well take the ship apart."

"They might if they knew the crown was on board."

"But *we* don't know, so there's no way the police would. And the moment the police show up on the pier, Peter goes into hiding, assuming he's aboard."

"So what do you suggest?" Dan asked.

"Sneak aboard. Hope to catch the crew unawares."

"By yourself?"

Gary looked up at the live picture. The time code said 20:14:22. The sun was low in the west, drawing long shadows across the port of Plymouth. Soon it would be sunset. The *Bhima* looked peaceful. A lone sailor stood watch on the quarterdeck beside the gangplank.

Gary turned to John. "I was hoping for some help."

John took a deep breath and let it out. "Wouldn't miss it for the world."

chapter 22

Gary pressed a button on his waterproof watch, and the backlit display showed 9:09 P.M. A deep red line on the western horizon was all that remained of sunset. From horizon to zenith, the blaze faded to purple and finally deepest blue. As dark shadows settled over Plymouth, three shapes climbed to the top of the truck.

"You ready?" Gary whispered.

"Yeah," John said.

The truck sat almost touching the port's western perimeter fence. Sully steadied the ladder while Gary stepped off the truck and started down. John picked up his pack and harness and followed. Sully waited until he reached the ground, then pulled the ladder back over the fence.

"Good luck, guys," he whispered.

Gary turned and waved.

Sully climbed down, stowed the ladder, and disappeared inside. The truck drove off into the night.

Snug inside his dry suit hood, Gary's earphone radio crackled. "This is Amphib Base, radio check," Dan's voice announced.

"Frog One, roger," Gary said.

"Frog Two, roger," John echoed.

Dan's voice gave Gary some comfort, but it quickly drained away as the reality of their mission finally hit him. They had to swim over five hundred feet across the outer basin to Trinity Pier and *then* board the *Bhima*, all without being seen.

Gary led the way through the gloomy shadows. The lighting increased a little as they approached the seawall, although at best it was dim since the moon was barely above the horizon. He reached the stone jetty and walked halfway down it where steps led to the water. He and John sat on the bottom step and pulled on their swim fins. Next came the face masks and snorkels. Without a word, they entered the restless black waters and pushed off.

Waves splashed over Gary's face mask, temporarily blurring the image of the distant target. His energy began draining away as the swim turned into a grueling chore. John slowly edged ahead. Gary kicked harder, then settled into a steady, determined pace.

Slowly the distance to the freighter decreased. Lights up high illuminated the quarterdeck but left the foredeck and stern in dark shadow. When Gary finally rounded the end of Trinity Pier, he caught a distant glimpse of the bright glare above the gangplank. Up ahead, the ship's bow rose out of the water like a rusty mountain. Gary looked all around but saw no sign of life on the ship or the pier; however, he knew there had to be someone on the quarterdeck.

Gary angled away from the pier and into the shadow cast by the *Bhima's* starboard side. He and John swam past the neglected steel plates until they reached the rounded stern. Gary stopped and looked up. The chain lifeline high over their heads was barely discernable against the night sky.

John pulled an air pistol out of his pack and fitted a grapple attached to a thin steel cable wound on a compact winch strapped to his chest. He raised the gun, sighted carefully, and pulled the trigger. The cable whined off the winch's spool, and the grapple shot straight up, the barely audible *swoosh* almost lost in the gentle lap of water against the ship's hull. The hook stopped even with the *Bhima*'s tall booms, then came streaking back down.

"Look out," John said in a harsh whisper.

He ducked and covered his head. Gary did the same and, after the soft splash, he surfaced in time to see the long loops of cable fall into the water and sink.

"Didn't allow for the wind," John said.

He engaged the winch and began reeling in the cable. The electric motor ground away, gradually filling the spool. Suddenly, John disappeared under the murky waters, leaving Gary gaping at the black ripples, wondering what happened.

Gary took a deep breath and dove, propelling himself downward with powerful kicks. Unable to see, he hit something hard and glanced off. He stopped. His lungs burned, but he had no idea which way was up. He turned about and swam, but the pressure on his chest increased. Realizing his mistake, he turned around and kicked even harder. His head rammed something hard, shoving his face mask down around his neck; his face scraped along the jagged surface. He pushed away and thrashed as hard as he could. His head broke the surface, and he drew great whooping breaths into his aching lungs. He looked around and saw John several feet away.

John swam close and pushed his mask up on his forehead. "Are you okay?" he whispered.

Gary shook his head. "Wait," he wheezed.

"What's that on your face?" John asked. "Looks like blood."

Gary touched his forehead and winced. His fingers came away dark and slick. He took a few more deep breaths. "Hit the hull," he gasped. "I'm okay, but what happened to you?"

"The grapple must have snagged on something," John

251

said. "The winch pulled me under, and I had trouble releasing the drum. Meanwhile you rammed into me when I was on the way up."

"Sorry, I was trying to help." Gary paused. "I thought something had you."

"What?"

"I don't know—a shark or something."

"In a harbor? Not likely."

"Time's wasting. Get on with it."

"Can't. The grapple's still stuck. Grab hold of me and kick hard while I reel it in."

"Okay." Gary replaced his mask.

John pulled his mask down, then reeled in the slack. "Now," he said.

He engaged the winch, and it immediately pulled them under. Gary held on, and even though he kicked as hard as he could, the pressure kept increasing. Gary kicked harder, but still the cable dragged them down. Finally the tiny scream of the winch cut off, and their combined thrusts propelled them upward. Gary broke the surface and released his hold.

"Man, that thing's really stuck," Gary said. He looked the ship's hull over, but there weren't any handholds he could see. Then his eyes drifted to the rounded stern. "Over there," he said, pointing.

John released the winch's brake and followed. Gary swam along the sheer cliff of the hull and under the stern's towering overhang. There, deep in shadow, was the top portion of the massive rudder.

"I'll get on the other side and hold onto your harness," Gary said. He swam around to the other side and reached around. The underwater portion of the rudder formed a solid surface to brace against. John swam backward until Gary could reach him.

"Got you," Gary said.

"Okay. Taking in the slack."

Gary felt the vibration as the cable drew taut, dragging John lower in the water. The pull on his arms went from light to heavy to painful. John sank lower and lower in the water. Gary's arms felt like they were being torn out of their sockets. Suddenly the pull released. Moments later the grapple surfaced.

Gary let go of John's harness and swam around the rudder. They positioned themselves under the stern, lined up with the deck above. John pulled out his air pistol, set the grapple in place, took careful aim, and fired. Once again the grapple and line arced up. John snubbed the cable, and the grapple fell across the chain lifeline. He tugged, and one of the hooks caught the chain.

"Nothing to it," John whispered.

"Yeah, right."

John shook his head. "I'm surrounded by Philistines."

Gary snapped the strap from his belt to John's harness. Without a word, John engaged the winch, and the powerful motor hauled them both out of the water. The gap between the swimmers and the rust-streaked hull decreased until they touched and scraped along the rough surface. Finally the winch stopped. John twisted in his harness and reached down. Gary pulled himself up on the strap and grabbed the outstretched hand. John hauled him up until he could grab one of the lifeline posts. Gary unhooked the strap, pulled himself up, and slipped under the chain. He sat on the deck and removed his swim fins and mask. The rough steel felt cold against his bare feet.

Gary sat down next to a locker and looked all around. The moon was higher now, and its cold, hard light flooded the deck, leaving them quite exposed if anyone happened to look aft. John sat beside Gary, struggled out of his winch harness, and removed his swim gear. Gary tucked their equipment under the canvas covering of a life raft.

John leaned close. "What about the guy on the quarter-deck?" he whispered.

Gary nodded. He stepped carefully around and between the cluttered deck equipment and took a quick look down the port side, then down at the pier. He jumped back behind the locker.

"Still there, but he's not looking this way. Also, three dock-workers standing near the transit shed."

"They see you?"

"Don't think so. Go up the starboard side."

"Right."

Gary pressed a button on his watch and felt a jolt of adrenaline. It was 9:35, less than an half hour from sailing time. He led the way through the deck gear and past the cargo hatches, now battened down. The towering superstructure loomed ever larger as they approached. Rows of portholes lined each level, some blazing with light, but most were dark. Finally they reached the deckhouse. According to Ann's diagrams, drawn from surveillance videos, the bridge was three decks above. Light streamed through the window in the nearest main deck door. Gary crouched, crept forward, and pressed his ear against the cool metal. Hearing nothing, he chanced a quick peek.

"See anyone?" John whispered.

"No. The passage goes all the way across, with ladders on either end. You ready?"

"Go."

Gary pushed the door open and stepped inside, trading the fresh saltwater tang for the pungent smell of paint, wax, and grime. John came in and shut the door. The distant whine of fans and an electrical hum seemed to come from everywhere. As Gary expected, the steep ladders went both up and down. He moved to the coaming and looked down. The ladders descended deep into the ship in a zigzag path through propped-open hatches. Seeing no one, Gary looked up. It was clear as well.

"Come on," he whispered.

He stepped onto the first tread and felt the ridged surface dig into his foot. He ignored the discomfort and continued up.

Behind him he heard the sound of a door opening. He glanced back and saw John motioning for him to hurry. The sound of heavy shoes carried clearly over the ventilator whine. Gary reached the next deck, turned, and started up the next ladder. Halfway to the next deck, he heard footsteps on the ladder below. He dashed up the remaining steps, rounded the corner, and continued upward. The ladder ended on the bridge with nowhere else to go.

Gary looked all around. In the center stood the surprisingly small ship's wheel, and beside it the engine order telegraph. Arrayed around these were the gyrocompass, magnetic compass, and hooded radar scopes. Various electronic readouts lined the overhead and surrounding consoles and bulkheads. Slow, steady footsteps drifted up from below.

"This way," Gary whispered.

He hurried to the door, pulled it open, and dashed outside. John followed and carefully closed the door. The starboard wing of the bridge extended out about fifteen feet from the towering superstructure, sheltered in front by a waist-high windscreen topped by a handrail. The light coming through the bridge door window illuminated the first few feet, leaving the rest in moonlight and shadow. A large pedestal stood near the end, supporting something covered by a ratty canvas cover.

Gary hurried over the cold, steel deck and ducked behind the pedestal. John squeezed himself in behind. Gary peeked around the tapered metal cone and caught a glimpse of a man as he passed the door, and again when he appeared in a window farther forward. The man walked over to the wheel and picked up what looked like a phone.

"They're about to get under way," Gary said.

"Then we're trapped, unless that guy leaves," John said.

"He's not going to leave."

Gary duckwalked to the aft deck edge, stuck his head between the lifeline chains, and looked down at the main deck, three decks below. Then he put on his night-vision goggles and examined the underside of the bridge wing.

"Hey, there's an angled beam going down to the superstructure and a ladder beside it going down to the deck. Come on."

"Right behind you," John said.

Gary turned, slipped under the chain, and held onto a lifeline support while he felt around with his feet. He hooked his right foot over the beam, then wormed his way around until he could climb on top. He slid down to make room for John. A dull booming sound rose above the soft murmur of the wind. The short, squat shapes of two tugs rounded the *Bhima*'s bow. A door opened, and heavy footsteps clanged across the overhead deck.

Gary slid down the diagonal brace to the deckhouse bulkhead and leaned way out, eyeing the steel rungs that ran from the main deck, past the aft edge of the wing, and up to the top of the bridge. John tapped his shoulder, held out the radio transmitter, and pointed to the beam they were standing on. Gary took the tiny box, uncoiled the wire antenna, then removed the tape and stuck it to the metal. John attached the tiny camera and turned it on.

"Receiving video and GPS data," Dan said in Gary's earphone.

Gary looked at the approaching tugs and decided they were too far away for the crews to see anything in the dark shadows of the deckhouse. He stepped sideways off the support and onto the ladder. The rusty rung felt like sandpaper to his bare feet. He started down, moving as quickly as he dared but stopped when a shaft of light appeared on the deck below. A sailor came out and walked to the lifeline. Gary looked up at John's startled face and pointed. John started climbing. The man on the bridge wing had his back to them, and Gary's eyes never left him until he and John reached the bridge's overhead. Gary followed John onto the roof.

Halfway across, the sheet metal gave, emitting a loud twang. Gary stopped and looked back. He strained to listen, but the only sounds came from the wind and tugs. Then a deep clattering rumble erupted from somewhere deep below, accompanied by a pervasive vibration. The *Bhima's* diesel engines were now running.

John looked back and beckoned. Gary crawled past and kept going until he reached the port side over the bridge wing. He looked down and, seeing no one, stepped down onto the windscreen's rail, then to the deck. He caught a glimpse through the bridge of the man on the opposite wing and saw he was looking down toward the water. Gary ducked down, and John slipped in beside him.

Now came their real business. "We'll start with the deckhouse cabins," Gary said. "I'll take the next deck down; you take the one below that."

"Okay," John said, but he didn't sound very hopeful.

Crouching low, Gary opened the door to the bridge, sprinted for the port-side ladder, and took it down to the next deck. There he waited. He removed his goggles and stowed them in his belt pack.

He pushed back his dry suit hood to clear his radio mike. "Stay in touch."

"Right." John continued down the ladder.

Gary listened, then pushed open the door to the athwartship passageway and stepped through. His watch now said 9:47, less than fifteen minutes to sailing time. He hurried to the first door, pulled a small LCD screen from his pack, unwound the cable with its tiny camera, and stuck it under the door. The image bloomed as the camera adjusted to the darkness. Gary pivoted the camera by swinging the cable. The cabin was empty. He moved on and found the next two vacant as well.

A sliver of light shone under the fourth door. Gary took care slipping the camera through the crack. The image slowly opened up, showing an Asian man resting on his bunk reading a book. Gary pulled the camera out, tiptoed back to the port side, and stepped through the door to the ladder.

"This deck's clear," he whispered.

"Same here," John replied.

"Where are you?"

"I'm on the right side."

"Meet you on the main deck."

Gary hurried down the two ladders, wondering what they would do when they finished with the main deck cabins, assuming they didn't find Peter. A quick peek at his watch showed it was 9:52. They were almost out of time. Gary slowed when he reached the door.

"Oh, no!" John shouted, his voice loud over the earphone.

Gary slid to a stop. "What's wrong?" he whispered.

Instead of a reply he heard rapid speech in a foreign language—Hindi, he guessed. He hesitated.

"What's happening?" Dan asked.

Gary ignored him. He wrapped up the camera unit and stuffed it into his pack, then felt around inside to make sure the pepper spray was handy. He looked up and down the ladder well, wondering which way to go. The main deck passageway was out, that was for sure. Going back up would probably get him trapped, but going down wasn't appealing either. A loud clatter of boots came from somewhere overhead.

Gary whirled around and dashed down to the next deck, taking the steps two at a time. There he found two doors, one leading forward and one aft. A sharp crash sounded above him. He chose the aft door and slipped through. He paused and looked down the long passageway, through the series of oval openings, each with a watertight door, latched open. To his right, a transverse corridor connected to a starboard passageway. He heard muted sounds coming from that direction and thudding of boots behind.

Gary stepped to the side, pulled out his pepper spray, and waited. The crewman hurtled through the door, and Gary hit him full in the face, then jumped back. The man screamed and rubbed his eyes frantically, which only made his agony worse. Gary whirled around and ran all-out for the starboard side, turned aft, and skidded to a stop. Down the passageway, two men were holding John.

Gary rushed to the next bulkhead, then took a quick look through the oval opening. He considered charging John's captors until he saw the pistol one of them was holding. Gary ducked back behind the bulkhead and waited. When he looked again, one crewman was holding his pistol to John's head while the other led the way farther aft. Finally they turned right and disappeared.

Gary raced aft, jumping through each bulkhead opening. Up ahead a jumble of mechanical sounds burst forth, then attenuated with the slamming of a door. He slowed as he reached a transverse passageway, stopped, and listened, but it was hard to hear over his labored breathing. He peeked around the corner. The passageway was deserted. There were two doors in the aft bulkhead but only one forward. He hurried over and placed an ear against the forward door and heard the same sounds as earlier.

Gary turned the locking handle and pulled the door open. A warm, moist breeze blew past, redolent of oil and ozone. The metallic whines and clatters seemed almost physical, and underneath it all lay a dominant thudding sound. He stepped over the coaming, closed the door, and swung the locking handle. A steep ladder led down to a steel-grating catwalk. He started down, and with each step he saw more of the engine room. Machinery of every size and shape lay arrayed two decks below, dominated by the immense diesel engines.

Gary stopped when he reached the catwalk and looked down. An engineer sat, his back to Gary, at an elaborate console set against the forward bulkhead. The man scanned the readouts and occasionally changed a control setting. Gary looked all around but saw no one else. The catwalk extended all the way around the engine room, and at periodic points, ladders led down to the engine room deck plates.

A sudden squealing noise came from somewhere aft, barely audible above the screaming blowers and the heavy clatter of the idling diesels. The engineer looked back but fortunately did not look up. He turned back to his tasks. Gary breathed a sigh of relief and began creeping aft. More and more of the rear bulkhead came into view. Down below, a watertight door appeared and a man stood beside it, one of the men he had seen earlier. But where were John and the other crewman? A ladder led down, but Gary knew he'd never be able to surprise the man. Then he saw that the perimeter catwalk passed directly over the door, and an idea formed in his mind. It did not seem promising, but he couldn't think of anything else.

Praying the man would not look up, Gary hurried along the catwalk and rounded the corner, slowing as he neared the spot over the door. He looked down through the grating at the man and his gun, and his heart sank. There was no way he could jump his opponent without climbing underneath the grating, and that was impossible. But, if the man were to move away. . .

Gary looked all around until his eyes fell on a tin can suspended under a leaking hydraulic line. He carefully undid the wires and hefted the half-full container. The dirty fluid sloshed around and almost spilled over. He scanned the deck below and finally spotted a large tool chest about fifteen feet forward. Gary tossed the can in a high arc, his eyes following it all the way until it hit with a loud, wet clatter.

The man lunged forward, then slid to a stop, and his head started turning, tilting up at the same time. Gary leaped to the safety rail, crouched, and then jumped off, dropping almost straight down. The man's pistol swung around. Gary watched in horror as the gun came to bear. A split second later his feet slammed into the man's shoulders. His opponent stumbled backward and started to fall. Gary landed squarely on top. The man's head slammed hard against steel, and his gun skittered off across the deck plates. Gary rolled off, staggered to his feet, and reached for his pepper spray, but his opponent was out cold.

Gary looked around, wondering if the engineer had heard, but decided it was unlikely amid the engine room din. He turned back to the watertight door, and another thought hit him: Where was the other man? The locking wheel turned, and with a loud screech, the door began to open. Gary grabbed the edge and pulled as hard as he could. The man on the other side gave a startled yelp, tripped over the coaming, and fell. Gary followed him down and with his knees, pinned the man to the deck. A blast of pepper spray finished the job. Gary jumped up and away to avoid the chemical fog. He looked inside the cramped equipment locker and saw John sitting on the deck.

"Man, am I glad to see you," John said.

Gary stepped into the room. "Likewise, guy." He eyed the nylon straps binding John's hands and feet. "We gotta get out of here."

He scanned the shelves, grabbed a pair of diagonal cutting pliers, and snipped the ties. As John stood, Gary noticed that something was missing.

"Where's your radio?" Gary asked.

"Creep with the pistol smashed it. Say, where is he?"

"Unconscious. Come on."

Gary turned, jumped over the coaming, and ran past the still-squirming crewman. Where they would go he had no idea. Then it hit him: John's guards had not reported him as a stowaway, so the *Bhima*'s crew obviously expected them. Gary groaned inwardly. They had fallen for another of Peter's traps.

A blur of motion high up caught Gary's eye. Two crewmen were descending to the upper catwalk. The lead man pointed at the intruders and pulled a gun as he ran toward a ladder leading down.

Gary scanned the engine room's aft bulkhead and saw a door near the starboard side. "Follow me," he shouted.

He raced to the door, threw the locking wheel's handle over, and pulled the door open, revealing a smaller engineering space. He jumped through, and John followed. Gary caught a glimpse of the lead crewman, his pistol raised. Gary slammed the door and swung the handle to engage the sealing rollers. Two shots rang against the steel surface.

"Gimme something to jam this with," he shouted.

John dashed off. The handle moved. Gary forced it back and held it. It jerked again. "Hurry up."

John ran up with a coil of wire cable and threw it down. "Here. You tie it."

Gary moved over, and John seized the handle. Gary let go, grabbed the cable, and bound the locking lever to a pipe.

"Okay," Gary said.

John released the handle. It jerked repeatedly against the bindings, but the cable held.

Gary ran aft through the towering mechanical maze, scanning the overhead as he went. The deck plates began to vibrate, and the insistent thudding sound increased to a bellow.

"What's that?" John asked.

Gary spotted a large rectangular hatch, high overhead. "The engines. The ship's getting under way."

He raced up the ladder, his feet pumping like pistons, until he was inches from the hatch. He glanced down at the deck far below, trying not to think of what would happen if he slipped. He turned back to the hatch. It was secured on the other side but had a circular escape hatch in the center. Gary spun the locking wheel and pushed the hatch open. It clanged against its stop.

"Hey, they've come through another way," John said. "Move it."

Gary looked down and saw the crewmen weaving their way through the room. He turned back and propelled himself through the hole, stood, and reached down. John's head and shoulders appeared. Gary grabbed his hands and pulled. John staggered to the side while Gary slammed the hatch. Gary looked around and saw they were standing in a transverse corridor. He ran down to the starboard passageway and looked both ways. The aft bulkhead was less than fifty feet away, and halfway there, a ladder led upward to a hatch.

He dashed down the passageway and up the steps, opened the hatch, and climbed out into the cool moonlight. The fresh salty breeze seemed to blow away the oily smells of the ship. He turned to help John out, then closed the hatch and turned the wheel.

Only then did he take time to look all around. They were standing about a hundred feet from the fantail, and the *Bhima* was past Trinity Pier and approaching the sound. Gary stepped to the starboard rail. A tug plodded along near the bow to provide assistance in case of emergency. Diesel smoke wafted aft, making Gary's eyes water. Behind him something squealed. He turned and saw the hatch wheel turning.

Gary ran aft through the clutter of deck gear.

"Gary, is that you?" Dan's welcome voice said over the radio.

"Yeah."

"Where are you? I was about to call the police."

"Later."

Gary fell to the deck beside the life raft, reached under the canvas, and pulled out his swim gear. John did the same, including the winch and harness. They ducked behind a locker.

"Leave that," Gary said.

"I can handle it."

Gary heard a sound, looked around the locker, and saw two men coming aft. One tripped over a coiled rope and hit the deck hard.

Gary stood and ran to the fantail, carrying his swim gear. John joined him. Gary sat down and pulled on his swim fins. Then he placed the face mask about his neck so it wouldn't be snatched off when he hit the water. "You ready?" he whispered.

John looked over the rail at the churning black water below. "Oh, man."

Gary stepped over the rail and held on to the chain. John joined him.

"Now!" Gary shouted.

He stepped off into midair and began his long fall. A rush of air whistled past his ears as he flailed with his arms to remain upright, feet together. He plunged beneath the surface, and everything went black. The roiling waters seized him and spun him around until he had no idea which way was up. The water pressed against his chest like a huge vise. He waited. The pressure decreased, and he caught a glimpse of a reflection. He swam hard in that direction. Moments later his head popped above the surface, and he took a deep breath. John surfaced some distance away, spluttering.

"You okay?" Gary asked.

"I'll survive."

Gary treaded water and turned all the way around. The moon looked huge, hovering just above the eastern horizon. They were several hundred feet from where they had entered the water, what seemed like hours ago. They had not found Peter or the crown, but they were alive when they very well could have died. He closed his eyes and silently thanked the One who knew all things, who knew what they were going through and how it would all come out. *With thanksgiving let your requests be made known to God,* he thought. Requests—not demands. Accepting this was not easy, he knew, but it was the right thing to do.

Gary pulled his face mask up and drained the water. "Dan," he said.

"I'm right here. You guys all right?"

"Yeah, we are now. Come pick us up."

"We'll be waiting."

Gary and John began swimming for the shore.

chapter 23

Sully helped John step onto the top of the truck, then gave Gary a hand. "What happened?" he asked.

"Wait until we're out of here," Gary said.

Sully pulled the ladder over, repositioned it, and the three men climbed down. Gary helped him stow the ladder.

"I want you up with Ann," Gary said to him.

"Where are we going?"

"Out of Plymouth. Go west."

"Right, boss." He loped forward, got in on the passenger side, and shut the door.

Gary and John entered through the hatch, carrying their fins and masks. Gary ignored Dan's inquiring look and began the cumbersome process of unzipping and peeling out of his dry suit. The task was onerous and tiring, but finally the suit lay at his feet. He scratched, grateful to be free from the hot, bulky swimwear. He grabbed a towel and dried his hair, then wiped his face. The white terry came away streaked with red.

"Better put something on that," John said. He turned and went forward.

"I'm all right," Gary said.

John opened the first aid kit, got out several alcohol gauze pads, then returned and examined Gary's face.

"Doesn't look too bad," he said. "Hold still."

He wiped the abrasions with a gentle touch, but to Gary it still felt like multiple bee stings. John finished cleaning the wound, dabbed it with dry gauze, then applied a liberal coating of Neosporin. "There, that should do it."

"Thanks," Gary said.

"You're welcome." John packed up the first aid kit, then returned to stow his dry suit.

Gary tucked his away beside John's, then sat in a folding chair and began pulling on his clothes. The truck lurched and swayed as Ann drove them north away from Plymouth Harbor.

"Where's the ship?" Gary asked.

"Clear of the breakwater and heading out to sea," Dan said.

John came and stood behind Dan. "On course for Gibraltar?" he asked.

"So far, but it's only a few miles out." Dan held out his hand to John. "Here."

John cupped his hand, and Dan dropped an earphone radio into it. "How'd you know?" he asked.

"I saw it die." He pointed to a bank of meters.

Gary got up and stood beside John. "Camera show anything?" he asked.

Dan pressed a switch, and a grainy image appeared on a monitor. "Great picture," he said. "Those low-light cameras John got us do a nice job." The *Bhima*'s bow rose and fell with the ocean swells. Whitecaps dotted the restless waves. Dan activated the servo control and used his mouse to swing the camera around for a 180 view from bow to stern on the starboard side. Westward, there wasn't another ship in sight.

"Nice," Gary said. "How long can you maintain contact?"

"Video is pretty much line of sight, say fifty plus nautical miles. It depends on the height of the antenna above the water. The GPS data link will stay with us a bit farther than that, but if Peter's aboard and they're headed for home, we'll lose them in three or four hours."

Gary frowned. "Yeah, that's the big question, all right."

Dan turned and looked at him. "You think he is?"

That was the very question Gary had been wrestling with ever since he and John had escaped. The fact that Peter had laid a trap seemed to suggest he wasn't, and that would mean a rendezvous with the ship somewhere else, or he'd have to find another way out of England.

"No, I don't," Gary said finally.

"But in case he is, why not tip the authorities?" John asked. "The navy could stop the ship and board it."

"No, they wouldn't, not without solid proof."

"Hey, guys," Ann said over the speaker. "I need some directions. We're approaching A38."

"Cut Ann and Sully in," Gary said to Dan.

Dan flipped two switches.

"Sorry," Gary said, "didn't mean to leave you two out of the loop. We need a vantage point near the sea, somewhere west of Plymouth. What do you recommend?"

"Is this to track the *Bhima?*" Ann asked.

"Yes. I want to keep our data link open as long as possible."

"So, Peter *isn't* on board."

"That's what I'm assuming."

"What happened to you guys?"

"Two crewmen jumped John when we were searching the deckhouse cabins and held him in an engine room compartment. I followed and sprang him. They were *definitely* expecting us. Listen, we need a lookout point on the west side of Plymouth. What would be good?"

"Just about anywhere," Ann said. "There are roads all along

the coast. A38 takes us over the river Tamar; then we can drop down at Trerulefoot."

"Okay, let's do that."

Gary settled back and watched the video monitors. Although the low-light cameras provided adequate detail, the pictures were grainy and lacking in color. The sparse traffic lulled him into a state of drowsiness he found hard to fight.

"We're coming up on the Tamar," Ann said.

Gary's eyes flicked to the forward monitor. The truck swept onto the long, high suspension bridge. Off to the side, a tall, narrow bridge ran parallel to the highway span.

"Look at that," Gary said. "I didn't realize the Tamar was this wide."

"It's an estuary," Ann said. "This whole area is divided up by them, so it isn't until Trerulefoot that there's a decent way down to the coast."

"Is that the old highway bridge off to our left?"

"No, that's a railway bridge, built by Brunel sometime in the nineteenth century."

Gary smiled. "That recently?"

Ann laughed. "For England, yes. Remember, C. S. Lewis had his lodgings in New Building at Oxford's Magdalen College—"new" because it was built in 1733."

"When was the college established?"

"Mid-fourteen-hundreds—that's before Columbus sailed the oceans blue."

"That makes the railroad bridge brand new."

"I guess that's one way of looking at it."

Gary's eyes followed the bridge's long arches of steel resting on tall masonry piers, wondering at the difficulties of building such a structure so long ago.

"Did you want any particular point along the coast?"

"No. You choose."

Gary settled back in his chair and followed their progress

westward into Cornwall on the various displays. Dan disconnected the audio feeds to Ann and Sully.

"Why don't you get some rest," Dan said. "The ship's still on course for Gibraltar, so there's nothing doing right now. I'll wake you if something happens."

Gary had to admit that the suggestion was appealing since he was not just tired but bone-weary. But the torment of not knowing where Peter was or what he was doing wouldn't let him rest.

"Maybe later." Gary turned to John. "No reason why you have to stay up."

"I can't sleep either."

Despite his decision, Gary still had to deal with his fatigue. He eyed the coffeepot up forward. The black liquid sloshing around inside seemed almost viscous. "Is that pot fresh?" he asked Dan.

Dan raised his eyebrows. "Compared to the railroad bridge, yes."

"Hmm. Better brew a fresh pot." Gary looked at John. "Want some?"

"If you're buying."

Gary poured out the old coffee into a plastic jug and started a new pot.

"Well, well, well, would you look at that," Dan said, pointing to the GPS overlay map with the *Bhima*'s position plotted. The truck was parked by the side of the coast road, east of Downderry. "The good ship *Bhima* has just altered course and slowed down. They're sailing almost due west now."

Gary glanced at his watch. It said 12:30 A.M., officially Saturday, and the ship had been under way for a little over two hours. "How interesting," he said slowly. He leaned forward in his chair. "Looks like Peter really *did* miss the sailing. Wonder what he'll do now."

"Have the ship pull in at another port?" John asked.

"Not likely. I doubt the captain would chance it, since he has no valid reason. Besides, there aren't that many ports west of here, and none of them large. No, I think Peter will take a boat out to them."

"But the ship's out in the ocean."

"No problem for a large fishing boat. Besides, the seas are moderate right now."

"Where would Peter leave from?"

Gary glanced at the map of England spread out on the work-table. "Good question. I guess we'll have to wait and see where the ship goes." Gary looked closely at the computer-generated map. "Looks like it's about thirty nautical miles offshore."

"Close enough," Dan said.

"What's happening?" Ann asked as she sat up in her sleeping bag.

Gary looked around. "Sorry, didn't mean to wake you. The *Bhima* has turned west. We're thinking Peter will be taking a boat out to meet it."

"Man, is it morning already?" Sully asked.

"Yeah," Dan said. "It's past midnight."

Sully squirmed out of his sleeping bag and stood up. "Sure glad I'm getting union scale for this."

"Quit griping and grab some coffee," Gary said. "We've got work to do."

Sully poured coffee into two mugs and gave one to Ann. "Then let's do it. I wanna see this Peter dude's wheels come off. Like right now."

"Couldn't agree with you more. Any suggestions, remembering they've got guns and we don't?"

"Did I hear you say old Pete's going out in a boat?"

"We think it's likely."

Sully's expression grew serious. "Where's he leaving from?"

"We don't know."

"That makes it kinda hard, dudes. We don't know where he is, and he and his best bud are armed to the teeth."

Ann sipped her coffee. "We may be able to figure out where Peter is when we see where the ship goes. There are lots of fishing villages along the coast, but only a few that are fair sized."

"Wouldn't he pick a small one?" John asked.

Ann examined the computer-generated map. "Maybe, but he's more likely to find a boat for hire in, say, Polperro or Fowey or Mevagissey."

"Maybe we could intercept him by boat," John said.

Gary shook his head. "No. We don't have enough time."

"What if those dudes get fired on?" Sully asked. "You know, shots across the bow."

"Sully, what in the *world* are you talking about?"

"Could John make us some explosives?"

Gary's mind raced ahead with the idea. "Oh, I see where you're going. Make them think the Royal Navy's firing on them." He turned to John. "Could you?"

"To answer your question, yes, since we still have quite a bit of C-4," John said. "What exactly do you have in mind?"

"Could you make some bombs that would go off when they hit the water?"

John thought a moment. "Yeah, no problem. I'll get right on it."

"When do we move out?" Ann asked.

"Now," Gary said. "They're already past Polperro's longitude and still heading west."

"Correction, they're coming around to the north," Dan said.

Gary and Ann looked over his shoulder at the computer map. The large numerals displaying the *Bhima*'s computed course increased rapidly, past 359, finally coming to rest at 002 degrees true. Dan clicked on a button to display the course projection.

"They're headed toward Polperro," Dan said.

Ann and Sully went out the hatch. Moments later the engine started, and the truck lurched into motion. Gary stared at the computer map, watching the slanted numerals that marked the *Bhima*'s position change. The computed speed read five knots.

"They aren't exactly trying for a speed record," Dan said.

"Yeah," Gary said. "Probably waiting on Peter to get his act together."

chapter 24

Hello back there," Sully announced over the speaker. "We're here. Ann says A387 ends up ahead. We take a left on a road called the Coombe, and that goes down to Polperro's harbor."

Gary checked his watch. It was almost one-thirty, and he had been fighting drowsiness for quite a while. "Cut Sully and Ann in," he said to Dan.

Dan flipped the switches.

"Take it easy going down the hill," Gary said. "I don't want to spook Peter if he's down there."

"Roger."

"Oh, he's down there, all right," Dan said. "I've been picking up encrypted radio signals for the last half hour. One line of bearing runs through the ship's position, and the other through Polperro."

Gary watched the forward monitor as the sleeping village gradually came into view, dark, with only a few lighted windows. But the low-light camera provided a surprisingly good picture, aided by the near-full moon. "Must be beautiful during the day."

"It certainly is," Ann said. "Polperro is probably the best of the Cornish fishing villages, and pretty much unspoiled. Most of the streets are too narrow for cars."

"Been here before?"

"Yes, once on a holiday from Cambridge. I had never seen houses like this before. They're all around the harbor and extend up into the hills. You can see how steep it is. They're made of lime-washed stone and have slate roofs. At high tide, the water covers the foundations of the ones along the harbor. They've got every kind of boat in the harbor, from skiffs to sailboats to large fishing boats."

"We're coming to an intersection," Sully said.

"Bear around to the left, then angle right just before we reach the harbor."

"Got it."

Gary leaned back in his chair and turned to Dan. "Any more transmissions?"

"Not recently. The last one was about twenty minutes ago."

"Who initiated it?"

"The shore transmitter. The ship's reply was short, probably an acknowledgement."

"Sounds like Peter is set to go."

"All done with the bombs," John said. He got up from the worktable, walked over, and filled his coffee mug.

Gary turned. "Thanks."

"You're welcome." John smiled, but it seemed strained. "I made you a bombsight too. It's crude, but it should get the job done."

Gary returned the smile. "I'll need all the help I can get."

John pulled out the chair beside Gary and sat down. "You ready for me to brief you?" he asked.

"Let's wait. Maybe I won't have to go." Gary's tone was light, but he believed it was inevitable. It was just a matter of when.

"There's the harbor," Sully said over the speaker.

Gary looked up at the monitor. "Slow down."

"Yes, boss."

The brakes squealed a little. Gary watched as more and more of the compact waterfront came into view. Several seconds later he said, "Stop here."

The truck came to a halt on an incline. Below them on the right, a stone quay formed a narrow V with a long row of multi-story houses on the opposite shore, many jammed together with no space in between.

Gary stood up and turned to John. "Ready for a little reconnoitering?"

"I'll grab the gear," John said.

"Well, well, look at that," Dan said.

"What?" Gary asked.

"The ship's turning."

Gary looked down at the computer map. "So it is. About twenty nautical miles out, and turning to port."

"Maybe they're heading for home after all," John said. He handed Gary a can of pepper spray.

Gary slipped it into his pocket. "We should be so lucky. They probably don't want to come any closer to British waters."

Gary put in his earphone radio and turned it on. He went to the hatch, opened it, and stepped out into the gentle sea breeze. It was cool and seemed almost cold after the snug warmth inside the truck. John came out and closed the hatch. They took the steep path leading down to the quay. The moon was high overhead, which removed the cloak of darkness except for occasional deep shadows.

"Over there," Gary whispered. He ducked into the narrow gap between two buildings. "Not any way we can hide in all this light."

John joined him. "Let's hope they're not looking for us. Here." He handed Gary a pair of night-vision binoculars.

Gary eased forward, sticking close to the stone wall, and raised the binoculars. The magnified green image danced before his eyes. Dozens of boats packed the confined harbor, many tied up at the quay but others moored out in the middle or near the houses that lined the far shore. The tide was in, he noted, since the water was well up on the foundations. The wind kicked up cat's-paws on the calm water. He lowered the binoculars, turned his head, and listened.

"You hear anything?" Gary asked.

"Yeah, sounds like an engine. Here." John handed him an infrared monocular.

Gary panned it slowly around the harbor, starting with the eastern shore. The only heat sources on that side came from the occasional light. He continued on around the cove and down the quay. A large fishing boat swept into view, and a large heat plume rose from its rear deck. Gary examined the boat and the adjoining quay but didn't see anyone.

"It's one of the boats on the quay," he said.

"Which one?"

Gary lowered the monocular and pointed. "It's that large, light-colored one."

"Anyone on board?"

"Not out on deck." He raised the night-vision binoculars and trained them. "Don't see—wait a minute. Yes, someone *is* moving around in the cabin."

"Only one?"

"That's all I see." Gary took the binoculars away. "That boat is certainly large enough for the open ocean."

"Could be a night fisherman."

"Maybe, but if so, he's going out by himself. There aren't any other boats warming up."

The man appeared on deck, took in the aft mooring line, then ran forward and loosed the bowline. He returned to the cabin, and the boat backed away from the quay.

Gary sprang out into the open and ran a few steps to get a better view. The boat angled across the harbor.

Gary pointed. "He's heading for a house on the other side. Come on."

Gary raced up the steep hill and around behind the truck. John threw open the hatch and jumped inside. Gary took one final look across the harbor. The boat was slowing down as it approached a light-colored house with dormer windows. Gary clambered inside the truck and shut the hatch.

"Cut Ann and Sully in," he said to Dan.

"Already have," Dan replied.

"I think Peter and Ian are being picked up at a house on the harbor. Is there a way over there?"

"Yes, there's a road that runs along behind," Ann replied.

"Give Sully directions. We *have* to cut them off."

"Roger."

The truck lurched forward in a tight turn, then slid to a stop inches from a house. The tires spun as the truck swerved backward, then roared back up the hill.

"Turn right here," Ann's voice shouted over the speaker.

Gary held on. The truck leaned over to the left, and for a moment he thought they would spin out, but Sully managed to recover.

"How far down?" Ann asked.

Gary looked at the forward monitor. Dan angled the camera more to the right. Gary felt panic rising inside. The houses looked so much alike, and most of them were light-colored.

"I'm not sure," he said finally. "Say two hundred feet."

A few seconds later Sully slammed on the brakes, making no attempt at stealth. Gary winced at all the noise they were making.

"Let's go," he said to John.

Gary led the way outside and down the narrow path between two houses. A cool breeze carried a saltwater tang with a hint of marine rot. Up ahead, moonlight glinted off a thin sliver of water. Gary pulled out the pepper spray can as they neared the end. He slid on the slick paving stones and nearly toppled into the water below. John snatched the back of his shirt and pulled him back. Gary eased forward and peered around the corner. There, three houses down, sat the boat, standing off about twenty feet. Two silhouetted figures crawled over the side from a rowboat and disappeared into the cabin.

"We're too late," Gary whispered.

The engine's sullen chugging picked up. The fishing boat backed into deeper water, turned, and headed for the rocky entrance to the harbor. Its wake spread out, rocking the nearby boats.

Gary ran back to the truck with John right behind him. When he turned the corner, he looked up. Several upstairs windows were lit in the nearest house. He opened the hatch and climbed inside. John followed.

"Sully, get us out of here," Gary said.

"Where?"

"Up in the hills. Ann will guide you."

"Yes, boss."

"What happened?" Dan asked.

"We were too late," Gary said. "Peter and Ian were already getting into the boat."

"You sure it was them?"

"I couldn't see their faces, but it has to be. And we have to assume they've got the crown."

Gary watched the forward monitor. The truck leaned alarmingly as Sully followed the curving road. They continued on the Coombe, past A387, and up the steep hill.

"Where are we going?" Sully asked.

"Look for someplace quiet—and hurry."

"Roger."

The truck roared up the hill. What Gary had hoped to avoid was now thrust upon him, since the only possible way to stop Peter was to turn back the *Bhima*. To succeed, he had to fly twenty miles out to sea, locate the ship, then convince the captain he was being shelled by a warship. He knew it wouldn't be easy but was determined to make it work. He removed his clothes and began pulling on his dry suit.

"Are you serious about this?" Dan asked.

"You bet I am," Gary said. "Where is the ship?"

"Twenty miles out, still turning circles."

"Okay, let's lay this thing out. We've got a narrow window here, and it's getting narrower every second."

"Any idea how fast the boat is?" John asked.

"As a guess, say, ten to fifteen knots."

"So, worst case, you have a little over an hour to intercept the ship."

"Yeah, maybe a bit more. I'd be surprised if that boat can do fifteen knots on the open sea."

John's serious expression became even more strained. "I need to brief you on the bombs." He brought one out and set it on the worktable beside Dan. The truck lurched. The round object rolled off and bounced across the floor.

Dan started to get up. "Hey, watch that."

John picked it up. "Don't worry. It won't go off accidentally."

Dan sat back down, but his eyes never left the bomb. "Sounds like famous last words to me."

Gary eyed the gray object.

"Now pay attention," John said. "Each bomb is a sphere of C-4 encased in a hard plastic shell with the detonator embedded in the center and wires leading out to this." He pointed to an attached circuit board. "This is the firing circuit. It has two exposed leads that will trigger the charge when immersed in salt water. See this tape?"

"Yeah."

"It covers the leads. Remember to pull it off before you drop the bomb."

"What about water vapor?" Gary asked. "I might have to fly through clouds."

"Freshwater doesn't have enough conductivity." John paused, his expression very serious. "The tape is there as a precaution. Look, this stuff is dangerous. I can't change that, but it's as safe as I can make it. Now, be careful, okay?"

"Don't worry, I will." Gary took the bomb from John's hand. "What's this thing?" he asked, pointing to what looked like a tiny parasol.

"That's the drogue. It keeps the bomb upright for water entry without slowing it much."

"How many did you make?"

"Ten."

"Well, that should certainly be enough. What about any left over?"

"They're safe to bring back. Now, here's your bombsight." He held out a thin board with a movable wooden arm.

"You can't be serious," Gary said as he eyed the device suspiciously.

John managed a nervous grin. "What do you expect on short notice? Listen, pilots did quite well with sights like this during the First World War."

"Come on, that was a long time ago."

"True, but the principle is still sound. It will do the job if you use it right."

Gary moved the wooden arm. "Okay, how does this contraption work?"

"Simple. First comes the bomb tray." John held up a plywood board with clamps on either end. "It attaches to the control bar down tubes just under your chest, and these bungee cords hold the bombs in place. The bombsight bolts onto the tray and extends forward. You move the sight to correspond with your altitude. I marked it in units of twenty-five hundred feet up to ten thousand. It assumes the ship's speed is five knots and an approach from directly ahead or behind. There are two sets of scales, clearly marked. Once your altitude and approach direction are set, you aim through the two eyebolts and drop when they're centered on your target."

"That's it?"

"Almost, and don't worry. I'll mount everything for you. The only other thing you have to do is make sure the bombsight is level. See these two bubble gauges?"

"Yeah."

"They're for leveling the sight, fore and aft and side to side. Once you get to cruising altitude, make sure the control bar is set for straight and level flight; then use these two thumbscrews to center each bubble."

"But what if I have to maneuver?"

"Try to get lined up ahead of time. Just make sure the control bar is centered when you aim." John forced a laugh. "Hey, no problem for an experienced aviator like you."

"Yeah, right." Gary paused. "You sure this is gonna work?"

John smiled. "Assuming my trig isn't too rusty, yes."

"Don't forget the wind," Dan said.

"Oh, yes, thanks," John said. "Dan will radio you the wind velocity and direction based on your true course and speed and what he receives from your GPS transponder."

"How do I apply that?"

"That you have to figure out for yourself."

"What effect will the wind have on the bombs?"

"Some, but not a lot, since the drogue doesn't slow the bomb all that much."

Gary turned to Dan. "What's the weather forecast?"

"There's a front moving in," Dan said. "Clouds will start rolling in about three or so, with rain around midday."

"Shouldn't affect me, then."

"When are you planning to attack?"

"Shortly before Peter and Ian get there."

"Let's see, if the boat is doing ten knots, that will make it around four in the morning. Any chance they could see you?"

Gary shook his head. "Almost impossible. The clouds should cover the moon, and it'll be quite dark overhead with dawn over an hour away."

"They've probably got night-vision devices."

"I'm sure they do, but the hang glider is painted light gray, so even at twenty-five hundred feet, it would be almost impossible to see. And with that fancy muffler, the engine makes almost no sound at all."

"Hey, guys, we're here," Sully said.

The truck leaned over in a turn, then came to an abrupt stop.

"Hey, Sully, Ann, come on back here," Gary said.

"Be right there."

Gary opened the hatch, and Sully and Ann climbed inside.

"Gotta make this quick," Gary said. "If this works, Peter and Ian will be forced to return, and we'll have to stop them."

"How?" John asked.

"Ambush. If we can get close enough, pepper spray will bring them down."

"You and John?" Dan asked.

"Yes."

"Didn't we have a tranquilizer dart gun for the Fort Knox job?" Ann asked.

Gary's mind raced ahead. "Yes, we did, in case we had trouble with guard dogs." He turned to John. "Did we bring it?"

"Yeah, I think so," John said. "Let me check." He hurried to the shelves and began digging through the equipment. "Aha," he said, grabbing a long nylon bag. He unzipped it and pulled out an air rifle, nightscope, and a bag containing the darts and tranquilizer vials.

Gary looked at Ann. "Thanks, that may come in handy."

She smiled. "You're welcome."

Gary took the gun from John and looked it over. "Listen up," he said. "If the ambush works, it'll go down fast, so I want every advantage." His eyes turned to Ann. "You're the only available shooter. Can you handle the dart gun?"

"I don't know; I've never handled guns." Her expression grew determined. "But I'll do my best."

Gary grinned. "That's what I want to hear."

"I'll check her out on it," John said.

"Good," Gary said. "The dart shooter will be off to the side. If we can knock one of them out, it'll make our job a whole lot easier." He looked all around. "But first, we've got to keep Peter from reaching that freighter." He looked at Sully. "How about some help with the hang glider?"

Sully jumped up. "Sure thing, boss."

John gathered up the bombsight parts and the sack containing the bombs. Sully hurried over to where the hang glider was stowed. Gary grabbed one end of the bundle, and Sully pulled the other end out. Ann moved aside to let them by. Gary stepped down from the truck and shuffled along until Sully was out.

"Where's the launch spot?" Gary asked.

"Straight ahead," Sully said. "We're on a lane leading up to some houses. You can launch on the road we came up."

Gary walked a few more feet and set the bundle down. He pulled out the Dacron wing and all the tubes and rigging and began the assembly. Although he hurried, he still checked each bolt and cable carefully since his life depended on it. Finally he stood up.

"Get strapped in," John said. "I'll take care of the rest."

Gary struggled into his harness, then slipped under the gilder, attached the straps, and stood up. John attached the tray and the bombsight, then pointed to the bombs nestled under the restraining bungee cords.

"Remember to pull the tape," he said.

"I will."

Gary slipped on his night-vision goggles. "I guess I'm ready."

He trundled down to the end of the lane with the hang glider heavy on his shoulders. There wasn't a light in sight when he reached the road. Gary set the choke, pressed the starter button, then let it go. A muffled *thrum* came from the propeller. He waited a few moments, then turned off the choke. A gentle vibration reassured him that the engine was running. He checked all the instruments. Everything was working, he was relieved to note, including the GPS.

Gary pushed the throttle wide open and began running down the steep road. A few steps later the billowing wing lifted him into the air. The hillside continued to fall away, revealing rows of houses paralleling the coast. Up ahead, Polperro Harbor formed a modest indentation, full of boats that reminded Gary of sleeping birds on a pond. He left the throttle at full power and decreased his rate of climb. He had plenty of time to reach twenty-five hundred feet, his planned attack altitude. Until he located the boat, he needed all the speed the glider could muster.

"Star Chamber, this is Gooney Bird One," Gary said. "Radio check."

"Gooney Bird One, this is Star Chamber. Read you five-by-five. Be advised we are moving to a new location on the ridgeline."

"Roger, Star Chamber. Gooney Bird One out."

Polperro crept past off to the left. Gary looked down at the houses arced around the harbor but didn't see any lights. Apparently, the earlier commotion was now forgotten. Gary felt a pang a few moments later as he crossed the coast.

"Star Chamber, Gooney Bird One is feet wet."

"Roger, Gooney Bird One."

The radar altimeter now read five hundred fifty feet, and it was slowly but steadily increasing. He looked at the magnetic compass. The hairline rested on 193 degrees, which was 6 degrees off. He was supposed to head due south, 180 degrees plus 7 degrees of magnetic variation, giving a magnetic course of 187 degrees. Once he reached cruising altitude, he had to hold that course so Dan could measure the wind speed and direction. The compass wheel turned slowly until it read 187 degrees.

Gary glanced at his watch. The digital readout said 02:51:33. The hang glider hummed along over the empty seas, leaving the land behind. The light dimmed suddenly. He looked up and saw heavy clouds covering the moon. Thirty minutes later he reached his cruising altitude of twenty-five hundred below feet.

An hour into the flight, Gary finally spotted a V-shaped wake dead ahead. He looked down and watched as the distance dwindled. Whitecaps dotted the restless waves. He suspected the boat's occupants were receiving a pounding. He smiled at the thought. His flight, so far, had been as smooth as glass.

"Star Chamber, this is Gooney Bird One. Fishing boat is directly below."

"Roger, Gooney Bird One. You ready for wind calculation?"

"Roger, Star Chamber. My heading is 187 degrees magnetic."

"Roger. Stand by."

"Gooney Bird One standing by."

Gary wondered what the answer would be. He knew the forecast said south-southwest winds at fifteen to twenty knots, which would make reaching the *Bhima* in time a chore. But catching up with the boat this soon suggested the wind had moderated. A few minutes later Dan called back.

"Good news, Gooney Bird One, the wind has dropped. It's from 172 degrees at five knots. Looks like smooth sailing."

Gary relaxed a little. The weather was cooperating, and he knew who was in charge of that. Maybe things were not as bad as they seemed. Then he thought about all he had to do. If everything went according to plan, and he *did* manage to spoil the pickup, what then? Peter and Ian would *still* be on the loose, and they would have to catch them—somehow. The wind in his face seemed to blow the momentary encouragement away.

"Gooney Bird One, do you copy?"

"Roger, Star Chamber. I copy 172 degrees at five knots. What is the ship's position?"

"Ship is circling at 49 degrees, 58.415 minutes north, 4 degrees, 30.897 minutes west. Do you require a vector?"

"Negative, Star Chamber. GPS is working like a champ, much to my surprise. Give my regards to our shade-tree mechanic."

"I heard that," John's unmistakable voice said.

"Star Chamber, this is Gooney Bird One. Please maintain correct radio procedure."

"Roger, Gooney Bird One."

"Thanks, Brother John. Gooney Bird One out."

As Gary expected, the wind had carried him to the west a little, but it wasn't all that bad, less than a mile. He altered course to 170 degrees. According to his GPS readout, he was about eight nautical miles from the ship. He pulled the throttle back to cruising power. There was no point in rushing things since he would get there well before the boat, and he didn't want to give Peter any time to think about their new crisis. A few minutes later the GPS longitude reading matched that of the *Bhima*, and Gary changed course to 186.

A little over ten minutes later, Gary spotted a creamy, green streak in the water below. His eyes followed it up to the stern of a ship. The position matched. It had to be the Indian freighter.

"This is Gooney Bird One; I have the ship in sight."

"Roger, Gooney Bird One. Confirm, that is the target. Look for a turn to the north in about a minute."

Gary punched a button on his watch to start the timer. A little later the ship started a ponderous turn to starboard. Gary stopped the timer. *Fifty-seven seconds,* he thought. *Not bad.*

He intercepted less than a minute later. The ship seemed like a toy from nearly a half-mile up. Gary turned and began a wide orbit. As time dragged on, he changed his pattern to a long oval that took him several miles to the north so he could watch for the boat. The contact seemed hours in coming, but finally he caught sight of a green V approaching.

"This is Gooney Bird One; the boat is in sight. Estimated

range to the ship is three miles."

"Roger, Gooney Bird One. We're picking up encrypted radio signals on your line of bearing."

"Roger that. Let's see what the Royal Navy has to say about it. Gooney Bird One out."

"Roger and good luck."

Dan's last words stuck in Gary's mind for a moment. He appreciated the sentiment, but what he *really* needed was help—not luck. Gary offered up a silent prayer for success, but even as the silent amen went up, he understood the Lord could very well say no; and if that happened, he had to be prepared to accept it.

The boat continued its slow approach. Gary looked down at the bombsight and remembered the leveling task. He examined the two spirit bubbles and found both were nearly level. He turned first one thumbscrew and then the other until the bubbles were perfectly centered.

Gary brought the hang glider around in a broad right turn, flew north for thirty seconds, then came around to a course of 187 degrees, lining up a little to the left of the ship's course to allow for the wind. He checked the altitude marking on the movable sight and verified it was set for a head-on approach at twenty-five hundred feet. He glanced back at the fishing boat. It was closer now, and the freighter was heading right at it with a combined closure rate of around fifteen knots. Time was fast slipping away.

Gary picked up the first bomb and removed the protective tape. It was now live, and he held onto it tightly. He made a slight course correction to line up with the *Bhima* and sighted through the eyebolts. He checked the bubbles and saw they were centered. He returned to the constricted view through the bombsight. The circles crossed the freighter's bow. Gary waited a few seconds, then dropped the bomb. He looked down immediately but only caught a fleeting glimpse of the tiny drogue.

"This is Gooney Bird One; bomb one is away."

"Roger that."

Gary continued to look down, as he wondered how long it would take the sphere and drogue to fall twenty-five hundred feet. John would know, he realized, probably down to a tenth of a second. He kept his eyes glued on the target. The seconds ticked on, and he began to wonder if the bomb was a dud. Then a towering gout of water erupted far below. The first "shot" landed about one hundred feet from the stern on the starboard side. A few seconds later the sound reached him, surprisingly loud.

Gary quickly changed the bombsight for an approach from astern, then waited impatiently for the range to lengthen. Finally he came around in a tight turn and rolled out on 7 degrees. Again he had to make several corrections to line up. He wanted this "shot" near the bow and on the port side to simulate a straddle.

"This is Star Chamber. I'm receiving encrypted signals from two sources. I think you've rattled their cages."

"Roger, Star Chamber. Kinda busy right now. Gooney Bird One out."

Gary peered into the distance. The fishing boat was still coming on, and the freighter showed no sign of changing course. That had to change, and soon. He pulled the tape off the second bomb and squinted through the bombsight. He held his breath as the hang glider crept up on the target below. The sight crossed the bow. Gary dropped the bomb and began counting off the seconds. Water shot into the air off the ship's bow, and a little to port. The delayed sound was just as convincing as the first bomb. Still the freighter plodded along.

Gary decided on a three-"shot" salvo. When his turning point came, he cranked the hang glider into a tight turn and rolled out on his third pass. He tore the tape off the next three bombs and picked up the first one. This time he aimed even closer to the ship. The bombsight crossed the aiming point. Gary dropped the bomb he was holding, then quickly dumped the other two. The first bomb exploded about twenty feet off the starboard bow. The second hit right next to the hull just forward of the bridge. Water shot over the rail and doused the bridge wing. The third bomb erupted even with the bridge, also very close.

Gary kept watching as he came around in a gentle right turn. He knew the simulated shellfire had been quite realistic, and if this did not turn the freighter around, nothing would. Still the ship plodded along. He looked beyond it to the approaching fishing boat, still over a mile away and steady on course. Then the *Bhima* began a ponderous turn to port. Gary watched, wondering if this were only to facilitate the rendezvous with Peter and Ian, but the ship's turn continued. Foam churned at the stern, evidence that the freighter was increasing speed.

"Star Chamber, this is Gooney Bird One. Target is turning back."

"Roger, Gooney Bird One. I confirm. Target changing course, speed increasing. Still receiving encrypted signals."

"Roger, Star Chamber."

"Gooney Bird One, any further reports? Over."

Gary knew Dan was asking about the fishing boat, which was still on its original course. What did that mean? Was the *Bhima* going to return? The fishing boat plowed on through the surging seas, riding up one wave only to plunge into the following trough. It looked peaceful at twenty-five hundred feet, but Gary knew those below were having a hard time of it. The boat continued on for a few more moments, then came about and settled on a northern heading.

"Small fry is heading for home," Gary said.

"Roger, Gooney Bird One."

"Will follow. Gooney Bird One out."

Gary looked at his watch and saw it was 4:05. Dawn was still over an hour away, and although it was still quite dark in the east, he decided to start climbing to seventy-five hundred for his return trip. He didn't think his light-colored craft could be seen, but it would be even less likely higher up. He nudged the control bar forward and went to full throttle. The bold numerals on the radar altimeter began slowly increasing. The earlier excitement gave way to the boredom of following the boat, which was still plodding along at ten knots. The only variety came in periodically circling around to keep from getting too far ahead. Gary jumped a few minutes later at the sound of Dan's voice in his ear.

"Gooney Bird One, this is Star Chamber. Be advised we have lost all telemetry from the ship."

That was not good news, but Gary had been expecting it. He looked down at the fishing boat from a vantage point of just over thirty-one hundred feet. The boat's heading had not varied since turning back.

"Roger, Star Chamber."

Gary was still worrying over Peter's next move when he noticed an odd sensation. There was less wind on his face, but he hadn't moved the control bar. Then he noticed the propeller's incessant thrumming was missing, along with the ever-present vibration. The engine had quit.

chapter 25

Gary's hang glider mushed along and almost stalled before he remembered to pull the control bar back. He then settled into a sedate glide at a little over eleven knots, the minimum sink speed. At that airspeed, the glider had a glide ratio of seven-to-one, seven feet forward for every foot down. Theoretically. Although his actual speed was over sixteen knots, thanks to a five-knot tailwind, this wasn't enough to enable him to reach the shore. According to his rough calculations, land was almost nine nautical miles away, and he was less than thirty-one hundred feet above the restless Atlantic waves.

He did the math again and came up with the same answer. He could fly a little over five nautical miles, but this left him almost four miles short. Not good. Although he could see the shore in the distance, he could not reach it.

"Star Chamber, I've got a problem."

Dan's reply was slightly delayed. "What's wrong?"

"My engine just quit."

"Any idea why?" John's anxious voice was unmistakable.

"Negative. It was running like a champ, then packed it in. No warning whatsoever."

"Did you run out of gas?"

Gary turned his head and examined the engine. It looked okay. The gas line was attached to the carburetor, and he saw no signs of leaking. He reached back, unscrewed the gas cap, and let it fall to the side on its chain. He reached inside the tank and felt liquid. The smell of gasoline sullied the pure ocean air. He replaced the cap.

"Negative," Gary said. "The tank's got plenty."

The radio remained silent.

"Star Chamber, do you copy?"

"We copy," John replied. "Try this: Turn the ignition switch on and off several times; then crank the engine."

"Roger."

Gary flicked the switch repeatedly; then turned it on. He looked back and pressed the starter button. The starter whined, and the propeller became a blur. He released the button, and the propeller coasted to a stop.

"That didn't do it," he said.

"There's only one other thing I can think of," John said. "The ignition switch might be shot. Take your knife and cut and strip the wires. Then twist them together and try again."

"Roger."

Gary pulled out his pocketknife, opened a blade, and cut the wires where they entered the switch. Then he began working on the insulation, mangling it and cutting some of the wire strands. He twisted the remaining wires together, looked back, and pressed the starter. Again the propeller spun up, then coasted to a stop.

"Negative, Star Chamber. What's *wrong* with this thing?"

"Hard to say. It's probably an ignition problem, or something's stopped the gas flow. Either way, it's not something you can fix." John paused. "Can you glide to shore?"

"Wait one."

Gary already knew the answer, but he forced himself to go through the calculations again. Perhaps he had made a mistake, but even as he held out a faint hope, he felt sure the answer would be the same. He looked at his watch again. It was 4:17. He looked down at the radar altimeter. It read nineteen hundred sixty-two feet. He had lost a third of his altitude while trying to restart the engine. He checked his current position on the GPS readout. He finished the math and found there was no change. He would have to ditch, four nautical miles off the rocky Cornish coast.

"No change. The closest I can come is four miles."

"We'll get a boat," John said.

"Negative."

"We've got no choice." The radio's tiny earphone hid none of John's intensity.

"I said negative. There's no time. I'll be down in twelve minutes."

"All the more reason to get started."

"There's too much chance you'll get caught. Then where would we be? Look, I'm wearing a dry suit, and I'm a good swimmer."

"Can you swim four miles?"

"I think so."

"You *think* so. Have you ever done it? And what about the currents?"

"I can rent a boat without getting caught," Ann added.

"I say again, negative. Gooney Bird One out."

Gary looked down. The water was definitely closer now, seventeen hundred eighty-one feet away according to the radar altimeter. The fishing boat lagged behind, cutting its green V in the water, pointing toward the shore that Gary would never reach, unless something happened. He felt an inner prodding, but in his gloom, he ignored it. Instead he concentrated on maintaining optimum airspeed. But the still, quiet urging continued, and he realized that John and Ann were undoubtedly praying.

He knew he should be praying as well, but how could he? For a brief moment his thoughts burned hot with accusations against the One who made him. Then, realizing his error, the heat turned to shame, and he did pray. When he finished, he felt better, but he still didn't believe he would reach shore.

Gary looked back at the engine. Should he give it another try? He pressed the starter button, and the propeller whirled. He held the button, giving the engine every chance to start; but when he let go, the propeller spun down and stopped. *So much for that*, he thought.

He turned back and scanned his instruments. His course and speed were almost dead-on. He looked back. He was continuing to draw ahead of the boat, but it would catch up and pass him once he ditched. He wondered absently if the skipper would see this, and what he would do if he did. Thoughts of rescue flitted through his mind until reality came crashing in. He must at all costs avoid Peter and Ian.

Gary stared at his instruments. The radar altimeter continued to count down, slowly but relentlessly, finally dropping below one thousand feet, the down-counting numerals bringing him ever closer to ditching. He glanced at the GPS readout, then looked more closely. The position it gave seemed off.

"Gooney Bird One, this is Star Chamber," Dan said in his ear, jarring him out of his morbid reverie.

"Go ahead, Star Chamber."

"Is your airspeed still eleven knots?"

"Yeah, why?"

"Have you checked your position lately?"

"Just did, but it doesn't look right."

"Remember how the forecast wind was twenty-five knots from the south-southwest?"

Gary felt a glimmer of hope. "Yeah. I was worried I wouldn't reach the ship in time, but then it turned out the wind was only five knots."

"Correct. Well, it's kicked back up to twenty-five knots again. You're actually doing thirty-six knots, and have been for about six minutes. I didn't call earlier because I wanted to be sure."

"Star Chamber, wait one."

Gary checked and found he really *was* going that fast, thanks to the wind. Something arrested his thoughts. No, it was thanks to God answering prayers. Earlier, the wind had dropped when needed. Now that the mysterious twenty knots was back, how would that affect things? He checked his watch. It was now 4:23. According to the GPS, he was now 3.35 nautical miles from land, but would his present altitude carry him that far? He did the calculation twice to be sure.

"This is Gooney Bird One," Gary said. "Providing the wind holds, I should make it with a third of a mile to spare."

"Roger, Gooney Bird One. Where do you plan on landing?"

That, Gary decided, was a good question. "Someplace along the shore. I can't make it to the launch point."

"Gooney Bird One, recommend Colors Cove," Ann said. "It's a little to the west of Polperro. Stand by for the coordinates."

"Gooney Bird One, standing by."

A few moments later Ann said, "Colors Cove is at 50 degrees, 19.467 minutes north, and 4 degrees, 32.75 minutes west. We will meet you there."

"Roger that. Gooney Bird One out."

Actually, the only coordinate Gary really needed was the longitude, since it would be obvious when he reached the correct latitude. He banked slightly to the left to intercept the correct heading. The GPS latitude readout slowly counted up toward safety.

Gary looked back. The fishing boat was still plowing along through the seas, quite far back by now. Then he noticed something odd: The boat was on his heading, and unless it changed course, Peter and Ian would also land at Colors Cove.

"Star Chamber, this is Gooney Bird One. The boat is making

for the cove. Recommend you look for a car on the way."

"Roger, Gooney Bird One."

Gary turned back to his instruments. The GPS longitude ticked over to 4 degrees, 32.751 minutes west. He corrected to the right. The hang glider continued to lose altitude, bringing the wave-tossed Atlantic ever closer, but his glide path looked promising, unless something happened.

The rocky coast loomed ever closer in Gary's night-vision goggles. His projected glide slope ended above the crashing breakers, but just barely. He looked back. The boat was miles behind and still heading for the cove. Doing a rough estimate, he figured it would take Peter and Ian at least a half hour to reach shore.

The surging waves seemed almost at Gary's feet. He turned his head to the side and heard the sound of waves crashing against the rocks. The glide slope now ended where rock and surf met as his precious altitude bled away. The angry ocean seemed to reach upward to snatch him out of the air. Now it appeared his earlier estimate had been a little optimistic. Finally the radar altimeter dropped to one hundred feet, and with almost a mile to go, he could only fly about half that distance, even with a twenty-five-knot tailwind. The altitude dropped to fifty feet and kept going.

Gary's mind raced as he reviewed his ditching procedure, tasks he had to perform perfectly or risk being drowned, wrapped up in the hang glider's rigging. He looked back to locate all his harness connectors, then faced forward to wait for the inevitable. The glider stopped descending as it entered ground effect, but Gary knew it would not be enough. It might put off the inevitable for a few seconds, but no more. Then he felt the solid jolt of a rising air current, followed by another even harder, and the altimeter now read three hundred feet.

Gary swallowed hard. "Star Chamber, I'm almost down, guys."

"John and Sully are on their way," Dan said. "Over."

"Roger that. Gooney Bird One out."

A movement above the shore caught his eye. Two figures scampered into the open and traced a zigzag path between the rocks. Gary hoped it was John and Sully and not part of Peter's crew, but it was impossible to tell with the night-vision goggles.

The hang glider swept ashore at thirty-six knots still fifty feet in the air but coming down fast. The jagged rocks streaked past in a blur. Gary knew he risked injury if he landed downwind but wasn't sure he could do anything about it. Scant feet above the rocks, he came around in a tight right turn into the wind. The brisk wind brought the glider to a stop, then began pushing it backward. Gary pulled the control bar back and dove for the ground. He hit hard and braced his legs, but a gust lifted the glider and threw him over on his side. He collapsed in a heap of aluminum tubing and Dacron. The sound of boots on rocks carried faintly over the crashing surf and the wind's incessant moaning.

"Hey, dude," came Sully's familiar voice. "Awesome landing."

Gary unsnapped his harness and struggled out from under the flapping wing. "Hey. Any landing you can walk away from is a good landing."

"I sure am glad to see you," John said. "Ann and I were praying."

"Yeah, I know. Thanks." Gary turned and looked out to sea, but the boat was hidden among the tossing waves. He knelt down and started disassembling the hang glider. "Did you find Peter's car?"

John squatted down and started helping Gary. "Didn't see it on the way here, but there are lots of places he could have hidden it."

"Sully, sing out if you spot the boat."

"You know I will."

John loosened a turnbuckle and unhooked a cable. "How far away are they?" he asked.

"Between seven and eight miles. They're doing around ten knots." He glanced at his watch. "It's 4:35. They'll probably make landfall around 5:15." He looked around. There was no sign of dawn through the heavy overcast. "We'd better get a move on."

John gathered up the hang glider's engine and stood up. "Think they can see us?"

"Not yet."

Sully took some of the tubing. Gary wrapped the Dacron wing around the remaining parts and followed John off the beach.

"Is the ambush still on?" John asked.

"Yes."

"What about calling the police?"

"No. Too much can go wrong. Assuming they could get here in time, which I doubt, what do we tell them—'Uh, hi. We're not the dudes what pinched the crown, but I can tell you who did'? Meanwhile, Peter and Ian sneak out the back way while the country constables haul us off and call MI5. Listen. We *have* to catch Peter with the crown, or it's 'no go.' Now we've got work to do."

Sully led the way through a gap in a dense copse of trees and heavy bushes and turned left. In a clearing up ahead, Gary saw the truck, hidden from the beach by a line of trees. He skirted a tree and crossed deep tire tracks. Sully loped to the hatch and opened it. Ann stood and looked out at them, obviously relieved.

"Thank God, you're safe," she said.

Sully jumped through the hatch.

Gary stepped up and hauled the hang glider parts inside. He moved forward and laid them on the floor.

John followed and set the engine down.

Dan turned from one of the monitors. "Welcome back," he said. "You had us worried." His words were subdued, but Gary knew he meant it.

Gary forced a grin. He started to say something when he

saw the monitor above Dan's head showing the ocean from the low-light camera mounted on the telescoping mast. The image of a fishing boat jiggled because of the strong wind. "Well, there they are," Gary said.

"We'd better get ready," John said. "How do you want to do this?"

"Dan, how about a quick scan of the beach," Gary said.

Gary grabbed the joystick, tilted the camera down, and panned it around the cove, then back along the rocky path leading up to the tree line. Dan zoomed in on the narrow gap surrounded by trees and dense bushes.

"Is that the only way through to the road?" Gary asked.

"Yeah," Dan said, "unless they decide to hack their way through a bunch of brush and trees."

"Good." Gary looked at John. "We'll hide in the bushes and come at them from the sides. Dan can monitor their approach on the tower cam."

"Won't they see the mast?" John asked.

"I'll lower it until the camera is just above the treetops," Dan said. "They'll never spot it."

"Agreed," Gary said. "The resolution on night-vision goggles isn't that good." He glanced at Ann. "Now we need a place for our shooter to hide."

Dan tilted the camera up and to the right. "How about that?" he asked.

It was a large boulder on the other side of the trees hiding the truck, not far from the gap leading to the road.

"That'll work," Gary said. "Ann can hide behind it and pop Peter and Ian as they go past."

"One of them," Ann said. "I probably won't have time to reload."

"Make it Ian, okay?" Gary said.

"I'll try."

"Then when they're distracted, John and I will rush them."

"So, where do you want me?" Sully asked.

"Behind the wheel."

"Yes, boss."

Gary looked up at the monitor. The boat seemed no closer as it wallowed along, its bow buried in the waves much of the time. He knew Peter and Ian were having a rough time of it. Maybe that would give the team an edge when the two came ashore, but somehow Gary doubted it. He moved forward, grabbed a pair of dark blue coveralls, and went outside to remove his dry suit.

When he came back inside, Dan was alternating between monitoring the boat's progress and the approaching dawn. It was now 5:00 A.M., but the heavy cloud cover made it seem like midnight. Dan turned the tower cam back to the sea. The boat was nearing the shore.

"Looks like they're headed right for us," Dan said.

Gary stared at the shaky video. "Yeah. Wonder where they stashed the car?"

"No telling," Ann said. "There are roads and trails all through these hills. We could search forever and never find it."

The boat slowed several hundred feet offshore and came about into the wind.

Gary turned to John. "Time to go. Got the pepper spray?"

John held out two cans. "Two for you and two for me." He patted his pockets.

Gary took the cans and look at Ann. "Is our shooter ready?"

"Ready," Ann said.

"Okay, let's do it."

chapter 26

Ann crouched low and scurried through the gap in the trees and across the rocky ground, keeping the boulder between herself and the fishing boat. Only when she reached her cover did she realize how enormous the rock was. It would hide her with ease, provided she didn't stand up. She crawled cautiously around the side and peered down the steep slope at the surreal green image provided by her night-vision goggles.

The fishing boat wallowed along, headed away from the cove as two men threw an inflatable boat into the tossing sea. One pulled it alongside with an attached line while the other jumped, lost his balance, and tumbled into the bottom of the rubber craft. The man holding the rope jumped, kept his footing, and pushed off. The fishing boat, its mission complete, increased speed, turned to port, and pounded through the seas toward Polperro. The rubber boat bobbed and tossed as each comber carried it nearer the shore while the two occupants paddled furiously. The craft drew ever closer until a breaking wave threw it onto the rocks. The man in front jumped up, slipped, and fell sprawling on the beach. Another wave lifted the boat and pushed it higher. The other man jumped, staggered a few steps, and then turned to help his partner up. A wave crashed around them, almost knocking them down. The men struggled through the water's suction until they reached the high-water mark.

"Both of them have guns, and one's carrying a bundle," Dan said over the radio.

Ann watched the men approach. They were walking surprisingly fast despite the rocky shore, obviously in a hurry. Ann checked the air rifle to make sure the safety was off, then removed her goggles and sighted through the night-vision scope. The crosshairs danced around a little, but Ann found she could hold them on target. Her main concern was the wind and how much the dart would drop after firing.

Ann crawled slowly around the boulder, keeping the men in sight as they passed her position and continued toward the gap in the trees where Gary and John waited. Finally she reached the rock's seaward side. She eased into her shooting position and sighted through the scope. The men's backs were to her now, and they were almost in line, one carrying the bundle trailing behind. Ann knew from his size that it had to be Peter. Although she would have preferred to target Ian, Peter blocked the shot. Deciding to take what she could get, Ann lined the crosshairs on her target and waited as the men neared the opening in the trees.

Gary waited in the dense stand of trees on the east side of the gap. On the other side, John waited, unseen, and beyond him was the truck. To the right, a narrow road ran along parallel to the rocky coast. Gary peered around a tree and scanned the wild Cornish scene, aided by his night-vision goggles. Although official sunrise was past, the heavy clouds made unaided vision difficult.

The men were much closer now, working their way toward the gap. Gary concentrated on the one in front, quite sure it was Ian. The one trailing behind carried the cumbersome bundle. Gary's eyes followed the object for a few moments, wishing the nightmare were over and done with. Finally the men were so close Gary could make out their faces. Ian led the way, and both were being very cautious. Their clattering footsteps carried clearly over the moaning wind.

A soft *pop* sounded, followed by a yell of surprise. Peter jumped and whirled around. Ian stopped and started to turn. A sudden movement caught Gary's eye, and he looked over and saw John running toward Peter. Fear etched every detail into Gary's brain, along with the certainty his friend was dead unless he did something. He grabbed a rock, jumped up, and lunged out of his hiding place. Ian's long, silenced pistol started coming up, swinging around to line up with John.

"Ya–a–a–a!" Gary yelled.

Peter brought his gun to bear on this new threat. Gary hurled the rock as hard as he could, striking Peter's goggles and knocking them off. Peter's pistol whipped up, and brilliant green flashes bloomed in Gary's goggles, accompanied by the sound of deadly *thwips*. Gary zigged toward Ian, whose gun wavered between the two threats. Gary grabbed for a can of pepper spray but missed his pocket. Ian's gun swung around. Gary dove under it, hit the ground, and rolled, gasping as rocks dug into his side and shoulder. His goggles flew off, and he saw muzzle flashes above him. He scrambled to his knees and sprang at Ian, ramming into his legs and knocking him down. Gary staggered to his feet and whirled around.

Two shadowy figures faced each other. One raised its arm.

"My eyes!" came Peter's unmistakable voice. "Help me, Ian!"

Ian jumped to his feet, and Gary saw the silhouette of his gun.

"John!" he shouted. "Duck!"

Gary grabbed a rock and threw as hard as he could.

The figure on the left started falling. The rock hit Ian, and three spasmodic shots briefly illuminated John and Peter. The latter stumbled about, obviously in pain.

"Ian! Come here. Now."

Two of the black shadows merged.

"Stay down, John!" Gary shouted.

Somewhere off to the side an engine started.

"No. Wait," Gary heard on his radio, and it took him a moment to realize it was Dan speaking. Headlights flashed on. The truck turned around and came roaring toward the fight. Peter and Ian were hobbling along the road going east. A gun flashed repeatedly, each shot like a squirt of light. Glass tinkled and metal screeched.

"Stop, Sully!" Gary yelled.

The truck slid to a stop minus one headlight.

"Kill your lights," Gary added.

The remaining light cut off. Several more flashes illuminated the fleeing men, accompanied by the sound of breaking glass. Then all Gary could hear was the moaning wind. Ann ran toward them, carrying her rifle.

"Are you all right?" Gary called out.

"Yeah," John replied. "How about you?"

Gary hobbled over to John, wincing at each jarring step.

"Anyone hurt?" Ann asked.

"Sore, but otherwise okay," Gary said. "Do you see my goggles?"

"Yeah. I'll get 'em."

She hurried past, bent over, and grabbed something on the ground. "Here," she said, handing them over.

Gary slipped them on and ran into the road. Peter and Ian were over a hundred feet away now.

"They're getting away," John said.

"Come on," Gary said.

He turned and they hurried back to the truck. One headlight was shot out, and dark gouges marred the flat, sheet-metal front. Three large holes starred the broad windshield. Gary continued on around to the driver's door.

"Are you okay?"

Sully looked down from his window. "Yeah. Let's go, man," he said. "We gotta nail those dudes."

To the east, a powerful engine roared to life. Gary turned in time to see a dark green shape shoot out onto the road. He looked around at Ann.

"I'll take that," he said, taking the air rifle. "Now move it, everyone."

Ann ran around the front of the truck and jumped in beside Sully. Gary ran to the back with John, and as he rounded the corner, something caught his eye. It was the telescoping mast, bent over and trailing along the ground with what remained of the camera and antenna. He shook his head and jumped through the open hatch. John followed and closed it. Gary removed his goggles.

Dan glanced their way, then picked up the mike. "We're ready, Sully."

The truck lurched into motion, and Gary had to grab the worktable to steady himself. He looked up at the forward monitor. The retreating taillights were quite distant now, and as he watched, they disappeared around a curve. He shifted to the rear monitor. The remains of the finely machined mast bounced and sparked against the road and weaved from side to side like a metallic tail.

"I see we lost our telescoping mast."

Dan looked at the monitor, then around at Gary. "Yeah. Sully took off before I could lower it."

Gary remembered the earlier radio transmission. "Oh, *that's* what you meant."

Dan turned back to the rear monitor. The battered remains

of the camera hit the road, separated, and went tumbling off into the roadside brush. "Uh-huh. *That's* what I meant. No more sky cam."

"No, I guess not." Gary nodded toward the front. "Cut Sully and Ann in."

Dan flipped the switches.

"Did you hit Peter?" Gary asked.

"I think so," Ann said. "He sure turned around in a hurry."

"But he didn't fall down," John said.

"He was hobbling, but that could have been from the pepper spray," Gary said.

"Or the dart could have nicked him."

"Yeah, I suppose. At any rate, that stuff's not instantaneous."

"We're coming back into Polperro," Dan said.

Gary looked at the forward monitor. The truck screeched around a curve, then slowed with squalling brakes. Sully made the tight left turn where the road doubled back on itself. The tortured mast followed, trailing sparks. They roared up the Coombe, and Gary caught a glimpse of taillights in the distance.

"They're heading back to A387," Gary said.

"It's the only practical way out," Ann said.

"Sully, how're you doing?"

"No way I can catch 'em, boss."

"I know. Just keep them in sight as long as you can."

"Roger that."

The truck veered right on A387. Almost a minute later the taillights turned to the left.

"Where are they going?" Gary asked.

"Just a minute," Ann said. A few moments later she added, "It's a shortcut to B3359."

"Where does that go?"

"Up to A390. It's the southern route to Land's End. It meets up with the northern route at Penzance."

Sully hit the brakes. The truck leaned over hard as it made the sharp left turn. Gary looked up at the monitor. The taillights, far ahead now, rounded a curve, and disappeared. He waited for them to reappear at each turn, but they didn't.

"They've lost us," Sully said.

Gary felt the last glimmer of hope fade. "I know. Pull over somewhere. We've got to do something about that mast."

"Roger."

A few minutes later the truck slowed. "How about this?" he asked. "I think I can make it under those trees up ahead."

Gary examined the picture on the monitor. The gap looked tight but possible. The truck slowed to a crawl, and limbs began scraping along the top and sides. Finally they stopped. Gary looked at the rear monitor and could not see the road.

"Very good," he said.

Gary led the way to the back, opened the hatch, and stepped down into the chill, dark bower. Beyond the leafy canopy, the sky was finally turning gray. He looked down at the bedraggled mast all kinked and soiled.

"What all have we lost?" he asked Dan.

"Not a lot," Dan replied. "Two cameras and the parabolic antenna."

"The cameras we can do without. What about the antenna?"

"I can't spoof mobile phones or receive weak microwave signals, but I still have all the other systems; our communications gear plus regular mobile phone service."

"Could be worse, I guess." Gary turned to the others. "Come on. Let's get this thing off."

"I'll do it," John said.

He got a socket wrench, climbed up on the side of the truck, and began removing nuts. A few minutes later the last one came free, and the base of the mast crashed to the ground.

"Okay, spread out and grab on," Gary said.

Together, they pulled the mast in under the trees and hid it.

—●—○—●—

Gary stood before them in the midst of the arbor. His first thought had been to hold the meeting in the back of the truck, but that seemed too gloomy, not that he felt especially cheerful under the heavy clouds. He frowned as he thought about Peter, still on the loose with the heisted crown, despite all their best efforts. Then, unbidden, a snatch of memory flitted through his mind: "Give thanks in all circumstances; for this is the will of God in Christ Jesus for you." Gary knew it was from one of Paul's letters, but he couldn't remember which one. With the thought came a feeling of peace. He became aware that John had said something.

"What?" Gary asked.

"Oh, nothing, just that here we are again, holding the bag, while Peter and Ian slip through our fingers. It's over. That was our last chance."

"It's *not* over," Gary said.

John only shrugged.

"I mean it," Gary said. "Now snap out of it. There must be *something* we can do. Come on; what do we know?"

A wry smile came to John's face. "You mean like start at the beginning?"

"Maybe a *little* further along. How about: Is Peter done with that Indian freighter?"

"That's a good question," Ann said. "Knowing Peter, he probably has options on top of his options, but escaping on the *Bhima* sure would solve a lot of his problems. But he could also have another way out."

"No, I say we check out the ship option first," Gary said. "That took *some* doing to set up, and I don't think Peter's going to give up on it that easily. Now, the *Bhima* was going west when they discovered our spy gear. Where could it pick them up?"

John shrugged. "Another fishing port?"

"I don't think so," Ann said. "I mean, they must believe the Royal Navy's after them."

"Maybe Peter figures we did it," John said.

Ann turned to Gary. "How convincing was your attack?"

Gary thought for a moment. "Very, actually." He glanced at John. "The explosions surprised even me."

John grinned.

"Do you think anyone saw you?" Ann continued.

"No, not a chance," Gary said. "I'm sure of that."

"In that case, I wouldn't expect the captain to risk coming close to shore, no matter *what* Peter says."

"I think Ann's right," John said.

Gary nodded. "I do too. Okay, so what if the ship stays *way* out, like forty, fifty miles or so? How would Peter. . . ?" He stopped when he spotted Ann's puzzled expression. "What?" he asked.

Ann looked up at him. "I think I know where Peter's going," she said slowly. "It's the perfect place, actually." She smiled. "Remember when we were in Peter's office, and we got to talking about vacations?"

"Uh-huh," Gary said after a brief pause. "And what does this have to do. . . ?"

She hurried on. "You told Peter we were thinking of the Orkney Islands, and he said the Isle of Man and Isle of Wight were quite popular."

"I remember. He was defending merry old England since he was working with the Tourist Authority."

"Correct. And Peter—methodical, one-track-mind Peter— left out one of the most popular islands of all—the Isles of Scilly."

Gary's mind raced ahead. "That's right, he did."

"And Scilly would be perfect. The islands are off Land's End, right out in the Atlantic, as far from British authority as he's likely to get."

"Interesting," Gary said slowly. "How do you get there?"

"We can check the Internet, but I know there's a ferry from Penzance, and you can get there by air."

Gary looked all around. "Any other ideas?"

"I say we check Scilly out," John said.

"All right, then," Gary said. "Let's get a move on."

Sully coughed. "Uh, dudes. It might be a good idea to do a makeover on the windshield. You know, bullet holes and all that. Might cause questions."

Gary looked past him to the front of the truck. "Yeah." He turned to John. "What can we do?"

John looked at it a few moments. "I can patch the metal, but the windshield is a real problem. Let's take it out. Probably won't be noticeable except up close."

"Okay. Hope you're right."

chapter 27

Gary tried to get comfortable in the passenger seat but found it impossible with a chill wind blasting through the opening in front of him. He and Sully wore sunglasses, which helped some. The overcast grew heavier as the morning progressed.

Ann was in the back researching the Isles of Scilly while John worked on the hang glider's engine, which left Gary the job of navigating. They had continued across A390 and turned southwest on A30, since the northern route into Penzance, besides being more direct, was a better highway, and Gary wanted to get there as soon as possible. So far the traffic had been light. They had already passed Camborne and were approaching Hayle, well down in the narrow green neck of land that led to Penzance and the fortresslike cliffs of Land's End.

"Gary, I've located most of the ways to Scilly," Ann said over the radio.

"Go ahead," Gary said.

"Scratch the ferry. It takes almost three hours, and there's only one trip a day. More likely are the Scilly SkyBus, light aircraft out of Land's End Airport, and the British International helicopter service from the Penzance Heliport."

"Okay, which one?"

"I'd go with British International. They run on a set schedule and are less up close and personal, if you know what I mean."

"Less likely to remember old Pete and his sidekick."

"You've got it."

"Any way we can check?"

"How about I quiz the British International chaps, eh what?"

Gary laughed, grateful for something to relieve the tension. "Ms. Edwina Dunn, I presume."

"Actually, Marjorie Evans, since MI5 is on to Edwina." Then she dropped the British accent. "Well, what do you think?"

"I say go for it." Gary glanced at his watch and saw it was 7:34. "How long will it take to get ready?"

"I'm putting on the final touches now."

"What does their schedule look like?"

"The first flight is at 7:30."

Gary sat up straight. "Wait a minute. What if Peter and Ian missed the earlier flight? You need backup."

"No. I'll be careful. If I spot Peter, I'll come back out."

"But. . ."

"It would take you too long to get ready. Look. I can handle it."

"Okay, how do you want to do it?" Gary asked.

"A30 goes right by the heliport. Drop me off; then go hide off A3071, west of town. I gave Dan a map."

"You'll call for a pickup?"

"We're taking enough of a chance as it is. When I get done, I'll make my own way out."

"But. . ."

"I'll be all right."

"If you two are through, I fixed the engine," John said.

"What was wrong with it?" Gary asked.

"Wire broke off the coil terminal. I soldered it back on."

"Good."

The traffic built steadily, and a short time later Sully began slowing for the merge with A394. Off to the left, gray Atlantic combers rolled past scattered rocks and into the cozy harbor. Boats and ships lined the docks or anchored out in the sheltered waters. A little farther out, St. Michael's Mount rose two hundred feet out of Mount's Bay, surmounted by a castle, which had once been a fortified Benedictine house. Up ahead, in a sweeping curve around the bay, nestled the compact town of Penzance.

"The heliport is just past the roundabout," Ann said. "Take the street to the right and drop me off at the car park."

"Got it," Sully said.

Gary held on to the armrest as the truck leaned around the traffic circle. Sully took the side road and slowed down.

"We're almost there," Gary said.

"I'm ready," Ann replied.

The truck stopped, and Gary heard the sound of the hatch opening and closing. He looked out his window and saw Ann stride past and start down the sidewalk leading to the terminal. Her disguise looked perfect: blond hair and a blue pantsuit.

"Move out," Gary said to Sully.

The truck lurched into motion and accelerated rapidly.

"Dan, we need directions."

"Roger. Left at the roundabout up ahead, and in a little more than a mile, bear right on A3071."

"Got it," Sully said.

Ann paused inside the terminal and looked around. A handful of passengers sat in chairs reading or looking out through the windows at the tarmac, and several stood in line at the counter, waiting their turn with the ticket agent. But Peter and Ian were not among them. Ann held back until the agent finished, then hurried up to the young man. He seemed friendly and wore his crisp uniform with obvious pride. He smiled as she approached.

"Traveling to St. Mary's today?" he asked.

Ann maintained her severe, professional smile. "Marjorie Evans, MI5," she said, holding up her ID for him to see. She lowered her voice. "If I could have a word." She struggled not to smile at his serious expression.

"Yes, of course. Anything to help."

"Good. We're looking for two men, both young. One is five ten, 140 pounds, black hair, black eyes, light brown skin. The other, six feet, 200 pounds, blue eyes, and long blond hair, usually tied in a ponytail."

"Two men did go out on our seven-thirty flight, but the descriptions don't match exactly."

"Oh?"

"The shorter man had a beard. He was wearing sunglasses, so I couldn't see his eyes, but he had black hair. Seemed ill."

"I see. What about the other chap?"

"Close to what you said, but with medium-length hair. No ponytail."

"Did he have a diamond ear stud?"

"Yes, yes he did, now you mention it. He wore sunglasses as well."

Ann felt a jolt of excitement but maintained her professional composure.

"Very good," she said. She lowered her voice. "You *will* keep this to yourself, won't you? Hush-hush, and all that."

"Oh, yes, of course. Anything else?"

"No, not at this time. Carry on."

"Yes, ma'am."

Ann nodded, then turned and walked out of the terminal.

Gary stood back, looking out through the gap between the

truck and the dilapidated building to his left. Sully had parked between two abandoned buildings, facing in to hide the damage. Gary approved of Ann's choice for a hiding place. It was several miles from the heliport on a narrow side street of light industrial shops. Traffic was almost nonexistent, and no one had shown the slightest interest in the truck. With nothing to do, time seemed to stand still.

"I'm at the road."

Gary jumped at Ann's voice in his ear. He breathed a sigh of relief. "Glad you're back. We're several hundred feet down, on your right."

"Roger."

Gary hurried up and took a quick peek. There she was. He stepped back and waited and soon heard the sound of footsteps on the pavement. A few moments later she rounded the corner.

"What did you find out?" Gary whispered.

"Peter and Ian flew out, all right," she said.

Sully opened the hatch and looked out. Ann stepped up, and Gary followed her inside. Sully came around beside Dan.

"They were wearing disguises and shades, and Peter had a fake beard," Ann continued. "Ian cut his hair, but the goof-ball forgot about his ear stud. Peter was apparently still a little woozy from the tranquilizer, but I suppose that will wear off soon."

Dan leaned back in his chair. "Okay, now that we've tracked them down, what can we do about it? There's no way we can follow with all our gear."

"Hold on," Gary said. "*First* we figure out Peter's next move, *then* worry about what we do about it."

Dan crossed his arms and frowned. "Okay. So what's Peter going to do now?"

"Obviously, rendezvous with the *Bhima*. I'm sure there are plenty of boats he could rent or steal." Gary turned to Ann.

"Unfortunately," she said, "St. Mary's has the most, since it's the main island. But Tresco, St. Martin's, Bryher, or St. Agnes might be better."

"Less likely to be spotted," Gary said.

"That's right, but take a look at this." She turned her laptop and called up a saved Web page. "Remember Peter's client?"

Gary frowned. "The Tourist Authority."

"Right. Look at this."

Ann brought up an aerial shot of an hourglass-shaped island, bare except for a stone building under construction. A steel pier jutted out into the sea.

"This is Samson Island, uninhabited, and one of the westernmost islands. And that," she tapped the screen with a fingernail, "is a faux castle the Tourist Authority is building." She looked at Gary. "Suggest anything?"

Gary zeroed in on the pier. "Wouldn't that be convenient."

"Couldn't ask for anything better. Samson is uninhabited, it has a pier, and there's nothing to the west but ocean. There's a construction crew, of course, but I doubt they work weekends."

"Perfect." Gary looked around at John. "This has *got* to be it. Everything fits."

"I think you're right, but what can we do?" John asked. "Flying there is a good way to get caught, plus we'd have to leave all our equipment behind."

"I know, but if we don't, Peter and Ian skate, and we take the rap."

"Guys," Ann interrupted.

Gary turned to her. "Yes?"

"How about a boat? Wouldn't that work?"

"Yeah, and so would our own personal helicopter, but we're as likely to get one as the other."

"Maybe not. I think Marjorie might be of some assistance."

Gary looked at her steadily. "Exactly what does Ms. Evans have in mind?"

Gary sat beside Ann in the cramped backseat of the tiny cab. He twisted his head about but resisted the urge to scratch. He didn't know which itched more, the beard adhesive or the fake scar on his neck. *We must look a sight,* he thought. She still wore her blue pantsuit, while he resembled a Cornish fisherman, in his canvas pants, striped cotton shirt, scuffed boots, and soft hat.

The cab slowed coming down the steep hill into the fishing village of Mousehole, south of Penzance. Mousehole Lane narrowed where it entered the village. Ahead lay the town, crowded up against Mount's Bay as if it had slid down the hill. Two masonry breakwaters protected the compact harbor, and beyond that, St. Clement's Isle rose out of the bay like a sentinel. The cab slowed even more and angled to the right near the shore. The driver stopped beside a lime-washed stone building with mullioned windows and a weathered red sign that said "THE MOUSEHOLE" in faded black letters. He turned to his passengers.

" 'Ere we are, then," he said with a broad smile. "The Mowzel in Mowzel, you might say."

Ann handed him the fare plus tip. "Thanks ever so much."

Gary got out and walked around to stand beside Ann, facing the pub. A brisk breeze blew in off the bay. The cab drove off.

" 'Mowzel?' " Gary whispered.

"That's how 'Mousehole' is pronounced," Ann replied softly. "Now don't forget, you can't talk."

Gary fingered his scar. "Oh, yeah. I be a tough dude, I be. Ar–r–r–r, matey."

"Hush."

Gary thought about what they had to do, and his smile disappeared. He walked to the heavy wooden door, opened it, and nodded for her to enter. He followed her inside the dimly lit interior and over to the bar. Rough-hewn oak beams, blackened with age, supported the building's second story. Iron chandeliers with grimy lightbulbs added scant light to what came through the windows. The hefty bartender finished pouring a pint and slid it over to his customer. He turned to face the strangers.

"How may I assist you?" he asked.

"Looking for a boat to hire," Ann said. "A large boat. Could you direct me?"

The man's eyebrows shot up. "Hello, odd request, that is. Let me see. I believe Bill Purves hires his boat out, now I think of it." His duty done, he smiled and looked at Gary. "How about something to wet the whistle?"

"Thanks, no," Ann replied. "About Mr. Purves." A ten-pound note appeared on the bar.

A large hand scooped it up. "Ah, yes," the man said. "Half a moment." He pulled out a mobile phone and punched in a number. A few moments later he said, "Bill, Douglas here. Got some folks here wants a word with you. Can you pop over?" His eyes seemed to echo the reply. "Capital. See you then." He pressed a button and returned the phone to his pocket. He nodded toward a vacant table in a corner. "Make yourselves to home. He'll be right over."

"Much obliged," Ann said.

Gary followed her over to a sturdy wooden table that seemed as old as the pub, and they sat down. A few minutes later a tall, thin man entered and slipped through the tables to the corner. Ann and Gary stood.

"Lookin' for Bill Purves, are you?" He peered first at Gary and then Ann. The man had a leathery face, well supplied with creases.

"Yes, I am, Mr. Purves," Ann said. "Marjorie Evans, MI5." She held out her ID. He drew back a little.

"Hold on, now. Don't want nothin' to do with you chaps."

"You haven't heard me out, Mr. Purves."

"Don't want to, neither." He started to turn away.

"*Please* sit down. I think I can change your mind."

He hesitated.

"Please. I shan't bite."

He pulled out a chair and sat cautiously. Gary and Ann took their seats.

"Who's he?" Bill asked, nodding toward Gary.

"He works for me," Ann replied. "Now, what I want to do is hire your boat."

Bill's scowl relaxed, and he almost smiled. "Do you now? Well, no better skipper in all Cornwall than Bill Purves. Ask anyone."

"Allow me to point my question. It's your *boat* I wish to hire. MI5 business, don't you know."

"Well, I don't know about that. Who would be operatin' it then?"

"My man. Quite capable, I assure you."

"*Is* he now?" Bill turned to Gary. "How about that, mate?"

"He can't speak," Ann explained. "Knife fight."

Gary tilted his chin up so Bill could see.

"Well, what do you say?" Ann continued. "We really do have pressing business. How much?"

"Five hundred a day and five hundred deposit. Take it or leave it."

"We'll take it. Now we'll need a way to get to shore."

"There's a rubber dinghy and outboard stowed up forward."

"Good." Ann pulled a stack of crisp hundred-pound notes out of her purse, counted out ten and handed them to Bill. "There, shall we conclude our business, then?"

Bill stood, and the notes disappeared into a pocket. Gary and Ann followed him out of the pub. They walked north to the harbor under dreary gray skies, then down the gentle slope and across the rocky bottom, exposed since the tide was out. Bill helped them into a skiff and rowed them to a large white boat moored between two buoys. He held the side while Gary helped

Ann aboard. Bill followed and tied the skiff to a stern cleat. He showed Gary where the controls were, then turned a switch and pressed a red button. The engine turned over a few times then rumbled to life.

"I'll cast you off, mate," Bill said. His eyes bored into Gary's. "And then we'll see," he added ominously.

He went over the side and into the skiff, rowed to the aft buoy, and released the line. Gary took it in. Bill did the same for the forward line and came back aboard. He took an oar and pushed the skiff away, parallel to the shore.

"Now, mate," he said, "come up to that bow-on, and I'll let you go."

Gary nodded but was not at all sure he could do it. He had driven outboards, but nothing as big and cumbersome as a fishing boat. He backed the boat in a wide arc until the skiff was dead ahead about fifty feet away. With a nearly slack tide, all he had to worry about was the stiff breeze, which was now from the east. It blew through the narrow gap in the breakwaters, directly on the port beam. Gary came around to leeward, between the shore and the skiff, pointed the bow into the wind, and waited as long as he dared, then shifted into reverse and backed hard. He brought the throttle to idle and shifted into neutral. The bow brushed against the skiff.

"That'll do," Bill said, obviously impressed.

Bill brought the skiff around with the oar, got in, and departed for the rocky shore.

Gary pulled out his radio, turned it on, and placed it in his right ear. "Star Chamber, this is Popeye. Meet us at the north breakwater."

"Roger, Popeye," Dan said.

The truck, large bundles lashed to its side, turned onto the massive stone breakwater, and drove slowly toward Gary and Ann. Sully sat behind the wheel, with John and Dan beside him. He wheeled the truck around and parked facing the harbor. Gary paired up with John to help haul the equipment and supplies down the interior stone steps to the waiting boat. When they were done, Gary ducked inside the cabin, removed his disguise, and turned Sully into a reasonable facsimile.

"There," Gary said. "That should satisfy Mr. Purves if he spots you."

"I sure hope so," Sully said. "This thing itches like crazy."

"You can take it off when you're clear of the harbor." Gary turned to the others. "Everyone clear on the operation?"

"As much as we can be," John replied. "Transport the team and gear to the north side of Samson Island and wait for you."

"Right. I'll ditch the truck, then fly over with the hang glider and recon the castle and ship."

"Yeah." John paused. "Well, this had better work, since it's probably our last chance."

Gary nodded but didn't say anything since he had been thinking the same thing. They might catch up with Peter; in fact, he thought it extremely likely. But what then?

chapter 28

Gary stood on the breakwater and watched the boat pass through the narrow gap and turn south into Mount's Bay. From there it would enter the Atlantic Ocean. The bow plunged into a gray wave, throwing spray over the top of the cabin. Gary looked up. The clouds were lower now and even darker. He knew the rain would not hold off for long.

He returned to the truck and climbed up into the cab, facing the gaping hole where the windshield had once been. He backed up and turned, then drove down the breakwater and up the long hill leading out of Mousehole. He reached the top of the hill, turned left, and followed the narrow road until he came to a rutted path that meandered down a gentle slope. Tree limbs brushed against the sides, and the wheels crunched through deep holes. Finally he stopped when he could go no farther.

Gary stepped down and looked all around. He couldn't see the road above, so he figured the truck was safe from immediate discovery. He followed a path leading south and found a clearing with a steep drop-off to the tumbled rocks below and a panoramic view of the bay. Waves crashed and foamed all along the shore. Wind blew past Gary as if to push him back from the precipice. He returned to the truck, pulled on his dry suit, and began hauling the hang glider parts to his launch point. After the last trip, he assembled the aircraft with care. When he finished, he looked at the engine, wondering if he could trust it to take him to the Isles of Scilly.

Gary crawled under the flapping Dacron wing, shouldered the cumbersome frame, and fastened his harness. He stood up fully and looked down the short takeoff path. In the distance he saw rain clouds riding above the restless sea. He set the choke and engaged the starter. The engine started instantly. He waited a few seconds, then turned off the choke. He took a deep breath, opened the throttle, and ran as hard as he could, jumping when he reached the drop-off. The hang gilder mushed a little, then lifted him skyward. The trees and brush fell away rapidly as the steep hillside tumbled down to the rocky shore far below. Gary angled south to bear away from Mousehole, a course he would hold until he was clear of the landmass south of Land's End, where he would turn west. Several minutes later he spotted a boat.

"Malibu Surfer, do you read?"

There was a slight pause. "This is Surfer dude," came the clear reply over the radio. "Comm boss says he reads you five squared."

Gary smiled at Sully's reply. "Roger."

"That's five-by-five," Dan said. "Stand by, Gooney Bird One."

"How's the engine?" John asked.

"Running like a champ."

"Good. We're praying for you."

"Thanks. Gooney Bird One out."

He soon left the plodding boat behind and followed the craggy coast as it wrapped around the brown mass of Gwennap Head. He looked back to the northwest and saw Land's End. Ahead lay twenty-six miles of open ocean and a handful of tiny islands, barely visible through the haze. His radar altimeter read twelve hundred seventy-three feet now. He looked up and estimated the rain-laden clouds were less than two hundred feet above him. All around him slanting gray shadows marked patches of rain, and the open corridors between squalls grew ever narrower with every passing minute.

Gary leveled off at thirteen hundred fifty feet, scant feet below the clouds. Because the hang glider was visible at low altitude, his present course would take him south of the islands. He knew Peter would be watching.

As the miles ticked off, the ceiling continued to drop, forcing Gary ever lower. He passed south of the green-and-brown smudge of St. Mary's, the main island, and a few minutes later the smaller St. Agnes. Gary continued on for five miles, then came around in a gentle right turn, flying just below the ragged clouds. The clinging gray mist obscured the islands at times, and up ahead a gray curtain of rain blocked his path. A few minutes later he plunged into it, and the ocean disappeared. Raindrops splattered against his goggles and ran off to the sides.

Almost a minute later he flew into the clear with Samson Island barely visible. The island, less than a mile long, was shaped like a malformed hourglass. It was ringed by a yellow sand beach, and a gray stone fortress sat atop South Hill with a construction crane overhanging the roof. A narrow waist separated this hill from the smaller North Hill. Gary peered through the intervening rain and haze at the pier jutting out from the island's southwest point. He held his course a few more seconds, then came around in a broad left turn.

"This is Gooney Bird One," Gary said.

"This is Malibu Surfer, go ahead," Dan replied.

"Just flew past Samson. Looks exactly like the Web pictures."

"Roger. Any sign of target?"

"Couldn't get close enough to tell, but the pier is empty."

"Copy that."

"Will reconnoiter other target, then return for rendezvous."

"Roger. What's the weather like?"

"Intermittent rain, and the ceiling is dropping fast. Sea state is moderate."

"I copy."

"Roger. Gooney Bird One out."

John braced himself as the boat rode down one wave and plunged into the one following, throwing foaming white spray high over the cabin. "If this is moderate, I don't want to see bad," he grumbled.

Sully turned the wheel to maintain course. "I've seen worse off California," he said.

"I'll take your word for it. How much longer?"

"About another hour. Why?"

"I'm not sure my stomach can last that long."

"Hey, man, don't be hurling any pizza in here."

John gulped. "Your compassion is noted." He turned to Dan. "Picking up anything?"

Dan shook his head. "Nope. But then I don't have any of my fancy antennas."

"You okay?" John asked Ann.

"I'm making it."

John forced a smile. "That's good. I hope I do."

Gary kept checking his position, wondering when the *Bhima* would show up. He was over fifteen nautical miles from Samson and still no sign of the freighter. He was down to eight hundred seventy-seven feet now, and the rain squalls were becoming widespread. He threaded his way through the narrow corridors between storms, looking toward the west whenever possible. Finally he spotted a creamy white line cutting across the white-caps, and turned toward it. A few minutes later he was sure; it was the Indian freighter, all right. He hauled the hang glider around in a tight right turn.

"Malibu Surfer," Gary said. "Target Two sighted, approximately twenty miles south southwest. Looks like we're in business."

"Copy that."

"Gooney Bird One returning to base."

Gary set his initial course for Annet Island, an uninhabited bird sanctuary and the westernmost Isle of Scilly. Using it as his guidepost, he planned on approaching Samson in a broad western arc to avoid prying eyes. He was below six hundred feet now and descending rapidly.

He dodged the dark squalls while he could, until he encountered a solid gray wall directly in his path. The cloud loomed ever closer with no way past. He gritted his teeth and plowed into it. Rain lashed at him, and the wind currents thrashed the hang glider around. Gary wiped his goggles so he could see the instruments and tried not to think of what would happen if he became disoriented or something broke. A few minutes later he flew out, but up ahead the clouds were even lower.

Gary dropped down to two hundred feet and finally sighted the yellow-and-green sliver of Annet Island in the distance. He overflew the island at barely one hundred fifty feet and turned north. A squall hid Samson, but he stuck to his plan of circling it well to the west. He dropped down to one hundred feet and began his long arc out over the sea. Almost immediately he plowed into the storm. He wiped at his goggles. He *had* to concentrate on his instruments. The wind currents shook the aluminum frame like a terrier with a rat, and at each bone-crunching jolt, he expected something to give way. Several minutes later he came out the other side. Storm clouds formed random dark walls all around, hemming him in.

Gary was northwest of Samson now and just south of Bryher Island. Beyond that was Tresco with its Abbey Gardens, a rich blend of dark green trees and subtropical plants. Off to his left Gary saw a boat plunging through the waves from the west. He banked in that direction and flew toward it. He smiled. This was good news, indeed.

"Malibu Surfer, this is Gooney Bird One," he said. "I have you in sight."

"Roger that," Sully replied. "Saw you pop out of that storm. Cool, dude."

"What's with the western approach?"

"Hey, you should check out these charts; shallow water all over the place. Figured going around was safer."

"You're the skipper. Everyone okay?"

"Three-quarters."

Gary felt a pang of concern. "What?"

"John had to speak to Ralph a few times. Hold on, I think we have a late-breaking report."

"Hush up," John said. "I'm fine, now that I can see land."

Gary grinned. "Copy that. I'll meet you on the beach. Gooney Bird One out."

He overflew the boat, turned around, and dropped down to within ten feet of the restless waves. Gary turned south, and up ahead, North Hill rose out of the shallow water and surrounding sand. Beyond that, storm clouds hid the castle. White combers crashed all along the narrow beach. Moments later Gary crossed the shore, switched off the engine, banked hard into the wind, and pushed the control bar forward, killing his forward speed. The hang glider slowed, then began to mush. He pushed the bar full forward, forcing a stall, and landed heavily on his feet. He slipped out of his harness and began disassembling the frame, bundling the parts and lashing them securely. Last, he removed his dry suit and pulled on his coveralls.

●—○—●

John braced himself as he scanned the shallow waters ahead. "Bottom's coming up fast," he said.

"I know what I'm doing," Sully replied. He had the wheel in constant motion to keep the boat's wild gyrations under control. "I need someone to drop the anchor."

A pang of anxiety mixed uneasily with John's seasickness. "I'll go."

"Are you sure?" Ann asked.

"I'm okay. What do I do?"

Sully pointed. "See that hump?"

"Yeah."

"That's the anchor windlass. First unlash the anchor; then make sure the rope is over the gypsy; move the operating level to 'free fall,' and throw the anchor over. The bottom's about ten feet, so pay out at least fifty or sixty feet before you engage the windlass."

"What's a 'gypsy'?"

"It's the pulley the rope goes over. Sure you can handle it?"

"I'm sure."

He wasn't, but John stumbled out of the cabin anyway. The fresh sea breeze caught him in the face and brought some relief. The boat made a ponderous turn into the wind. He crept forward, holding the rails fastened to the cabin roof. On reaching the foredeck, he tottered over to the windlass and knelt down. The nylon anchor rope came up through a hole in the deck, over the gypsy, and forward to where it attached to the anchor. He struggled to maintain his balance. The bow plunged into a wave, drenching him. He set the windlass control, unlashed the anchor, and threw it over the bow. The rope made a buzzing sound as it raced over the spinning gypsy. A few seconds later he locked the windlass and looked back. The engine sounds fell off abruptly.

Sully sprang to the side like a monkey and came racing forward. He knelt down, examined the vibrating rope, and paid out more.

"Will it hold?" John asked.

Sully nodded. "Should, unless the weather gets worse." He looked toward the shore. "There's the boss man."

John followed his gaze. "Let's go find that rubber boat."

Gary watched John and Sully move aft, then disappear inside the cabin. A few minutes later they emerged dragging two bulky objects. The black rubber boat inflated quickly. John threw it over and held the rope while Sully jumped inside. John handed down the tiny outboard and the first equipment bundles. Sully turned, pulled the starter rope, then pulled it again. The engine sputtered to life, and Sully sat down. Ann stepped into the bobbing craft. John threw in the line, and Sully drove the boat ashore, raising the outboard just before impact. The boat crunched up on the sand.

Gary helped Ann out and hauled the equipment ashore. "How much more?" he asked Sully.

"I don't know, two or three more trips."

Gary pushed the boat back into the surf. Sully lowered the motor, started it, and backed out. It actually took five trips through intermittent rain, with Dan coming last, cradling his precious communications gear. Another squall rolled over them as Gary helped carry the rubber boat above the high-water mark.

"Anything happening?" Gary asked Dan.

"Yes," he said, raising his voice to be heard over the rain and surf. "I was picking up encrypted signals on the way in. Can't be sure without precision antennas, but the bearings seem to come from Samson and the ship."

Gary rubbed his hands together. "So, we've found them."

"Sure looks like it."

"Now what?" John asked.

"Reconnoiter the castle, and make sure that's where they are. Have we got the pepper spray?"

"Yes, it was on the list."

"Isn't it time we call in the police?" Ann asked.

Gary thought it over. They hadn't dared do this before, because without Peter *and* the crown, they were holding the bag. However, Gary still wanted proof Peter was on the island.

"Let's make sure first." He paused. "Scilly *has* a police station?"

"A sergeant and a constable over on St. Mary's."

Gary couldn't help smiling. "Twenty-four-seven?"

Ann laughed. "I guess that depends on whether or not you can find them."

Gary turned to John. "Let's get moving."

They divided up the bundles and started out.

Sergeant Arthur Ivey shivered involuntarily. He slammed down the phone and stood, all in one motion, then paused. The downpour rattled against the windows, and wind moaned around the eaves. He was snug inside the St. Mary's Police Station, but not for long. He hurried to the steel cabinet in the corner, unlocked it, and retrieved the revolver he rarely carried. In fact, he couldn't remember the last time he had handled it. He stared at his constable's gun a few moments, then took it as well.

His first order of business was to locate Hubert, then arrange for a boat to take them over to St. Martin's. He sat down at his desk again. At first he thought of trying Hubert's home, but instead punched in the number for Bishop Rock Inn, a public house in the heart of Hugh Town. It rang twice.

"Bishop Rock Inn, may I help you?" a female voice asked.

"Elizabeth, Arthur here. Have you seen Hubert?"

"Yes, he's at the bar. Shall I fetch him?"

"Yes, please."

He waited impatiently, listening to the random sounds of the bustling pub.

"Hello, Arthur." It was impossible to miss Hubert's apprehensive tone. "Anything the matter?"

"I'm afraid so. Emergency call from St. Martin's. Tourist rang up from one of the chalets—said someone was breaking in. Then he got cut off."

The line remained silent.

"Hubert, are you there?"

"Yes. Where shall I meet you?"

"On the quay. I'll arrange for the boat."

"See you there."

"Right. Oh, wait. Put Elizabeth back on."

A few moments later she said, "Yes, Arthur?"

"If anyone asks, we're going to St. Martin's. Trouble at one of the chalets."

"Oh, sorry. I'll remember."

"Thanks. Bye."

Arthur hung up and punched in another number.

Despite the pouring rain, the team had made good time crossing low-lying Samson Island. Gary led the way up the east flank of South Hill, guided by the black silhouette of the tall construction crane. He called a halt when the dim outline of the castle's roof came into view against the dark clouds. Dan and Sully turned to the side and began setting up tents on a rocky shelf.

"Come on," Gary said to John. "I want to see what's up there."

John knelt down, opened his backpack, and pulled out a pair of binoculars. "Lead the way."

Gary crouched low and began working his way up the rocky slope, dropping to the ground when the upper-story windows came into view. He shivered as his icy, soaked clothing sapped the heat from his body. He wriggled over the mud and rock, and a few moments later saw a lighted first-floor window, a subdued yellow through the rain.

"There they are," John said.

"Maybe," Gary said. He turned his head and heard a deep rumbling sound. "Diesel generator."

"That explains the light. Here."

John held out the binoculars. Gary took them and put them to his eyes. Rain streaked the lenses. He wiped them and focused on the window. A worktable sat in the middle of the room, and on it rested a nylon bag and an open laptop.

"I see a computer," Gary said.

"Guess that cinches it."

Gary lowered the binoculars. "Maybe, but where's Peter and Ian?" He heard a sound behind. It was Ann crawling toward them.

"Dan wants to see you," she said. Her expression looked grim.

"What about?"

"Better let him tell you."

Gary crawled down the slope after her, then stood and ran the rest of the way. He knelt before the tent and scrambled inside. A battery lantern bathed the interior with a bright glaring light. Dan sat cross-legged, cradling several electronic boxes on his lap. Sully squatted next to him. Dan removed his earphones. John came in and made room for Ann beside him.

"We've got a problem," Dan said.

"What?"

"Two problems, actually. One, Peter isn't on Samson."

"You *said* his transmissions came from here," Gary said in irritation.

"I said they *seemed* to come from here." He held up a small loop antenna. "I don't have my best gear anymore."

"Okay, so where is he?"

"The signals are coming from southwest of here, which is what fooled me. On the boat, the line of bearing passed close to Samson, but it was actually from farther out."

"Do you know where?"

"Most likely Annet Island," Ann said. "It's an uninhabited bird sanctuary south of Samson."

Gary turned to her as he fitted the pieces together. Peter had even allowed for them tracking him to Scilly. The castle under construction, the pier, the running generator, the light on, and the laptop computer—all planned out, just in case. Then he remembered something else, something that sent a chill down his spine.

"I'm afraid Peter and Ian know we're here," he said.

"How?" John asked.

"I flew right over Annet at one hundred fifty feet. That hang glider may be hard to see, but at that range they couldn't miss it."

Dan cleared his throat. "There's more."

"What?"

"The freighter is approaching. Its radio bearing has changed."

The rain pattered against the tent's nylon roof and ran down the sides. Gary turned to each team member in turn.

"What can we do?" John asked.

Gary knew they *had* to do something. They had come *so* far, endured *so* much. This was their very last chance. They couldn't let Peter and Ian escape after all they had been through. He made his decision. "Pack up the gear. We're going to Annet."

"Gary?" Ann said.

"What?"

"The police. We should call the police."

"Okay," Gary said, "but how? It's all over if they haul us in before we can explain what really happened."

"I know," Ann said. "What if Marjorie calls and asks them over to Annet on MI5 business, then we explain when they get there? Surely they'll check it out, hold Peter and Ian, and search for the crown."

"That might work, but I hope they're up to the job." But even as he said it, doubts rose up in his mind. Could two island policemen really take Peter and Ian?

"I do too."

Gary turned to Dan. "Have we got phone service?"

Dan dug around in a bag and hauled out a handset attached to an electronic box. He set some switches and checked an LED meter, then gave Ann the handset. "There," he said. He pulled out his mobile communications analyzer and attached the directional antenna.

Ann retrieved her PDA and looked up a number.

"You've got the police number?" Gary asked.

"Of course," she said. She punched it in and waited. Her expression of concentration turned to a frown. She punched the End button and looked at Gary. "I got a recording."

"Maybe they're off on weekends," Gary said.

"Perhaps. I'll try the public houses."

She consulted her PDA again. The first two calls came up negative. She punched in the third number and waited while it rang. She went through the same inquiry, identifying herself as Marjorie Evans. She listened; then her face brightened. She held the handset to her ear with her shoulder while she made furious notes on her PDA.

"Yes, thank you, ever so much," she said finally. "Bye." She punched the End button.

"That was Bishop Rock Inn. Constable Chester was there when Sergeant Ivey called him away. Ivey told the hostess there was trouble at one of the chalets on St. Martin's."

"Where is that?" Gary asked.

"St. Martin's is the farthest north and east of the inhabited islands. A farm on the east side has chalets for let—rent."

"How convenient for our friend Peter," Gary said sarcastically.

"Isn't it, though," John said.

"Can we can reach Ivey?" Gary asked.

"Not him," Ann said. "He doesn't like mobile phones, but Constable Chester has one, and I've got his number." She started to punch it in.

"Just a minute," Dan said. He tilted the communications box so he could see the readouts and adjusted his earphones. "Okay."

Ann finished entering the number and pressed the Talk button. A few moments later she said, "Hello, Marjorie Evans, MI5 here. Is this Constable Chester?"

Her eyes became animated as she listened. "Capital. I need your assistance." The earphone buzzed with the long reply. "Yes, I'm aware you were called out to St. Martin's. Have you reached the chalet, then?" She nodded impatiently. "You haven't? Well, I'm afraid you're on a wild goose chase. Listen, my investigation—" She stopped abruptly and looked at Dan. "I was cut off." She punched the number in again.

"You won't get him," Dan said. "His signal strength was dropping the whole time. I think his battery gave out."

Ann held the handset to her ear and waited. Finally she punched the phone off. "I got his voice mail."

"Wish his battery had lasted longer," John said.

"Yeah," Gary said, "but it didn't." He looked around at Dan. "How close is the ship?"

"Based on the last bearing, I'd say less than ten nautical miles by now."

The operational variables began to fall into place. "Okay, everyone. Start packing."

"What about the police?" Ann asked.

Gary turned to Sully. "I want you to drop John and me off at Annet, then you three go get the cops."

"Yes, boss," Sully said.

"Okay, let's move it, people. We haven't got much time."

chapter 29

Where do you want to land?" Sully asked.

Gary consulted the map Ann had given him. Annet was small, less than a mile at its longest dimension. The shape reminded him of a flying bird, with wings pointing north, the head facing west, and a long tail hanging down toward the south. Gary pointed to a cove on the east side of the island. "See if you can put us ashore here," he said.

John took a peek. "What if they're expecting us?" he asked.

Gary looked at the map again. Peter and Ian *had* to leave from the west side, since shoal waters barred the ship's approach from any other direction. That made this cove the logical place to reach them.

"Yeah, I see what you mean," Gary said slowly. His eyes drifted farther south. "How about along here?"

John nodded. "That's better."

"Sully?" Gary asked.

Sully glanced at the map. "I think I can do it."

The boat plowed into a rogue wave, and a torrent of white roared over the bow, slammed into the windshield, and cascaded over the cabin and down the sides. Off to the right, Gary caught a glimpse of the green ribbon of low-lying Annet just before another squall enveloped it. Sully leaned over Dan's laptop, following the GPS coordinates on the digital map.

"This is it," he said a few minutes later.

Gary grabbed his backpack and stood by the cabin door. John brought his pack over and leaned against the bulkhead.

"You okay?" Gary asked.

He winced and took a deep breath. "I will be when we get ashore."

"Coming about," Sully shouted. The boat wallowed and plunged all the way around. The engine sounds dropped off, and Sully looked back. "Go over the starboard side," he said. "It'll give you some shelter."

"Take care," Ann said.

Dan looked around. At first he didn't say anything, but Gary could tell he was concerned. "Keep us posted," Dan said finally.

"Will do," Gary said. He opened the door and staggered out, carrying his pack in one hand while he used the other to grab handholds. He reached the rubber boat, dropped his pack, and began removing the lashings while John freed the outboard. Together they threw the boat into the water and tied the line to a side cleat.

"Get in," John said.

Gary nodded and went to the side. The rubber boat tilted and bobbed, snubbing against the line. Gary waited, timed his leap, then jumped. He hit hard, slipped, and almost rolled into the churning waves. He scrambled upright and turned around. John handed down the packs. Last came the tiny outboard. Gary lowered it into place and secured the clamps. John jumped, landing cleanly. He untied the boat and sat down.

It took three pulls, but Gary finally got the motor started. He faced forward and caught a brief glimpse of the shore through the downpour before it disappeared again. He fought to maintain course despite the boat's wild gyrations. The sound of crashing surf grew louder, and then he saw the beach. A wave lifted the boat, and Gary tilted the motor and held on. The boat slammed onto the sand and slid to a stop. Gary jumped out, and he and John dragged it up on the beach.

Ann waited impatiently for the Internet data to download over Dan's radio link. She watched Sully struggle to maintain a northeastern course past St. Agnes Island. Finally the laptop's speakers chirped, announcing the download was complete.

"Malibu Surfer," the radio speaker announced. "We're ashore."

Dan grabbed the mike. "Beachcomber, we copy. Take care."

"Roger that. Beachcomber out."

"That's good news," Ann said.

Dan looked up from the jumble of electronic boxes arrayed about him. "Yes, it is," he said.

"We're going to St. Martin's, right?" Sully asked.

"Yes, we don't have time to wait for them at St. Mary's."

"Cool, but I'll need some GPS data soon or we'll be plowing up rocks big-time."

"Coming right up." She temporarily attached her computer to Sully's and copied over the files.

"Thanks."

Ann turned to Dan. "Where's that freighter?" she asked.

"Getting close now," he said.

It had taken fifteen minutes to reach the cove. Gary's eyes followed the curve of springy turf that outlined the cove, and there near the center was a dark smudge that didn't belong. He dropped down, and John crawled in beside him. Gary pulled his binoculars out of his backpack, propped himself up on his elbows, and swept the beach carefully. The dark object was still there, barely visible through the heavy rain.

"Looks like you were right," Gary whispered. "It's a camouflaged one-man tent, and it has a rifle barrel sticking out. It's got to be Ian." He lowered the binoculars. "Peter's probably on the west side. I guess we could try an end around and come at him from behind."

"I don't know. Peter's bound to call Ian back at any time. I'd hate to be caught between those dudes."

Gary had to agree with that, but what could they do about an armed and alert enemy? "I'm open to suggestions here."

John pulled out a can of pepper spray. "What if I circle around Ian and come at him from behind?"

Gary shook his head. "That's asking for it. You'd have absolutely *no* cover."

"How about a diversion?"

"Like what?"

"Sherlock still has his flash-bang gear."

"You brought Sherlock?"

"Well, yeah. Thought he might come in handy."

Under the circumstances, Gary couldn't argue the point. "I guess we could try. Haul him out."

John removed his backpack, pulled out the robot, and set it on the sand.

Gary took the controller. "Okay, now listen. I'll bring Sherlock in from this side, and the moment I see you coming in, I'll hit the flash and explosion."

"Got it."

John started to move.

Gary reached out and grabbed him by the shoulder. "Take care."

"Don't worry, I will."

John crawled well clear, then sprang up and ran inland, disappearing into the rain. Gary started Sherlock on a slow, steady approach toward the tent. He wiped the lenses of the binoculars and swept the beach behind the tent, alert for any sign of movement. He corrected the robot's course and looked at the controller's TV display. The image jittered as the robot trundled over the sand. The exposed rifle was still there.

"It's a trap!" John shouted.

"Shut up," said another voice over the radio, faint but unmistakable. It was Ian. The radio made a few crackling sounds, then nothing.

An icy tingle shot down Gary's spine. He dropped the controller, jumped up, and started running toward where he thought Ian was, then slid to a stop. Ian surely knew he was here, so there would be no sneaking up on him down the narrow neck of land leading to Annet's western point, and getting captured wouldn't do John any good. But what could he do?

"This is Malibu Surfer. Status check."

"Stay off the air. Beachcomber out."

Gary turned off his earphone radio since further transmissions might help Ian. Then he ran to the tent and looked inside, finding it empty except for a painted wooden dowel. Sherlock was still scooting along, obeying its last orders. Gary scooped it up and ran back to the controller. He shut Sherlock off and stuffed it and the controller back in John's backpack.

As he considered what to do, his eye fell on the rubber boat, barely visible through the rain. Then he remembered the map Ann had shown him. He was standing on a narrow spit of land only a few hundred feet wide. If he hauled the boat across it, he could loop around to the south and come at the western point from the sea. He looked down at John's pack, wondering if he needed it. He had almost decided to leave it when he thought of Sherlock. He grabbed the pack and ran for the boat.

Ann peered through the windshield but couldn't see much through the driving rain. A wave crashed over the bow and plowed into the windshield. Ann shivered, but it wasn't from the dank, musty air inside the cramped cabin. A morbid silence had settled over the team members after Gary's last transmission.

"How much longer?" Ann asked.

"A little more than a mile," Sully said. "Lower Town is due north of us."

Ann knew this was St. Martin's western town. "What's that?" she asked. A dark object had just appeared through the rain, directly in their path.

"Hope it's not a rock," Sully said. He brought the throttle back to idle.

"It's a boat. Sound the horn, and pull alongside."

Sully pressed a button, and a surprisingly loud air horn sounded over their heads. "Man, *that* ought to get their attention," he said. He advanced the throttle and turned the wheel. The boat turned reluctantly.

Ann threw the door open, stepped out into the pouring rain, and ran to the side. She held a hand over her eyes and squinted. The distance dwindled slowly, and the deck vibrated as Sully backed the engine. A man in a yellow slicker stood out on the other boat's deck.

"Ahoy, do you require assistance?" he shouted.

"Yes." Ann's mind raced. How could she possibly explain? "Two men on Annet Island. We need—"

"Did you just ring us up. . . ?" the man interrupted.

"Sergeant Ivey?" she asked.

"Yes."

"No time to explain. I need your help on MI5 business. Follow us to Annet Island."

341

"Half a sec."

Ivey disappeared into the cabin and merged with two others while Ann waited impatiently. Finally the sergeant returned.

"Skipper won't take us there."

"Come with us, then."

Sergeant Ivey just stood there, swaying with the wallowing boat.

"Now, mate! Lives are in peril."

"Right."

Ann raced to the cabin and threw open the door. "Bring us alongside, Sully. They're coming with us."

Sully looked around. "Hey, we don't have a boat."

Ann had forgotten. "Oh, yes. I'll see what I can do." She slammed the cabin door.

Sully brought the boat around in a tight turn, wallowing up to the lee side of the other craft. Ivey came out on deck with another man. The distance between the boats dwindled until they bumped together.

"We need a boat to get ashore," Ann shouted to make herself heard over the wind and driving rain.

Sergeant Ivey looked pained but returned to the cabin. A few moments later he returned. "Skipper says we can use his."

Constable Chester jumped over and took one end of the yellow rubber boat and wrestled it over the side. Then Ivey jumped over with an agility that surprised Ann.

"Come inside, and I'll explain everything," she shouted.

"Right," Sergeant Ivey replied.

Gary reached the opposite shore breathing hard and with a sharp pain in his side, wondering why he had not dumped John's backpack to lighten the load. The heavy rain raised countless geysers on the restless waves. He pulled the boat into the water, jumped in, and paddled out into the surging surf. He yanked the starter cord, and the outboard motor started. He squinted into the driving rain and steered the unwieldy craft along Annet's southern shore. Ahead lay the western point and beyond that, the trackless Atlantic.

Gary was sure he knew where Peter was, and although the downpour might help his approach, his opponents knew he was near and would be watchful. And all he had was pepper spray, Sherlock, and whatever else might be in John's pack.

The boat pitched and plunged, making agonizingly slow headway. The boat seemed to have a mind of its own, and it took Gary's full attention to maintain his course. Finally he drew even with the western point. He scanned the beach between squalls but saw nothing. Peter and Ian were probably up among the grass and heather, he thought, and that made his approach extremely exposed. *Well, nothing I can do about that.* He swung the motor over and headed for the point.

About a minute later the outboard hit bottom and quit. Gary tumbled over the side and, keeping low, scrambled up on the sand and pulled the boat ashore. He looked into the boat at the two backpacks, knowing he couldn't carry both. He almost picked his own but decided he couldn't leave Sherlock behind. He retrieved his binoculars and stuffed them inside John's pack along with two cans of pepper spray. Inside, he spotted a nylon bag he didn't recognize, but he couldn't spare the time to look at its contents.

Gary rolled onto his side and struggled into the backpack. He flopped over on his stomach and crawled over the sand, low grasses, and heather, with no cover except what the pouring rain provided. He paused and pulled out his binoculars. Although he saw no signs of life, he knew Peter and Ian could be camouflaged or simply hidden by the rain. And where was John? Was Ian holding him as hostage, or was it already too late? Gary felt a tightness in his throat together with anger.

He removed his backpack and pulled out Sherlock and its controller. He yanked up grass and heather and festooned the low-slung robot in an attempt to hide it, then turned on the controller and started Sherlock on its way across the point. The video display bounced and jiggled as the robot trundled along the beach. Halfway across, Gary stopped it and zoomed in on the terrain ahead, but all he saw was sand and sparse vegetation. He looked up and tried to spot Sherlock but couldn't since the camouflage was more effective than he had realized.

Ann knew the time had come to disabuse Sergeant Ivey and Constable Chester of their belief they were assisting MI5, but how? So far, Sully and Dan had not said a word, for which Ann was grateful since it gave her time to think.

"Sergeant Ivey," she said finally, "there is something you need to know."

"Oh, and what might that be?" he asked.

"The men we're after are the ones who pinched the Crown Jewels."

Ivey's eyes grew very round. "What? The Americans are here? On Scilly?"

Ann took a deep breath and dropped her British accent. "As a matter of fact, we're three of them. The other two, Gary Nesbitt and John Mason, are on Annet going after the men who *really* stole the crown."

Ivey stepped back and drew his revolver. "What's the meaning of this?" he demanded.

Ann held up her hands. "That's what I'm trying to tell you. The crown is on Annet, and we're not the ones who have it."

Ivey's eyes narrowed. "Is that so, now? Then who?"

"Peter Watkins and Ian Hayford."

"Watkins? Wasn't he the MI5 chap what got killed?"

She shook her head. "He faked it. I'm telling you, he's *on* that island, and he *has* the crown. Now, if you don't *do* something, he and Ian will escape with it."

"I don't know. . . ," Ivey said slowly.

"Look. If *we* had the crown, do you *really* think we'd be stupid enough to invite you to capture us? Would that make sense?"

Ivey took his time answering. "No, can't say that it would," he said finally.

"Oh, one other thing; he and his partner are well armed, whereas we aren't. Now, what do you say?"

"Tell you what. I'll go ashore and check it out whilst Constable Chester guards you blokes."

"No good," Ann said. "I *told* you. Peter and Ian are armed to the teeth. It will take *both* of you, and you need us to guide you."

"And leave him aboard?" Ivey asked, nodding toward Sully.

Ann turned to Sully. "Can you come with us?" she asked.

"Take a while to anchor, plus it might not hold."

"You don't have time," Dan interrupted.

Ann turned to him. "Why?"

"The ship is here. I'm receiving strong radio signals on a bearing just off Annet."

Ann looked into Ivey's eyes. "Okay, it's your call, but if you *don't* act now, the crown is gone forever, and it'll be *your* fault."

Ivey winced at that. "All right, all right," he said finally.

Gary stopped Sherlock, zoomed the camera in, and peered into the controller's video display. Not far from the robot, two humps nestled amid the grass and heather. Gary panned around to the left, and there was another hump. There were three oblong objects, all perpendicular to the shore, and beyond them what looked like a large, flat rock. Gary knew his imagination could be running away with him, but the more he studied the display, the more convinced he became he had found Peter and Ian—and John, he hoped.

Then a movement beyond the humps caught Gary's eye. There, at the very edge of visibility, dark shapes were approaching, almost certainly his friends, and they were walking right into a trap. He turned on his earphone radio.

"Look out," he whispered. "They're in front of you."

One of the humps moved, and a long, thin object appeared and slowly swung around to the north. Gary rammed Sherlock's motor controls full forward. The rifle barrel stopped moving. Gary jabbed a button on the controller and looked up. A blinding flash stabbed at his eyeballs, and the reverberating sound hit like a trip-hammer. The rifle jumped violently as the shot went wide. The distant objects had disappeared.

Gary jumped up and ran all-out. The dark shape nearest the water rose and threw off its covering. It was Peter, and the pistol he held came around swiftly. Gary dove for the ground and rolled. The silenced automatic spat fire three times. A bullet slammed into Gary's right boot, and it felt like a red-hot poker had impaled his big toe. He gritted his teeth and looked up, half-expecting to see Peter lining up for the kill. Instead, he was hunched over, throwing off a cover and tugging at the rubber boat underneath. A few feet away, Ian was firing at something to the north. Peter threw a bundle into the boat and began dragging it toward the water.

Gary struggled to his feet but almost passed out from the pain. Peter was at the water now. A wave crashed over the boat and swirled about his feet. Gary limped back to John's backpack, fell to his knees, and pulled out a can of pepper spray. Then his eyes fell on the package he had seen earlier. He hesitated, then opened the bag and blinked in surprise. Inside were two of the bombs John had made to turn back the *Bhima,* only minus their drogues. Gary looked up. Peter was in the boat now and paddling furiously.

Gary pocketed the pepper spray, grabbed a bomb in each hand, and staggered to his feet. He limped toward the tossing waves, each step shooting razor jabs deep into his brain. When he finally reached the surf, Peter was about fifty feet out and indistinct in the heavy rain. Gary threw the bomb in his right hand. The heavy sphere arced up high, then splashed down ahead of the boat. Gary winced. He had forgotten to remove the tape. Peter stopped rowing and reached for something.

Yellow flashes marked Peter's unheard pistol shots. The wet sand erupted all around Gary. One shot snatched at his coveralls, and he felt a searing pain in his side. He tore the protective tape from his remaining bomb and threw it. The bomb lofted up and over, landing right in front of Peter. The blast's huge white geyser demolished the boat and hurled the pieces high into the air. A torrent of water and debris thundered down for several seconds. Peter popped to the surface and started swimming for shore.

"Drop your weapon!" a voice commanded.

"Look out, Gary!" Ann shouted.

Gary whirled around, caught a glimpse of Ann, Dan, and two strangers, then spotted Ian taking dead-aim with his pistol.

"I said, drop it," the policeman repeated.

Gary threw himself down at the same moment Ian fired. Then a second gunshot rang out. Behind Gary, a muffled cry of agony carried over the wind, merging with Ian's scream as he collapsed. Gary turned his head and saw Peter flailing in the water. *Ian shot him,* he thought.

Gary struggled to his feet and hobbled into the water. The salt water set his toe on fire. He clenched his teeth and kept moving until the water surged about his waist; then he dove. Peter went under, then surfaced, retching and coughing. Gary dug into the water with powerful strokes, kicking with one leg, but his energy was fading fast. Peter was thrashing the water frantically. Gary ducked, swam underwater, and came up behind

Peter. Gary threw his right arm around Peter's neck. Startled, Peter cried out and tried to break Gary's hold. Gary squeezed harder and began swimming back to shore. Up ahead he saw Dan swimming out to meet him.

"Need any help?" Dan spluttered as a wave splashed over him.

"I think I can make it," Gary said. "See if you can find the crown."

Dan swam past.

Gary knew he was almost spent, but seeing the shore gave him a fresh adrenaline jolt. Finally he touched bottom and struggled to his feet. Peter tried to break free, but it was a feeble attempt. Blood mingled with seawater flowed down his jacket. Gary spotted Ann.

"I need help!" he yelled. "Peter's hit."

Gary pulled him up on the sand. Ann dropped to her knees, removed Peter's jacket, and tore away his shirt.

"This looks bad," she said. She wadded up the shirt and pressed it into the gaping wound in Peter's chest. He screamed in agony, and Ann had to fight to keep it in place. "Send down something to put over him."

"Okay," Gary said. He hobbled over to the two strangers. One was holding a gun on Ian while the other tore multiple layers of duct tape off. It was John.

The man working on the bindings turned. "Hello, mate. Constable Chester, at your service."

"And I'm Sergeant Ivey," the other man said.

Chester stopped when he saw Gary's bloodstained coveralls. "Here, you've been injured."

"I'm okay," Gary said. Right now, all he wanted to do was rest. A sudden wave of dizziness swept over him, and he sat down quickly. He pointed toward the shore. "That guy down there is hurt really bad."

"We'll tend to him as soon as we take care of this chap," Ivey said.

Gary pulled at the hole in his coveralls and saw an ugly red gouge. Although it looked nasty, he knew it was only a flesh wound. The toe wasn't serious either, but it shot searing arrows of pain into his brain with every movement. He looked up and saw Ian holding his arm.

"I see big bad Ian got it too," Gary said.

Ian glared at him with hate-filled eyes.

"You might say that," Chester said. He finished freeing John and stood up. "Hold out your hands," he ordered Ian.

"I'm injured," Ian complained.

"Do as I say." Chester picked up a roll of duct tape and began binding Ian's wrists.

Sergeant Ivey lowered his pistol and grabbed two sopping wet blankets. "Don't know how much good this will do, but it's all we've got." He took them down to Ann and helped her bind the shirt into Peter's wound.

Gary looked past them and saw Dan emerging from the water carrying a package. Gary felt some of his strength return. He struggled to his feet.

"I think this is what we're looking for," Dan said.

"I sure hope so," Gary said. He turned to Ivey. "Can you call for help? Peter Watkins will die if we don't do something."

"Don't have a radio," Ivey said, "and Hubert here, his phone's give out on him."

"I think I can help," Dan said. He set the package down, reached into a nylon tote bag, and pulled out an electronic box. He flipped a few switches and gave Ivey the handset. "Be my guest," he said.

Ivey looked at the lighted keypad. "How. . . ?"

"Trade secret," Dan said.

It took several calls, but Sergeant Ivey finally reached the pilot of a Ministry of Agriculture, Fisheries, and Food helicopter at St. Mary's Airport and convinced him to fly over to Annet Island.

"Shouldn't be long now," he said as he gave the handset back to Dan. Ivey's eyes fastened on the box wrapped inside a clear waterproof covering. "I say. Is that the crown?"

Dan picked up the package and gave it to Gary.

"We certainly hope so," Gary said with feeling. "We'll find out as soon as we get out of this rain." He wanted to rip the package open immediately, after all the trouble it had caused them.

A few minutes later Gary heard a droning whine approaching. The helicopter flew over, circled, then settled in a gale of spray and grit, the high turbine whine attenuating rapidly. The pilot jumped out, lowered his head, and hurried over.

"Sergeant Ivey?" he shouted, to make himself heard.

Ivey held his hand up. "Here, mate. Got three wounded, one serious."

The pilot looked around. "I can take six, but the other two will have to wait."

"I can go back with Sully," Dan said.

"Constable Chester will accompany you," Ivey said, "till we get things sorted out."

John and Dan carried Peter over to the helicopter and eased him onto the cabin floor. Then Ann, Gary, John, Ian, and Sergeant Ivey clambered aboard. The pilot shut the door, then ran around and entered the cockpit. Gary felt his stomach lurch as they lifted off and flew through the rain toward the airport.

"Here," Ivey said, handing Gary a pocketknife, his eyes on the package Gary held so securely.

Gary cut away the clear wrapping and saw the box he had last seen when he had turned it over to Peter what seemed like ages ago. Taped to the side was the key. Gary trembled as he opened the box revealing the red crown. The fabled Koh-I-Noor twinkled in the cabin lighting, surrounded by a court made up of thousands of diamonds.

"Coo, *what* a sight," Ivey said.

At that moment, Gary realized it was finally over, the

nightmare Peter and Ian had put them through. All that remained was to submit to whatever official red tape the Brits would deem necessary. He groaned inwardly, anticipating a detailed process, but at least they had established the actual perpetrators.

"You okay?" John asked.

Gary looked at him and smiled a weary smile. "Yeah, I'm just fine."

chapter 30

Gary stared out the window of the Royal Air Force Merlin HC3 helicopter as it clattered along under dark English skies on its way to Battersea Heliport in London. Amid all the things that had happened this day, two stood out: the ferocious speed of the roused British Lion, and the official cloud that still hung over the team. There had been no question of Peter's and Ian's guilt, for which Gary was grateful, but MI5 was having trouble working out the Americans' exact status.

Within a hour of their arrival at tiny St. Mary's Airport, two Merlins had swooped in, landing beside a British International Sikorsky. One whisked the crown directly to London, while the other flew the team, Peter, and Ian to the Penzance Heliport, accompanied by two MI5 agents. Two police cars and a van met the helicopter. The police van took Peter and Ian to West Cornwall Hospital for surgery, pending transportation back to London to face charges. One of the cars took Gary to the hospital to be patched up, while the other drove John and Ann to the truck, where they retrieved the team's personal effects and Peter's MI5 paperwork, including the advance and bonus checks. Then, at 8:40 P.M., they had been on their way with their MI5 escorts.

The rain had stopped by the time they left Penzance, and as the helicopter neared London, the skies cleared up, revealing bright stars and a nearly full moon. The city below formed an ocean of lights forming grids and outlining major arteries. But despite the beauty, Gary couldn't shake his feeling of gloom.

Finally, the Merlin slowed and began its approach to the rooftop heliport beside the river Thames. Gary looked out his window and saw the lighted splendors of Buckingham Palace, Parliament, and Big Ben. The sinuous black ribbon of the Thames carved the city in two on its journey to the sea. Less than a minute later the helicopter touched down, and Agent Frederick Grint stood up, blocking the door. He was tall and thin, and immaculately dressed in a light gray suit, white shirt, and what Gary suspected was a school tie. Gary frowned. Somehow, he suspected they weren't in for a "hope you enjoyed your flight" message.

"May I have your attention," Grint said. "As I explained earlier, it may take some time to set things right, so I ask for your patience. In the meantime, we've booked rooms for you at the London Bridge Hotel."

"Are we at liberty?" Gary asked. He already knew the answer, but he wanted the agent to say it.

Grint frowned. "That is rather a sticky wicket, I'm afraid."

Gary felt the heat rising in his face. "How so?"

"I offer you a choice: Either you agree to remain in your rooms, or I shall be forced to have you arrested, in which case you shan't be staying at the hotel."

"That's a Hobson's choice—take it or leave it."

"I'm afraid that is correct. Well?"

"We'll take the hotel."

"Splendid. I shall send cars round for you tomorrow."

Grint nodded to the RAF crewman who opened the door.

353

There, waiting for the Americans, was their police escort.

At 10:00 A.M. on Sunday, a two-car convoy delivered the SecurityCheck team to the front entrance of Thames House on Millbank. Majestic clouds sailed across a deep blue sky, but the springtime beauty was lost on Gary. Last night he had prayed about their situation, asking for God to be their advocate, but all he felt was gloom. A Special Forces officer led the way, and Gary hobbled along as best he could. Less than a minute later they were ushered into Frederick Grint's office. The agent, if anything, looked even more splendid in his dark gray, pin-striped suit. The Sunday *London Times* rested on his orderly desktop, and five chairs awaited his guests.

Grint looked past Gary to the Special Branch officers. "You may go," he said. He waited for the door to close. "Please be seated," he told the team.

Gary sat carefully and glanced around nervously at the others. Grint settled into his executive swivel chair.

"Well, I trust everyone had a restful night," he said. He tried a smile, but it wasn't very convincing.

"Agent Grint," Gary said.

"Yes?"

"Could we cut to the chase?"

"What? Oh, yes, that quaint American expression. Well, I suppose we should. I have good news. No charges will be filed, and the British Government will be paying your way home. In fact, your British Airways flight to Los Angeles leaves at 3:00 P.M. Now, I'm sure. . ."

"Hold on there," Gary interrupted.

"I beg your pardon."

"What about our pay for the work we did for MI5?" Gary suspected *that* wasn't going anywhere.

"And our bonus," Ann added.

"Yeah, *and* the bonus," John said.

Grint clear his throat noisily. "Well, of course there can be no question of payment, since the contract is illegal."

"Peter Watkins executed it while acting as an MI5 employee," Gary said.

"Now, see here. Her Majesty's Government is *not* responsible for the unauthorized actions of employees."

"We executed that contract in good faith."

He stood up. "I cannot help you. Now, I'm sure you have things to do before your flight."

Gary looked over at John and shrugged. He grabbed his armrests and levered himself up, putting his weight on his good foot.

Grint's phone rang. The agent frowned and picked up the handset. "I said I was *not* to be disturbed," he snapped. As he listened, his expression began a journey that went from irritation to surprise and finally to astonishment.

"Why, yes, of course, put her through." he said as he stood up straight. "Yes, Your Majesty, Agent Frederick Grint, at your service." He nodded as he listened. "That is correct, Your Majesty. If I may. . ." He stopped abruptly, but the nodding continued. "I see." He fell silent again. "I understand perfectly, Your Majesty, and I assure you, I shall attend to it personally." His head gave one further bob. "At once, Your Majesty. Good-bye, Your Majesty."

Grint looked thoroughly stunned as he set the phone down. He waved absently at the chairs. "Please, do be seated."

Gary eased back into his chair. Grint looked at him.

"That was Her Royal Highness, Queen Elizabeth," he said. "At her command, I extend to you Her Majesty's heartfelt thanks for rescuing the Queen Consort's Crown and her sincere sorrow for all your troubles and injuries. Her Majesty also instructed me to tell you that the Crown's obligations, vis-à-vis the contract, *will* be paid in full—*immediately*."

"Including the bonus?" Sully asked.

"But of course. Her Majesty was *most* explicit. And Mr. Nesbitt, it is Her Majesty's wish that you forward your medical bills to the British ambassador in Washington." He paused. "Or, if you prefer, you may complete your rehabilitation in London, all expenses paid."

Gary smiled in relief. "That's very kind of Her Majesty, but we really need to get home."

Gary started to get up.

Grint cleared his throat, looked at each of the Americans, and once more returned his gaze to Gary. "There is *one* more thing. Her Royal Highness, Queen Elizabeth, requests the pleasure of your company for tea at Buckingham Palace."

Gary blinked and for a few moments was speechless. Then he said, "We are honored, but we're hardly dressed for the occasion."

Grint's expression suggested the agent agreed with Gary's assessment, but he said, "Her Majesty instructed me to convey to you that it was 'come as you are,' I believe were the words she used."

"We accept."

"Very good. Your transportation awaits."

chapter 31

Gary read the engraved invitation over again as the Queen's Rolls Royce purred along down the Mall toward Buckingham Palace. "The Lord Chamberlain is commanded by Her Majesty to invite. . . ," the impressive card began. After listing their names in flowing calligraphy, the invitation gave the venue, Buckingham Palace, and listed the time and date.

"That's really something," Gary said. He handed the card to Ann, who read it quickly and passed it around.

John looked down at his California casual attire: slacks and short-sleeved shirt. "Yeah, but I wish we could have changed into our formal clothes."

"You heard what Grint said. It's come as you are."

"Command performance, I guess."

"Actually, that pertains to performing artists," Ann said.

"Hey, the *Kid's* in show biz," Sully said. "What if I. . . ?"

"No, Mr. Sullivan," Gary said. "Whatever you had in mind, better save it for southern California."

"Just a thought."

The black limousine swept past the Queen Victoria

Monument, through the black iron gates, and up to the palace steps where two liveried servants waited. The car coasted to a precise stop, and the men opened the doors. Gary waited for Ann, then stepped out himself, wincing at the lingering pain in his toe. John joined him, while Dan and Sully got out on the other side and came around. The Americans closed ranks and approached a rather formal-looking man, who seemed in no way surprised at the guests or their clothing.

"Lady," he said to Ann; then his eyes made contact with each of the four men. "And gentlemen. On behalf of Her Royal Highness, Queen Elizabeth, welcome to Buckingham Palace. If you would follow me, please."

He turned and led the way up the steps and through the massive front doors into the Grand Hall and up the Grand Staircase. Gary eyed the portraits set in the walls, and the tasteful art and tapestries on either side of the gleaming floor. They passed the huge ballroom and finally came to the Bow Room where a stately lady waited dressed in a casual, but still elegant, blue dress.

The guide stood to the side and said, "Mr. Gary Nesbitt."

As briefed before their trip, Gary walked up and held out his hand.

"So pleased you could come, Mr. Nesbitt," Queen Elizabeth said as she shook his hand.

"Thank you for inviting me, Your Majesty," Gary replied.

He stood to the side, and waited while the other team members were announced and greeted. The introductions went smoothly, including Sully, who seemed in total awe for a change. Their guide, his duty done, bowed to the queen and left the room.

Queen Elizabeth looked at each of them in turn as she spoke, "First of all, let me extend to you all my heartfelt gratitude for your service to the Crown." She paused. "As you may know, what's called the Queen Mum's Crown has very special meaning to me, since it was my mother's. I should have been very sad to see it lost."

"We're glad we could be of service," Gary said.

"You are very kind. I sincerely regret that Mr. Watkins and Mr. Hayford gave you so much grief."

"It was difficult; I can't deny that, but it's over now."

The queen paused and looked at Gary quizzically. "I have read a detailed account of what your team went through. I am *amazed* at how you kept on going, no matter what. It puts me in mind of a speech Prime Minister Churchill gave at Harrow School in October of 1941. Are you familiar with it, by any chance?"

Gary's mind went blank for a moment, but then a vague memory surfaced. "Didn't he give a speech where he said 'never give up' three times, and then sat down?"

Queen Elizabeth smiled, but Gary could tell it wasn't at his expense. "That is a common myth, I'm afraid. The quote I'm referring to came as closing remarks, and what he actually said was: 'Never give in. Never give in. Never, never, never, never—in nothing, great or small, large or petty—never give in, except to convictions of honor and good sense. Never yield to force. Never yield to the apparently overwhelming might of the enemy.' To my mind, the correct quote more accurately describes what you and your friends did."

"Your Majesty, what a kind and considerate thing to say."

"It's a true thing I say." Again she paused. "I lived within these walls when Nazi bombers blitzed London, and I remember and appreciate how Prime Minister Churchill led us through those dark days—by never giving in." She nodded. "Well done, *very* well done."

"Thank you, Your Majesty."

The queen turned to Ann and smiled. "Ms. O'Brien. I understand you led our police a merry chase—Ms. Edwina Dunn and Marjorie Evans, I believe you were called—impersonating MI5 agents."

Ann blushed. "Well, yes, we couldn't have caught Peter if we had been arrested."

The queen laughed. "I am certainly glad you carried it off so well, for all our sakes." She turned her head and brought John under her friendly gaze. "And Mr. Mason. I'm told you work wonders with explosives, electronic gadgets, and things of that nature."

John grinned. "Yes, Your Majesty. High-tech tools for testing security systems."

"Yes, now what is this machine I've heard mentioned—Sherlock, is it?"

John's grin grew even wider. "Sherlock is my pride and joy. It's a miniature, remote-controlled robot. With the right tools, it can do almost anything."

"MI5 and Special Branch agree with that assessment from what I've heard. I understand they are most happy to hear that you really are on our side after all."

"We're glad too, Your Majesty."

The queen turned to Dan. "And Mr. Thompson. Your exploits certainly played hob with our communications. I presume you *will* put things back as you found them, now that your work is done."

"Yes, of course, Your Majesty."

"Thank you," the queen said with a smile. Then she turned to Sully. "Mr. Sullivan, I presume."

Sully swallowed, and his Adam's apple bobbed. "Yeah—er, Your Majesty. That's me."

She laughed. "I thought it might be." She looked him in the eye. "But I believe you go by 'Sully' or 'the Kid,' is that right?"

Sully looked at Gary, who shrugged. "Um, yes, ma'am. I answer to either one."

"How interesting. I'm curious, how did this, ah, heist, compare with your work as a Hollywood stuntman? Exciting enough for a day job, would you say?"

"Oh, yeah, big-time—uh, Your Majesty."

Queen Elizabeth again made eye contact with each of her guests, her smile as sincere as ever. "You are quite a team, I see, and I congratulate all of you. And again, my sincerest thanks for your courageous service to the Crown."

"Our pleasure," Gary answered for them.

She turned and waved a hand toward the doors leading out into the garden. "Won't you join me for tea?" She started walking. "It isn't time for high tea, but since I understand British Airways doesn't observe it, I decided we could move the clock up a little." She looked past Gary to Ann. "Tea and scones with clotted cream. Does that sound good?"

"It sounds wonderful, Your Majesty," Ann said.

"Have you had it?" the queen asked Gary.

"Can't say as I have, Your Majesty."

"Well then. We must remedy that."

The queen led them out to an elegant white table set for six under a broad umbrella. A servant came out with the silver tea service and began his rounds.

Gary looked around the bright profusion of flowers and the immaculately trimmed lawn. What a difference a day made. Yesterday, a fugitive from British law enforcement; today, tea with the queen. He looked up into the dark blue sky. And in a few hours, they would be on their way back to Los Angeles.

The British Airways gate agent announced the boarding of their flight. Gary stood up. He looked around at each of them, and a tightness came to his throat that surprised him. "Thank you, everyone. I appreciate the sacrifices each of you made. What you did was truly above and beyond."

"It was a team effort," John said.

"Amen," Ann added.

Gary paused. "*Yes,* amen. Most of all, I appreciate God taking care of us, even when I doubted."

John smiled. "I can agree with that."

Gary cleared his throat. "Brother John?"

"Yes, Brother Gary?"

Gary's mind soared on ahead of them across the broad Atlantic, all the way to California. "I believe SecurityCheck is back in business," he said.

ABOUT THE AUTHOR

A former navy seaman, Frank Simon is a Texas-based computer consultant and technical writer. His action/suspense novels include *The Gathering Storm, The Third Dragon, Trial by Fire,* and *The Raptor Virus.* Frank and his wife make their home outside of Dallas, Texas.

ALSO FROM
BARBOUR PUBLISHING